Park Spring

Date Chec

M000187274

7-21-20		
2-3-21		

WITHDRAWN

P A R K   S P R I N G S℠

REAWAKENING REBEKAH

THE GIFT
of
THE CLAMOR GIRLS

REAWAKENING REBEKAH

THE GIFT
of
THE CLAMOR GIRLS

a novel by Deidre Ann deLaughter

Deidre Ann deLaughter
February 27, 2014

DEEDS PUBLISHING | ATLANTA

Published by Deeds Publishing
Marietta, GA
www.deedspublishing.com

Printed in the United States of America

Cover Photo by Matt King | mbk-photo.com
Design and layout by Mark Babcock

Library of Congress Cataloging-in-Publications Data is available upon request.

ISBN 978-1-937565-81-7

Books are available in quantity for promotional or premium use. For information, write Deeds Publishing, PO Box 682212, Marietta, GA 30068 or info@deedspublishing.com.

First Edition, 2013

10 9 8 7 6 5 4 3 2 1

To my three doe-eyed inspirations. Being mom to three of the classiest young women in the world is my great joy, honor, and privilege.

Acknowledgments

I WROTE THE ORIGINAL DRAFT of *Reawakening Rebekah* over a nine-month period in 2001-2002. Ever since then, as I would mention my "project," dear family and friends encouraged me, believed in my dream to bring this story to print, and realized, with me, the necessity of shedding light on a horrific topic. Aforementioned dear friends and family, you know who you are, and I earnestly thank you. It is my great desire that *Reawakening Rebekah* be a vehicle for divesting dreaded secrets of their power and to be a tool in healing. I'd also like to express my deepest appreciation to the Deeds Publishing team—Bob, Jan, and Mark Babcock. What a joy and a privilege it is to work with you, and may this be the first of many collaborations to come.

Prologue

THE CLOUDLESS SKY AND WANING moon made a natural night light in the bedroom where the two girls slept. When he stepped into the room, the light made shadows, moving as he moved first to the bed closest to the door. Watching the child sleep, he smiled then leaned over to push her bangs away from her eyes. "Good night, Lovey," he whispered, kissing her forehead. The girl sighed in her sleep and rolled to her side. He paused then went to the bed where the other girl slept. The moon cast a glow around him, illuminating the spot where he stood watching her sleep. A small puddle of drool had dried on the pillowcase where the girl's thumb had slipped partway out of her mouth. He smoothed her cheek with the back of his fingers. Reflexively, she stuck her thumb back in and sucked. He felt himself harden and he closed his eyes and waited for the sensation to flood him, then unzipped his trousers slowly, the sound of it barely audible. He inhaled deeply. His shadow shuddered and then moved over her, covering her face.

One

THE MARE WHIMPERED AS DR. Casey Greer examined her pregnant patient in the air-conditioned barn. Turning to the owner, she said, "She's in extreme distress. The foal is presenting sideways. I think I can turn it, but there are significant risks, and she's too fragile to transport. You said this is her third pregnancy, right, and that the other two were normal deliveries?" The owner nodded, ashen, but taking in every word of his young veterinarian. The other mares nickered in sympathy with their barn-mate's plight. "Then the likelihood of this rupturing her uterus is less than if she'd had difficulties in previous pregnancies. Would you like for me to try? If I'm not successful, I'll likely have to put her down." Again the owner nodded, his eyes imploring Casey to save the lives of both mother and baby.

Casey injected the mare with a mild sedative then disinfected her hands and arms and laid out her instruments, including an additional pre-loaded syringe, in case. She spoke soothingly to the mare, observing her vital signs as she waited for the sedative to begin working, and then began. Casey had slid one arm inside the mare when she was momentarily distracted by a movement in her peripheral vision. The horse's owner, a burly man in his mid-50's, anxious to help, took a smithy's apron off the hook close to where he stood. He unzipped his windbreaker. Casey felt as if someone had suddenly changed channels inside her head. She struggled to stay focused on the panting mare.

* * *

Dr. Lorelei Mackenzie crossed her legs, placing her hands in her lap. She smiled at her new client. "It's nice to see you again. Is there something in particular you'd like to talk about today?"

Without hesitation, Casey pushed forward in her chair, pupils dilated, voice pitched with pain, "If I know something about a terrible thing that happened years ago—20 years ago—but I never said anything about it then and I didn't do anything to stop it, would it cause more harm than good to say something about it now?"

"That depends on the nature of this terrible thing. Would you like to tell me more about it before you make that decision? Do you think that would help?"

"I've haven't spoken about it with anyone for years. I don't know if I can talk about it… I'll try."

"Why don't you start at a safe place in the story, and work your way toward this terrible thing. Want to try that?"

Casey nodded, squared her shoulders, and drew in a larger than usual breath. Fixing her eyes on an imaginary home movie screen, she provided the narration. "I want to tell you about Rebekah, Rebekah Wilkins. I met her when I was in the third grade." Casey smiled. "I noticed her right away. She had luminous green eyes, red hair that she wore every day in two French braids, and freckles across her nose and cheeks, and she wore matching Osh Kosh outfits. I envied her on all those accounts but even more for her laugh. She never squealed or tittered like other third graders; instead, she gave her whole body over to a wellspring of delight that bubbled out of her.

"I was new at Founder's Creek Elementary that year, and painfully shy. The first two weeks of school, during recess when all the other kids were playing together, I stood off to the side watching. Some of the girls invented elaborate princess stories, screaming hysterically to summon the boys playing nearby to slay imaginary dragons and rescue the fair maidens from their jungle gym turret. Other girls skipped rope, played on the slide and swings, gathered up roly polies and other insects, or walked in pairs around the playground, pausing occasionally to point, whisper, and laugh over a shared secret. During that first week, I fell under Rebekah's spell." Casey smiled, remembering. "For all her winsome charm and despite the desire of the entire third grade to be a part of her world, Rebekah possessed a sureness of herself and the ability to avoid aligning herself with any specific person or group, all without wounding anyone's sensibilities. Where I was concerned, though, I assumed she didn't know I existed.

"My father was the new preacher at Founder's Creek Community Church. When we arrived in early summer, neither of my parents was familiar with the community nor living in the Florida panhandle. Mama wanted to get settled immediately, so she started sewing new curtains for every window in the parsonage while Daddy worked toward his goal of visiting every family on the membership roster—active or not. On certain days he asked me if I'd like to ride along with him. I would look at Mama, waiting for her nod of approval. It wasn't until much later that I realized Daddy had asked me along on the visits where he would be calling on members who had a reputation for being difficult. I was a buffer of sorts, softening the tirade those members had planned to launch against the former pastor or some present church member or policy. During those visits, I would sit quietly, half listening to the adults in conversation, half distracted by the new surroundings and the private world inside my head.

"One visit in particular stands out in my memory. It was to the home of Mrs. Nusbaum, an elderly widow. She informed my father right away that she was chairman of the Altar Guild, president of the Sewing Circle, secretary of the Golden Agers Sunday School class, and probably some other things I've forgotten by now. She also pointedly mentioned she was a charter member of Founder's Creek Community Church. Mrs. Nusbaum's old cat, Henrietta, had never been around young people. Mrs. Nusbaum had never had children and I recall thinking that was probably a good thing," Casey smiled wryly. "Anyway, Henrietta hadn't developed the self-protective habit of running to hide when the doorbell rang, so while Daddy and Mrs. Nusbaum sat in adjoining chairs in what she referred to as her parlor, solving all the church's problems along with a few of the world's, I followed Henrietta around with my eyes. I was so engrossed in her indifference to the lowly human folk in her living room; I think that's the day I decided to become a veterinarian.

"By the time school started that August, I'd become bored with my summer routine of eating my Cheerios by the glow of morning cartoons while Mama sewed. Eventually, she'd walk over and stand between me and the television and ask, 'Haven't you watched enough television for one morning?' I would shrug and she would turn the TV off and then suggest I either play outdoors or in my room or read a book. I had long ago quit asking her to play *Candy Land* or *Chutes and Ladders* because I knew the 'maybe later' would never materialize. Fortunately, my collection of stuffed animals was always willing to play with me. I'd pretend I was a teacher and they were my students as I read Dr. Seuss to them. Or I was a very important businesswoman and they were my very important clients. Sometimes I'd pretend I was a preacher and they were my adoring congregation, but my favorite was playing circus-master to my show-stopping act. For a lonely kid, I at least knew how to entertain myself.

"In the late afternoon, Daddy would come home for dinner before his evening church meetings, and the three of us would sit around the little table in the eat-in kitchen, discussing the events of the day. Mama would report on the progress of her curtains or a telephone invitation she'd received to a ladies' luncheon, or she'd tell Daddy about something that had arrived in the mailbox that day. Then Daddy would provide his growing assessment of the inner-workings of the church and the membership. He was beginning to know who was who and what was what—in the church and the community, a vital link in pastoring any congregation. Then he would turn to me and ask, 'What did you do today, Lovey?' Halfway through my telling, Mama would invariably interrupt with, 'Wes, you'll be late for your meeting. Casey, help Mama clear the dishes from the table.' It's odd when I think about it now: she never referred to herself as 'me' or 'I' when she spoke to me. It was always, 'Help Mama *this*' or 'Show Mama *that*' or 'Mama says it's time to *whatever*.' I cannot remember when she ever acknowledged her first-personhood with me when I was a little girl."

Casey paused, looking up at Lorelei, who nodded *go on*. Returning to the imaginary screen, Casey continued. "After Daddy kissed me on the forehead and encouraged me to remember my bedtime prayers, he hugged Mama goodbye. 'Don't wait up for me,' he'd say. 'I'll probably stay after the meeting and work on my sermon. Casey, I'll peek in on you when I get home and make sure your special angel is still watching over you. Mind your Mama, okay?' Then he would leave and I would help Mama load the dishwasher and put the leftovers away. My nightly task was to wipe off the table while she hand-washed the pots and pans. Then she would sweep the floor while I held the dust pan. This would all be accomplished in virtual silence, but even then, I had the sense that things hadn't always been this way between us. I wasn't sure, but a fleeting snapshot image—of Mama smiling indulgently at me or her making a sing-song phonics lesson out of a chore or an errand—convinced me she did love me, once. I'd stop wiping the table and squeeze my eyes shut and try to imprint that image on my mind like a photographer's negative.

"Bedtimes were the best part of the day. After I'd finished brushing my teeth, bathing, and putting on my pajamas, Mama would have me get the book we'd checked out of the library and she would read to me. That summer, we had selected the *Anne of Green Gables* series. I would curl up on the sofa next to Mama and she would turn to a new chapter in the book. Before long, she had transported herself to Prince Edward Isle: her voice would be light and confident and tender, her body relaxed next to mine. While Mama read, a cloak of peace would cover us both, like a beloved baby blanket. At the close of the chapter, the bliss of silence would hang, timeless, in the air, punctuated only by frogs singing outside and our matched, even breathing. The moment was magical, but then the spell would break. I was ushered to bed, prayers heard, and lights turned off. If I hadn't been so captivated by Anne Shirley's spirit, I might hate Lucy Maud Montgomery for writing such short chapters." Casey smiled momentarily.

"One morning after Daddy left for the office and before I'd finished eating my cereal and watching *Sharon, Lois, and Bram's Elephant Show*, Mama announced we were going to Hancock's to buy fabric for school clothes. Mama made most of my clothes, as all the women in her family had done for generations. Homemade was all I knew, with the exception of an occasional gift from Grandma and Grandpa Greer or from a wealthy parishioner. Mama would buy two or three patterns and select material from several bolts of fabric, and the next few days would be a flurry of pinning, cutting, stitching, altering, and hemming. By the weekend, I would have six or seven new outfits, all mix and match, that I would wear the entire school year or until a growth spurt rendered them mission-barrel worthy. That day, I experienced my first twinges of dread and hope about a new school year in a new school. I was ready to relieve the summer tedium, but I was also uneasy about going into the third grade knowing nobody except Billy Murphy from my Sunday School class. Billy barely tolerated me at church; I knew he would completely ignore me at school when his parents weren't making him be civil to the preacher's daughter.

"So it was with this odd duet of eagerness and anxiety that I began school at Founder's Creek Elementary. That first week passed quickly enough as Mrs. Austin's students became familiar with her ways and she quickly learned all 26 of our names. The second week, Mrs. Austin was courageous enough to begin assigning group activities. Each activity was with a different mix of classmates and, of course, most students assigned to a group with Rebekah were grateful—she just had that kind of presence. Rebekah, though, always acted as if she were unaware that she was being worshipped, which made her all the more endearing to me. I was transfixed by her, but never expected her to notice me. So that's why, that Friday so many years ago, I was surprised to hear her call me by name on the playground. I had stooped to look at an inchworm on a leaf when I heard, 'Casey! Hey, Casey!' I turned to see Rebekah, upside down on the monkey bars, her braids forming little arcs at each ear, looking directly at me. There could be no mistake; she was addressing me. 'Yeah?' I answered, trying to sound nonchalant. 'Wanna play with me?' 'Yeah, I guess.' And from that moment on, we were best friends, inseparable. That school year, I learned about sleep-overs and tents made from bed linens. That was the year I saw how other families performed their rites of dinner and bedtime. That was the year Rebekah's family became members of Founder's Creek Community Church. And that was the year my father betrayed us all. She saved me from my mundane, flat existence and when I had the opportunity to save her, I didn't."

Casey stopped, the emotions of that year fresh. She moved her gaze from her memory-screen to Lorelei's face. "That's a very powerful story, Casey. And this betrayal—you believe you, at—what? eight, nine years old?—had the power to prevent it?" Casey nodded, her brow knit. "And this has something to do with Rebekah and your father?" Again, Casey nodded. "Are you and Rebekah still close?"

"No. We haven't spoken since the third grade. But I've never stopped thinking of her, wondering how she is. And then I heard that her father died recently—rather suddenly. She idolized him. If ever a father was a little girl's hero, Mr. Wilkins was Rebekah's." Casey leaned forward again, a sense of urgency in her voice, "What should I do?"

Lorelei paused, gathering her professional wisdom. "What is it you hope to gain by saying something now, after all these years? I want you to think hard about this. Do you want absolution for your eight-year-old self?"

"No! Not at all. I have worked so hard at achieving stability and peace in my life. I want to know if *she's* okay. But I can't just ask outright, 'Rebekah, about that thing with my dad—you okay?'"

Lorelei smiled, held Casey's gaze. "You're right. Still, it's possible that, with her father's death, she's mourning multiple layers of loss. You may have something to offer her, help her grief process, but there's no way of knowing for sure. How does this feel—test the waters, as it were? Write a letter to her, but don't discuss the betrayal. Just see how she responds to hearing from you. I believe you'll know more from her response, or lack thereof."

Casey nodded, already composing the letter in her mind.

Two

"MR. SANDERS," REBEKAH PINCHED OFF her words, "if I don't have the contract by 5 p.m. today, there will be no fall line-up of your company's Christmas formal ware at any of the Belk stores in Northeast Florida. People take their office parties and opera and symphony tickets very seriously here. Glossy ads in all the women's magazines will do you no good if customers cannot purchase your garments." She paused to listen, then "Yes, 5 p.m. today." As she hung up, she noted the time on her computer desktop—*4:35*. Reaching for her daily hand-written to-do list, she crossed off the final item: *secure contract with Sanders*, then sat back in her chair, waiting for the hum of the fax machine.

On the drive home, a wave of sadness washed over Rebekah, eroding the sense of accomplishment she typically relished at the end of a work day. Since the sudden death of her beloved father, Theo Wilkins, five months ago, Rebekah was often caught off guard by an encroaching sorrow. When the frequent bouts of lassitude began affecting her decision-making, and her libido, she sought the services of Hank Stone, Licensed Mental Health Counselor. *Big deal*, Rebekah mused, thinking of her therapist. *LMHC could stand for Lackluster Man Has Credentials*. In Rebekah's estimation, Hank Stone was completely average in every observable way. *I swear I don't know why I waste a lunch hour each week with that man. He's so attached to his precious note pad; he'd probably be completely ineffectual if he misplaced it. And he almost never asks me about Dad. How am I ever going to get over his death if I can't talk about him?* At the thought of her father, Rebekah continued straight on Arlington Expressway, skipping the turn at Cesery Boulevard into her neighborhood. Instead, she drove to Regency Square Mall and the cologne counter of Belk. She found herself making more frequent detours there so she could spray Acqua di Gio, the scent she associated with her father, onto a sample card. Inhaling the scent helped her feel connected to her father and filled her with the resolve she felt missing from her usual state of being.

Once inside her home, a comfortable two-story ranch house she shared with her husband of three years, Cliff Standifer, Rebekah listened to voicemails on the answering machine while flipping through the mail. *Catalog, catalog, magazine, junk, bill, bill, junk, letter. Letter? Who writes letters anymore? Who do I know from a vet's office in Ocala? Probably a sorority sister's husband, asking for money to save the old racehorses from the glue factory.* Rebekah poured herself a glass of Cabernet, kicked off her shoes, and settled into her favorite armchair. Opening the letter, she read:

June 9, 2008

Dear Rebekah,

I hope this letter finds you well. I'm sure I am one of the last people you thought you'd be hearing from. After all, it's been 20 years. Can you believe it?

Rebekah turned to the last page of the letter. It was signed, *Love always, Casey.* Rebekah's eyes widened. She continued reading:

I just recently heard about your father's death. I'm sorry it has taken me so long to send my condolences. Your loss must be terrible to bear. I know how much you loved him. He was a grand man, a true gentleman.

I wasn't sure you would welcome a letter from me, especially after all these years, but my therapist, Lorelei, encouraged me to write. I have told her how much I treasure the time we were girlhood friends. I've told her how cute and smart and outgoing you were and how you took me, the shy newcomer, under your wing. I couldn't believe you wanted to be my friend, especially since everyone wanted to be yours!

Do you remember how much fun we used to have together at your house? I thought you lived in a mansion, there were so many rooms. And your mom made the best chocolate chip pancakes. I always felt like I was getting away with something scandalous eating such a treat for breakfast. Probably my fondest memories are of the swing set in your back yard. Remember how we spent hours making a circus out there with our stuffed animals? Do you remember when you used to stay at my house, too, how we'd use the bedspread to make a tent between the twin beds and pretend we were the famous explorers Christina Columbus and Louise Clark? (Never mind that Columbus and Lewis and Clark were not contemporaries.)

I also remember that Mama would smile more when you were over at our house. Do you remember how quiet and timid she was? Your laugh and your smile were infectious, though. That's probably one reason my father insisted that I invite you to church with us

Rebekah's stomach lurched. She continued reading: *and one reason why he visited your parents so soon after your first Sunday at Founder's Creek. When your mom and dad joined the church, Daddy strutted around for weeks. The fact that Mr. Theo Wilkins, Esquire was such a prominent attorney in town made him think he'd staged a coup of sorts, especially when your father asked if we would be back-up if your mom went into labor at night.*

I'll confess; I liked having your family at Founder's Creek Community Church, too. It made being an only child less lonesome. And, honestly, I was in awe of the relationship you had with your parents. I felt like they <u>saw</u> you. I was never very sure whether Mama and Daddy felt my presence or not. When I was with you, I was somehow more of an entity.

Anyway, Mama and I went to live with her parents near Ocala after Daddy was arrested.

Rebekah felt her head become light, as if it might detach and bob on the ceiling like an errant birthday balloon. The room seemed to sway, pitching like a cheap carnival ride. Invisible fingers clawed at her stomach, acid burning the back of her throat. She forced her eyes to focus on the letter: *I lived with them until I graduated from high school, which was quite a record, considering we had moved five times by the time I was eight years old. It was strange—and good!—for me to finally be able to put roots down somewhere. After Daddy died, Mama had a nervous breakdown and was in the hospital for many months, so it was a good thing we had already moved in with Grandma and Grandpa Greer. Several years ago, she confessed that she had been hanging on to her sanity by a frayed thread years before her breakdown. I'm sad when I think about how lonely she must have been as a pastor's wife. Which makes me all the more grateful for having met you!*

Rebekah, I'm sorry if I've rambled. I hope my letter isn't too much of an intrusion, and that my memories bring some measure of comfort to you. Despite your loss, I hope, too, that you are happy. I have no doubt you are successful, whatever you are doing. I would love to hear from you. You have my return address, should you want to write.

Love always, Casey

Rebekah held the letter to her breast for a moment, moving through a peculiar waltz of emotions while the room continued to move, now in a slow-motion ooze, like one huge lava lamp. Grief and tenderness box-stepped across her heart. She felt like a paid mourner at the funeral of a child she knew of, but had never met. She turned the letter over. *No p.s., no email address, no phone number?* She smiled sorrowfully as she folded the letter, inserting it back into the envelope. *I'll tell ol' Hank about this at our session tomorrow. This should make him ask me questions about Dad. You may be a LMHC, but I'm a VDBD, a very determined bereaved daughter.*

Three

HANK HANDED THE LETTER BACK to Rebekah. "It's curious, isn't it? How many people hear from someone they were friends with in elementary school? Tell me about her. Casey," Hank nodded toward the letter.

Rebekah moved back from the edge of her seat and settled into the armchair. "We were really close in the third grade. Joined at the hip, my mom used to say," Rebekah smiled, remembering her friend. "She was extremely shy, but also sweet and gentle and smart. Different from most kids, but in a good way. I liked her instantly. Most weekends, I was either at her house or she was at mine. As a matter of fact," Rebekah's voice lightened with the sudden recall, as if she'd found a missing border piece to a puzzle, "I stayed at her house when Mom went to the hospital to have Robert, my brother."

"How long were you friends? Beyond third grade?"

Rebekah shook her head. "We lost touch when she moved. I don't remember all the details, but she left before the end of the school year, soon after Robert was born. Pretty abruptly, if memory serves. Mom ended up having an emergency C-section and had a difficult recovery, so I quit all my after-school activities to help her. I remember Casey telling me her last day of school that she was going to live with her grandparents."

A quiet sadness crept into Rebekah's voice as she remembered. "She was just as confused as I was by this. We both cried. When I got home from school, I wanted to call her but Mom told me they had already left and she had no idea how to contact them." Rebekah's voice caught, "That was a rough time. But Mom tried to keep me occupied helping with Robert." She smiled again, "He was such a delight. A good baby. Mom said I was born to be a big sister."

"Tell me about Casey's dad. What do you remember about him?"

Rebekah exhaled audibly. *Casey's dad? What about my dad?* "Not a lot. He was always doing something for church—meetings, visiting shut-ins, that type of thing—so he spent a good bit of time away from home, like my dad did building his practice. He was always there for dinner, but he usually left right after. Our fathers' busy-ness was just a fact of life for us. I assumed all fathers worked long, hard hours."

"Do you remember anything particular about your interactions with him?"

"Only at the dinner table. Oh, and at church. He was a pretty nice guy, I think. There was always a long line to shake his hand on the way out after services." Rebekah paused. "Hank, can we talk about my da… ?"

"Tell me about staying there while your mom was in the hospital," Hank interrupted.

Sighing, Rebekah answered, "It was like every other time I spent the night. Except…"

Hank waited while Rebekah allowed the memory to catch up. "I do remember being upset this time when Mom and Dad dropped me off. I pitched the only temper tantrum I can remember when they drove me there instead of taking me with them to the hospital. We'd been talking about the baby for so long; I assumed I was going with them and that I'd be the first person to hold my new sibling."

Rebekah smiled sympathetically. "Poor Mom. Here she was in labor and Dad was trying to stay calm, and I was standing at Casey's front door bawling and begging Dad to take me with them. When Casey's mom opened the door, she looked genuinely worried. Dad said something about adjusting to the new baby and hurried back to the car. After he left, I stood in the foyer and sobbed. Poor lady."

"Tell me about her—Casey's mom."

Jeez, what do I have to do to get you to ask me about my parents? Rebekah sighed, and relented. "She was very quiet, very demure. She was really great about letting Casey and me play all kinds of make-believe games in Casey's bedroom; she never seemed to mind the mess we made so long as we cleaned it up. My mom was a little more prone to sending us outside to play." Rebekah paused, another memory announcing itself. "Casey's mom made all of her clothes, and I thought that was so cool. She even made us matching outfits once." Rebekah stopped talking, her mind trying to decide what to do with a shadow that had fallen across her memory. She blinked hard and rubbed her eyes with her fingertips.

"What is it?"

"Huh?"

"Were you finished telling me about Casey's mom?"

"Yeah. No.... I don't know."

Hank waited, his pen poised over the legal pad.

"I have a sense that she was a woman of great sorrow…"

Again, Hank waited.

"… as if I had something to do with that somehow." Rebekah swallowed hard.

"Mm hmm," Hank responded.

After a brief lull, Rebekah clipped off her words, "That's it? Mm hmm? Look, Hank, I've been coming to see you for weeks now, feeling worse instead of better, crying at home and at work at the most inopportune times, sleeping every chance I get, and saying no to my husband's romantic overtures. I am not myself. How am I going to get through this depression if you won't let me talk about my own father for a change? You ask me questions about people I haven't seen in years, yet you seem to purposefully steer the conversation away from my father. But I answer your stupid questions anyway, and all you can say is, 'mm hmm'? What exactly does 'mm hmm' mean, Hank?"

Startled, Hank paused, glancing between the leather binder in his lap and his client's glare. "I'm sorry. That's therapist talk for *what do I say now?* I'm buying myself time and seeing if there's something more you want to add. I apologize if I've made you uncomfortable."

"You've made me very uncomfortable, Hank." Rebekah paused, trying to gain control of the warble in her voice. "If you can't help me, just say so. My father died too early and too suddenly. I lived a fairy tale life before then. I was not prepared to let him go, and I was not prepared to become Debbie Depression"

"I'm sor…"

Rebekah cut Hank off, "And another thing. I've always been a really nice person. Why do my visits with you seem to bring out the worst in me? I never used to be someone to boo-hoo or complain. As difficult as it was for me to come to you for help, I'll look for someone else, someone who *can* help me. Just say the word." Her voice cracked and fresh tears collected at the inside edges of her eyes.

"I apologize again. I just want to be very careful about not suggesting things."

"What is there to suggest, Hank? I am a woman who lost her father. Why can't we just talk about that? All this talk about Casey, Casey's dad, Casey's mom—it just confuses things."

"I apolog…"

Rebekah interrupted Hank again, "And another thing: don't you ever get mad? Are you always so damn nice, even when someone's been rude to you? Do you raise your voice? Does *anything* bother you?"

"Yes, there are things that bother me," Hank smiled wistfully. "It troubles me greatly that I seem unable to help you." Hank reached into a pocket in his binder and pulled out a business card, handing it to Rebekah. "I know you believe I've purposefully avoided discussing your father, but I had very good reasons for doing so. Maybe I should have shared those reasons with you, and I apologize if that has added to your pain. I think it might be prudent for you to see her," he pointed at the card. "Dr. Devoe is a friend of mine. She's a doctor, a psychiatrist. She can prescribe an anti-depressant for you, if necessary. She also specializes in women's issues. Maybe she can help you find out why losing your father has been so devastating, if there is additional grief buried beneath the loss of a parent." Hank smiled sadly at Rebekah.

Seeing Hank's smile, Rebekah wordlessly tucked the card into her purse, slipped her suit jacket off the back of the chair, stood up, and walked out of his office. *Treat me like you're the bomb squad, will you? Like you can't figure out which wire to clip. Like I might blow shrapnel all over your pristine office if you share your reasons with me.* As she waited for the elevator, Rebekah suddenly felt as if a critical coil in the underpinnings of her idyllic upbringing had snapped, as if the ballast of intelligent, involved parents, friendship, good moral direction and exceptional schooling had slipped, leaving her listing, sagging, adrift.

Trembling, Rebekah fumbled with the keyless entry to her Volvo. She pressed the remote with a vengeance and slid her body into the driver's side, pulling the door closed. She rested her hands and forehead on the steering wheel. A hundred wordless thoughts and impulses competed for articulation and lost; her breakfast formed a hard knot in her stomach. Despite the heat, she remained in the closed car trying to force the pinballs in her mind to cease firing. Suddenly, she slammed her palms on the steering wheel. Choking back a new onslaught of tears, she wondered through clenched teeth, "How is it that I can go to the Merchandise Mart in Atlanta, negotiate and close a million dollar deal like a pro, but I come out of this, this therapy," she spit the word as if it were an epithet, "every week and feel like a scared little kid? All I've done since I started going to him is cry. Why can't I get a grip? What is wrong with me? My God, he's reduced me to talking to myself. Why am I even putting myself through this?" Knowing the answer to her own question didn't still the pounding in her heart and head.

Four

REBEKAH STARTED HER CAR AND backed out of the parking space. She turned the air conditioner on maximum, in part to cool herself off, but more consciously to try to blast the evidence of tears from her face before returning to work. By the time she had driven through the maze of parking lots in the medical plaza and reached the highway, a profound fatigue had invaded every space of her body. Picking up her cell phone, she called her voice mailbox at work and changed her greeting. "You've reached the voicemail of Rebekah Wilkins-Standifer. I am out of the office the afternoon of June 12. Please leave a detailed message and I will return your call at my earliest convenience." Her voice was courteous, direct, no-nonsense, her accent indicative of her north Florida Panhandle roots and of refinement. With that, Rebekah turned her car into the street, heading home and to a nap she hoped would erase the picture that was attempting to paint itself onto the canvas of her mind.

A coma-like sleep enveloped Rebekah. Dark swirls of long-buried images danced at the edges of a dream. The curtain parted mid-scene: *A little girl skips through a meadow of waist-high wildflowers. Without restraint of self-awareness, she is smiling, singing to her doll, twirling and dancing, lost in her joy. She drops her doll and when she stoops to pick it up she sees a snake slithering across her doll's face. Panic seizes her. She loves her doll yet is repulsed by the snake. The little girl catches movement out of the corner of her eye. Her baby brother is crawling toward her, babbling and cooing, unaware of the danger the snake presents. Wild with terror and helplessness, the little girl tries to scream for help and finds herself mute. Her feet rooted to the spot where she stands, she watches as the snake coils itself on top of the doll, prepared to strike the unsuspecting baby. Squinting her eyes, gritting her teeth against certain pain, she reaches toward the snake to grab it before it can attack. Instead, the snake wraps itself around her wrist, its head resting in the valley between her thumb and forefinger; it leers at her as it flicks its tongue into the air in front of the little girl's face. She attempts to scream once more, to summon help.*

"Casey! Help!" Rebekah woke abruptly to the sound of her own voice. She jerked her body upright, drenched in sweat, heart jackhammering in her chest. Quickly sliding off the bed, she ran into her closet, shutting the door behind her. There, she folded herself up as tightly as possible in a back corner, wrapping her arms around her knees. A primal moan escaped from her. Although she felt sick to her stomach, she pushed her back into the wall behind her winter clothes, deep dread washing over her.

"Rebekah? Bec, I'm home. I brought Thai for dinner. Babe, where are you?" Cliff opened the closet door to hang up his suit coat. As he moved to close the door, he stopped. Hearing the whimpered keening of an animal in distress, he looked toward the sound and saw Rebekah's feet sticking out from behind a row of coats and jackets. "Bec? God, honey, what's wrong?"

In a childlike voice, Rebekah squeaked, "I'm scared." Cliff sat cross-legged on the closet floor and coaxed Rebekah out with his open hands, pulling her into his arms. Rebekah allowed herself to be held, resting her head on his shoulder, inhaling his scent and absorbing his strength until her breathing returned to normal. The smell of her husband was one of the first things that had attracted Rebekah to Cliff Standifer: a mixture of cleanness, gentleness, and virility, of expensive cologne and innate goodness. At times during their three-year marriage when they were apart overnight, she slept with one of his t-shirts just to be near his smell. When she breathed it, she knew she was safe.

Sitting up, Rebekah slipped out of Cliff's arms and turned to face him. "I had a horrible dream. I came home to take a nap 'cause I was so tired after seeing Hank. Then I had this dream about a snake—you know how I hate snakes—and I woke up from it screaming Casey's name. I've told you about when we were little girls, and about the letter I just got from her. Anyway, when I woke up, I ran in here. I didn't know what else to do." Rebekah blushed. "How embarrassing...." She pushed her eyebrows up with her fingertips then shook her head slightly, as if to clear her mind from the debris left by the dream.

"Do you think you need to call Hank and talk about this with him?"

"No. No, I really don't." Rebekah's answer sounded harsher than she intended.

"What's up? You and Hank have a tiff?" Cliff gently teased.

"No. Well, yeah, we did. I yelled at him today after he steered the conversation away from Dad—again." Rebekah grimaced at the memory. "Anyway, he sort of fired me. What I mean is, he referred me to a psychiatrist who," she made air quotes, 'specializes in women's issues'. I didn't realize depression was a 'women's issue'. Whatever. Besides, whoever heard of a therapist named Hank? Sounds like he ought to be a stable hand at a dude ranch—not that I can picture Hank doing that." Afraid to release the tenuous hold she currently had on her emotions, Rebekah quickly changed the subject. "Did you say you brought Thai? Let's eat. I'm starving."

Five

LORELEI AND CASEY QUICKLY EXCHANGED pleasantries, then sat down in Lorelei's spacious office adjacent to Ocala Regional Hospital. "So tell me. Did you write a letter to Rebekah?"

"I did. I expressed my condolences and did a little reminiscing about when we played together as little girls. I tried to keep it friendly and open, not heavy. Oh, and I purposefully didn't include my phone number or email address so she wouldn't feel obligated to share her personal contact information with me. I figured a letter would be hard to ignore, but would feel less threatening than if I'd found her in a Google search and emailed or called her." Casey shrugged.

"Good thinking. As I said last week, you can take your cues from her response, if you receive one. I do have one recommendation to make, though. If she does respond, set up some boundaries with each other. Like maybe snail-mail only. We tend to censor ourselves less when we have pen in hand, so we're more authentic, but the reader can also determine the time and place to open letters. Phone calls and unopened emails in an inbox could be too much of a distraction or a nuisance."

"That sounds good. I'm all for putting technology in its place anyway."

"Okay. If you feel up to it, I think it would be good for us to talk about what happened—the betrayal you mentioned. Were you caught off-guard by it?"

"If I'm to be honest, I'd have to say no, not entirely. I began sensing something was wrong when I was about six years old, before we moved to Founder's Creek. My father was occasionally invited to lead revivals or camp meeting weekends. We'd all go as a family - Mama, Daddy, and me. Since the revivals were usually held outdoors, they were scheduled during the warmer months, which varied, depending on location. Many times, those revivals were scheduled in rural areas—places so small and remote they weren't on the circuits of traveling evangelists.

"The congregations or the community would invite Daddy with only the promise that they would take up a collection to try to defray the cost of our transportation there and back home. If the money they collected amounted to more than that, they were able to offer him a small honorarium. And to save on expenses, we were invited to stay in the homes of church members, usually someone who was in charge of arrangements for the revival.

"Each revival began with an air of expectancy and my father didn't disappoint. He was quite the showman. Those people expected Bible-thumping and that's what they got. Daddy could whip a crowd of people into a frenzy of guilt just as easily as he could get them to lay every worry at the makeshift altar set up under the tent. He would walk through the aisles of metal folding chairs, holding open his Bible in one hand, thumbing through its pages, citing passages, shouting out verses of perdition and promise, raising and lowering his voice in a hypnotic cadence while the crowd tried to cool themselves off with funeral parlor fans or handkerchiefs.

"I was never sure whether they felt more heat from the temperature outside or from Daddy's message burning them inside. To this day, the smells of sawdust or inexpensive talcum powder and sweat instantly send my mind back to those days and make me feel like something is about to happen.

"Most of the people we met farmed for a living or earned their income through hard manual labor. They weren't simple people, though; they just weren't complicated. I mean that as a compliment. Most of them knew more about living a life of faith than people who aren't dependent on the whims of sun and rain. And although their faces were creased with years of working outdoors and worrying from harvest to harvest, they were also creased with more laugh lines and joy than I remember seeing anywhere else. They were easily delighted—by a timely rain or a cooperative combine.

"At any rate, once the revival service was over, we would be invited to spend the night at the home of a local pillar in the church community. Daddy would usually preach at a Friday night service, go on Saturday afternoon visitation with another church leader to the homes of those too old or too ill to attend, preach a Saturday evening service, then pull out all his pastoral stops at the Sunday morning service, after which there was usually dinner on the grounds and then a long ride home for us.

"When we'd spend the night at someone's house, I would usually share a room with the children, if there were children my age. If it was the home of older people, the host and hostess would usually give Mama and Daddy their bedroom while they would take the spare bedroom or sleep on a fold-out sofa in the living room, and I would be assigned to a cot on the screened-in porch. I'd lie awake as long as I could, listening to a concert of the bullfrogs and crickets and cicadas while the adults stayed up talking indoors. It gave me a lot of comfort to hear Mama's voice—her comments and her gentle, sincere laughter—as I knew even back then that she felt isolated in her life as a pastor's wife.

"It wasn't that she didn't have friends in every church Daddy served; it's just that she kept a part of herself reserved. I guess it appeared that she was dignified but, in looking back, I'd have to say it was also to protect the image that others had of Daddy, of our family. When we were away from home, though, she could ease up a little more and simply enjoy the company of those whose spiritual nurture she wasn't responsible for.

"Around the time I was five years old, Daddy began to slip out of our hosts' homes after everyone had gone to bed. He'd tell Mama he needed to take a prayer walk to get ready for the next day's service. Years later, Mama told me he seemed distracted and restless at those times and that she had admired his spiritual solution to his restlessness. When I had just turned six, Daddy abruptly put an end to the family coming along with him. He claimed it was because the travel left me too exhausted for school on Monday. That was the only time I remember Mama and Daddy arguing loud enough for me to hear them. Mama pleaded, 'But Wes, why? Please don't do this. Going with you is just as important to me as it is for the people you're going to serve.'

"And Daddy, emphatic, replied, 'No. I said no. End of discussion.' I remember thinking, 'Please don't do this to Mama.' When we moved to Founder's Creek, Daddy quit doing revival meetings altogether and focused all his pastoral energies on his congregation. He said it was too far and too expensive to travel to the places that invited him each year. So, yes, I did see something brewing, even though I was too young to know what exactly. Quitting those revivals was a huge loss for Mama. Whatever sparkle that was left in her before we lived in Florida got left behind in the move. It's too bad other things didn't get left behind instead."

Six

REBEKAH MINDLESSLY FLIPPED DR. MYRA Devoe's business card between her thumb and forefinger, debating the merits of trying to break in a new therapist. The imagery of the helpless girl in her recent dream and the fresh shame of rebuffing her husband's attempt at love-making that morning convinced her she needed to make the call. *I can always cancel if I change my mind.* What she did not expect is for Dr. Devoe's receptionist to inform her of a cancellation for the following day. Rebekah booked the appointment, cursing herself for joining a health plan that didn't require referrals and endless red tape and waiting.

The receptionist handed Rebekah a clipboard with papers to fill out. Rebekah allowed herself to be swallowed up by an oversized chair in the waiting room. The waiting area was shared by the patients of five licensed therapists—two men and three women, judging by the shingle on the outside of the building. Rebekah glanced around the room at the other clients waiting: one man, dressed in a business suit, tapped on his Blackberry; one watched CNN on the office television, stone-faced, elbows perched on his knees; one woman was absorbed in the task of cleaning out her purse while talking in animated tones on her cell phone; another stared into a place only she herself was privy to.

Rebekah completed the forms, delivered herself from the womb-like chair, and returned the clipboard to the receptionist. She selected an outdated magazine and resettled in the chair she had already warmed. Over the edge of the magazine, she studied the gentleman on his phone. As a fashion merchandiser, she always felt compelled to observe the placement of people and things. She considered her critiques a refinement of her skills. *I wonder what he's here for. He looks a little nervous. I'll bet he has a gambling problem; probably embezzled funds from work to cover his debts.*

Her gaze wandered to the other man, who continued to stare impassively at the television screen. *Marital problems. And who can blame her?* she thought, observing his scraggly two-days' growth of beard and his grubby jeans and t-shirt, both insufficient to cover a telltale beer belly. Eyeing the chatty woman, she mused, *Look at all the crap she's had crammed in her purse. And why in the world does she think any of us want to hear about her affair with her boss? She doesn't need a therapist; she needs a course in charm school. And a muzzle.* Noting the woman's badly outdated outfit, she added, *A subscription to Vogue wouldn't hurt, either.*

Censoring herself, she continued her assessment of her waiting room peers. *Better turn the page so they'll think I'm actually reading this magazine—that's how old? My God, I'd forgotten what Britney Spears looked like when she shaved her head.* Rebekah looked at the time on her watch, then turned her covert attention to the woman staring off into space. *I hope I don't end up like her. This Dr. Devoe had better be good or electroshock therapy, here I come.*

"Rebekah?" a refined voice with traces of Caribbean ancestry announced her name at one of the two doors leading out of the waiting room. Rebekah looked in the direction of the voice and saw an attractive, statuesque, 50-something black woman holding one of the doors ajar.

"That's me," she responded as she approached the woman.

They shook hands. "Hi. I'm Myra Devoe. It's nice to meet you." Her resonant voice was rich and reassuring. Dr. Devoe led Rebekah down the hallway of the U-shaped corridor that contained the therapists' offices, carrying herself with the mien of Nubian royalty. In her stride alone, she seemed to possess an inner peace and strength that made Rebekah yearn—for some unnamable thing time and circumstances had forgotten. *I think I like this lady already*, Rebekah allowed herself to feel hopeful as she looked at the back of this woman in possession of nobility and grace.

Opening her office door, Dr. Devoe motioned toward a set-up that resembled a den. "Please. Have a seat." Rebekah chose a comfortable-looking chair, one of four eclectically mismatched chairs, positioned, with a sofa, around a glass-top coffee table, all atop the handsomest Persian rug she'd ever seen. *Three thousand dollars, at least*, Rebekah mused.

Dr. Devoe settled herself into an adjoining chair, methodically glancing over the paperwork in a manila folder while Rebekah stole a look at her: this woman, with burnished ebony skin, creased by laughter and age, and close-cropped hair, flecked with gray, exuded wisdom and calm.

Rebekah's eyes scanned the room. Dr. Myra Devoe's office was a testament to her passion for jazz and travel. A massive mahogany desk with matching bookshelves and credenza took up one wall. Hundreds of books on every topic imaginable, matted and framed photographs of exotic scenery, artifacts, travel posters, and jazz memorabilia and concert playbills lent texture to the neatly organized, inviting office.

Dr. Devoe interrupted Rebekah's visual tour. "Let's get started, shall we?" Shifting her focus to Dr. Devoe's face, Rebekah nodded. "Just this once, I need to look at your paperwork and make some notes. I promise you after that, if you choose to remain with me, I won't seem so distracted. Okay?"

Rebekah smiled. "That sounds like a refreshing departure for me. I swear my last therapist was married to his precious legal pad. Like it was his blankie or something," she added sardonically.

Dr. Devoe smiled appreciatively, glancing down at the form in front of her. "That would be Hank Stone, right?"

Oops. Rebekah smiled in embarrassment. *That's right. They know each other. Better watch what I say.*

"What brings you here, Ms. Wilkins-Standifer?"

"Rebekah. Please. Call me Rebekah. I know my last name is a mouthful."

"And you must call me Myra," Myra Devoe smiled warmly. "So, what can I do for you, Rebekah?"

"Well, my father died this past November—it was very unexpected, he was only 59—and ever since then, I've been depressed. I went to see Hank for a couple of months, but I didn't feel like I was making any progress. He thought I might need a prescription for an anti-depressant and, possibly," she smiled weakly, "a different therapist. He's the one who recommended you to me."

Myra returned her smile. "Tell me about your father."

Yes! thought Rebekah. *Smart woman.* Rebekah proceeded to tell Myra everything she could about her father—that he was her hero, her friend, her protector, the standard against whom she measured all men.

"You do know how fortunate you are, don't you, to be able to say those things about your father?" Myra responded.

"Oh, yes, I do. And I suppose that's why I'm having such a hard time getting over his death, even though he's been gone nearly eight months now. Actually, my mom seems to be dealing with this better than I am, and she was absolutely devoted to him! I don't understand what's wrong with me. Why can't I get over it and get on with my life?"

Myra smiled sympathetically. "Different people have different ways of working through their grief," she said, "and different timetables for doing so. There isn't some magical formula for arriving on the other side of sorrow." Rebekah smiled appreciatively. Myra continued. "You said you've been depressed. How has your depression played itself out? What does it look like in your life?"

"At first I was so numb, I couldn't cry. Then I'd cry at the most inopportune times, like in the middle of business meetings. Now, I'm numb or crying or craving sleep. I do love my job and the life I have with my husband, but they aren't enough some days to make me want to slap that alarm clock and," Rebekah spoke with an animated flourish, drawing out her vowels for emphasis, "rise and shine. I still do—get out of bed—but I'd rather be asleep."

"Your husband. Has he been supportive of you throughout this time?"

"Oh, yes, very. I could *not* have made it through these past eight months without Cliff. And, frankly, he deserves better than what he's getting right now, which is a whole lot of nothing. Do you think you can help me?"

Myra smiled warmly at Rebekah. "Oh, I don't believe you're so far gone that you won't be enjoying your life a lot more again. Do you?"

Rebekah shrugged her shoulders. "I hope not. I do worry sometimes that I'm worse off now than I was right after it happened. And I'm so tired of going through the motions. I'm tired."

Myra nodded. "Let me ask you some more questions." For the next half hour, Myra asked Rebekah her standard getting acquainted personal and medical questions and Rebekah answered them as straightforwardly as possible, with little change or inflection in her voice. Myra concluded by asking, "What is your goal for our sessions? What are we working toward?"

"I want *me* back."

"And who is that, exactly?" Myra responded.

"Hmm. She's someone who's lively and energetic. Fun and interesting to be around, interested in other things and people instead of merely making it through another day," Rebekah smiled wryly.

Myra sensed the desperation in Rebekah's voice. "I have an assignment for you. One I hope you will find not only enjoyable, but therapeutic as well." Rebekah's interest flickered. "I'd like for you to get out as many photographs of yourself as you can, including ones with your father. Try to line them up chronologically and take your time as you look at them. I want you to determine who you were growing up—both in relation to your father and others and as an individual. What made you laugh, what made you cry, what made you happy, what made you mad… what made you tick? Do you think you can do that?"

Rebekah paused before she answered, poring over her Outlook calendar and daily task lists in her mind. "I guess I could do that. I'd probably have to go to my mom's, though, to get the pictures."

"Will that be a problem?" Myra asked. "Seeing your mother?"

"No, it's not that. I'm just trying to figure out when I can get over there. I have a couple of big projects at work...." Suddenly, Myra's assignment intrigued her, and a visit with her mother seemed like a very good idea. "No, I can do it. Mom already has the pictures in albums and scrapbooks. And I'm overdue for a visit with her anyway. This'll be good."

"Good. I'm glad. Now, Rebekah, I don't want you to skim over those pictures, all right? Take your time. Allow yourself to feel whatever each picture causes you to feel. Will you do that?"

Rebekah's eyebrows arched. "Why wouldn't I do that anyway?"

"Well, you said you've been sort of numb. There may be some strong emotion behind the numbness. Will you allow yourself to," she made quotation marks with her fingers, "'lose control'? Will you let your grief speak to you?"

Rebekah's brow furrowed. "Sure. It's not as if I haven't already cried about this. You do understand that, don't you?"

"Yes. You mentioned inconvenient bouts of crying, times when you may be more concerned about regaining your composure than listening to what your grief might be trying to tell you. This time, I want you to listen. And write down any and all impressions you have while you're looking at those photos. Will you do that?" Rebekah nodded. "If you'll do that, then we can begin working on getting *you* back, okay?"

As Rebekah walked to her car, with a prescription for Zoloft in her purse, a wave of apprehension overtook her, but she dismissed it as evidence of how inconvenient a weekend away from work-related projects would be. *All she has to do is listen to people all day. She doesn't have a clue what a real job is all about. She even has time to travel and go to concerts! But, if this will help me get my game back, I'll do it. Hello, World, get ready. I'm coming back!*

Seven

REBEKAH STABBED THE AUTO-DIAL BUTTON on her car radio with a freshly-painted fingernail, trying to find a satellite station whose mood matched hers. *And what is that, exactly?* she asked herself. She selected an Oldies station and, as the car covered the distance between Founder's Creek and Jacksonville, replayed the events of the weekend. Spending time with her mother in the Wilkins home had been both nourishing and exhausting. The very wallpaper and furniture were infused with memories of schools and playmates, Girl Scouts and ballet, school plays and recitals, boyfriends and cheerleading, slumber parties and proms, achievements and accolades, and a family that had loved and laughed together through it all.

Like two teen-agers at a sleepover, Rebekah and her mother, Faye, had spread the many photo albums and scrapbooks out on the floor of the living room, alternately howling at Rebekah's snaggle-toothed grin in the first grade and crying at pictures of her handsome father, Theo, walking her down the aisle at her wedding, his expressions of pride and tenderness unconcealed.

Rebekah had spoken honestly with Faye about her assignment and her new therapist, Dr. Myra Devoe, as well as her continued struggle to claw her way out of depression. And Faye had listened attentively, weeping with her daughter over the too-short life of the man they both loved and who, they both knew, loved them. Rebekah's mother served her daughter home-cooked meals and appropriate portions of motherly love and concern.

"How is it that you seem to be doing so much better with this than I am?" Rebekah had asked.

"Oh, I have my days, honey," Faye answered, "when I stay in my nightgown until noon. And I'm never very far from a box of Kleenex. I do think your therapist is right, though. Different people have different ways of dealing with grief. I got a lot of my crying done during the funeral and the days afterward. You were there taking care of me and Robert and all the details, and then you went straight back to work. I had the gift of time after everyone left."

Her silky Southern voice trailed off. "Not a day goes by that I don't miss your father, but I have very fond memories to keep me company, too. I'm glad to be sharing those with you this weekend." She patted her daughter's arm. "Do you know, it's been ages since we did this?"

"I know. I was thinking about that on the drive over. I don't think we've really hung out together since I was in college."

"I used to love it when you came home for holidays and long weekends. I've never been happier than when this house was filled with you and Robert and your friends. It's been pretty quiet this summer with him away at summer school. I'm glad he made the Davidson tennis team, though," her voice broke. Rebekah reached over to comfort her mother.

The first night at home, after her mother had gone upstairs to bed, Rebekah had stayed up late looking through the photographs again, this time with pen and paper nearby. Regardless of whether the assignment had come from a professor, a boss, or her therapist, Rebekah prided herself on her thoroughness, promptness, and attention to detail. *Reactions, thoughts, feelings. Okay.*

Rebekah thumbed through her earlier years, jotting down words and ideas: friendly, nice, accepting, popular, athletic, fun, golden. *Golden? What the hell does that mean?* She scratched through the word and continued. She flipped to a page that contained photos of her with Casey. Rebekah reached out and touched the page, tracing the outline of a picture showing her and Casey in Halloween costumes, their eyes twinkling. They had gone trick-or-treating as Tweedle-Dee and Tweedle-Dum, their costumes expertly sewn by Casey's mother. *Miss Annette*, Rebekah suddenly remembered the name she had affectionately called her friend's mother.

A pang of—what—she couldn't identify it, shot through her, and she quickly grabbed an entire section of scrapbook pages and turned past them, arriving at a page with photos of her in a cheerleading uniform. *I was pretty full of myself then. And in a huge hurry to grow up and get out of Founder's Creek. I sure didn't know then how well I had it here.* Rebekah started to cross though the indicting descriptions, but chose instead to keep looking at photographs.

The next section of photos included those of her parents helping her get settled into her dorm room at Wake Forest. Although all three of them were smiling in the photograph taken by her new roommate, a bookish girl straight from a Long Island prep school, there was an edge to Rebekah's smile. She wrote: impatient, aloof, guarded. *It didn't take me long to fit in, though,* she thought of her freshman peers. *I wowed 'em during Rush Week. They all wanted me,* she smiled.

Like a headache brought on by drinking something too cold, a thought suddenly stabbed Rebekah's brain. *But I didn't want any of them. Not really. I wanted them to like me, but I wanted to put in my four years and then get on with my future. I didn't want to get too attached.* To her list, she added: coward. Then: shallow. The truth of those words invited old hurts to announce their presence, but Rebekah shut the scrapbooks and albums, guzzled the last of her glass of wine, and curled into a fetal position, awaiting the bliss of sleep to override her memories and her consciousness.

The next morning after breakfast, Rebekah had ridden to the cemetery with Faye. They placed fresh flowers on Theo Wilkins' grave, both misting up when Rebekah said out loud, "I miss you, Daddy." After they had cried and hugged, they had driven to the outlet mall in Destin to shop away their gloom. As usual, Rebekah's impeccable eye for a fashion bargain enabled them both to leave five hours later with a trunk full of clothes and accessories, none of which they truly needed.

"Thanks," Faye enthused. Rebekah thought a little too brightly, "I needed that. I haven't had a good old-fashioned shopping therapy day in forever." Rebekah wasn't fooled by her mother's effusiveness; she knew her mother was trying to be brave on her behalf.

"It was good for me, too, Mom." She smiled at her mother. *Anything to delay finishing my assignment,* she thought. Then *I'm learning the fine art of procrastination rather late in life.*

While her mother was driving, during a lull in their conversation, Rebekah asked, "Mom, what do you remember about Casey? Do you remember her? She was my BFF in third grade."

Faye took a moment to answer. "Y'all spent every spare minute together—or so it seemed." Rebekah noticed a tightness around her mother's mouth. "And she was kind of peculiar. Not so much odd as she was quirky. Unique. But endearing. Why? Why do you ask?"

"No particular reason, except that I've been thinking about her a lot lately. I hadn't thought about her in years, but recently she wrote me a condolence letter, and then a few days later I had a horrible dream and I woke myself up calling out her name." Faye flinched, pursed her lips. Rebekah continued, "I haven't written back. I don't know what I'd say to her. I mean, we'd barely know each other now."

"What'd she say in her letter?"

"Other than she was sorry to hear about Daddy, she talked about how we used to play at her house and about when we used to play at our house. She remembers your chocolate chip pancakes," Rebekah smiled at her mom, whose hands tightened on the steering wheel. "She talked about how special you and Daddy were. And, let's see…. She's a veterinarian, in Ocala. Oh, and she mentioned that her father got arrested and that's why she had to move down there with her grandparents. Did you know that? I don't think I remember anything about that."

"Oh, Rebekah, that was so long ago." Then, "did she say anything else?"

"No. That was about it. Oh, Miss Annette had a nervous breakdown or something. And her father ended up dying. I wonder if he died in jail or after he got out. You sure you don't remember anything about that? His arrest had to have been in the newspaper."

Rebekah's mother relaxed her grip on the steering wheel and the pink returned to her cheeks. "Like I said, that was so long ago. And you must remember, I stayed so busy taking care of you and a new baby, I barely had time to wash my hair, much less read the paper."

"Well, that can't have been easy for them. I'll bet that's why Miss Annette had a nervous breakdown. Goodness knows, if Cliff ever got arrested, you'd have to scrape me off the floor."

Seeing a Baskin-Robbins sign up ahead, Faye blurted, "I feel like an ice cream cone. Want to indulge?" And with that, their conversation quickly drifted to calories and fat grams and their favorite flavors of Ben and Jerry's, and the need for just a spoon, not a bowl.

Rebekah, sensing a now-familiar heaviness in her throat, changed the radio station and allowed herself to be lulled into a state of suspended thought and feeling by the rhythmic thrumming of tires against asphalt.

Eight

"HOW WAS YOUR VISIT WITH your mother?" Myra asked, her tone genuine.

"Good. It was good. Thanks." *Thanks? For what? For asking? For making me do something I should have done months ago? For charging me an arm and a leg to listen to me talk—to be my friend?* Rebekah smiled weakly.

"Tell me what you've learned about Rebekah." Myra's smile was warm, inviting.

Rebekah pulled her homework out of her briefcase and proceeded to tell Myra her observations about herself, both then and now. She recounted the details robotically, devoid of emotions.

"If you don't mind my saying, you seem rather detached from your life," Myra noted.

"What?"

"Detached. You seem almost disconnected from yourself. As if you were telling these things about a stranger."

Rebekah started to protest. Instead, she surprised herself with the words she spoke. "I *am* a stranger. At least to myself. I look at those pictures of myself as a child and she in no way resembles who I am now. I have no idea who I am anymore. Or who I'm supposed to be."

Myra waited patiently for her client to absorb the impact of this self-revelation. Rebekah spoke again, "And I realized I don't have any true friends, other than Cliff. I haven't had a genuine friendship since elementary school. I've kept nearly everyone, including my mother, at bay."

Myra continued her silence, maintaining an open gaze with Rebekah, inviting her to keep talking, to keep listening to ideas that had remained in seclusion too long. As if she'd dusted off years and layers of debris from an artifact, Rebekah continued, "The sad thing is, probably nobody in all these years has known that my relationship with them has been superficial. That *I've* been superficial."

"Why do you suppose that is?"

"I have no idea. I seriously had no idea until now how shallow I've been."

"Rebekah, you are anything but shallow. Scared is more like it."

"Of what? I have nothing to be afraid of. If anything, I'm tenacious. Driven. Take charge. I push people away, but I'm so smooth about it, they don't even realize I've done it. I've drawn a circle around myself and the only person I've allowed in is my husband, and that's only because he sneaked his way in." Rebekah smiled sheepishly.

"Let's talk about that, then. Why do you think you push people away? How do you think you got to be so good at it?"

"I don't know. Maybe I was afraid they'd get in the way of my ambitions. I've known since I was 12 years old what I wanted to do and I've been determined to achieve it."

"Which is?"

"To be the best damn fashion merchandiser in the Southeast," Rebekah replied straightforwardly. She held up her hand in self-defense. "Don't get me wrong; I wouldn't trounce on anyone to get there, and I have no intention of doing anything illegal or unethical, but I wouldn't let anyone get in my way, either. Or slow me down." Myra again waited, sensing another personal revelation. "But somehow, after Daddy died, the wind has sort of gone out of that sail. Not that I don't still want to be the best at what I do, but I'm having a hard time getting as excited about my work as I used to."

"Why do you think that is?"

"I guess it's the whole mortality thing: is this all there is, and what's the point, and what will I have to show for all my success? As hard as my father worked and as much as he was away from his family, we still knew we were the most important part of his life. He didn't always do a good job of balancing that, though, and I see myself doing an even less admirable job than he did. What happens if I climb all the way to the top but there's nobody up there to share the victory with me?"

"Or nobody to share the climb?"

Tears welled up in Rebekah's eyes. "Yeah."

"So, what are you afraid of, Rebekah Wilkins-Standifer?"

"I'm afraid of getting too close to people, but I'm afraid of getting too far away, too. God, am I bipolar or something?"

Myra smiled indulgently. "No, you're not bipolar. You're a woman, but you're not Superwoman. It's not a bad thing to need people to share your life with. It's not a sign of weakness; it's a sign that you're human. You know, you can be extraordinary and ordinary at the same time. You're permitted." Rebekah smiled while dabbing at her eyes. Myra continued, "Do you think you know why you haven't had a close friend since, when did you say? Elementary school?" Rebekah shook her head. "Why don't you tell me about that friendship, then."

Rebekah told Myra everything she could remember about her friendship with Casey. She spoke in animated tones about the things they used to do together and her eyes sparkled. "It's funny, but I hadn't thought about Casey in years, and now it's almost as if I'm being drawn back to her, everywhere I turn." Rebekah told Myra about the photographs, the conversation with her mother, the letter she had received from Casey, and about the dream that seemed to have started her reminisces.

"Have you written her back? Or called her?"

"No. I've thought about it, but I don't really know what I'd say. I'm not even sure why I'd want to re-establish contact or if we'd have anything in common now. I mean, isn't it sort of ridiculous to try to rekindle a friendship based on the fact that you played with stuffed animals together 20 years ago?"

"Maybe that's ridiculous, maybe it isn't. How will you know unless you find out for yourself? At any rate, you've acknowledged that you need to begin cultivating friendships again. It might not be such a bad idea to do that with someone who already knows you. Or knew you. Someone you were once close to. Who knows; this might be just what you need right now to not only help with your depression, but also to give you some answers about yourself that you seem to be searching for."

"Yeah, maybe."

"You don't sound convinced."

"I'm not convinced of much these days. But maybe you're right. I'm not very decisive these days, either. Sorry."

"No need to apologize. This is the place you find yourself in now. Let's look at what you *do* know and we'll work from there. You want some depth to your life, right?" Myra used her hands to illustrate, and Rebekah nodded. "You have a husband who loves you and is supportive of you, true?" Rebekah smiled and nodded again. "You know you don't want to stay in this pattern any longer than necessary, isn't that so?" Rebekah nodded emphatically. Myra moved her hands apart, as if breaking a loaf of French bread, "And you also want some breadth, right?" Rebekah hunched her shoulders. "That's where relationships become important." Rebekah nodded. "I want you to consider something after I give you another assignment."

Oh, goody. More homework. Wearily, but obediently, Rebekah pulled her iPhone out of her briefcase, opened the Notes feature, and looked up at Myra. *Go ahead.*

"Your assignment is this: I want you to explore some more this relationship you had with Casey. Go back to those days when you two were inseparable. Take a mental tour of your home when she was there—what did it look like, what did it sound like, what did it smell like? Then do the same for her house. Try to see not only yourselves in both places, but also the other people involved. Who do you see? What do they do? What were their dynamics? Okay?"

Rebekah's expression said *whatever.* "Okay."

"And if you decide to communicate with Casey, I think it's best that you do so only in letters. You'll feel safer that way and less obliged to respond to any of her questions that you don't feel comfortable answering."

Rebekah nodded, mutely.

"And I want you to consider becoming a member of a new support group I have, beginning in August, just for women."

Rebekah's eyebrows shot up. *Whoa there, lady.* "A support group? What for? So I can make," Rebekah's tone was mocking, "friends?"

Myra continued to smile reassuringly at Rebekah, ignoring her wild-eyed expression. "Yes, a support group. For women in similar circumstances—in search of answers, in search of understanding. If for no other reasons than to reinforce to each other that you are not in this alone, nor are you as peculiar as you may sometimes feel. I just want you to consider it. Will you do that?"

"Yeah, sure," Rebekah said, gathering her belongings. *When camels fly.* She made an appointment to see Myra in a week and left in a cloud of desperation and confusion.

Nine

LORELEI SMILED AT CASEY. "HAVE you heard back from your letter to Rebekah?"

Casey shook her head.

"Give it time. Give *her* time. She is probably sorting through a cocktail of emotions right now, with her father's death and then hearing from you." Casey nodded. "So why don't we discuss the episode that prompted you to reach out to Rebekah. Shall we?"

"Okay. I think I have my own cocktail going on." Casey's smile was edged with confusion.

"Please. Tell me about it," Lorelei invited. "What emotions are in your cocktail?"

"When I think back on the night my father abused Rebekah, I remember being terrified, unable to move, but at the same time, my mind was whirring, trying to think of a way to make him stop. Why I didn't fake a cough in my sleep, or pretend I was having a nightmare, I'll never know. I felt guilty and helpless all at the same time. Those two reactions—*do* something, *don't move*—have been the hallmark responses I have every time I'm stressed."

"Talk to me about that."

"The first time I saw a therapist was when I was 16. After years of not talking about my father and what he had done, seeing the toll it took—still takes—on my mother, I was angry. Roots of bitterness and confusion had grown deep and were choking the life out of me. I also began having migraines, which interfered with my ability to concentrate at school which, in turn, affected the GPA I needed to get into the University of Florida's pre-vet program.

A doctor determined the headaches were from grinding my teeth at night, so she fitted me with a night splint. That fixed one thing, but then I lost all interest in even my favorite activities. Mama had never seen me indifferent to 4H or volunteering with the hippo-therapy program at Shepherd's School for Exceptional Children. She was the one astute enough to realize this wasn't typical adolescent ennui, and used what little strength she had to force the issue of my seeing a psychologist. She was determined to see that I not remain tethered to whatever my gene pool and family history might've conspired together to rob from me. She said, 'whatever is Greer and good about you *will* prevail.'"

"She sounds very wise."

"Oh, she is. I also think she's stronger than she gives herself credit for. At any rate, intuitively I knew what was at the heart of these problems but I could not bring myself to describe to Mama what happened that night and my silent complicity. I was afraid of what it would do to the fragile peace she had developed with the way her life turned out. But there's no doubt I still needed to talk about it. And she knew it."

"Was there any other time your," Lorelei made air quotes, "'cocktail' interfered with your life?"

"Yes. Right before I turned 21, after I'd been accepted to vet school, pending completion of my undergrad degree. I began waking up every morning with a cinder block of dread pressing down on my chest. I couldn't completely fill my lungs no matter how deeply I tried to inhale. I don't know what was most disconcerting, that this happened when I wasn't expecting it - it felt like a sniper attack, or that I could be rejected from vet school after working my tail off to get in. I like definitives. I've always had goals and deadlines for achieving those goals, with identifiable steps along the way, so engaging in a battle with panic attacks was, to say the least, a disruption. It wasn't on my agenda." Casey smiled sardonically. "Until this episode, my life had been an attempt to negate all the bad things that had happened to Mama and me. I kept looking for the erasure of those events by being smarter, more competent, successful.

"Suddenly, I felt like someone trying to secure tent stakes in a howling rainstorm, tarp flapping wildly in her face. As soon as I'd get one side secured, another would come loose. I was drenched with exhaustion, suffocating under the weight of my efforts. I finally slogged into the campus counseling office. It's because of Doc Brown that I learned to embrace life instead of trying to supervise my demons. She helped me see truth and honesty as my allies rather than barely-tolerated evil co-workers. I also started going to church again."

"And now, you're once again experiencing the *do* something, *don't* move response?"

Casey nodded. "I've at least learned over the years to push into the fray so inertia doesn't completely take over. To try not to get completely stuck while I'm sorting things out."

"Well, what do you need me for, then?" Lorelei winked.

"Oh, I think we both know this is something that's far too big for me to wade around in without you as lifeguard. I need you to help me avoid making things worse in my attempts to make things better."

For the remainder of their hour together, Casey and Lorelei discussed the cocktail of ambivalence and what the appropriate pairings were to serve with it.

* * *

Rebekah handed Myra a plate of brownies. The brownies were on a decorative disposable plate, securely and precisely wrapped in clear Saran wrap. "Here, these are for you," she said, trying to sound buoyant.

"What is this for?"

Grinning sheepishly, Rebekah replied, "It's a peace offering. For not doing my homework. And for wasting your time. I'm not even sure why I came today."

"Certainly it's not merely to deliver these brownies...." Myra placed the plate on the coffee table.

"No. I did think about cancelling, but I kept putting off calling you, hoping I'd get motivated enough to do what you asked me to do last time. Then I realized this morning that you wouldn't have had 24 hours' notice, so I baked these—hoping to appease you, I guess.

I really am sorry. I don't know what's wrong with me. I've never not done my homework before. Never."

"Rebekah, what is it you hope to get out of counseling?"

Rebekah was startled by Myra's directness. *What, no 'thank you for the brownies'? No polite segue into the session?* "What do you mean? I thought we already talked about that. Remember? I don't want to be depressed any more. I want my life back."

"Okay, let's talk about that. What do you mean by that? What life is that? Tell me what it looks like."

"Where I'm at the top of my game professionally, not distracted by my thoughts and feelings. Where it doesn't hurt like hell to feel. Maybe where I can loosen up a little, smile more, laugh more, make new friends." Rebekah's sigh was long, loud. "I don't know exactly what it looks like, but I do know it doesn't look like this," she sat forward, spreading her palms out in front of herself.

"*This* being…"

"I don't know. Flat? Dull, routine. Punching out on the proverbial time clock so I can go home and set my alarm clock and get up and do it all over again." Rebekah's voice rose. Myra waited patiently. "I guess I want to go back to doing the things I love without feeling like I'm one wave away from drowning in sorrow. I want things to be easy and innocent and meaningful." She sat back.

Myra's voice was warm, understanding. "That's a place everyone's trying to get to. It doesn't exist for us anymore. Not all the time, anyway. Call it the Fountain of Youth, Nirvana, Walden, Eden— we're all trying to find it."

Rebekah smiled weakly, gasping in mock horror, "You mean those aren't real either?"

"Sorry. Disillusioned?"

"Yes. Very." Then, "Seriously, what is it I should be working toward?"

"I cannot answer that for you, but knowing what you know about yourself and about your relationship with your family, friends, and co-workers, what are some areas you'd like to see some changes in?"

Remembering her early morning rebuff to Cliff's romantic overture, Rebekah answered without hesitation, "I'd like to be more responsive to Cliff again. We've talked about starting a family, but

I think we have to have sex for that to happen. I feel like he's the innocent victim in all this, and I turned him away again this morning to make these brownies. So far, he's been very patient, but I don't want to take advantage of his patience, his good nature."

Myra nodded. "What about your friends and co-workers?"

"We haven't done much socializing in a while. We both stay so busy at work." *Liar. Who are you kidding? Myra knows you're in seclusion.* She thought of the mounting phone messages and emails, invitations and overtures from her sorority sisters to which she had failed to respond. "When I'm at work, I'm pretty much a nose-to-the-grindstone kind of girl. If I had to guess, I'd say I probably come across to my co-workers as someone who's unapproachable. I suppose I should learn how to take myself less seriously there."

"Those are laudable goals. Achievable ones, too." Myra leaned toward her client. "Rebekah, I'd like to recommend that you get a journal and begin writing these things down. While they're fresh on your mind, write about what you're going through, including those ideas you just mentioned. Write about what your father meant to you. These journal notes will serve to remind you of where you're coming from and what it is you're working toward. They will help you when you hit a particularly rough patch. Will you do that?"

"You mean like a diary?" Rebekah smirked. "I haven't done anything like that since middle school."

"Does this make you uneasy?"

"No, it's just that… Well, yeah, a little. I don't mind jotting down ideas and goals, but I don't like the idea of memorializing my shortcomings or my bad days. Why can't I just write down motivational thoughts to keep me on track?"

"You're not a locomotive, Rebekah, you're a woman. A woman who has been deeply wounded by her father's death and who is searching to find her way out of a dark cavern of loneliness and grief. You don't need to be," she made finger quotation marks, "'kept on track.' You need to give voice to what you're thinking, how you're feeling, anything that comes up that feels like a loose end that we can discuss."

Rebekah squirmed in her chair. Myra continued, her voice firm but compassionate. "I know you pride yourself on doing things well and doing things right, Rebekah. In counseling, though, there isn't such a thing. You must leave yourself room to be inarticulate, frail, confused, messy, even. It's not only important, it's necessary to face those parts of yourself with honesty."

"I'll think about it."

"Good!" Myra's response was bright, enthusiastic, ignoring Rebekah's hesitation. "Now what do you say we get started on the assignment I gave you last week? You could begin by writing Casey a response."

"You're the doctor." Rebekah's voice was flat. Then, with more indignation than she meant, "Remind me again why I'm doing that? I'm a grown woman. Casey was my friend for one—less than one—year, when we were kids."

"Yes, you're a grown woman, but there is a change in your demeanor and your voice when you talk about your friendship with Casey, as if there's some part of you that still longs for the connection you two apparently had. And, remember, the past can provide important clues for understanding the present. Do you know what it was about your relationship with Casey that tugs at you?"

Rebekah closed her eyes momentarily. "I was drawn to her because she was smart, but so unpretentious about it. She was shy, but at the same time, she seemed comfortable in her own skin. I thought her so unique and utterly delightful in just being who she was."

"And what were you to her?"

"Huh? I don't know. What difference does it make? We were children. And I don't want to discuss this anymore."

"I'm going to be as blunt with you as you've just been with me. I think you are using anger and deadness to ward off something."

"Ward off what? I know my father died. I know I'm depressed. What does this third grade friendship have to do with that?"

"Since you asked, I think you need to prepare yourself for the possibility that something traumatic may have happened during the time of that friendship, something traumatic enough that you closed off part of yourself as a form of self-protection." Myra's gaze was penetrating, her voice more comforting than confronting. "Something in your life story is inextricably tied to this time in your life, maybe to Casey directly, and I do not think you will get to the root of your depression until you explore those ties."

Rebekah's head reeled. Unnerved by Myra's directness, a quality she usually found refreshing, her mind desperately tried to shut out the sound of her therapist's voice, as well as the implications of her words. *Shut up, shut up, shut up!* Then, just as quickly as she had thought those words, she straightened up, calmly matched Myra's steady gaze and replied, "Okay. Let's talk about that then." *I'll show you there are no skeletons in that closet.*

In the next half hour, Rebekah stoically responded to Myra's questions—about her relationship with each of her parents, her brother, Casey, Casey's mother, aware that, without these sessions, she would not be able to refill her Zoloft prescription. She detached from the room, patiently biding her time until the session would conclude. "Picture yourself now at the dinner table with Casey and her parents," Myra prompted next. "Tell me something about the interactions."

"Oh, God," Rebekah sat up straight.

"Yes? What is it?"

"I didn't think I remembered what Pastor Wes looked like, but just now I got a fleeting image of him. No, that can't be right." She shook her head.

"Tell me what you saw."

"He was looking at me, I don't know—funny. His expression made my skin crawl."

"How was he looking at you?"

"I can't describe it. It's sort of the same way I looked at that pan of brownies this morning when I took them out of the oven."

"And how is that?"

"Can't wait for them to cool so I can cut them."

"What would you call that?"

"Shoot, I don't know. Drooling? Leering?" Rebekah paused. Then, "Oh." She swallowed hard. "Lust." Then, "No, that cannot be right." She shook her head, scoffed. "That has to be my imagination playing tricks. And even if it's true, why not leave the past alone and help me get on with my future?"

"Rebekah, have you ever gardened?"

Excuse me? How did we get from brownies to gardening? Despite herself, Rebekah was intrigued. "Not a lot, but I have planted things in the yard—azaleas, flowers, things like that. Why?"

"When you are preparing a plant bed and you want to prevent weeds from growing, you put mulch down, right?" Rebekah nodded. "But if you don't pull up the existing weeds first, what you've actually done is create the ideal breeding ground for stronger weeds to grow. Isn't that so?"

"I guess."

"In much the same way, if we don't acknowledge what, at some level, we already know, pull it out by the roots or dig it out, shake the dirt off of it, and put it in a place we've designated for it, it will create greater problems for us in the long run, especially in the places of our relationships. Your marriage—it sounds as if that's very important to you. Right?"

"Oh, absolutely!" Rebekah's eyes danced. "Cliff is the best thing that's ever happened to me. He's strong and sensitive. He's been so supportive of me in everything I've ever attempted, personally and professionally. And so patient since Daddy died."

"I know you wouldn't intentionally do anything to jeopardize that. Am I right?"

"Of course."

"Then I'm encouraging you to find every weed in your garden not only for you, but also for him. The better you are," Myra leveled her index finger towards Rebekah, "the better off you *two* are." She emphasized her point by bringing her other index finger to rest side by side with its twin. "I know it's a scary proposition to give voice to your confusion, to talk about what feels bad and ugly and dark. And I won't kid you, it's unsettling and can be disruptive, but the cost of *not* doing so can keep parts of you locked away, vital parts of you."

Tears began to work their way down Rebekah's cheeks. Her voice squeaked, "I'm scared."

"I know you are. And that's one reason I'm here. You won't be doing this alone. You'll have me. And," Myra smiled warmly, "it doesn't sound as if Cliff is going anywhere."

Rebekah's head hurt. She felt as if her brain would burst if one more idea forced itself into the already-crowded spaces of her mind.

She was exhausted by the mental scramble to sort and file so many opposing thoughts, and she suddenly craved the escape of a long nap.

While Rebekah's defenses were trying to regroup, Myra added, "I want to invite you again to the support group I'm starting next month. I've already got five other women interested in attending." She sat forward and looked deep into Rebekah's watery green eyes. "I know this makes you uncomfortable, but I do think this would be good for you. I sense you're at the beginning of unearthing something profound, something that has remained walled off by the security of your family. Your father's death, I am guessing, has breached the wall, weakening your defenses, making you fearful of an unknown, unseen invasion of the past."

Rebekah's voice was weak. "I'll think about it." She was trying to decide whether she was being steamrolled toward a commitment she would regret or if she'd been blessed with the good fortune to find someone she could trust to help her find herself.

Ten

THE MORNING BEGAN TYPICALLY, WITH half-eaten bagels and half-finished coffee. Rebekah and Cliff had stayed up late the night before, discussing details of his recent business trip to Longboat Key and what he hoped to accomplish on his return trip today. They talked about Rebekah's upcoming commitments at work and her recent session with Myra, including Myra's allusion to a breach in Rebekah's emotional wall as well as the invitation to join a support group. Rebekah's enjoyment and abandon at their love-making had surprised and pleased them both. *Thank you, Zoloft,* Rebekah mused, as she dozed off into a blissful sleep to her favorite lullaby—post-coital contentment, Cliff's muffled snoring, and his top leg draped over hers.

Cliff kissed Rebekah goodbye as he fled the house in his usual hurry to beat the traffic moving in the same direction toward his downtown office at Robinette and Martin Consulting. He wanted to polish his prospectus before heading to the airport. Cliff had worked his way through college as a CAD operator at Robinette and Martin and had been hired there as an engineer after graduation from the University of Florida. The land engineering firm's projects were scattered throughout the southeast and he had been promoted to senior project manager just one week before Theo Wilkins' death.

His boss, Dave Robinette, had been very understanding about Cliff's need to be absent, encouraging him to take as much time as he needed. Despite the desire to begin working on the new projects that awaited him, Cliff had remained available to Rebekah and her family, being especially attentive to Robert.

At her childhood home after the funeral, while guests in the living and dining rooms had spoken in solemn tones and nibbled from a seemingly endless supply of funeral food, Rebekah had escaped to the kitchen to wash some dirty dishes. She had looked up from the window at the kitchen sink and seen Cliff and Robert standing together, talking in the gazebo in the backyard, Cliff's right hand on Robert's left shoulder. They had embraced; thumping each other's backs the requisite three times of males who had bonded.

Rebekah's love and admiration for her husband had enlarged her heart that day in a place she thought too numb with grief to respond. Now, once again, recalling portions of last night's conversation, Rebekah marveled at Cliff's ability to accept disruptions in their lives and incorporate them into the reality of his day-to-day existence without being resentful. She both admired and envied that. *I've got to be sure Myra helps me get things turned around for good.* Cliff's unwavering confidence in her ability to work through the shadows of her depression occasionally outmatched hers, but this morning she was hopeful. *I won't let him down. And I won't lose me—for both our sakes.* She rinsed out her coffee cup and loaded it into the dishwasher. She wished it was already tomorrow, already her appointment time with Myra. Despite a full calendar today, she planned to drive to Regency Square Mall during her lunch break and buy something to wear to surprise Cliff when he returned from Longboat Key tomorrow evening. She grabbed her briefcase off the kitchen island and left for work with a little more eagerness than she'd known for months.

For lunch, she quickly ate a Subway sandwich while walking from the food court toward Belk. *First I'll get Cliff another bottle of Drakkar Noir.* Rebekah remembered Cliff had mentioned running low on his favorite aftershave. In truth, she was getting it as much for herself as she was for him. It was a smell she especially associated with her husband—his virility as well as his gentleness. *Nope. Can't have him running out of that.*

She continued to stride purposefully through the mall. *Then I'll go to the lingerie department and see what'll stop him in his tracks.* She smiled as she imagined greeting him at the door on his return from his overnighter. Out of the corner of her eye, she saw a display of journals in the window of Barnes and Noble. "Write Your Life, Right Your Life" the ad proclaimed. Rebekah felt a quick pang of conscience as she remembered Myra's latest assignment for her—to jot down her goals for being in therapy, where she was now, where she wanted to go, *anything that comes up that feels like a loose end that we can discuss.* She could hear Myra's cadenced voice in her head and she smiled again. *Loose end,* she tried to imitate Myra's accent. *Loo send. Loosend.*

Catching her reflection in the window, Rebekah paused. She tried to glance casually over her shoulder to see if anyone had observed her lips moving silently to the motion of her mind. Convinced everyone else in her radius was as caught up in his or her own mall-objective, she turned and walked into the bookstore.

Rebekah absent-mindedly ran her hand over the bindings of the journals while she read the promotional poster by the display. *I had no idea journals were so chic. I wonder if I should buy two—one for the office and one for home.* She stepped back from the display rack and assessed her choices. Aware of her dwindling lunch break and the work waiting on her desk, she selected a journal with a padded, paisley-print cover and quickly made her purchase, stuffing it into her shoulder bag.

As Rebekah approached the men's cologne counter in Belk, a woman in front of her spritzed cologne from a demo bottle onto a sample card. Rebekah froze as a sense of dread washed over her. She momentarily felt light-headed and the sandwich in her stomach turned a somersault. *What the?* A bitter taste filled the back of her throat. *Oh, God.* She scanned the store for signs leading to the restroom and walked as quickly as her suddenly wobbly legs would allow, trying to maintain her poise, afraid of drawing attention to herself.

In the lounge area of the restroom, Rebekah noticed every angle of her stricken expression, thanks to the arrangement of mirrors—side views and front views superimposed on one another in continuous fashion. The images mocked her earlier hopeful mood in mirrored overlays. She rushed past the lavatory counter and into the first open stall. Kneeling before the porcelain bowl, she pulled her hair back with one hand, steadying herself on the toilet seat with the other. The waves of nausea made her perspire and she remained in her altar-like pose until her lunch was gone and the waves had subsided.

At the lavatory counter, Rebekah dabbed at her face and neck with a wet paper towel. She smiled weakly in response to the concerned expression of the matronly woman occupying the neighboring sink. "Are you ill, dear? Can I do anything to help?"

"No thank you. I'll be okay. I think I just need to sit down for a moment," she nodded toward the lounge.

"Well, okay, if you're sure. I can call someone if you'd like."

Rebekah strained to smile again. *I'll be fine once I don't have to pretend to be fine. Please hurry up and go.* She walked into the lounge and sat on a bench upholstered in bright orange vinyl. *God, this color will make me sick again. Where are my sunglasses?* Rebekah rested her elbows on her knees, her forehead in her palms. *I NEVER get sick. What is wrong with me?*

Her stomach settled down and her clammy skin dried, but she could not shake the sense of impending doom. The dread circled around her head like annoying no-see-ums at a summer picnic. Determined to elude the buzzing confusion, she resolutely stood up, straightened her skirt, smoothed the sweat-induced curls at her forehead the best she could, and returned to her car, intent on returning to work and the void of numbness her projects often generated.

Back at her desk, Rebekah spread out the various projects and proposals she was working on. She reshuffled the papers, opened, closed, and reopened documents on her computer desktop, trying to force herself to focus. *C'mon, you can do this. Concentrate!* Finally, she set the Kaspar account in front of her and stacked the remaining piles in the order of most important to least. *That was exhausting. Do I have any mental energy left to actually work? Thank goodness all this account needs is to tidy up loose ends. Loo sends. Loosends. Cut it out. Focus!*

For the next several hours, Rebekah read through the work she'd already done in anticipation of meeting with Glenn Averitt, the Kaspar representative, the first part of next week. She made notes in the margins and, on a separate Post-it, wrote *Kaspar to-do's*, all while trying to ignore a filmy haze trying to encroach on her concentration. Staring at the account, she strained to assess the impersonal diagrams, swatches, facts, and figures before her.

Hmm. I never noticed that before. Why don't the sketch artists draw more human faces on the models? Probably so distracted buyers like me don't become more distracted. I'd probably want to know their names, where they're from, why they picked that hideous color when it doesn't go with their skin tone. I'll just ask Mr. Averitt when he's here next week. Rebekah smiled at her private joke. She doodled on the Post-it: *Put faces on the unknown.* Suddenly and viciously, her stomach lurched; acid burned the back of her throat. Even sitting down, she felt lightheaded and disoriented. *Not again. What the hell is wrong with me?*

The physical distress was short-lived this time. Rebekah looked at her watch. *4:30. Soon enough to call it quits for one day.* She collected the papers she had been working on, pressing the Kaspar Post-it on top, and put them all into her briefcase. Standing slowly to make certain her legs would carry her, Rebekah picked up her briefcase and left her office. She walked the three doors down to her boss' office. Ross Williams was just finishing up a phone call. He looked up as Rebekah stood in the doorway. "What's up?' he asked, motioning his head toward her briefcase.

"I'm cutting out a little early today. I'm feeling a little crummy, so I'm taking the Kaspar account home. I'll tie up all the loose ends tonight." *Loo sends.* She forced herself to smile, not wanting her boss to perceive her as anything but the tough, determined, competent merchandiser he'd always known her to be. "I'll see you in the morning."

Ross returned her smile and nodded once. "Okay. Feel better." Rebekah turned and walked away, suddenly weary and very glad she had chosen to leave early. As she slid into the front seat of her car, she turned over in her mind the scene in Ross' office, replaying frame by frame, looking for any sign her boss detected how much she was struggling to perform up to her usual level of energy and commitment.

Satisfied he was as clueless about her state of mind as she was about how to manage it, she mused, *Someone should nominate me for an acting award. Meryl Streep hasn't got anything I haven't got. Home now, to Kaspar. And to loose ends. Loo sends. Loo... Okay, you win,*

Myra. She glanced at the Barnes and Noble package peeking out of her purse. *I'll write in my new journal just as soon as I get home.*

Once home, Rebekah changed out of her suit and put on her chenille bathrobe, then settled into her favorite easy chair, tucking her legs underneath herself. She reluctantly reached for the cloth-bound book. Absent-mindedly stroking its cover, she turned ideas and thoughts over in her head, trying to choose the ones that would find themselves in print. She clicked the ballpoint pen open and closed, open and closed. *This is crazy. Myra said to just write.*

"Okay, here goes," she spoke audibly, the dust bunnies and imagined journal gods her only audience. She opened the book, the gold-edged, unlined pages crisp, virgin. She wrote, *Dear Diary.* Rebekah groaned at the adolescent tenor. *I ought to add a heart to dot the i and a few curlicues for good measure*, she thought, then crossed out the words.

Dear, she wrote again. *Myra? Rebekah?* she wondered. *Nope.* Again, she crossed out her entry. *Quit editing already and write, coward!* She tapped the pen on the paper in a staccato rhythm then, annoyed with the sound she was making, started, hesitantly at first, then not quickly enough to capture the words that suddenly made themselves known—from where, she couldn't say.

July 21, 2008

I begin a new journey today—of honestly giving voice to threads of my life left unraveled by my Dad's death. The thoughts, ideas, reminisces, fears, joys, trepidations roaming around my head now seem to me like ghosts inhabiting a once-lively house, looking for a place to settle and make peace. I must find some way of helping them come to rest and Myra seems to believe that begins by introducing them to these pages. It seems on the one hand a daunting task and, on the other, an utter waste of time. I already know how much I loved Dad, how he gave me the best childhood one could hope for. He gave me perhaps the greatest gift a father can give his daughter—he loved my mother with intense and abiding loyalty and he loved me and believed in me and in nurturing any dream I had for the future.

Rebekah reached for a Kleenex to dab her eyes.

I just never envisioned my future without him in it. I pictured him and Cliff on the front lawn after Thanksgiving dinner tossing the football with Robert. I pictured him dandling my future babies, his grandchildren, on his knee—giving them horsy rides the same way he did for me. I imagined him throwing back his head and laughing that booming laugh of his at some clever joke, whether it was at his expense or not. God, I don't want to forget the sound of that laugh!

A tear plopped on the paper and Rebekah patted it with the tissue.

He was so strong and decisive, I know he would be disheartened to see me so restless, so upended this many months after his death. I've had ample time to mourn, so I cannot understand why I am still such a hostage to my moods these days, why I can't soldier through and get back in the groove. How can penning a litany of my short-comings help me to once again become the strong, determined, savvy young woman he raised me to be? What good will it do to admit I'm stitched together on the inside by Zoloft, my husband's love, and a therapist's concern—that all my original seams haven't held? What does this say about me? Where's that intestinal fortitude that got me through undergraduate school on four hours of sleep a night?

At the mention of intestinal fortitude, Rebekah winced. She took a swallow of water and continued:

And what was that episode in Belk all about today? I used to have the constitution of a horse.

In her mind, Rebekah heard Myra's gentle encouragement about loose ends. *Loo sends again? Okay, why not?* She wrote:

Perhaps this episode is one of those loose ends I need to trace back to its origins. It started at the cologne counter. I was there to buy a gift for my husband. Okay, I was there to buy it for him and for me. What went wrong?

Rebekah paused for a moment to run the details of the event through her mind. She wrote:

Oh, yeah. It started when that woman spritzed the sample card. Why did that make me sick?

Her mind flashed for an instant on the face of Pastor Wes and an insincere, malevolent grin. *What is he doing here? This is about me, about my dad, about Cliff, Myra, now, not another lifetime ago. God, I must really be losing it. Am I regressing?* She began clicking the pen again, a rapid-fire motion that matched her memories and thoughts colliding, caroming off doors long closeted in her mind. "Okay, I have work to do," Rebekah announced, standing up abruptly. The journal dropped to the floor and she left it there to rest, determined to ignore it and the door it had nudged open.

She strode purposefully into the kitchen and propped open her briefcase on the kitchen table. She forced herself to focus on its contents. She poured herself a glass of Merlot and put a *Tuck and Patti* CD in the stereo. Tuck and Patti had been the featured musical duo on the cruise she and Cliff had taken for their honeymoon and the CD always made Cliff seem nearer. She located the Kaspar contract and opened the folder, immersing her energies into cold statistics and impersonal details.

Several hours later, Rebekah woke; her face in a puddle of drool on the opened folder, her wine half finished. Looking up at the clock on the microwave, she saw the time was 2:10 a.m. She pressed her fingertips into her eyes, trying to rub reality into her reluctant consciousness. She grabbed a napkin and dabbed at the folder. Placing the folder back into her briefcase, Rebekah shuffled upstairs to the master bathroom.

She pulled her hair back with a claw clip and turned the water on in the bathroom sink, letting it overflow the cup she made with her hands. Rinsing her face with the cool water, she looked up at her face in the mirror. *I want my life back—the way it used to be before Dad died.* She remembered what Myra had said about his death being a breach in the wall. Now she fully considered the truth in that. *If I have to poke around in the past to assure my future, then so be it. If I have to write down every loose end until they knit themselves into a sweater, then that's what I have to do.*

She padded back downstairs to the living room and retrieved her journal, carrying it back up to her empty bedroom. Rebekah propped herself up with pillows on top of the queen-sized bed, not bothering to turn down the bedspread. She began writing again:

July 21, then crossing that out, *Tuesday, July 22, 2008*

Dear Dad,

I miss you. Things have taken an interesting turn here since you left. I think I need you in ways I could never have imagined. I speak for myself and I know I also speak for Mom and Robert when I say thank you for working so hard to provide us with what you didn't have growing up. But we would rather have you here now, with us, instead of the things and the lifestyle. You have left us richer materially, but impoverished in intangible ways.

I know you kept promising to take more time off, but it just never quite happened, did it? Now that Robert has made the tennis team at Davidson, I wonder what it will be like for him when he plays his matches and wants to call you afterwards to go over them point by point. Nobody could encourage him like you. Nevertheless, he's done a pretty good job of adjusting to your absence.

I wish I could say the same about myself. I'm seeing a therapist to help me. I got really depressed after you died and I just can't seem to get that cloud to lift. After each good cry, I think maybe I've turned the corner, but the resolution, the acceptance, the letting go have continued to elude me.

My therapist, Myra, believes that's because your death has made me get in touch with a part of the past that, while you were alive, you tried to protect me from. At least that's what she's hinting at. She says your dying has left an area of vulnerability—a breach in a wall is what she called it.

If that's true, part of me wishes I could remember what it is; the other part of me doesn't know what to think or hope for. What I wish is that you were here to help me sort this out. I know you and Mom always tried to do what you thought best for me and Robert. I hope I can live up to that when Cliff and I have children of our own. But right now, I'm floundering and I miss you and I need you.

Love, Your Little Princess

Rebekah wiped her nose on the edge of her sleeve, turned out the light, hugging the journal to herself. She slept the fitful sleep of a child with a fever. When the alarm announced the beginning of another day, Rebekah started. The haze between the world of sleep and the world of work quickly burned off as she showered and got dressed. Skipping breakfast, she grabbed her journal and briefcase and headed out the door, determined to get in several hours of work before 11:30. She found herself actually looking forward to her appointment with Myra. *Myra, my Patron Saint of Sanity. She gives Zoloft to the zany!*

When she arrived at her desk, she picked up her phone to check her voice mailbox. There was an urgent message from Ross Williams to see him "ASAP." Rebekah left at once for his office. She tapped on his door and was summoned inside. "What's up, boss?" she asked, smiling.

"Do you have the Kaspar account ready?"

Remembering the spittle-warped folder in her briefcase, she answered, "Not quite. Why? What's up?"

"Glenn Averitt called. He's already in town. We've moved the meeting up to noon today. I need the contract to be ready and I need you to meet us here for lunch."

"Noon? Today?" Her voice quavered. She cleared her throat. "Um, I already had plans to take my lunch hour early. Is there some way we can move the meeting to later in the day—dinner, perhaps?" Her mind felt like it had been processed in a blender.

"Nope. Glenn's flight leaves at 3:00. It has to be noon. You can have it ready, can't you?"

Rebekah prided herself on her professionalism. It was one of the attributes that had set her apart early in her career and had contributed to her rapid advancement in her occupation. Right now, though, she hated her job and her boss with his demanding tone and disingenuous smile.

She placed her fingertips on Ross' desk as much to stabilize her knees as her mind. "I'll have it ready," *you sorry son of a bitch.* She looked out the window of his fourth story office at the St. John's River below. *I'd love to shove you out of that window; not just for this, but for all the times you dump stuff like this on me. How well can you swim? I wonder if I could make it look like a suicide...* She gave Ross her best *eat shit* smile. "Lunch in your office at noon, then."

"That's my girl."

Rebekah waited until she reached the sanctuary of her office to release the hot tears of frustration. Clenching her teeth, she swore under her breath. She located Myra's number in her iPhone and dialed, swiping at her runny nose with her forefinger. When Myra's voicemail greeting picked up the call, Rebekah spoke haltingly, "Um this is Rebekah Wilkins-Standifer. I have an 11:30 appointment with you today. Something has come up at work and I need to reschedule for later in the afternoon, if possible. Please call me back at your earliest convenience."

Rebekah left her phone number, then hung up, attempting to turn her attention to her work. All the things she had wanted to discuss with Myra—the episode at the perfume counter, her midnight resolution to be completely open and honest, her fear that her imagination was playing games with her tenuous hold on sanity—contended for attention with the Kaspar contract, demanding their utterance, asserting their importance.

And the morning passed in the tug of war between duty and a call that was beginning to declare its urgency regardless of its inconvenience. By the time Myra was able to return Rebekah's call, Rebekah had accepted that she would retain sole custody of those urgencies until her session with Myra next week.

Eleven

"WHEN I WAS IN THE pre-vet program at UF, one of my favorite classes was Anatomy and Physiology—A&P. I loved learning about all the various parts and functions of the body, loved learning how everything worked together. In fact, I loved everything about the class except for the dissections. As much as I understood the need to, it still bothered me to slice into a once-living creature, regardless of the knowledge that their lives had been planned and nurtured to be offered up for a nobler purpose.

"One time, we had to do a dissection on bulls' eyes. I had done my homework before the lab, but that hadn't prepared me for the shock of seeing the lab set up with rows and rows of small metal, rectangular pans, each with a golf-ball sized eye in it, staring up at us. I imagined herds of blind bulls roaming the gentle pastures of central Florida's countryside, relying solely on their senses of hearing and smell to negotiate the terrain, to find food, to mate. Then as I sliced into the smooth, rubbery orb, I couldn't help wondering, *if eyes are the window to the soul, what could this eye tell me? What kinds of unconfessed sins would a bull be burdened with?* And then I wondered if, as a little girl, I had only studied my father's eyes more carefully, what might I have known?

"Another time, we did a lab on live frogs, but we pithed them first, inserting a sharp needle into their spinal cords at their necks, rendering them quadriplegics. Then we pulled their massive, vascular tongues out of their mouths, pinning them to the waxy base of a microscope so we could study the effects of different stimulants and relaxants on the capillaries.

"For a long time afterward, I had nightmares about that lab; the frogs' expressions of total helplessness would gradually change and, suddenly, I'd be dreaming about the night my mother couldn't stop screaming. If someone had dissected my father's soul, would that have helped us figure out what lay deep inside of him that made him appear so normal on the outside but so dark and wretched on the inside? It's odd that it didn't bother me to think about him being dissected. I guess I figured there were enough of us who, for the rest of our lives, would be dissecting what he had done to us."

Casey sat back, folded her hands in her lap, and allowed Lorelei time to process these revelations. "Are there times in your life when you forget to dissect and allow yourself to just be?"

"Absolutely. The Daddy-dissections seem to come in waves, with long stretches of calm in between."

"What precipitates these waves?"

"Something that activates my memory, usually. And the regrets and unanswered questions that accompany the memories."

"Talk to me about memories, Casey. How do they present themselves to you?"

"Memory is a peculiar thing. There are some things about the past I remember better than what I ate for dinner last night. My friendship with Rebekah is like that—because it stood in such stark contrast to previous and subsequent friendships, I have gone over every detail of it many times. It was a touchstone for me. Plus, my grandparents encouraged me to talk about her, which further emblazoned that year into my consciousness.

"There are other things, though, that are so hazy that, despite Mama's detailed descriptions, I cannot firmly grasp them in my mind. Like Daddy's face, or what he did in his spare time. To be sure, there are certain things about him that are firmly imprinted in my mind—how he smelled when he came into my room late at night to tuck me in and kiss my forehead, and how he strode through the hallways and up and down the aisle at church with such authority, but crept around so tentatively at home.

"It's as if he was a houseguest in his own home or, worse yet, an intruder—a mouse fearing being found in the pantry. How could he have such assurance in the lives of relative strangers, but such caution and hesitation around his own family? Weren't we the ones who would always be there for him, while his parishioners were more than happy to make him their Whipping Boy for every grievance they had against the church and against God? I guess if memory is a peculiar thing, so is assurance. I'm sorry. I got off track there a little."

"No. You hit on some important things. Like the role your grandparents played in helping you and your mom restore some normalcy to your lives. And your mother's willingness to speak openly about your father. And your father's seeming dual existence. All this would be difficult for an adult to process, to put words and feelings around. More so for a child. I would like to explore these further, if that's okay."

"Sure. What first?"

"Let's start with your mother, your primary care-taker when you were younger. What images come to you when thinking about her when you were a young girl?"

"Sorrow. Deep sorrow. I'm remembering the summer between Kindergarten and first grade, when Mama and I selected the Pippi Longstocking books to read at bedtime. As captivating as Pippi's adventures were to imagine, I often felt sad after we read together, like there was an unformed tune behind my heart, begging to be discovered, played. Pippi's high-spirited nature, her acceptance of her near-orphaned circumstances, her innocence in the midst of mischief, all contributed notes that were out of concert with the way our lives were constructed and played. All was predictable and well-ordered, sterile. Barren, really.

"But I came to see that was Mama's way of trying to keep our world from spinning out of control. In her mind, it was better to keep things safe and sedate than to acknowledge any glimmers of doubt she had. What I longed for, I couldn't have put into words, but the hunger was there, gnawing at my heart, gradually siphoning off hope and expectation, just as I'm sure that was happening to Mama. Routine and ritual are superficial comfort in the absence of mystery, discovery, and joy.

"In the brief time Rebekah and I were friends, the haunting and gnawing subsided. I was Annika and she was Pippi, and I was alive with wonder, while Mama's spirit died a little more each day."

"You seem to hold no grudge against your mother for what she didn't provide you."

"Not didn't. Couldn't. And what other existence, up until Rebekah and I became friends, did I have to compare my life with? Maybe I was wise beyond my years; maybe it was the love that Grandma and Grandpa Greer gave me; maybe it was that brief interlude of joy I felt when with Rebekah and her family—all I know is I never blamed Mama. She became world-weary and resolved to her lot in life out of self-protection and, even as a little girl, I think I understood that at a level I couldn't express.

"Don't get me wrong. I often felt like a burden to her, but everything was a burden. Emptying the dishwasher, answering the phone, plastering on a smile to go to church. So, you see, she wasn't singling me out in her misery."

"I still find it admirable that you are as objective about your relationship with her as you are. I…" The sound of Casey's pager cut short Lorelei's pronouncement.

"I'm so sorry to have to cut our session short. I'm on call and it appears I'm needed at one of the horse farms. May we continue this at our session next week?"

"But of course. Hope all goes well at the farm. See you next week."

* * *

Rebekah's hands were sandwiched between her knees, her face upturned to Myra's warm gaze. "I'm sorry to bail on you last week like that."

"I'm glad you called to tell me, Rebekah, and I'm glad you're here today." Her voice was resonant and reassuring. "You look tired."

"I am. I haven't been sleeping well, which is sort of an interesting departure for me of late. But I have been journaling." Rebekah eyed her closed journal resting on the coffee table. "Would you like to read it?"

"Wouldn't you like to tell me yourself what you'd like to share?"

"I'm too tired to decide what you get to know about me and what awful things I get to keep private. It's too exhausting to figure out. Read. Please." Rebekah leaned back and closed her eyes while Myra scanned the pages, nodding.

When she had finished reading, Myra spoke. "Rebekah, what you described at the perfume counter sounds like an olfactory memory. Sometimes, memories are locked inside our bodies, our senses." Myra made a tight fist with her left hand. "And then something occurs that begins to unlock the memory." She turned her imaginary key at the fisted thumb, releasing its hold on the other fingers. "This is a good thing, Rebekah, for memories that are not locked deep inside you no longer have their power over you."

"I don't understand. What could I possibly be keeping secret—from myself?"

"When we are young and something happens that we don't have the vocabulary, nor the age, nor the experience to understand, this is our very clever way of protecting our tender souls. We store it in a safe place until we can fully process what it means. This memory, Rebekah, is not only a gift to you, but a message from your body, from your mind, that it is time to look at the past."

"What am I looking at from the past?" Rebekah's voice was a whisper.

"If you follow the thread—the smell, the sound, the image—it will lead you where you need to go. If you ignore it," Myra clamped one hand tightly into a fist and tapped it with the other forefinger, "the secret stays in here, where it controls you in ways you cannot imagine." She paused. "I won't lie to you, Rebekah. Following those threads can feel frightening. Remembering can feel frightening. Or it can feel like a waste of time. But you must persevere. Look here," she turned Rebekah's journal around and pointed to a passage. "You were on the verge of discovery. 'It started when that woman spritzed a sample card. Why did that make me sick?' What did you do after you wrote this particular line?"

"I stood up and left the room. Went and got some work out of my briefcase," Rebekah's smile was sheepish.

"What happened when you actually had this experience?"

"I threw up."

"Can you see why it might be worth pursuing?"

Rebekah's shoulders slouched. She nodded.

"Rebekah, look at me." Rebekah looked up into Myra's liquid brown eyes. "I'm not scolding you. I'm here to help you. I will walk every step of the way with you, but I cannot make you take steps you are unwilling to take. I don't counsel with a cattle prod, nor am I indifferent to whether or not you choose to do what's ultimately in your best interest. We are partners in this. Okay?"

"Okay."

"So, let's go back to that cologne counter, shall we?"

For the next few minutes, Rebekah haltingly recounted her experience of the previous week, stopping and starting, hesitating and continuing under Myra's steady, soothing encouragement.

"I believe this means you have kept your secret long enough, Rebekah."

"What secret?"

"There are times when we keep a secret so long, so hidden, it is safe even from ourselves. I think your secret is begging to be exposed, to be allowed light and air long enough for you to know it for what it is, for you to decide what to do with it."

"But what *is* it? What do you know that you aren't telling me?"

"Let's follow the thread some more. How did you feel when the scent made you sick? What were you thinking?"

"I wanted to get away. I wanted to make myself as small as possible. It felt like something bad was about to happen."

"What? What bad thing?"

Rebekah's eyes implored Myra to stop asking questions. Her stomach churned. Her throat closed and opened in spasms. "I don't know. I don't know. I just needed to get out."

"What will happen if you don't?"

"Something bad."

"When you were younger, a little girl, what would you do if you felt afraid?"

"I'd call for my mom or my dad." A tear slipped down Rebekah's cheek.

"And if neither of them was available?"

"I'd hide, curl up in a ball, shut my eyes tight, and suck my thumb."

"And if there's nowhere to hide? What would little Rebekah do then?"

"I'd, um, try to be very still and quiet and hope not to be noticed." Rebekah's voice was a girlish whisper.

"What happens when you are noticed, Rebekah?"

"Bad things. Naughty things. Icky things."

"Tell me. You can tell me. You're safe here."

"I, I don't know. Things I can't tell. Things that will make Mommy and Daddy sad." Rebekah shuddered.

Myra looked at her fragile client, whose gaze was fixed on a point in the past. "What do you see, Rebekah? Things that will make Mommy and Daddy sad—what do you see? What things?"

"I don't... I can't... It's dark."

Myra let the words linger in the air. Every contortion of Rebekah's face testified to her struggle between not knowing and not wanting to know. Finally Rebekah's focus began to return to her therapist and the quiet ticking of the clock on Myra's credenza.

"When is the last time you hid, Rebekah?"

Rebekah's voice trembled. She tilted her head down, staring at her lap. "In the closet. Just recently. After a bad dream." She looked up at Myra. "Do you think that's related to The Cologne Counter Encounter?" Her smile was weak.

"I do. I think they are very much related."

"Please tell me what you're thinking. Hank seemed afraid to be honest with me. I need you to tell me what you think."

Myra paused. "Very well. I will tell you. I think now a greater part of you wants to know than the part of you that doesn't want to know. You exhibit some hallmark signs of someone who has suffered a childhood trauma—one you were not allowed to speak of, something you were encouraged to keep secret for so long, it has leached out into every facet of your life. Now it demands your attention. And," Myra paused again, "I think that trauma was sexual in nature."

Myra heard Rebekah's sharp intake of breath. "I also think this trauma is a large contributor to your depression."

Rebekah gulped for air, hungry for stillness and calm in her mind. Her thoughts tumbled over one another. Her stomach felt as if she had just stepped off the Tilt-a-Whirl at the county fair. Her head reeled in confusion.

"Wait a minute, wait a minute. Wait." She held a hand up to Myra. "Stop." Her chest heaved as she struggled to breathe. "How can you say that? A little depression. A bad dream. An episode at Belk. Somehow all that adds up to sexual trauma in my childhood? Don't you think I'd remember something like that?"

Rebekah's eyes darted around the room; she clenched and unclenched her fists. "I just don't know how you could say something like that. My father—my parents—gave me everything I needed. Everything. You're wrong." Suddenly wracked with sobbing, she looked fully in Myra's face. "You just have to be wrong. Please. Tell me you're wrong."

Myra moved to sit beside Rebekah, offering her a box of tissues. Rebekah took the box and one of the pillows from the sofa. She held the pillow to herself, rocking, keening, mourning a loss she had been avoiding for twenty years. Myra sat patiently, allowing Rebekah her grief and confusion.

As Rebekah's breathing returned to normal, Myra clasped her hands around Rebekah's. "I know I've dropped an atomic bomb on you today. It's a huge shock for you to consider. But," she pressed her hands closer around Rebekah's to make sure Rebekah was looking at and not past her, "now you can begin to break the hold this awful secret has had on you. You can begin to choose what you will do with this revelation. You can decide how this will influence you instead of it making those decisions for you. The power," she smiled, "has begun to shift back toward you now."

"I don't feel very powerful right now. As a matter of fact, I don't feel much of anything."

"That's to be expected—to feel numb with shock. This will take some getting used to—thinking of yourself in these terms."

"What am I going to tell Cliff?"

"What do you usually tell him about yourself? About your sessions here?"

"Everything. But this is huge and horrible and I'm still not certain it's true. No offense, Myra. I mean, who would do such a thing?"

"No offense taken. Your response is actually quite normal. As for who did this—you will know when you know. It would be only conjecture on my part to guess. And unprofessional at this point. I would encourage you to tell your husband exactly that—what we talked about and how that makes you feel. Tell him as much as he needs to know to support you in this. Help him know you as you are right now."

"Which is a mess. Tell me something. Why would I want to open this, this Pandora's Box, if it makes me feel so crazy? Won't the Zoloft help me function like a normal person?"

"How does a normal person function, Rebekah? What does that look like?"

"Someone who can get her work done; someone who has energy left over at the end of the day for her husband and her life. Someone who can keep the house clean. Someone who likes her life."

"Rebekah, you over-estimate the power of an anti-depressant. It is not a battery and you are not the Energizer Bunny. You have been given the opportunity to learn who Rebekah is really meant to be, and the energy you have spent in avoiding having your armor penetrated will need to be used elsewhere. You cannot avoid pain altogether. Rather, you can learn what to do with your pain. When you put labels like 'normal' on your life, you may be preventing yourself from seeing yourself as so much more—a wonderful, human, fallible, passionate woman."

"Am I really that awful?"

"I didn't mean to imply you are awful. I would simply like for you to give yourself permission to live your life without condemning yourself for not measuring up to this impenetrable, perfect expectation you seem to have. There's good stuff that happens in the messiness and unpredictable nature of really living. Does that make any sense?"

"I think so." Rebekah's brow furrowed as she tried to imagine herself embracing life instead of trying to manage it. "But I have no idea where to begin."

"You already have. You've begun by facing the worst secret imaginable; you've been honest in your journaling and with your husband. And you're here," the sweep of Myra's hand indicated her office.

And not in some padded room at Chattahoochee, Rebekah smiled wanly. "So what do I do next?"

"Keep being honest with yourself. Allow yourself to let things be disorganized—as much in your physical world as in your mental world. And in here," Myra tapped her chest. "And please tell me you'll check out this support group."

Before Rebekah could protest, Myra continued, "In the past, the women who have opened themselves up to the group work have pieced their lives back together much quicker and with better results than those who don't. Please say you'll attend. Just the first time. What have you got to lose?"

Rebekah hadn't the energy to launch an argument, to continue defending the crumbling fortress of her world gone awry. She nodded, thinking, *Just my mind, Myra. Just my ever-lovin' mind.*

Twelve

THE FOUR WOMEN HESITANTLY LEFT the security of their cars, gathering at the back door of the clinic building. Myra had left a note on the door: *Be back soon.* With elevator-like etiquette, the women avoided each other's eyes and, to the best of their abilities, the invisible boundaries marked by each one's body language.

One woman, petite, 60-ish, with short, thick, stylish salt and pepper hair, attempted to slice into the tension, "Aren't the mosquitos horrible tonight?"

Rebekah found the cultured Southern lilt of the woman's voice comforting. It reminded her of voices she had heard at a family reunion many childhood summers ago. She couldn't remember the myriad names of the aunts, uncles, and cousins, nor all of their faces, but she remembered the way the syllables of their words slipped over each other, their genteel drawl matching the pace of the family gathering—easy, fluid, infused with love and unspoken ties to long-dead ancestors.

Rebekah turned her head toward the woman and smiled. "I'm Libby," the woman introduced herself. "And I have to tell you I'm sort of nervous about this group. I've never been in something like this before."

Befowah, Rebekah mused, turning the word over in her mind. *I love it.* She smiled at the woman. "I know what you mean. This is new to me, too. I only met Myra a few weeks ago and now, here I am. By the way, I'm Rebekah," she extended her hand to Libby.

The other two women watched the exchange then lowered their gaze, almost in unison, one returning to the study of her cuticles, the other to some unseen focal point on the threshold of the door. Rebekah guessed that the young, heavy-set woman with stringy peroxided hair was about her age. Her hands and complexion revealed her youth, but her eyes betrayed a fatigue borne not of years but of sorrow and defeat. The other woman, an attractive black woman with a flawless mocha complexion and elegantly braided hair, was dressed in scrubs. Judging from the whimsical print of her outfit, Rebekah guessed she was a pediatric nurse. *Lucky her. She gets to hold babies all day.*

Rebekah's hastily eaten Taco Bell dinner performed a digestion-defying somersault. Two other women arrived in the parking lot almost simultaneously and as they walked up to the sidewalk to join the others, Myra drove into the parking lot in a late model Buick Century. *Myra drives a Granny car!*

Rebekah glanced at her watch. It was 6:55. While Myra exited her car, Rebekah surveyed the last two arrivers. They were a study in point-counterpoint. One was a tall, slender woman, fashionably, albeit a little provocatively, dressed, probably in her early 30's. Her honey-colored hair was piled into a clip, casual yet sensual. Although she wore more makeup than Rebekah thought necessary, it was easy to see she was beautiful without it.

Rebekah had a more difficult time appraising the other woman. She was average height and athletic looking, despite being dressed in a dark, tailored skirt and a plain cream-colored blouse—an outfit, it seemed, she was not entirely comfortable wearing. Other than a large watch suitable for diving, she wore no other adornments such as earrings, bracelet, or necklace. Her wavy hair fell to her shoulders without design or any seeming intent and she still wore sunglasses, despite the shade provided by stately oaks. Her expression was just as unreadable as her eyes.

Myra arrived at the door. "Evening, All," she said in her deep, lustrous voice. They all acknowledged her in silence and waited until she unlocked the door, removing the sign. "I'm usually already here, but I had an errand I needed to run. I hope you haven't been waiting too long. I know it's humid and hot out here."

Once inside Myra's office, the women evenly arranged themselves in the chairs and sofa around the coffee table. Myra rolled her desk chair to the circle. "I'm sure some of you are a little apprehensive about being here." She sat down. "I assure you that's quite normal. As you get to know each other, though, Thursday nights will become a place of security for you. Just how safe you feel here and how much work you get done will depend on you. So what do you say we get started?"

Myra's comments were met with silence, not uncomfortable, but expectant. She continued, "Next week you'll each have an opportunity to share a little bit of your story, about what brought you here. Tonight I think we'll just start with introductions and group ground rules and expectations. All of you know who I am, so now just tell the group what your name is and one or two things about yourself. Like, 'I'm Myra and I have a cat and I love to travel.'" She gestured to the woman on her left and indicated it was her turn.

"I'm Libby. I have two grown children, a son and a daughter, and one precious granddaughter, Courtney. My husband, Bud, and I are retired and enjoy volunteering at our church."

"And Libby makes a killer peach pie," added Myra, which elicited an embarrassed smile from Libby. "Okay, next."

The woman to Libby's left, the tall willowy one, introduced herself. "I'm Celeste," she said, with no discernible origin of accent. "I'm a hairstylist. And, um, I like . . .," she said, searching for some bit of innocuous information, "I like going to the beach."

"Neptune? Atlantic? Jacksonville?" asked Myra.

"Ponte Vedra"

"Upscale, huh? Next time you go, maybe we'll all go with you," Myra joked. "Celeste, did you make the outfit you're wearing?"

"Yes, I did."

"Celeste designs a lot of her own clothes."

The looks of admiration from the others brought a flash of warmth to Celeste's eyes. Myra looked at Rebekah.

"I guess it's my turn." *Duh.* "I'm Rebekah. I'm married and I'm the North Florida market representative for Petite Clothiers, Inc., a resident buying office. That's a glorified way of saying I'm a merchandising liaison between the manufacturers and the buyers. In this case, mostly department stores. I spend about half my life behind a desk and the other half divided between my car and meetings with clients." Rebekah realized she had been speaking as if introducing herself to the Rotary Club. Suddenly embarrassed she'd said too much, she looked down into her lap, the repository of her shame.

She lifted her head as Myra spoke her name. "I just met Rebekah recently, so the only thing I can add is that something tells me we are going to rediscover the fire in Rebekah to match that red hair." Rebekah blushed appreciatively. *Aw, teacher's pet.*

In a voice that was neither warm nor devoid of feeling but, rather, professional and guarded, Andrea of the tailored skirt and athletic build reported, "I'm Andrea. I'm an investigator for the sex crimes unit of the Duval County Police Department. And I like to cycle on the weekends."

Depahtment. Rebekah smiled to herself. *Bet she's from Bahston,* she thought, as she listened to Andrea's rapid-fire speech, punctuated with soft r's.

"That's bicycles, right?" asked Myra, aware that Andrea's profession came as a surprise to the others. Andrea nodded. "I also happen to know that Andrea is a star player on the police league volleyball team." Andrea volunteered a quick smile, the only one of the evening.

Margot was next. "I'm Margot," she said in a quiet, gentle voice with minute traces of mid-Western inflections. "I'm a registered nurse for a local pediatrician. I like to read and swim."

Knew it! I'll bet children like her, Rebekah thought.

"And I believe it's Margot's dream to become a nurse practitioner, isn't that right?"

"Yes, that's right. Although that dream is a long way off from happening."

Olivia was last. In a timid, almost apologetic voice, she self-consciously pushed the words out of her small mouth, betraying her north Florida Cracker roots with a soft-spoken twang. "I'm Olivia," she said, pronouncing her name Uh-liv-yuh. "I'm married and I have a 7-year-old son, Tyler. I work at Publix, as an assistant manager."

She looks more afraid than I am, but if she keeps tugging on her t-shirt like that, she's going to ruin it, Rebekah thought. Then, sending a mind message as much to herself as to Olivia, she mentally chanted her self-calming mantra, *Composure, girl. Composure.*

"I'm going to have to get Olivia to bring pictures of her little boy. He's so cute; like a little man." Olivia smiled at Myra gratefully.

"Good. That wasn't so bad, was it? As I said before, next week you'll be telling the group a little more about yourselves, as little as you want or as much as a few minutes. So be thinking about what you want to share. The things you share about what led you to ask for help may help someone else in here. That's one reason we share. Not to be gratuitous or sensational. You'll likely find there are common themes in your stories. Your stories will overlap, and you will find you have more in common than you think possible and that you're not as unusual as you think you are. And," Myra continued, "you will help each other to find authentic ways of expressing your sorrow, your pain, your anger, and your triumphs." She stopped and looked around the room at the mixed expressions of fear, indifference, and agitation.

"Everyone okay so far?" They all nodded mutely, and Myra continued. "I know I'm doing a lot of talking tonight. As of next week, that will shift, although I do find it difficult to resist teachable moments." She smiled.

"Now, about the ground rules for group work. Everything, e-v-e-r-y-t-h-i-n-g," she carefully enunciated, "that is shared in these sessions is to be kept in strictest confidence. It is not to be discussed with anyone else, anywhere else. Please be sensitive to each other's need for privacy. Also, if this is to be a safe place, I insist there be no sexual contact between group members." The women looked at each other and Myra, surprised, embarrassed.

Myra smiled, slightly amused, "You'd be surprised." Then, "In addition to guarding each other's trust, honesty is a must, as much for yourself as for each other. We must all know we can count on each other to deal in the truth. Any questions or comments yet?" The women quickly glanced at each other, shrugging their shoulders and shaking their heads, *No.*

Stupid! You didn't even think about having to trust total strangers with potentially damaging information. Rebekah felt queasy. *And what if it isn't even true?!*

Myra interrupted Rebekah's self-flagellation, "Okay. When I work with women who have been abused, I like to talk about growth rather than recovery. Recovery means you get back what was lost or stolen. Growth implies that we struggle, we learn, we become. There will be times when relief will elude you. We are not here for relief but to grow, to work toward becoming who you were meant to be before you were betrayed. Does that make sense?"

Rebekah looked around the room. Silent tears slipped down Olivia's cheeks. Margot winced as if in physical discomfort. *Worse yet*, Rebekah thought, *what if it is true?* Libby smiled a knowing, compassionate, maternal smile. Andrea continued to be unreadable, a mask of clinical indifference on her face. Celeste wore inurement comfortably, like a favorite pair of old Levi's. Rebekah made a mental note to consider Myra's words when she was able to examine them in the privacy of her own thoughts, without the distraction of so much newness. *I'm a regular Scarlett O'Hara. Fiddle dee dee, I'll just think about all this tomorrow.*

"You will have many things in common, but what you feel, how intensely you feel it, how you express that, all of those will be unique to each of you. You will learn from each other," Myra swept her arm across her body. "You will grow with each other. And you will learn from yourselves." She tapped her chest. "As to my role, I am here to help, to facilitate, but not to babysit or cajole. So, let's wrap us this session with each of you sharing how you feel right now about being here, part of this group."

No one volunteered any information, so Myra tried another approach. "Who here feels sad?" Olivia raised a tentative hand, as did Margot. "Who feels angry?" Celeste flipped her index finger. "Who feels fearful?" Rebekah, Olivia, and Libby acknowledged with slight nods. "Anyone feel hopeful?" Again, Libby responded. "Confused?" Rebekah and Margot both nodded. "How about skeptical?" Celeste, Rebekah, and Andrea's subtle gestures admitted that Myra had found a target. "So, as you can see, you are all at different places.

"You've each acknowledged how you feel right now. I would also like you to try to become aware of ways you try to avoid dealing with your pain. When we feel so out of control over what was done back then," Myra flipped her right hand over her shoulder, almost as if tossing an imaginary ball, "and over how that's making us feel now," she spread both hands out in front of her, palms up, "we might try to overcorrect by seizing control of what we can, retreat and do nothing, or numb ourselves. Either way, the message is that there is pain lurking about. Don't ignore it."

Rebekah glanced over at Margot, whose neatly plucked eyebrows were etched together by unspoken hurt. Her expression caused a brief flicker of memory to invade Rebekah's casual observation. *Casey, standing by herself on the playground, watching all the other children playing. She needs a friend. I will be her friend.* Rebekah inhaled sharply. Only Andrea seemed to notice, arching her eyebrows in bored observation, then shifting her attention back to Myra. For Rebekah, the rest of the evening slipped by in a fog, with voices from the past and those in Myra's office presenting themselves as cast members in a play, beckoning her to join them in the drama. *My name is Rebekah and no one is home. Please leave a message.*

Thirteen

"WHAT DID YOU THINK OF the group Thursday night? You were rather quiet when you left." Rebekah was sitting in Myra's office, twirling one strand of hair in continuous motion around her index finger, her journal resting on her lap.

"I had a lot to think about. And I'm starting to remember some things." She tapped her journal.

"What kinds of things?"

"Mostly good. Playing at Casey's house, her at my house, us at school and in Camp Fire Girls together. The rest is just really vague sensations—of something being not quite right in that family."

"How so?"

"I think her mom was very unhappy. I don't recall her saying much or smiling much. She seems muted to me."

"Anything else?"

"I think I felt uneasy around her father. He looked at people strangely."

Myra probed, "Can you remember specific incidences?"

"Not really. Not clearly. Maybe it had more to do with being that age and feeling awkward around any male who wasn't my own family member. Maybe."

"Maybe. Anything else?"

"Yes, actually. There are a couple of things I'd like to talk about that, I think, fall under your 'loose ends' category," Rebekah couldn't help a tiny smile.

"By all means. What's on your mind?"

"First of all, about the group. I think I might be a little out of my element. I mean, just looking at Olivia and Margot, I can tell they know exactly what happened to them, who did what. I spent most of the hour looking at everyone else's reactions than thinking about myself in those same terms. And that's what I wanted to ask you about. Is it normal—me sizing everyone up all the time? Not critically, really, but just sort of evaluating them?" *Okay, so maybe I'm a little critical, but I'm not catty.*

"I used to think my eye for detail was part of my job, one of the things that makes me good at it. I'm pretty good at assessing the aesthetics of objects, especially clothes," her eyebrows arched upward, "but I don't think I've ever been so aware of, um, assessing people, of trying to evaluate them. What's up with that?"

"First question—is it normal?" Myra slid to the edge of her chair and leaned forward, resting her elbows on her knees. "Normal is really difficult to define. Maybe a better question might be, 'Is it unusual?' And, no. I've led lots of groups for post-traumatic stress disorder and for abuse survivors, and one of the things I find that trauma brings about is hyper-vigilance. For example, some people, whenever they're in public places, scope out where all the exits are." Myra demonstrated by visually scanning the room. "It's not something they choose to do; it seems to be automatic.

"Other people scrutinize every aspect of their lives—people, places, things. Their radar seems to be stuck in the 'on' position." She sat back. "I wouldn't get overly distraught over it. These reactions are ways of trying to figure out whom to trust, how to stay safe, or how to move to safety. As you begin to defuse some of the triggers associated with your abuse, you will find the tendency to, as you say, assess, will probably decrease."

"So why was I doing it Thursday night? What was the, uh, trigger?"

"How do you typically respond to novel situations?"

"Ah." Rebekah nodded. "I usually do a mental 360-degree walk-around, as if I'm not actually a part of what's going on, but an impartial observer, trying to get the lay of the land."

"And in your walk-around last Thursday, did you come away with any particular negative impression?"

"Not really. Actually, I wouldn't mind getting to know everyone in the group. There's nobody who particularly offends me, and a few who particularly intrigue me," she smiled at her quasi-confession. "I think there are a few who might be harder to get to know, but I'm still not convinced this support group is the right thing for me."

"Rebekah, in all my years of doing groups, I have never met anyone who didn't question whether or not it was the right thing to do—for a multitude of reasons. You're just going to need to trust my experience on this. I won't force you to continue, of course, but I would like to encourage you not to dismiss it so soon. Not for my sake, but for yours."

"Okay. If you think so."

"Good," Myra said expansively. "I'm glad you'll be a part of the group. I know you'll bring a lot to it. You'll gain a lot from it, too. I promise."

"Okay. There's something else I wanted to ask you about. I don't know how exactly to describe this, but at some point in the evening, I kind of zoned out. I was aware of what was going on, but I was somewhere else at the same time. How normal, uh, usual is that?"

"Again, not so unusual. Remember when I said you were detached from some of the events in your story?" Rebekah nodded. "You were probably feeling a bit overwhelmed Thursday night, so you went to a safe place. Again," Myra leaned forward again, "as you begin to deal in earnest with your abuse, number one," she grabbed the tip of her raised index finger with her other hand, "you will want to escape to that safe place more often but, number two," she repeated the gesture, raising two fingers this time, "you will reach a point in your growth where you'll want to stay fully present more than wanting to retreat. If, however, you begin losing track of time and place, you need to tell me. That could be a sign of something more serious."

Rebekah swallowed hard. "Okay, that leads me to something else. I have a very real fear that I could completely fall apart. What if I get worse instead of better?" *What if I end up in a rubber room at Chattahoochee? Men in white coats? Tended by Nurse Ratched?*

"Several things, Rebekah. First, keep journaling in some form or fashion. Draw, write, talk into a tape player—something. And be consistent about it. Don't wait until you are completely at your wits' end. Stay current with yourself."

The rhythmic nod of Myra's head emphasized the import of her counsel. "Second, there will be times when you think you have made the wrong decision to enter into counseling and face the damage that was done to you. You will be tempted to walk away from it all. But remember the weeds. You can walk away from counseling, from journaling, from the group, but you will still carry the weeds. Merely wishing them away doesn't destroy them.

"And thirdly, try to remember that feelings are not always the most accurate gauge of reality. By that I mean your feelings are precisely that—yours," she handed Rebekah an invisible package, "feelings," she touched her chest. "But they do not present the entire picture of who you are and you are not entirely at their mercy."

She smiled warmly at Rebekah. "You will turn many corners in your growth journey. What I ask is that you stay with it, moving forward. An inch one week, ten inches the next."

Rebekah released a stored-up sigh. She felt tension leaving her shoulders and neck, relief climbing up inside her mind. "Okay. A few more questions then?"

Myra nodded.

"I haven't contacted Casey yet, but I think I'd like to try. What do I say?"

"What is it that you hope to receive as a result of contacting her?"

"Well, I think it'd mean a lot to her. But I also think she may be able to help me round out some pictures I have in my mind, help me to know I'm remembering details instead of making stuff up in my head. You know, like the color of her bedspread, the layout of her room. And, I don't know," Rebekah smiled shyly, "I guess part of me wants to know if there's still some connection between us. I've had lots of girl pals, but there was something quite special about Casey and me. At least there was 20 years ago. I could use a real friend right now, especially someone who already knows what I'm facing."

"I think those are all valid reasons for reaching out. I encourage you to move on that."

"Okay. I think those are all my loose ends."

"Well, do let me know if others arise. Now, if you don't mind, I'd like to return to your observation that Casey's father looked at people strangely. Do you remember mentioning this to me when you brought me the brownies, Rebekah?"

"Yes, I do."

"Do you remember how you referred to it?"

Rebekah scrunched up her eyes, trying to remember, then her face fell. "Yes. I do. Leering. Lust. My God, Myra. Is it Pastor Wes? He was a minister! That just can't be right. If this thing happened, as you think it did, it had to have been someone else. My best friend's father?" Rebekah shook her head.

"I'm not saying it is. Again, you will know when you know. For now, keep the possibility open, minister or not. Ministers are made of the same stuff as the rest of humanity."

"I figured I felt uncomfortable around him because he was so unlike my own father. That, and how Miss Annette was so strange and quiet, especially when we were all together, like at meal time. He was a minister, for God's sake!" The tug of war between disbelief and anger made Rebekah's head hurt. She rubbed her eyes.

"Rebekah, even if the so-called *only* thing he did was leer at you, you had every right to be uncomfortable. Besides that type of behavior being wrong, an eight-year-old simply isn't equipped to know what to do about it."

"Oh, that is so gross! I will never understand how a grown man can look at any child that way. What did I ever do to make him look at me that way?"

Myra's eyes flashed. She leaned toward Rebekah, her words crisp, "You did not do a thing to *make* him look at you like that. He *chose* to see you as someone other than the eight-year-old friend of his daughter. Do you understand that?"

"I think so," Rebekah nodded. "Oh, that's so disgusting. Myra, I feel," she gulped, "sick. Could I have some water, please?" Rebekah took a tissue from the box on the table and dabbed at the moisture on her forehead and upper lip while Myra poured from a pitcher of water she kept on the coffee table.

Rebekah sipped tentatively then set the glass down on the table. "Thank you. I seem to be doing that a lot lately," she attempted a smile. "I think I'll be okay now."

"Are you certain?"

"Yes, thank you."

"You're welcome. Now, I want you to tell me, again, out loud, what you want out of our sessions together. In my experience, if we don't articulate our reasons frequently, the temptation to scrap the whole thing will be strong, especially after a particularly difficult session, like today's."

Rebekah thought for a moment, then said, "I want my life back, to not feel so one-dimensional. I want to not be depressed anymore, and not have to take medication for it. No offense." She smiled wistfully, "And Cliff and I would like to have children, so I need to get my bearings in the world again. You know, Cliff and I had been trying before Daddy died; now we're mostly trying to try. So far, he's been very patient with my erratic interest in having sex." Rebekah's smile was sorrowful.

"I understand. You may not need the Zoloft forever, but at the same time, many women are able to have healthy pregnancies while on certain anti-depressants. I do have quite a few patients who ultimately are able to manage their depression with counseling and good nutrition and exercise. Meanwhile, if you decide to go off the Zoloft, we'll need to decide that together."

"Okay. I understand." *Counseling—check. Diet—check, sort of. Exercise—bad girl. Well, one and half out of three is not bad. For a batting average.* Rebekah studied Myra's face for signs of her mind-reading capabilities. And in the waning minutes of her session, she began to feel the tug of war between walking away from ideas too preposterous to imagine and walking, instead, into an inferno to reclaim her life.

Later that evening, while waiting for Cliff to return home from work, Rebekah wrote:

August 12, 2008

I think I've been nailed with the truth—right between my mind and my heart. Then again, I can't be sure. How maddening! I almost had a meltdown in Myra's office. She knows more than she's letting on and I don't know whether to thank her or browbeat her into telling me. I left her office feeling like I have a fungus growing on me. I can't see it, but I know it's there, just out of my peripheral vision. Or maybe it's a scarlet letter emblazoned on my forehead: S for Survivor. It's still so weird for me to think of myself in those terms, and I will not be sharing this with Mom until I'm absolutely certain, one way or another. How can I deal with something I don't remember? This phantom mold keeps encroaching on my consciousness, toying with me, taunting me. Now I really sound like I'm cracking up. Can I trust Myra that I won't go off the deep end?

I'm considering writing Casey. Can it be true about her father? Does she know? What does she know? Do I want to know?

Upon hearing the garage door open and Cliff's car pull in, Rebekah set the journal aside, but not her swarming suspicions.

Fourteen

"LET'S RESUME TALKING ABOUT YOUR mother, if that's okay." Lorelei's expression was warm, welcoming.

"Sure. Anything specific you'd like to know?"

"After you and she moved in with her parents, after your father's arrest, did anything about her demeanor change? Did she seem less, uh, remote?"

"Not really. You have to understand, Mama became a pariah, a widow, and a psychiatric in-patient all within a very short period of time. Imagine spending years making a life with someone who was so utterly charming in public but so mysterious and insular in private that you ended up tucking away all your fleeting scraps of suspicion and concern, almost like they were coupons you clipped, but then never redeemed.

"The cycles of hope and expectation then disappointment, self-doubt, and confusion were relentless. She has told me she chose to ignore signs because she thought she had an over-active imagination. She would think that especially after seeing him 'perform' on Sundays. Gradually, though, an incident, a subtle gesture, a scent, or a strained silence would be too much to ignore, and with each wave of suspicion, her pride, her dignity, and her peace of mind eroded a little more.

"The first time I visited her in the hospital after her nervous breakdown, she held both of my hands in hers, trying to explain to her bewildered daughter what she was doing there. She simply said,

"My coper's broken, Casey. My coper's broken." The dike she had constructed to keep the floodwaters of intuition from drowning the persona of capable mother and devoted pastor's wife had sprung a leak—and she had finally referred to herself in the first person.

"In addition to her coper being broken, she believed her intuition was irretrievably broken. After she was discharged, she continued to second-guess her ability to know pretty much anything. I think she knows herself, but does not, to this day, completely trust herself to read people or situations well. So she keeps life as monotonous and routine as possible—to prevent any surprises.

"Some days are easier than others for her to emerge from the quiet world she has sequestered herself to. I wish she weren't so fearful, but she has told me she doesn't think she can live through another crushing disappointment. So she doesn't venture out much, doesn't interact with others much. On those occasions when I'm able to convince her to go somewhere with me, we usually go to dinner and then walk around the mall and just window-shop and talk. Whenever she sees babies in their strollers, she smiles wistfully, looking not so much at the babies or their parents, but at a mythical place just beyond them where every baby is wanted and loved and no parent ever fails. Honestly, I think she's relieved I'm not married with children, but at the same time, she's also relieved that I'm a grown-up and her child-rearing duties are finished."

"Does that bother you?"

"It's something I accept."

"So has *anything* about your mother changed since you went to live with her parents?"

"Sure. She's not as mechanical as she was before Daddy was arrested. I absolutely know how much she cares for me. At the same time, she realizes her reserves of emotional energy are easily spent just in the business of keeping her life as ordinary as possible. She will always, I believe, live with one foot in *what if?* and the other in *what happened?*. This deprives her of genuine joy. And makes her reluctant to take even the slightest risk.

"For example, about a year ago, someone abandoned a kitten at my clinic. I offered it to Mama, thinking it would be a good companion for her. She declined, saying she was afraid of it getting hurt due to her negligence. So, you see, the grieving process continues for Mama."

"Since you've mentioned them before, what can you tell me about your grandparents? It sounds as if they took over most of the child-rearing duties. Am I right?"

"Grandma and Grandpa Greer," Casey smiled broadly, "are two of the finest people I've ever known. I know I'm biased, but I cannot imagine how my life might have turned out if I hadn't gone to live with them. My coper might've broken, too, if it were not for them.

"Grandma is a typical housewife who's truly at her best when she is doting on those she loves. Grandpa's expertise is in letting Grandma's gifts flourish," Casey's eyes twinkled, "and in animal husbandry. He still collects and freezes bull semen, which he sells to cattle ranchers and dairy farmers. It was his matter of fact way about animals and life cycles and his regard for all living creatures that helped shape my desire to practice veterinary medicine from the primordial ooze of childhood idealism to the evolved respect of hard work, education, and practiced craft.

"That Grandma and Grandpa Greer love me and believe in me has always been undeniable. In the absence of an involved mother, I thrived on their encouragement, attention, and discipline. It was my idea to take their last name on their 40th wedding anniversary. It was the best way Mama and I could think to honor them and the sacrifices they've made on our behalf."

"They sound like extraordinary people, Casey."

"They are. And wise, too. Their entire approach to life and its grandeur as well as its heartaches kept me on solid footing, anchored me. Their ethic is infused into all they say and do. There is nothing false or pretentious about them. For instance, they firmly believe in not working on the Sabbath. For as long as I can remember, Grandma Greer doubled her domestic efforts on Saturdays so we could all enjoy a huge meal on Sunday afternoons. She shelled peas, snapped beans, and shucked corn when they were in season; she baked biscuits and cornbread and two kinds of dessert; she peeled, sliced, and boiled potatoes for mashing; she brewed enough tea to make several quarts of iced tea, thick with sugar; and she cut up and dredged several chickens for frying. That way, she said, all she'd need to do after church was put on the finishing touches. Of course, the 'finishing touches' entailed almost as much labor, but she didn't see it that way since she'd done so much advance preparation.

"After Sunday dinner, Grandma would take her only nap of the week and Grandpa Greer would engage in his ritualistic activity of checking all his machinery and implements. I'd usually follow him out to his work shed and watch him carefully sharpen blades, oil parts, and check and fine-tune adjustments, helping him when he'd allow. He was particularly conscientious about the settings and connections on the liquid nitrogen tanks ever since the accidental death years prior of a friend and fellow bull semen supplier. One of Mr. Adrien's tanks developed a leak. His 12 year old daughter found her father, a hulking man of 6'5", 240 pounds, dead beside the tank—killed, the medical examiner said, moments after switching the valve on. Grandpa was meticulous in his maintenance, repeating the story to me from time to time. He said his life and his reputation depended on it.

"And Grandpa's known to his neighbors as a handy man; he's always enjoyed tinkering with recalcitrant lawn mowers and tillers on his Sunday afternoons. Once, I asked him if this wasn't breaking the Sabbath. He responded, 'This is where I get some of my worshipping done, Casey. The Sabbath is about rest and recreation.' And he'd emphasize each syllable—'ree cree aye shun.'

"Another Sunday, on the anniversary of my father's death, as I watched Grandpa sharpening the blades on a neighbor's reel mower, handing him an occasional wrench or screwdriver while he put the mower back together, I asked him about Daddy. 'Grandpa, why do you think my Daddy turned out so wrong?'

"Grandpa thought and continued tinkering before he replied. Then he pointed to a cotter pin in the mower. 'See that?' he asked. I nodded. 'Without it, this mower will start to fall apart. It'll work okay for a while, even though it ought to be fixed. Then one day it just won't work. I think your daddy had a defective cotter pin. Whether he was always that way or some big jolt knocked it loose—either way, there wasn't anything you or your mama could've done to fix it or prevent it 'cause if he'd wanted it fixed, he'd 'a' done something about it. Instead, he tried to pretend it wasn't important.'

"Now, each Sunday while I sit in church, not only is it a time of worship and reflection, it's also a time to do inventory of my emotional and spiritual cotter pins, making sure the connections are solid and sound."

"Extraordinary. Truly extraordinary. And they're still living?"

"Yes. Mama still lives with them. They're not quite as active as they used to be, but their lives are largely unchanged from when I was a little girl—with the exception of those huge Sunday meals." Casey smiled.

"What good fortune that you and your mother both ended up there with them."

"Agreed. As you've noticed, I could go on and on about them for hours," Casey smiled, unapologetically.

"Do you mind, now, if we discuss your father? I want to know about all the people who were with you in your formative years."

"Not at all. I still have more questions than answers where he's concerned, but you can ask me anything you'd like."

"You mentioned before that you've done multiple 'dissections' of his life. What's one of your questions?"

"Well, one of the things that still bothers me is how my father came into possession of his distorted desires. Was it a genetic fluke that lay dormant for generations and then insidiously twisted itself into the spiraled combination of his parents' DNA? Parents I never met, by the way. Or was it some rogue wind that blew through his personality, sowing seeds of perversion into a vacant patch of soil in his soul? Either way, what would keep the same thing from happening to me? How can I guard against a silent, deceitful vapor that seeps in, leaving poisonous deposits of mutated self-absorption where noble intent ought to reside?"

Lorelei sat forward, looked Casey intently in the eyes. "First of all, as insightful and self-aware as you are, I highly doubt you will develop the same predilections as your father. If there's any 'rogue gene' in you, you'd already have determined its presence. Secondly, as you no doubt know, abuse doesn't spring up in a vacuum. There must have been some precipitating event or events in your father's life that set this in motion. Thirdly, I agree with your grandfather: he had choices about addressing his impulses but, apparently, chose to do nothing."

"I'm relieved to hear you say that. I sometimes wonder if he went into the ministry to appease God in some way. 'Look at all the good I do. Will it not offset those occasions when I cannot keep my thoughts and actions in check?' I've heard some people say that people who like sex with children are too sick to distinguish between what's right and wrong. I disagree. Maybe someone ends up that way, but in its very genesis, the secrecy associated with perversion indicates that the person *knows* it's wrong.

"This became clear to me in high school when I volunteered for the hippo-therapy program. I helped some of the children with horseback riding. Occasionally, when some of the more profoundly mentally handicapped children would get excited, they rubbed or touched themselves, right there in front of other people. There was no reservation to their actions because they didn't know to be ashamed. When there's tremendous secrecy attached to someone's actions, though, it's because they don't want to be found out—because they know it's wrong. Over time, perhaps the secret person stops communicating with the public person and they live a dual existence. How convenient is that?"

"Casey, what would you say to your father if he were still alive today?"

"I've fantasized about that, you know? I have no desire to have a relationship with him, but I would like to see a look of contrition on his face, a flicker, even, of repentance for choosing, cafeteria-style, that which he would and would not confront about himself, then leaving the rest of us to wade through the garbage heap of those choices. He carried himself with what was often assumed to be self-assurance, a sort of theological confidence moored to seminary education and earnestness.

"He thrived on being a pastor; he enjoyed being indispensable. A lot of people really liked him; he could be so charming and sincere. You wanted to believe him, to believe *in* him. In reality, his demeanor wasn't so much confidence as it was swaggering defiance—a smirk in the face of God and my mother and anyone else who made him aware of his inadequacies. If he felt any regret before he hanged himself, that acknowledgement died with him.

"My God, even in the act of ending his life, he deprived his family and flock of the opportunity to at least lay to rest our concerns about his conscience. So, my question? 'Are you genuinely sorry, or sorry you got caught?'"

"What does it mean to you, now, as a young woman, to be the daughter of a sexual predator?"

"Oh, wow. While I'd like to think my identity isn't much wrapped up in his shameful acts, it does mean I lost my father to an unseen enemy, an undiagnosed soul-cancer. Who could have known the dark part was winning the war inside him? As he gave his vigor over to this sinister force, I very nearly lost my mother. She is haunted by a sense that she let her love for her husband cloud her judgment; but also because she loved him, she thinks she should have known better what was happening inside him, by him.

"Grandma and Grandpa Greer keep a framed photograph of Mama and Daddy on their wedding day. When I was younger, I studied that picture almost as if I were an archaeologist searching for clues. I wanted to know who these two people were who made me. The young woman in the picture is radiant in her beauty; not starry-eyed, but serene and sure, possessed of great aspirations for herself and the future with her young, handsome husband. Her devotion to him and all that he stands for is evident, not just in the way she looks at him but also in her carriage and the softness around her mouth and eyes.

"She staked her life and her identity on being part of what he claimed to stand for. It's difficult for me to reconcile that photograph with the woman she became—both the mother I knew as a young girl and the one I now know. Being the daughter of a sexual predator means I was very nearly orphaned, I was deprived of a healthy childhood, and I discovered things about the darkness that exists in this world at a far too young age."

Fifteen

AT 7 P.M., THE WOMEN of the Thursday night support group began to forge a sisterhood over secrets finally revealed, allowed out of musty closets of quiet despair into the light of self-disclosure. For some, it was the first time they had spoken of events in their lives outside the safety of their counseling sessions with Myra; one could almost smell the pungent odor of mothballs, the secrets had been stored away so long.

For others, the telling was almost by rote, and the poignancy of their stories was in seeing the elaborate armor they had constructed to keep the long-ago arrows from re-piercing their hearts.

Rebekah heard accounts of extraordinary heroism, so astounding she listened intently, allowing their stories to seep into crevices where only cobwebs of her story lingered. She both envied and pitied her fellow group members for their ability to recall sordid details. Myra merely had to invite one woman to start and what followed was, in Rebekah's estimation, profound, riveting, dreadful and, yet, magical, as one story of struggle and survival segued into another, weaving a tapestry of tenacity amidst brokenness.

Libby began, her cultured drawl again drawing Rebekah in, each cadenced syllable sliding smoothly over the next. "Well, I first starting seeing Myra after my daughter, Rachel, ended up in the hospital with an eating disorder at the age of 30. She had fought it most of her life, but after her daughter, my little granddaughter, Courtney, was born and Rachel couldn't get the weight off, she started purging—you know, making herself vomit. Then she couldn't make herself stop.

"I went to take care of her family while she was in the hospital; Courtney was still a baby. One of the things that came up while she was in therapy in the hospital was the subject of sexual abuse. Rachel asked me if she had, to my knowledge, ever been abused. I was shocked," Libby clasped her hand to her breast. "I couldn't think of anyone who would ever do such a thing to her." Her voice became quiet, "and that's when I remembered I had been molested by an uncle when I was a little girl. I was only five years old at the time."

As if narrating the mental video playing on her screen, Libby continued. "My whole family—parents, sisters, brother, aunts, uncles, and cousins—was visiting my grandparents for Christmas in Mississippi. Everyone was lying down to rest after Christmas Day dinner. I sneaked out of the room where the children were supposed to be napping and went downstairs to the living room. I wanted a piece of candy. I knew I should have waited and asked permission, but it was my favorite candy—lemon drops.

"My Uncle Walter—really my mother's uncle—was sitting in the living room drinking. All the rest of the adults were still resting upstairs. I didn't see him until I popped that lemon drop into my mouth. I turned around to go back upstairs and saw him sitting there, looking at me through a liquor-induced stupor with this sickening crazy smile on his face. He called me over to him and pulled me onto his lap."

As silent tears filed down Libby's face, gravitating toward laugh lines around her mouth, other women joined in the silent keening, sensing what she would share next. "He slurred something about little girls who should be napping and how he could keep a secret if I could keep a secret. I remember feeling ashamed—ashamed for not wanting to be near him and for sneaking downstairs. Then he turned me around on his lap so I was facing him and told me to give him a big hug. Which I did, even though he reeked of whiskey. And he didn't let go. He slid one hand under my bottom and with the other one held on to me tightly, moving me back and forth, side to side across his crotch. I didn't know what he was doing at the time, but I knew it felt wrong.

"Then he groaned real low, like a dog does when you find that spot where he likes to be scratched. Then he picked me up off his lap, set me down, patted me on the head and said," she imitated his gravelly voice, "'now you go on upstairs like a good girl and ol' Uncle Walter won't tell nobody you been downstairs snitchin' candy.' And I did. I never told anyone, but the shame I felt about my secret with Uncle Walter nearly suffocated me—like wearing a winter coat in the middle of summer.

"Over time, I quit thinking about it, probably after his funeral, but it definitely did something to me. I told Rachel about it and I asked her if anything like that had ever happened to her. She didn't think so, but her psychiatrist thought maybe some of my unfinished business became hers. I hate the idea that when I gave birth to her, I may have passed that ugly secret on to her. So I started seeing Myra," she turned and smiled at Myra, "to finish the Uncle Walter business." In her voice, there was a measure of defiance against a very real but unseen enemy. "And to help my Rachel and Courtney." Libby took a Kleenex and patted at her eyes then blew her nose.

There was a respectful silence and then Margot cleared her throat and began speaking with a catch in her already tremulous voice. "Something sort of similar happened to me, only it wasn't a relative. My father left when I was real young, so it was just my mom and me. She worked two jobs just so we could have a place to live and food to eat. I was on my own after school for as long as I can remember. I'd let myself in the apartment and watch TV or do homework until she got home. She was always so tired, but we cooked dinner together and she'd ask me how my day was at school and I'd ask her about her day."

Margot's smile was sorrowful. "While we were eating, she'd look at my homework and help me if there was something I didn't understand. After dinner, I would take my bath while she cleaned up the kitchen, then we'd sit together and read or watch a TV show. She would usually nod off before 9:00 and I'd have to wake her up so she could tuck me in. Then she'd drag herself to bed and start the whole thing over the next day before sunrise. She never complained, but I remember her telling me on Friday nights how tired she was and how glad she was that it was the weekend.

"One day, when I was nine years old," Margot paused, took a deep breath, "I got home after school and couldn't find my key. I had been to the building superintendent's apartment a few times before, with Mom, to drop off an overdue rent payment. That day I knocked on his door to ask him to let me in my apartment and he invited me inside. It was nasty. He was nasty." Margot shuddered involuntarily. "He talked about what a pretty girl I was and how it would be a shame if my mom and I got evicted because of her frequent overdue payments.

"Then he unzipped his pants and started playing with himself—while he was talking to me. I was mortified. Until then, I didn't even know what a man looked like underneath his clothes. He must have seen how shocked I was because he laughed and said, 'Don't tell me you've never seen this before. I figured a girl as pretty as you has lots of boyfriends.' I was only nine. I didn't know what he was talking about. I just wanted to get out of there. But I didn't have a way of getting into my apartment.

"So I asked him if I could borrow the key and I'd bring it right back. He laughed again and said I'd have to come and get it. Or I could wait there until my mom got home and he could tell her how careless I was with my key. I didn't know what to do. I didn't want to add to my mother's worries, and I had been taught to respect adults. So I went over to get the key. He was standing up, leaning against the table in his kitchen, holding himself with one hand and the key with the other, like it was a carrot and I was the bunny. When I held out my hand for him to give me the key, he grabbed me and made me touch him."

Margot closed her eyes, wincing with the memory. "I can't talk about the rest, but I will tell you he began dropping by our apartment after school on a regular basis, always talking about how pretty I was and how many people would be glad to live here and how difficult it was for people who were late with their rent payments to find another place to live. He got what he wanted and I never, ever told my mom. I never told anyone until I started seeing Myra," Margot nodded in her direction. "I came for help getting over my divorce and Myra encouraged me to become part of this group."

Margot swallowed hard and seemed tempted to crawl back inside herself, turtle-like, to watch and listen from the safety of her shell. Instead, she drew strength from Myra's gaze of approval, sitting up straighter with her hands relaxed on her lap.

Celeste sighed, letting her breath escape through pursed lips. Her voice, matter of fact, temporarily lost some of its acerbic edge. "I'm a single mom, like your mom was," she looked at Margot, "only I haven't been so good at it. I'm seeing Myra because I was court-ordered to get counseling so I could get my son, Justin, back. He's in foster care because I had to go through drug rehab. I don't know who his father is; I didn't get names when I was turning tricks for drugs."

She paused long enough to gauge the reactions of the other women, who were listening attentively and without judgment. Then, softer, "I'm lucky he wasn't born with anything wrong with him. Now I'm just trying to put my life in order, change some things; learn how to be a better mom. I'm in this group because Myra says the drugs and the sleeping around are markers of some kind of abuse. Until I met Myra, I never thought of it as abuse for my mother's boyfriends to barge in on me in the bathroom while I was taking a bath or changing clothes or sitting on the toilet.

"Or when I would wake up during the night because my mother and her boyfriend-of-the-month were making so much racket screwing on the sofa and they wouldn't quit, even though I was standing there, telling her it was too loud for me to sleep."

With a measure of defiance, Celeste continued, "I left home when I was 18, determined to make something of my life, be somebody." She sat up straighter, tossing her hair. "First I went to cosmetology school and then I was working on an AA degree at the community college in Anaheim. I had a pretty good job and a couple of decent boyfriends until I went on my first crack binge. Then I turned out to be just like her." She sat back. "But I'm trying to make things right for Justin."

Olivia was smiling through tears, nodding. She looked at Celeste and said, "I have a little boy, too. Tyler. He's seven. We call him Ty." She reached for a Kleenex then continued, looking at a focal point just beyond her nose, her voice timid and girlish, "I started seeing Myra after my sister committed suicide back in January. I did my best to take care of her after Mama died—she died when I was 12 and my baby sister—Elise, that's her name- was only four. My daddy tried to turn me into his wife—you know, um, sleeping with me," Olivia tugged nervously at her oversized shirt.

"That went on until I left home to marry my husband, Clay. I was 18 and already pregnant with Tyler when Clay and I got married. I didn't even finish high school." As if reading the thoughts of some of the others, Olivia added, "Tyler is Clay's son. I'm sure of that. Anyhow, I begged Elise to come live with me, help me with the baby. I didn't want Daddy doing the things to her that he had done to me. But she didn't want to leave her school and her friends. When she killed herself, she was pregnant."

Olivia paused and cleared her throat. "As far as I know, she didn't have a boyfriend. I had to get help; I almost went out of my mind blaming myself for letting that happen to her. So I've been dealing with her death and now I'm ready to deal with everything else, too. I have to. For Ty's sake," she said, fervency in her voice. "I need to be strong for him."

Rebekah waited for a moment, then spoke, her voice filled with emotion and admiration. "I thought I had it really bad when my dad died suddenly a couple of months ago, but I cannot imagine what it must be like to lose your sister—and to suicide. I'm so sorry." She looked at Olivia, who raised her eyes momentarily to receive Rebekah's condolences.

Rebekah continued, fidgeting with her wedding band like it was a talisman, "I started seeing Myra because I've been depressed since my daddy's death. She thinks I might've been sexually abused, but I don't remember. The girl who was my best friend in third grade—Casey— it might've been her father. If it was, I would've been eight, nine years old," Rebekah nodded momentarily toward Margot. "I guess I've blocked it out of my mind, but I think my body is beginning to remember. At least, my nose is," she flashed a grin at Myra.

"Casey sent me a letter. I hadn't heard from her in 20 years. Maybe if I contact her, she'll be able to tell me if our suspicions are out in left field or not. Anyway, I'm here because I'm tired of being depressed and I want to move on with my life, but this abuse thing seems to be a logjam that keeps me from getting anywhere. And because I think my husband, Cliff, deserves to be with a woman who's not moving through life like a robot. I want *me* back, the me he fell in love with, the me I think I'm supposed to be, whoever she is."

"Wow," Andrea said, without so much as a pause, "I've been the way I am now for so long I can't remember being anything other than pissed and practical. I channel my anger into my job to catch perpetrators and nail their asses to the wall." Andrea's Boston accent was made even more pronounced by the stony, harsh edge in her voice, as if any hint of vulnerability in her treatise might tip the first domino. "I left home early, too—at the age of 19," she glanced at Olivia and Celeste, "but I never looked back. Haven't spoken to any of them in 15 years.

"Let's see, my story.... I was the middle child of five children born to your typical working class parents. I have two older brothers and two younger brothers." Her voice remained emotionless as she clipped off her story. "My father never could seem to keep a job for more than a year or so." She rolled her eyes. "Between him and my two older brothers, someone was always in trouble or in a crisis. I was the invisible child. Stuck in the middle and too damn nice for my own good.

"So when my oldest brother started bringing his buddies around to have their way with me, Mom was too preoccupied taking care of my baby brothers and my father and with bailing my older brothers out of their messes to notice anything wrong with me. I stood it as long as I could and then I left and got into law enforcement. My way of saying, 'You bastards won't mess with me now.'"

Andrea paused. "I'm good at what I do, too. But recently I let one case get to me. I let my anger cloud my objectivity, so I decided that before I jeopardize my job, I'd better get a handle on my anger. Myra says this group should be good for me, that I might learn how to get past my anger instead of just keeping it in check. So that's why I'm here. I guess."

Myra let their words remain untouched for a moment, allowing them to have a life and a power of their own. Then she began, softly, "Isn't it interesting that many of the reasons for seeking counseling aren't the abuse itself, but manifestations of the abuse? If you are ever tempted to believe that your abuse wasn't all that bad, let these symptoms remind you of the toll abuse takes on people's lives, of the toll it has taken on *your* life."

Come on, Rebekah coaxed herself, *ask your question. Open your mouth and speak.*

"May I ask you something?"

"Sure. Go ahead," Myra faced Rebekah, her expression encouraging and inviting. Rebekah looked surprised, not sure if she had thought it too loudly or actually spoken.

"I guess I don't understand why we do things that make our lives more complicated. You would think we've suffered enough. Why do anything to make life harder?" Rebekah looked lost.

Myra waited, watched, then probed, "Can you give us a for instance?"

Rebekah's brow furrowed. *Should've kept my mouth shut.* Then, "If depression isn't healthy for me, for the relationships I care about, why do I stay that way? Why can't I pull myself out of it?"

Myra looked around the room. "What do you all think?"

"When Rachel was in therapy at the hospital, they talked a lot about that," Libby offered. "She said nearly everyone in her support group for eating disorders talked about using food to kill pain."

"Oh, Lord, that's the truth," Olivia said, almost to herself. "When Clay and I aren't getting along, I go straight for the ice cream, even though he tells me how fat I've gotten."

Andrea spoke. "Doesn't that make you mad that he tells you you're fat?"

Olivia nodded, her eyes downcast.

"Why do you put up with it, then?"

"I guess 'cause I'm afraid he'll leave."

"My thing is, if someone wants to leave, who needs him? I mean if he leaves that easily...." Andrea's voice trailed off.

Margot found her voice. "It hurts when people leave, especially without a good enough reason."

After a brief lull, Myra said, "Our typical response to pain is either get out, get even, or get control. Depression is one way of getting out. Does that help answer your original question?" She looked at Rebekah.

"Yeah. But just because I understand it a little better doesn't mean I like the answer."

Myra looked at Rebekah, then the others. "This may be a good time to check in with yourself and see how you're feeling. There were likely times when your feelings were not considered in the environment of your abuse, whether intentionally or not. Your feelings then, and now, need to be validated. *You* need to be validated. Who feels sad right now?"

Olivia and Margot both nodded.

"Olivia, how else would you describe your sorrow?"

Olivia thought a moment, then said "Like I'm lost. And alone. All alone." Her voice drifted off, small and childlike.

"Margot? How else would you describe your sadness?"

Margot closed her eyes briefly, then, "Like I've been at the bottom of a well for a long time, and the well is so deep that nobody can hear me. I am cold and afraid. And scared I'll give up."

Myra waited a moment, then asked, "Andrea, what is your anger telling you right this moment?"

Andrea clipped off her words. "You know me. I'm pissed." She faced the other women with a smirk. "Myra keeps trying to get me to find out what's beneath my anger. I don't know how, and I don't want to. Anger works for me; it's my partner. I just want better control of it."

Rebekah mused, *I wonder how her real "pahtnah" feels about that.*

Libby spoke. "Oh, Sugar, don't you know anger will eventually destroy you, from the inside out?" *And don't you know you're lecturing?* Rebekah thought. Andrea, bristling at being addressed as "Sugar," merely shrugged.

Myra turned to Libby. "How are *you* feeling right now, Libby?"

"Oh, I'm hopeful. I see how far I've come in such a short period of time, so I'm encouraged." Rebekah's brow furrowed. *I don't remember what that feels like.*

Interrupting Rebekah's running mental commentary, Myra asked, "How about you? How are you feeling?"

Rebekah scanned the faces in the room, then answered. "I'm amazed at how strong everyone is. I'm scared that if I start to remember, I won't be able to handle it as well as all of you. Part of me wants to remember and part of me doesn't. I feel caught. Stuck."

In a rare moment of unguarded honesty, Celeste said, "I'm with you. I don't really want to poke around in the past. I haven't been out of rehab very long. I'm afraid of relapsing and never getting Justin back." Before anyone had the opportunity to respond with warmth, Celeste quipped, "I'm also a little afraid I'll end up hating men, and that'd be really unfortunate," she smiled, her voice throaty, "'cause I really like being around them." Andrea snorted.

In the ensuing flow of conversation about how each might deal with their feelings after leaving the group meeting, Rebekah entered a private space, no longer engaged in the discussion. Something in Andrea's comments and Casey's letter fused together and Rebekah knew she needed to follow the outlines of an idea back to the night her brother was born. *Follow the thread. Wouldn't Myra be proud?* The determination started as a whisper and by her next session with Myra, it had raised its voice to an audible pitch.

Dear Diary, Dear Self,

How am I feeling right now? Exhausted. Feelings are exhausting. Maybe that's a hidden benefit of depression—it mutes everything.

That Andrea is a real ringer. She's not only rough around the edges, she's coarse through and through. But I think she shoots straight, and I admire that. I don't think she necessarily only hates her family or "perps," I think she just hates. I'll bet she's a hell of a volleyball player, though. I certainly never want to be on the other side of the net from her.

Olivia is sweet—and fragile. But resilient. I guess I never thought you could be both. I wonder what her favorite flavor of ice cream is....

So my choices are: forget about the past, don't even try to remember, and probably stay depressed for the rest of my life, or stick with this group, keep seeing Myra, and watch the nightmare unfold. Oh, crap. I'm so glad I got out of bed this morning. And that's where I'm going now. More later.

Sixteen

August 19, 2008 a.m.

Diary, Dearest,

I dreamed all night about little girls. There was a tea party in my backyard in Founder's Creek and a young Celeste was there, chasing butterflies with a net. Little Olivia was serving ice cream. Little Libby was teaching Margot how to play jacks. Casey was swinging a stuffed giraffe on the swing set and singing "It's a Hard Knock Life." And a youthful Andrea was trying to get us all to play volleyball, while Myra kept trying to tell me something important. I wanted to listen, but I also wanted ice cream and to catch butterflies and watch jacks and volleyball and swing with Casey. And I couldn't do any of the things I wanted to; all I was capable of doing was to stand in the middle of the festivities, walking in a slow, small circle, observing, but not participating.

When I woke up, I realized that I have to know what happened the night Robert was born. I don't really want to, but I need to. Myra has told me that the more receptive I am to remembering, the more the memories will honor me with their presence. Honor me? Disgust is more like it. But I want to know how to play again, how to experience joy in simple things. So I begin with what I know, what I do remember.

I remember Casey. Her mom and her dad I don't remember so vividly. And as much as I loved being with Casey, I vaguely remember some reluctance to go over and stay at her house the night Mom went into

labor. Mom told me he was an unscheduled C-section. How I wish he'd
been born during the day. . . .

If Casey's father, if Pastor Wes, did something to me, maybe it wasn't
too bad—or else I would remember it, right? Maybe there was just a
big misunderstanding. Besides, he was a minister. A minister! They don't
do things to hurt little children, they protect them. And my dad was an
attorney, with a lot of clout. None of this makes sense, and I am about to
be late for work, and if that happens, I can't use my lunch break for my
appointment with Myra.

Myra looked up from Rebekah's journal, open on her lap. "Despite
your ambivalence, I'd say you're on to something. And once you pay
attention to one of those puzzle pieces, others will follow. If you're
so inclined, you might want to either draw some pictures of what
you do remember, or go into your closet and talk as if you're little
Rebekah, being dropped off at Casey's house. Try to *be* the reluctant,
confused child; listen to what she needs to tell you."

Rebekah blushed. "I'd feel kind of foolish going into the closet
and talking like a child. Besides, what if I'm making too big a deal
out of this?"

"Ah. Cleopatra Syndrome. I see it all the time. Great protective
device."

"Excuse me?"

"Rebekah, as you remember your abuse—as those pieces of
the puzzle begin to create a picture, you will also remember more
graphically. Along with remembering come greater attempts to
minimize or deny what occurred. Cleopatra, the Queen of de Nile,
denial." Myra smiled sympathetically. "I know. It's corny. But the
truth is everyone who has been sexually molested battles this. Tell
me. Where do your doubts lie? What makes you think you may be
making too big a deal out of what happened?"

Rebekah motioned to her journal, her brow knotted, "What
possible interest would a grown man have in a little girl? He was
married, so it's not like he wasn't getting any, you know? And he was
a pastor. *Our* pastor. *If* I was molested," she shuddered, "maybe I need
to look elsewhere. The whole thing doesn't make sense."

Myra listened thoughtfully, then asked, "And because something doesn't make sense, it means *you* are the one who has made a mistake?"

"I don't know, Myra. I almost convinced myself that I'd overreacted, but now I'm confused again. I just don't know."

"Rebekah, abuse takes many forms. From a look, a comment, or the brush of a hand, to overt contact. It is wrong for any grown man to look at a child sexually. As to him being a pastor," Myra pointed to the journal entry, "pastors are not immune from pedophilia just because of their profession. Maybe he got a thrill out of getting away with his behavior while his daughter was in the same room and his wife asleep down the hall. Maybe he was careless. Or just stupid. His age, marital status, or profession do not mean abuse could not have happened. Do you understand that?" Myra was sincere, but emphatic.

Rebekah sighed, nodding, trying to talk over the catch in her voice, "So why don't I remember, then?" Sorrow was etched in her eyes.

"For some time now, for 20 years, you have been treating remembering as if it were the enemy. Truthfully, the greatest promise for you is in facing how terrible things really were, not in avoiding it. Is it painful? Absolutely. But your enemy is not the remembering or the pain, it is the denial. You must stop fighting the pain and fight the denial. And I am here to help you."

Tears slid down Rebekah's cheeks. In a small voice, without looking up at Myra, she said, "Thank you." In the waning minutes of their session together, Rebekah spoke of her concern that this hazy occurrence from her past was taking up so much of her time and attention, like slowing to wait for the distant sound of an approaching siren to catch up, being unsure of when to stop, pull over, or go. With Myra promising safety, and as the wail and flashing lights were growing in intensity, Rebekah agreed to surrender to the noise and emergency signals, at least in the confines of her therapist's office.

* * *

"Before I go, I wanted to tell you about a bit of an epiphany I had during church this past Sunday," Casey spoke in measured tones, but her eyes sparkled with discovery.

"Do tell," Lorelei encouraged.

"The Scripture passage was about when Jesus asked the crippled man if he wanted to be whole. I always thought that was a rather stupid question. Who wouldn't want to be whole? Why else would he be lying close to that pool for the last 38 years, hoping to be the first one in the healing waters? But then I realized something. Maybe being an invalid wasn't, in his mind, so bad. At least it looks like he's trying, lying there, waiting. But really, if he's crippled, if his options are seriously limited, so what? So are expectations of him. Whom can he disappoint? In his current condition, he has an excuse for every failure in his life. It's been 38 years, too. He knows how this works. He may not know how to be responsive or how to be successful, but if he is not an invalid, what or who can he blame? This is his cloak and it fits. Maybe he doesn't want to be examined or known—not really. So tomorrow, maybe he'll be the third person in the pool, and next time he'll be the second, or the fourth, but he'll have to really think about being first.

"Being whole is a choice. That's why Jesus asked. Some people would rather be defined by their inadequacies than by the deficiencies those particular inadequacies conceal."

Seventeen

THE WOMEN WERE EXCHANGING LIGHT-HEARTED conversation in the moments before their Thursday night meeting began. September and the promise of fall were nearing and the mood in the comfortable room was airy and easy, unlike the stifling summer heat outside, where the humidity still had its oppressive arms draped around Jacksonville. Libby said, half-joking, "I think we should come up with a name for our group. Something like 'Sisters of Survival.'"

"That's a cool idea. How about 'Mavens of Molestation,'" offered Celeste, arching her eyebrows playfully.

Olivia winced, but whispered in mock seriousness, "'Secret Society of Shame.'"

"I'm thinking 'Sob Sisters,'" Rebekah grinned. "Or am I the only one who owes Myra a case of Kleenex from Sam's?"

"Oh, oh. How about 'Withered Womanhood' or 'Broke-down Beauties,'" suggested Libby.

"Speak for yourself," Celeste responded. "I'd prefer 'Sassy Survivors of the Wrecking Ball.'"

"More like 'Whimpering Women of the Wilderness,'" offered Margot.

"Ooh, I know. 'Ladies in Wraithing,'" said Libby, enjoying the game. "Or 'Damaged Damsels in Distress.'"

"Devastated Dames," offered Andrea.

"I think we need an acronym," Margot said, smiling.

"Well then, how about 'People Interested in Saving Themselves.' You know, PIST," Andrea said.

"Or 'Ladies Out Saving Themselves,'" said Olivia, shyly, her eyes twinkling as she enjoyed the unfamiliar territory of camaraderie.

"Or how about 'Society of Outcast Ladies," said Celeste. "You know, S.O.L."

"Nah. I like 'Females Under Cataclysmic Trials, Understandably Pissed,'" said Andrea as Myra was rolling her desk chair from behind her desk to join the women seated in the circle.

There was a pause as they each figured out her hidden meaning. Libby gasped, looking embarrassed. Celeste smiled appreciatively. The rest sat in stunned silence, unsure of how to respond. Myra sat down and, without reacting to Andrea's statement, looked at Margot. "You suggested an acronym. Let's hear yours."

"I thought about 'Survivors of Abuse Finding Encouragement' because I feel safer here than anywhere else, but it's not very catchy. How about 'CLAMOR?' That's the first initial of all our names and it describes the confusion and noise that being molested has brought into my life."

"What do the rest of you think?" Myra asked, scanning the room.

"I like CLAMOR. That's a pretty good description of my life right now," Rebekah said, smiling at Margot. "CLAMOR time."

"I like it, too," said Olivia.

"Yes. That's good," said Libby, nodding.

"I could live with that name," Andrea said. "And hey, I apologize for getting carried away. I didn't mean to offend anyone," she looked at Libby, who smiled maternally in return.

"How about you, Celeste?" Myra asked

"Alright by me," she answered. "CLAMOR Girls."

"Then CLAMOR Girls it is," declared Myra. "Here is where you may talk freely about the noise and confusion. And this is an appropriate time to begin discussing what elements of your childhood made you vulnerable to abuse. Think about your upbringing, the dynamics in your family. What are the sorts of situations in your family that made you… clamor," she nodded in Margot's direction, "for attention, that left you feeling needy, unfulfilled? To an outside observer, what would your home life as a young girl look like? And what was it really like for you?"

Olivia volunteered to speak first. "After Mama died, people thought Daddy was a hero, such a devoted and wonderful father to raise me and Elise without any help from his family or Mama's side of the family. Of course, they didn't know I was the one doing most of the cooking and cleaning. And I was the one who took care of Elise. Mama had been the real glue in the family before she got cancer. She tried to teach me everything she thought I'd need to know. I think she realized Daddy was incapable of being any more than a breadwinner."

"I don't want to sound nosey, so you don't have to answer this," Rebekah broached, "but was he molesting you before your mom died?"

"No. He didn't start that until about a month after her funeral. When she knew she was dying, Mama taught me how to cook and do laundry and stuff like that. She had no way of knowing I'd be taking over *all* of her wifely duties." There was sorrow in her matter-of-factness.

"I was so fortunate to have two very loving parents who had nothing but my best interest at heart," Rebekah said, shaking her head. "I cannot imagine what it must have been like for you." She continued, "I guess what made me vulnerable was that my best friend's father was a minister. You're taught, you know, to trust your minister, to respect authority. That, and my parents' temporary preoccupation with my mother's pregnancy with Robert, my brother."

"He was a minister?" Libby's voice trembled. "Gosh, if you can't trust your parents and your minister, who can you trust?"

Olivia and Rebekah answered in stereo, "Good question." They looked at each other and smiled.

"I was so blessed with very caring parents," Libby explained. "There's no way they could have known that just because Uncle Walter drank too much that he was also a dirty old man." She shrugged her shoulders. "It was Uncle Walter who took advantage of a situation. Do you know I haven't eaten a lemon drop since that day almost 60 years ago? I won't even put lemon in my tea. Isn't that crazy?"

"Oh, I don't think so. When I was 13, I started locking the door when I was in the bathroom, and I still lock the door, even though there's nobody else at home. I guess if you're crazy, so am I." Celeste smiled conspiratorially at Libby.

Andrea lifted one corner of her mouth, arched her brows, confessing, "I sleep with two pair of underwear on."

"Taken out of context, those actions might sound pretty peculiar but in this room, we understand them," Myra spoke in comforting tones. Then, "Anyone else?"

"I've already told you all about how self-absorbed my mom was. She didn't think she was anybody unless she had a man in her life. What I needed was of secondary concern, if that. I think she resented me because I represented a 'package deal' to any man she was dating—and I use the term 'dating' lightly," Celeste said, "and we all know I understand the difference. You know, it's a sad thing to both love and hate the person you need in order to survive. There you have it. My childhood in a nutshell."

"Which is why I don't need anyone. I've made sure of that," Andrea said, the practical hardness returned to her voice.

Myra gently responded, "Certainly there was a time when you did need someone, though. When you were younger? Your mother? How did she let you down? How did she set the stage for your brother and his friends to abuse you?"

"By being too wrapped up in my father and my brothers," Andrea answered, speaking slowly and controlled. "By not noticing that I was dying a little more each day. By not having the guts to kick my oldest brother out of the house." The words came faster, louder, with increased fury, betraying a hairline crack in her emotional armor. "By not caring enough to stop and see that I needed her to protect me." Andrea took a deep, deliberate breath, releasing it slowly. "By choosing to be blind."

"I guess I'm the one who encouraged my mother to be blind," Margot said, almost to herself. "I felt responsible for her having to work so hard; if she hadn't had me to provide for, she wouldn't have had to work two jobs and she wouldn't have had to worry about keeping the apartment. I didn't want to add to her burdens. I was enough of one already...."

Libby interrupted Margot. "I find that hard to believe—that you were a burden. It sounds to me as if you were the ideal daughter. I have children. I know."

Margot smiled at Libby. "Well, I tried to be good and to do well in school, to make my mom proud of me. I guess at some level, I blamed myself for my father leaving when I was little. He never tried to contact me, so he obviously didn't want me. If it hadn't been for me, Mom's life would've been easier. At least, that's what I believed growing up. I understand now that she willingly made sacrifices for me and that we were better off without my father, but I didn't know these things when I was younger. So, in a sense, I was protecting my mom."

"It sure is hard to be an adult when you're just a child, isn't it?" said Olivia.

"Yes," Margot responded, "I think I lost a lot of my childhood that way."

"So," Myra inserted, "abuse rarely occurs in a vacuum. Often there is already a void, an emotional hunger, a need. And the set-up can be as subtle as wanting to please the adults in our lives, or not offend them, or to appease them. Abusers seem to be able to smell the void, to use it to their advantage. They can lay a trap through pleasant exchanges that cause a young child to drop her defenses, or with a promise of a privilege or with a threat. When you think back on the particular dynamics in your life, how does that make you feel now?"

"I'll go," Andrea's perfunctory manner had returned, her voice nearly robotic with the telling. "When my brother Lance would bring his drinking buddies by the house, they'd tease me a little, tousle my hair. Sucker that I was, I lapped up their attention like a kitten starved for milk. When Lance started bringing his buddies up to my room after a night of drinking, I thought it was just to tease me or tickle me some more. I liked the attention. But it got out of hand really quickly, and Lance got really mean when I tried to fight back. He'd say stuff like, 'You don't want Mom to know what a dirty little bitch you are, do you?'"

"What'd you do?" Olivia asked, alarm in her voice.

"I just took it. I turned off my mind and went numb. But I started planning my escape. Hell, I would've grown testicles if I could have, just to keep them off me."

"Your brother," Margot spoke, "what happened to him?"

"Last I heard, two of them were in prison. One for rape, one for attempted murder. I'm not surprised. They were always a bunch of screw-ups. I hope they rot there."

"Do you feel at all sad for the little girl you used to be?" Margot wondered.

"Not really. I feel angry toward my family, and angry with myself for being a defenseless, needy girl who let them get away with it."

Olivia implored, "But you couldn't help it! They took advantage of you."

"I should've found a way to make them stop. I should not have had to leave to make it stop."

"Is that why you pursued law enforcement?" asked Rebekah.

"Yeah. It's too late for me, but I'll be damned if I'll let someone else get away with this. I figure it's one way to make some good come out of it."

Libby, her drawl gentle, offered, "I don't think it's too late for you, Andrea. I think you need to find a way to love that little girl."

Andrea looked at Myra. In a voice tinged with fatigue and sarcasm, she said, "You paid her to say that, didn't you?"

"I'm serious, you've got to find a way to love her," Libby leaned forward, emphatic. "To help her know how special she is, how much Jesus cares for her..." The hardness in Andrea's eyes made Libby shift her attention to Myra. "I don't think I was necessarily set up, except maybe by the way society operated back then. We didn't discuss funny uncles."

Myra nodded, looking around the room. "What's more important here isn't necessarily how it could have happened but that it did happen and what your life has been like as a result. How you felt then; how you feel now."

"When it happened, I felt dirty. Even though what Uncle Walter did to me was wrong, I thought it happened because I had disobeyed. To this day, when I really want something, I think I'm being bad."

Rebekah's brow knotted, "I don't follow. Can you give me an example?"

"Hmm. Let me think… Okay, when I see an ad in the paper for a dress or some new kitchen gadget, there's a part of me that says I'm being naughty, that I shouldn't want it."

Myra coached, "So to want something means…."

"To want something means," Libby searched her emotional database. "Oh, dear. To want means something bad will happen. Oh, dear. I'm sure I've raised my children to think the same way. Appreciate what you have, but do not want."

The silence in the room was respectful, each woman matching her experiences of desire against Libby's, determining when cravings had become caustic. Myra waited, then said, "So desire can be dangerous, no?"

"Sure can," Celeste stated. "My mom messed up her life and mine because she couldn't get a handle on what she wanted. So she gave herself away. At least I made men pay for my affections," Celeste's smirk was tinged with sorrow.

Rebekah leaned forward, as if peering into a dark cave. "I hope this doesn't offend you but I cannot imagine selling my body. I think I would find it degrading. Why did you do it?"

"Aside from the fact that I needed money for my cocaine habit, I turned tricks because that allowed me to be in control of what men wanted. I could call the shots that way. They got what they wanted, but they had to pay for it and they didn't get to hook my heart. By the way," her tone was brazen, but not disdainful, "I don't offend easily. Don't worry about being careful around me."

"So your heart has never gotten in the way before?" Myra asked.

"Nope. Not really. I really liked some of my boyfriends, but I could take them or leave them. I never got emotionally involved with them, and especially not when I was doing johns."

Libby squirmed at Celeste's frankness, but continued to smile her most maternal smile. While surprised at her bluntness, Rebekah found Celeste's honesty engaging. Olivia and Andrea, each in her own way, appreciated Celeste's cavalier manner. Margot winced, but determined not to retreat into the security of silence. She spoke softly, "There's a part of me that envies that sort of emotional detachment. I'd like to find a way to turn off my heart. At least turn the volume down a bit."

"How in the world did you tolerate what that man was doing to you if you didn't shut a part of yourself off?" Celeste asked Margot.

"I just endured it. My heart broke a little more each time, and I hid more and more behind a façade of skill and good grades and self-sufficiency. When I met my husband, it felt like my heart regenerated and started to bloom again... until he told me he couldn't love me anymore. Not didn't," she held up a finger to make her point, "couldn't. Like I was a broken piece of furniture he needed to get rid of." Margot was crying now. Libby, Rebekah, and Olivia all reached for a tissue.

"I understand that," Olivia sniffled. "I wanted my Daddy to pay attention to me. When Mama was alive, he barely noticed me. After she died, all I seemed to be good for was cooking and cleaning and looking after Elise. I felt like an old used-up paper towel. And then he started visiting my room at night, stroking my hair, telling me how pretty I was, how much I looked like Mama. I soaked up his attention, but the price I had to pay for being his Little Princess...." Olivia looked up at Margot. "I just endured it, too." Her voice broke.

Daddy called me his Little Princess, too, Rebekah thought, fighting the urge to retreat into the privacy and security of her memories of her father. Olivia continued, interrupting Rebekah's thoughts, "I didn't feel like I had a choice. But the thing is, I feel like I betrayed myself because I enjoyed those few scraps of attention as much as I hated what I had to do to get them." Olivia wept now, her body shuddering involuntarily at the release of her torment.

Hesitatingly, Libby placed her arm loosely around Olivia's shoulders, cooing in a whisper, "It's okay, Sugar. Just let it all out."

As Olivia's crying subsided, she continued, "All my life I've been afraid. Afraid to love and afraid of not being loved. Afraid to not go along with what my daddy said. And afraid to go along. Afraid to get mad. Afraid that if I did, I'd start screaming and never quit. But all that's changed since Elise died. Now I don't know which of those fears to tackle first."

"What about your husband?" Rebekah asked, "Where does he fit in?"

"Things aren't so good between us right now. Haven't been for a long time," Olivia confessed. "There are times when I think he hates me, there are times when I feel like he can hardly stand me, and then there are times when I feel like he really loves me. These days, we mostly seem to stay out of each other's way. I'm usually pretty tired from working and taking care of Ty. I catch myself, though, wishing Clay would talk to me, help me feel important, not because I'm his wife or the mother of his son but because I'm me. I don't know. I just don't know." Olivia shook her head, defeat in her voice.

In the remaining time, the members of the CLAMOR Girls spoke honestly about what the other group members could do to best help them. Their candor was the closest to liberation that most of them experienced in a long time, blowing like a sea breeze across the stagnant waters of repressed dreams and resurrected wounds.

August 21, 2008

The Queen of Denial reigns. But for how long? For a while, going to my appointments with Hank was something I did every week or so, and then I returned to my life. Now I feel like the whole abuse thing has taken over my life, moved from the edges to the center, even though I'm not 100% convinced it really happened. I told Myra I'm afraid that everyone will notice this cloud hovering around me like the dust around Charlie Brown's friend, Pigpen. They'll point and whisper and hold their noses.

Margot said she feels like she was robbed of her childhood because her innocence was stolen. I have wonderful memories of growing up. Not like Olivia, who was like Cinderella without the ball and the glass slippers and the prince. I don't understand how Margot's husband could hate her, how Olivia's father could hate her. They're both so genuine and good. Are there really people who want to hurt you or leave you just because you give them your whole heart and they can't handle it? So they—what—try to destroy you?

Celeste amazes me. She and Andrea are both very direct, but Celeste does it in a way that's kind of disarming. If she thinks something, she says it. Me, I just think. All the damn time. I can see me in some nursing home 50 years from now, sitting in a wheelchair, my brain-to-mouth editorial processes shot to hell by Alzheimer's. The people who know me now will be stunned at all the random—and mean-spirited—things I say, most likely about them. Why is it so easy for me to see things about other people, but so difficult to figure my own self out? I should write Casey for some clues.

Eighteen

August 22, 2008

Dear Casey,

I guess you were beginning to wonder if you would ever hear back from me. It hasn't been because I haven't wanted to write, I just haven't quite known what to write. I appreciate your letter more than I can adequately express. It came at a time when I truly needed it. Daddy died so suddenly last November. A few months later, I realized the depression I was experiencing was getting worse, so I began seeing a therapist. I'm now on my second therapist. This one, Myra Devoe, is a psychiatrist. If you had told me a year ago that I'd even consider such a thing, I would've rolled my eyes at you.

So, the niceties: I'm married to Cliff Standifer, who is a wonderful man. As you might guess, I measure all men against my father, and Cliff is a keeper. He is a civil engineer with contracts throughout the southeast. I work as a fashion merchandiser and I have accounts mostly in Florida. It's what I've wanted to do since I was 13 years old. I enjoy what I do, even though my boss can be a prick sometimes. Did I just say that? Please destroy this letter after reading *wink*. Cliff and I don't have children, but we very much want a family. Soon. Until then, we don't so much as have a goldfish to take care of. How about you? Are you married? Do you have children?

Myra—she insists her patients call her by her first name. How cool is that?—has me poking around in my childhood to unearth any reason besides my father's death that might be contributing to my depression. Since I have mentioned you several times, she suggested I check some of my memories with you to see if they're correct. For instance, I seem to recall that your bedroom had Strawberry Shortcake sheets and curtains. And you had an impressive stuffed animal collection. I hadn't met anyone whose stuffed animals could rival my collection until I met you.

I don't remember much about Founder's Creek Community Church. My family stopped attending around the time you moved away. I also don't remember very much about your parents except that your dad was the pastor and your mom was really quiet, but a great seamstress. If I may ask, what stands out in your mind when you think about your life in Founder's Creek? Seems you told me once that it was the 5ᵗʰ town you lived in, and you didn't even live there an entire year. I noticed the Ocala postmark. Is that where your roots are now?

I do hope this letter finds you well, happy, and leading a charmed existence. If you would like to write back, I know I'd like that, but if not, please don't feel any pressure to do so.

Fondly,

Rebekah

Lorelei finished reading the letter and handed it back to Casey. "It seems friendly enough, without divulging much either. It feels a little bit, too, like she's fishing. What do you think?"

"She seems cautious to me. I'm having a difficult time squaring the Rebekah I remember with a woman who is depressed and seeing a psychiatrist. No offense. Actually, I feel a bit sorry for her."

"How so?"

"For years, because it shone so luminously in my memory, I carried an image of Rebekah in my mind—of the open way in which she accepted people, receiving them, me, into her dazzling presence so that even when we moved out of her aura, we still felt a glow about us. Like when Moses came down off the mountain after visiting with the Lord. It was that image of Rebekah that gave me courage to break out of my shyness and my shame, to stop being so wary, to cease automatically expecting rejection because of what my father did. I would imagine myself poised like Rebekah, more spectacular than I felt I deserved to be, more confident, more lively. More like her. It's how I got through high school, how I got through undergrad scholarship cattle calls, and how I made it through my graduate school interviews. How I landed this job I love so much. Now, not only does she seem guarded, she seems a little lost. And rather like, despite being depressed, she's trying to convince me that her life is good. Or convince herself, maybe."

"That may be so. So what's your next move? Will you respond?"

"Yes. I think I have something to offer her. She rescued me from my small existence years ago, brought laughter and light into my life. Maybe now I can repay her. I'm not sure if she was fishing or not, but I do know that I will hold nothing back if she asks. I used to long for a bottle of Cosmic White-Out, but I have worked far too hard to own my story and not let it direct my course in life. If she needs me, I want to be there for her."

* * *

Myra seated the CLAMOR Girls around a conference table and presented each woman with a can of Play-Doh. "I want each of you to sculpt yourself as a child, at an age when your abuse occurred. I'll give you a little while to work on your sculpture." She watched the women work the formless lumps into some semblance of humanity while Mozart played through the speakers connected to her iPod. Some worked tentatively at first but eventually all of them participated thoughtfully in the activity. As they mashed and molded, their playful banter gave way to quiet introspection.

Rebekah was the last one to finish. She became aware that the others were patiently waiting, alternating between watching her, looking at their own sculptures, and stealing looks at each other's. She blushed, pinching one more feature onto her likeness, and then looked at Myra apologetically. Myra turned the music off and looked admiringly at her artistic flock. "I'll bet it's been a long time since some of you have played with Play-Doh, huh?"

Olivia and Margot protectively kept their hands near their sculptures as if, by keeping them from being seen, the little children they represented could be kept safe. Rebekah and Libby occasionally touched theirs with traces of tenderness. Celeste and Andrea kept their hands in their laps, ignoring their sculptured selves.

Myra continued, "We are all born with the need to be accepted, valued, enjoyed. Ultimately *everyone* experiences a deficit there. When an assault to those needs occurs in the setting of abuse, though, the resulting shame causes us to adopt survival strategies. For women in particular," she looked around the room, "our bodies are a great source of shame, either occasionally or as a theme woven throughout our lives. Shame says you are incomplete, unimportant, disgusting, used goods, or too needy; and the great effort we expend to try to keep people from finding this out is just greater evidence that shame exists. We will do nearly anything to avoid feeling exposed and defenseless."

She paused, smiling. "It is not my intent tonight to become Toto and pull the curtain back on your fraudulent Great and Powerful Oz act, but to help you see where shame steals from you. So, has anyone ever felt betrayed by her body? Or, what have you found shameful about your body?"

Myra's observations marched a legion of vulnerability through the room. The silence was palpable, as was their recognition that speaking held-in secrets might provide a scouring to some of the dark, stubborn stains in their souls where the faucet of shame had silently dripped for years. Myra waited confidently. Finally, Libby offered, "I guess the worst I ever felt about my body was when I started my period. Gracious, that was so long ago," she laughed nervously. "My family didn't talk about the facts of life, so I was completely unprepared for what happens in puberty. I was in the bathtub shaving when all of this blood appeared. I thought I had severed a vein, for Pete's sake. I cried out for my mother to come quick, thinking I was bleeding to death. She came in the bathroom and figured out what was really happening. Her explanation was awkward. I think she was more embarrassed than I was. So, instead of celebrating the wonders of womanhood, I felt freakish." Libby smiled through her pang of regret. "I made sure my Rachel wasn't caught off guard like I was. She was ready." She touched her Play-Doh person maternally.

Myra pointed at the sculpture, "May we see her, Libby?"

Libby lovingly scooped the figure into her hand and held it out for the others to see. She had sculpted a girl standing with her hands clasped together behind her back, her face angled toward the ground.

"What does she say about you?"

"I don't really know." Libby looked at the others. "What do y'all think?"

Margot said, "She doesn't want to look anyone in the eyes."

Celeste asked, "Why are her hands behind her back?"

"I think it must be because her hands got her in trouble. She doesn't want anyone to see her sticky hands. Then they won't know." "Won't know what?" asked Myra.

"Won't know... won't know that... that she's damaged goods." Libby's voice caught, laced with sadness and surprise at this self-revelation.

Olivia spoke. "That's exactly how I felt." She hesitantly removed her hands from around her Play-Doh self-portrait. It revealed a normal head and feet with a body that was round and rumpled, like rags tossed into a heap. Tears began to form at the inside edges of her eyes. "I'm garbage. Used up and thrown away."

Celeste asked, "Why do you say that?"

"That's how I felt every morning after Daddy made his nighttime visits into my room. He would completely ignore me except if he needed me to pack his lunch for him. I pretty much learned to stay clear of him those mornings because he was so hateful—like it was my fault. The only—the only—time I broke the silence first was when I was 16 and thought I was pregnant." She exhaled slowly, remembering. "I was, and it was his baby." Libby gasped. A lump formed at Rebekah's throat so that she found it difficult to swallow. "Talk about feeling betrayed by your body...." Olivia's voice was sad, flat. She stared straight ahead. "He picked me up from school the next day and took me out of town to get an abortion, acting all mad and put out by the inconvenience of it. He never said he was sorry and he never promised me it wouldn't happen ever again, and he never asked me if I was okay or if it hurt." She paused. Then, "I was almost 18 when I got pregnant with Ty. I know people thought Clay and I were just two dumb kids that got caught playing grown-up games, but I didn't care. I think in the back of my mind I meant to get pregnant with Clay's baby. I just wanted my daddy to leave me alone and I wanted Clay to get me out of there." Her voice a mixture of maternal fierceness then defeat, she continued, "Don't get me wrong. I love my son. I can't imagine life without him… Lord, I just hope he doesn't turn out like me."

"And how is that?" asked Myra.

"Scared, weak. Uneducated. Fat." She pulled self-consciously at her shirt. "He's such a cute, smart little boy. I hope he has more ambition in life than just making do, getting by…."

"You're being pretty hard on yourself," Andrea remarked. The other women nodded.

"I can't help it. I feel like a failure."

"But look at all you've been through. And you've survived. There's a lot to be said for that, you know?" Celeste offered. "And you're a good mother to your son. I just know you are."

"Thank you. He's the world to me. If it weren't for him, I'm not sure I would have had the strength to go on after Elise died." Suddenly embarrassed at the attention offered her, Olivia said, "Enough about me. It's someone else's turn."

After a pause, Margot cleared her throat and shared, "About a year after I was married, I had a miscarriage. My body let me down and I hated it, and myself. My husband didn't understand why that was so devastating. Of course, he didn't really want the baby in the first place…. His heart wasn't even large enough to make room for me, so I guess it's just as well that we didn't have a child together. But losing that pregnancy hurt and it made me feel so defective."

Myra asked gently, "Would you like to show us your sculpture?"

Margot's person was flat, but curled inward at the edges, and she had poked a hole in its chest where the heart should be. "I feel flat. Well, except for these," she indicated her well-endowed breasts. "Emotionally. I feel like there's a hole in my heart, and I'm turning in on myself. I'd like to be filled up, but I'm also afraid to be."

"What are you afraid of?" asked Myra.

"Afraid of getting hurt again. Of caring more for someone than he cares for me. Of feeling foolish for loving someone. I don't want my heart filled up just to get it drained empty again. That hurts too much. So I'll remain one-dimensional for now—where it's safer."

"That seems like a waste to me. I think you must have a lot to offer—to the right person," Rebekah said.

"Thank you. I hope you're right. And I hope I get to find out some day."

Rebekah showed Margot her sculpture. "See, I have a hole in mine, too." Rebekah's self-sculpture was of a saucer-eyed child sitting cross-legged, sucking her thumb. There was a small hole where the throat should have been. "I feel like I betrayed myself with my silence. If I could've found my voice, maybe nothing bad would have happened. And I'm also ashamed for whatever I did that might have led him on."

"Whoa! That is such a lie," interrupted Andrea. "There is nothing that children do to lead on a perpetrator." The intensity in her voice sounded both scholarly and angry. "Just because they get turned on doesn't mean a child has done anything to warrant that. They're just sick bastards who didn't bother to get help before their problems became too big for them to handle alone."

Myra nodded. "What she's saying is true, Rebekah. You didn't do anything to deserve what happened to you. Okay?"

"My head agrees with you. How do I get my heart to agree, too?"

"See it for the lie that it is. You were a child, acting like children do. He was an adult who chose to use you, abuse you." Myra's voice was forceful, "Ladies, remember, don't fear the truth; fear the denial. The truth, no matter how messy it is, is your best ally for moving forward. Okay?"

They looked stunned, wary, like elementary school students called into the principal's office. Then Andrea spoke again, "Giving a perpetrator an excuse for what they did is like protecting him. That would be like saying Hitler shouldn't be held responsible for what he did because he was born illegitimate."

Myra asked, "Andrea, would you like to show us your sculpture?"

Andrea shrugged and barely glanced at her artwork. The Play-Doh child was an amorphous blob with indefinite features.

"What can you tell us about her?"

"Not much. There's not much to tell. She's pretty much a non-person, a nobody. More like a piece of furniture."

Margot observed, "There's not anything to indicate she's a girl. Is that on purpose?"

In a voice that was dull and detached, Andrea answered, "Being a female has got to be one of the most dangerous things. It's better to be nothing."

"Honey, do you really believe that?" asked Libby, concerned.

Myra gazed around the room. "How many of you have felt it wasn't safe to be female?"

"Well, yeah," Celeste answered. "How many guys have to worry about getting raped?"

"Or getting pregnant," added Olivia.

Rebekah, eyebrows knit together, asked, "So why do we care how we look? Why do women want to be pretty? I'm serious. My career is to make sure stores have clothes that help women feel beautiful. Why bother?"

"We are born inherently beautiful," Myra answered, hands clasped to her chest, "and somewhere deep inside each of us is the longing to return to that place where it's safe to be beautiful."

"Well I don't feel beautiful," Andrea said, slowly pressing down on her sculpture with an open hand. "And I don't want to, and I don't care," she added with a finality that didn't even fool herself.

"And you don't want to have feelings either, do you?" Margot asked gently.

"Right."

"I brought something for you from work. I was going to give it to you later. You don't have to take it but if you want it, it's yours." She pulled a magnet out of her scrubs pocket and handed it to Andrea. The magnet bore the logo of a childhood vaccine. On it were 30 caricatures depicting different emotions, with a movable frame that said, *Today I Feel.*

Andrea looked at the magnet and, without looking at Margot, smirked, placing the magnet on the table. "Thanks."

Celeste, her voice more buoyant than she intended, said, "That is so cool! I want one." She smiled at Margot, who suddenly remembered to be self-conscious.

"I'll see what I can do."

Myra looked at Celeste and said, "We haven't talked about your sculpture yet. What can you tell us about her?"

Celeste's likeness was only a face—bewildered, waifish, with one large tear beneath each eye.

Childlike, Olivia said, "You haven't given yourself a body."

"I know. I couldn't think of how to do that. I'm not ashamed of my body." She sat up a little taller, smiling, smoothing her hands down her hips. "I just kept picturing myself with breasts and hips, and Myra said to sculpt ourselves when we were younger..."

"Maybe that face belongs to you when you're older," offered Rebekah.

"Could be. To tell you the truth, I'm not sure why I made that face."

Olivia asked, "Are there pictures of you when you're a young girl that remind you of that face?"

"No. The pictures of me when I'm younger are of a girl who's clueless and really pretty carefree."

Libby suggested, "Maybe your sculpture's trying to tell you something about when you're a little olde-"

"Omigod," Celeste interrupted.

Calmly, Myra asked, "What is it, Celeste?"

"That picture of me... My senior picture. Taken the summer before the 12th grade. That was the summer I dated Bobby. He was older, already finished with college." Focusing on an imaginary screen, her projector replaying an archived film from the cold storage vault of her memory, Celeste intoned, "I met him at the beach right after school got out for the summer. We hit it off right away. He called or came over every night."

Her mouth formed a wry smile. "I'm pretty sure my mom was attracted to him, too. I was completely in love with him. He wanted me to sleep with him the first time we went out and I told him no. I didn't want to be too easy, like my mom. We dated all summer and he would talk about us being together forever. What girl doesn't dream of hearing that? He kept pressuring me to 'take our relationship to the next level.' I wanted to, but like I said, I didn't want to be too easy.

"Finally one night, I couldn't wait any longer. I wanted to give myself to him, to show him how much I loved him. My mom was out tying one on and we were alone in my bedroom. We were talking, then making out, then getting undressed, and this time I didn't say no. We were going at it like two starving people with an all-expenses-paid trip to Ryan's. I felt so alive, so beautiful, so whole. There I was making love to Bobby, giving him my heart, when I looked deep into his eyes and suddenly realized—he was just getting laid."

Tears decorated the lashes of Celeste's luminescent eyes like dainty droplets of crystal. "The next day was senior picture day. I was a wreck. When the proofs came back, all my mom could say was, 'God, Celeste, you look awful. Can't you get a retake?' That was probably when the idea of using my body as bait started. I could enjoy men and enjoy sex, but if they wanted it—me—they would have to pay for it. And I wasn't going to let them destroy me."

Her voice had a finality to it. "That was definitely a turning point. All along, I've blamed my addiction because that's when I started turning tricks, but that isn't entirely accurate. I see that now." Celeste reached for a Kleenex, her usual defiance momentarily supplanted by a delicate openness.

"You poor dear," mothered Libby. "I'm so sorry." The others were mute in their compassion, their eyes conveying shared sadness.

"Yeah, so am I," Celeste sniffled.

Myra, using her exquisite hands in explanatory gestures, spoke. "To someone whose trust has been exploited, the fear of abandonment sends confusing messages to the longing for love. It says, *You are not whole, but this is where you will find completeness. Achieve this accolade, love this person, get this degree, own this house, and others won't leave you.*" Myra paused, allowing them to dress their experiences with her words. "Now would be a good time to talk about longing. What do we tend to do with longings? Do we kill them? Do we feel as if they will kill us? How do you handle your desires? Not necessarily sexual, but the yearning to be special and significant."

Andrea volunteered, "Well, I think we all know that I just don't have them—longings, I mean. I wouldn't know a longing if it came up and bit me on the ass."

"But you can learn to have them, don't you think?" Libby offered, looking intently at Andrea, then turning to Myra for affirmation. "I think that's what God would want for you."

Andrea cringed, but responded, "I suppose. If I wanted to. What do *you* do?"

"I'd have to say I probably rise above them."

"What does that mean?" asked Celeste.

"It means I, uh, gosh," Libby laughed nervously, "I don't know. It means…"

". . . that you ignore them?" asked Margot.

Libby looked crestfallen. "I guess so. I've been so conditioned to mistrust wanting anything, I probably do ignore them. Get real busy. Clean a closet or something."

Olivia cut in, "Hey, next time you have that urge, call me, will you?"

"Yeah," Rebekah agreed.

Margot suggested, "I'd be willing to bet you tend to use efficiency to cover your longings."

Hurt, Libby replied, "I'm not sure what you're saying, Margot. And I see nothing wrong with being efficient."

"I mean you do things for other people, almost make yourself indispensable to them, so it looks like you're involved, but that you're hiding behind your busy-ness. I hope I'm not way out of line here," Margot glanced in Myra's direction.

"What do you all think about what Margot just said," asked Myra.

"I think she's very perceptive," said Rebekah, smiling at Margot, then looking at Libby apologetically.

"Yeah, I think she's right on," said Celeste. "As a matter of fact, I think you're probably way *too* nice," she said to Libby. "Approachable, but unattainable."

Libby looked wounded. "Is being nice to other people, helping other people, suddenly so wrong?"

"Wouldn't that depend on why?" said Andrea. "I mean, what if you're doing nice things for other people so you can always be on the giving end and not on the receiving end, or to make you feel good about yourself? What if you're being nice so they'll believe the same way you do? That would make your life easier, wouldn't it?"

Libby started to speak, but closed her mouth into a thin, hard line.

"I'm sorry," said Margot. "I didn't mean to start anything. I do think you're a really nice person and you probably get a lot of joy and satisfaction out of helping other people. I just wondered if you ever let them see that you have needs, too." She turned to Myra. "I guess the reason I brought it up is that I see some of the same tendencies in myself. I get to help other people professionally and I like to do that. But when *I* have needs, I tend to withdraw. It's like my longings are quicksand and the more I thrash around, the faster I sink, so I do nothing. I don't trust others or myself enough to talk about what I need or to ask for help."

"Are you asking this group to help you reach out?" asked Myra.

"I guess so."

"Shoot. I can help you loosen up," Celeste interjected. "And maybe you can help me put a harness on my mouth."

"But I envy the way you just say what's on your mind."

Celeste smiled her appreciation. "Yeah, but Myra says I use my gift of gab to...," she turned to Myra, "how do you put it? Oh, right. Deflect pain. Myra thinks I'm not letting my pain talk to me. I need to practice the Myra Mantra: 'Fear the denial more than the pain.'" She performed a rendition of Myra's earnestness, perfectly matching her voice and mannerisms.

Myra smiled good-naturedly at Celeste. "Beautifully done. It appears that I will soon be out of a job. Before I take down my shingle, let's hear from Olivia and Rebekah."

The two looked at each other, each politely, awkwardly yielding her turn with subtle shoulder shrugs and quick eyebrow raises. Celeste playfully chanted, pointing alternately between the two quiet women, "Appa bappa soda cracker, appa bappa boo, appa bappa soda cracker, I pick you." Her finger came to a stop on Olivia.

Olivia smiled bashfully. "What do I do with my longing? Good question. I don't think I've ever thought about my longings. I guess I eat. And smoke. That means I kill them, right?" her voice was small and uncertain.

"Could I ask you something?" Rebekah said. Olivia nodded. "Are you aware that you're trying to shut off your feelings when you're doing those things—eating and smoking?"

"Not always. It's usually afterwards that I realize what I've done. Then I get mad at myself."

"Then I guess I kill my longings, too, and I wasn't aware of that until this evening. When I want to crawl into a dark hole and sleep for a hundred years, the main thing I'm aware of is the pain and frustration, but not that there's longing underneath them."

"Is it possible to do both? I mean, is it possible to sometimes misdirect the longing and at other times try to numb it?" asked Margot.

Myra answered, "It's not only possible, it's probable. You are all intelligent, resourceful women. I'm sure you've learned lots of ways to cope," she smiled indulgently, "and have settled on a few favorites."

"So I could do something that's actually good and use it to take a detour around my pain? Like work? Or working out?" Margot asked.

"Oh, absolutely."

Rebekah spoke again. "I've always been able to lose myself in my work but I'm finding that harder to do. What does *that* mean?"

Myra looked at the group and repeated her question, "What does that mean?"

Celeste said, "I think it means you're off automatic pilot; you're alive…"

"Give me back the automatic pilot! I had no idea being alive could be so hard. Is it supposed to be this way?" she directed her question to Myra.

"Whether or not it's *supposed* to be this way is less of an issue than the fact that it *is* this way. In that respect, pain is your friend. It tells you that there are wounds, and wounds need to be properly bathed and bandaged in order to heal. Ignoring them only allows them to fester."

"I wish I still believed in the Fairy Godmother," said Rebekah. "With one wave of her wand, she could make all my dreams come true and all the nightmares disappear."

After the session broke up, the CLAMOR Girls stood and talked informally, reluctant to return to the heat and humidity of the August dog days and the interior chambers of their neglected longing. Libby stood off from the others, listening, but not participating in the chatter. She was first to leave. As the others filed out, still talking on the way to the parking lot, Andrea slipped the magnet into the pocket of her skirt, an action only observed by Myra, who was pretending to be occupied with some piles on her desk. All the Play-Doh people had been taken except one, the leveled blob of Andrea.

Nineteen

REBEKAH TOYED WITH THE HAIR tie on her wrist while Myra read her most recent journal entry. She studied first the clock on the wall then squinted to try and read the diplomas hanging discreetly to the right of Myra's credenza. Having no luck with that, she attempted to distract herself from watching Myra's facial reactions by studying the texture and pattern of the ornate Persian rug under their feet. Her eyes traced the intricate zigzag of lines from one edge of the rug to the opposite while Myra read:

August 28, 2008

At the meeting tonight, Myra had us make a sculpture of ourselves at the age we were when abuse occurred. She said they would tell us about our shame and reveal our longings. She also says shame is the package that longings and the fear of abandonment come wrapped in. I felt like Myra was talking directly to me when she talked about "buy this house, get this degree...." I know I can be intense (was I always?), but are there necessarily fears and longings lurking behind my intensity? If so, what are their names?

On the way home, I talked to my Play-Doh alter-ego as if she were the possessor of all secrets, sordid and glorious. I told her I'm not aware of any genuine longing and, if that's so, how can I determine what I do with them? What I do know is that I'd like for my life to be a romantic comedy where I can wrap up every dilemma before I run out of popcorn and Coke. I don't like lack of resolution. I pride myself on getting results. And I don't like having so many contradictory emotions happening at the same time. How impolite they are! They don't take turns to talk, they just start yammering at once, and I wind up feeling like a weary parent with a passel of bratty children who bully each other around, demanding attention. Willful creatures, these emotions.

I also told Play-Doh Polly that I like that Myra believes we are all born beautiful. What a pity some of us learn to equate seductiveness with beauty, like Celeste. Or sabotage their beauty, like Andrea and Olivia. Do they know—or care—that underneath the brazenness or oversized t-shirts or stoic sneers lies real beauty?

In discussing all this with Polly, I got a very strong image—a monster face, a bed, a scream. I was afraid to "look" further while I was driving. So now I'm sitting here waiting for Cliff to come home, while this arts and crafts project stares at me with vacuous eyes, sucking its—her—thumb. What do you need to tell me, First Person Past Perfect?

"So, Rebekah," Myra said, handing her the cloth-bound journal, "what did your little dough girl teach you?"

"After I wrote this, I closed my eyes and thought about the image I'd had in the car. When it shot across my mind again, at first I wanted to get up and wash dishes or something, anything to divert my attention. But I kept my eyes closed and waited. It was like an old timey movie, silent, sort of jerky and out of focus. I saw enough, though, to know that it was Casey's father and what he did must've been horrible. Scary. Wrong. I know you say truth is our friend and denial is our enemy, but I'd much rather continue to be the editor of the unhappy outtakes of my life and leave them on the cutting room floor. I don't like looking at them."

Myra smiled. "Wouldn't we all like to rewrite our history in our own way? But what would that accomplish? Now tell me about what you saw, how you felt, anything you heard or sensed...."

Rebekah recounted her discovery—of remembering the dread of staying with Casey the night Robert was born, of her fitful sleep, of being awakened by a scream. She alternately cried and ranted, pushing past the catch in her throat. When she had finished, she slumped back and exhaled deeply, temporarily emptying herself of the last urge to fight against what was stored somewhere behind the clutter of daily care on a back shelf in her memory closet.

Myra was quiet for a moment, then asked, "What does this suggest to you?"

"That it happened more than once," Rebekah said, her voice tinged with defeat, "or else I wouldn't have been so upset about spending the night. And that there must have been something really wrong with me to go back there after the first incident. That I must have asked for it or wanted it in some warped way." Her voice cracked, "And that I've lost some part of who I'm supposed to be in the process. I want her back."

Myra chose her words carefully, used her expressive hands to illustrate. "The last thing you said and the first thing you said are biographical bookends." She held up both hands, palms parallel and apart. "What you said in between is fiction." She swished her right hand back and forth. "Let me ask you, what could be wrong with what a young girl would want from an adult male? It isn't sex. If you wanted anything at all from him, what could it have been?"

Rebekah thought. "I guess I wanted him to treat me the way my own father treated me, like a princess. Like a precious little girl who was smart and delightful. Isn't that the way all daddies should behave toward their daughters?"

"Exactly. The fact that he took advantage of you and your trust of him in no way means that there was something wrong with you or warped about your desires. Do you understand the subtle mind game going on here?"

"I guess I don't. I do not understand why I returned to that house after what he did the first time, whatever it was."

"It's not because you were stupid or bad. You were a little girl. And," Myra emphasized, "apparently you were half asleep. When you really think about it, Rebekah, what a terrible dilemma that was for a small child—to be with her best friend also meant not knowing what to expect from her father. Even adults can't handle that kind of uncertainty. How could one expect a child to? Unfortunately, your perspective on that today doesn't erase how you felt then."

Myra paused to allow Rebekah's mind and emotions to catch up with what she had said. "In order to protect yourself from further shame, you have, since that time, focused on some imaginary inadequacy in yourself that 'caused'," Myra made finger quotation marks, "the abuse in the first place. It's much easier to try to fix ourselves or order the world around us than to try to understand a person or a situation that we have no categories for. Trying to fix things gives us the illusion of control, and who doesn't like to feel in control? Do you see that, Rebekah?" Myra's eyes implored Rebekah to understand.

Hesitantly, Rebekah shrugged, a wrinkle of confusion remaining where her eyebrows met for consultation. "Sort of."

"What do we need to clarify? Where are you still confused?"

Rebekah tried not to sound defensive, but failed. "How do you think I've tried to fix myself? I've always tried to do my best."

"You may not have necessarily tried to fix yourself. You might have tried to order your world in such a way that you don't ever feel like things are out of your realm of control. Perhaps you tried being the nicest or the smartest or the most successful, whether that was in athletics, business, academics, or whatever. The goal is the same," Myra leaned forward and spoke in a low, hushed tone, "and that is to trust no one else for the outcome of our lives and to concentrate on achieving rather than working through our grief."

She leaned back in her chair and templed her fingers. "It's also a very handy device for keeping people at arm's length. It allows us to permit people into our lives only when it's convenient for us. This way, no one ever has to know about the perceived glitch in our makeup. Very clever, really, don't you think?"

Rebekah sighed, closed her eyes and gazed down a corridor of time, a sorrowful smile playing at the edges of her mouth. She knew Myra had pegged her. *She must have her spies out working overtime.* Rather than feeling cornered, Rebekah felt relieved of a duty that had taken on its own life, gradually moving her out of its way. *She knows me. Who I am and who I was.*

"What are you thinking right now? How are you feeling?"

"I'm remembering when I was a little girl.... When did I lose my sparkle?...." Rebekah's voice was wistful. "I mean," a fresh tear slipped down her cheek, "it's exhausting, really, to try to make everything turn out nice and even. It doesn't leave much room for spontaneity—unless," she smiled wryly, "you consider the sudden decision to run out and rent a DVD and maybe even splurge on an ice cream cone spontaneity."

She shook her head, "God, what a shitty way to live. I didn't always have to have everything so safe and so defined." Rebekah stopped, looking intently into Myra's eyes. "Can you help me? Can you help me learn how to live without having to calculate everything first?"

Myra smiled, returning Rebekah's gaze with warmth. "I'll let you in on a little secret, Rebekah. You are well on your way. We're all refugees from our own war-torn countries, from a holocaust against the soul. We all spend the rest of our lives learning to take back what was ours while letting go of the schemes we adopt to keep our lives on an even keel but that rob us of the real essence of living."

"You said 'we.' What are you telling me?"

"Just exactly what you think I'm telling you, my dear."

After her appointment, Rebekah rolled down the windows in her car and drove around, letting the wind and warm Jacksonville air toss her red curls and blow kisses on her cheeks. Exhilaration wooed her, beckoning her to recall carefree days of hopscotch and reading primers, of such weighty concerns as choosing between Cocoa Krispies or Lucky Charms for breakfast. She drove to Wolfson Park and strolled around, trying to become better acquainted with the fresh sense of wonder that had slipped its hand into hers—a wonder that felt new but she knew was an ancient treasure. Hearing laughter, she stopped to watch two children, a brother and sister, twin replicas of their smiling mother, swinging. Their rapture at being airborne but anchored stirred a delighted restlessness in her. She sat on a bench nearby and let her heart soar with every pump of their energetic legs, then pulled her journal out of her purse and turned to a clean page.

Tuesday, September 2, 2008

Just finished a session with Myra. Something wondrous has shaken itself loose in me. Can't describe it adequately, but I feel like a bird in a cage and the cage door has been opened. I'm not free yet, but freed. Both exciting and scary. Some of the pressure I have placed on myself to be perfect has been relieved. I can see now the rapids of rage that provide the current for perfectionism. Myra said I've been trying to fix myself and my world ever since whatever happened with Casey's dad.

At first, I didn't see what she meant, but I kept seeing myself as a young girl, secure and carefree. I want to embrace life like that again. I want to be radiant in my actions. Not necessarily precise, but radiant. I have spent too many years looking for the definitives in life—THE right college, THE sorority, THE career, THE house. Every decision I've made has been considered as if Atlas himself was looking to me to take a load off his shoulders. And all under the guise of being this really nice person who is savvy and pleasant and inerrant.

There really are so few definitives in the world, and it certainly isn't up to me to determine what those few are. I need to learn to just be who I started out to be and stop worrying so much about how it's all supposed to look when it's over. I've missed out on so much by focusing on the ends without enjoying the means. I have a lot of learning—and unlearning— to do, but for the first time in a very long while, I WANT this.

The journey begins today—without a compass and a map, but in the company of several women who are also arriving at the same conclusions, I think. And with a husband who has always believed in me. I supposed it's a good thing Cliff isn't here right now because if he was, I'd rip all his clothes off and give this park a fireworks display more memorable than any Fourth of July.

Twenty

CASEY PLACED BOTH ELBOWS ON her knees, propping her chin in her hands. "Sometimes, I just cannot figure out what makes my mother tick."

Lorelei's eyebrows arched and she nodded *go on.*

"I showed her the letter I got from Rebekah and told her I was planning to write back and she came very close to shutting down. I thought she'd be glad that I might have the opportunity to rekindle my friendship with Rebekah and, if not that, at least she'd understand why I want to communicate with her. Instead, she seems threatened by it. I know she is haunted by the sense that she let her love for her husband cloud her judgment and also that, because she did love him, she should have known what was happening to him. By him. She believed in everything he said he was, staked her life and her identity on being a part of that. Do you suppose it's just too painful for her to have to think through all of that again?"

Lorelei replied, "Perhaps she is less threatened by your communication with Rebekah than she is disturbed—for herself and for her daughter—about reliving it?"

"Hmmm. Maybe. I hate to say this, but I think what she really wants is absolution. She doesn't think that's possible, but so long as she doesn't have to relive every day of the past, she can at least find some peace, acceptance, or whatever. But now that the past has come back to occupy a part of my life, she's actively looking for absolution again, and I cannot give it to her. My father gave his vigor over to an unseen, unknown sinister force, and she has given hers over to continual penance and self-flagellation. What can I do?"

"Actually, I have something for you and your mother to consider. I was going to mention it today, as a matter of fact. This might not answer your mother's quest for, as you say, absolution, but it may provide her a venue for making something good come from something so awful. You interested?" Lorelei asked.

"Very."

"I serve on a professional board that has been created by a sub-committee of the state legislature to help them craft new laws governing sentencing guidelines for sexual predators. They have another group working on similar recommendations for sex offenders but, as you know, predators can never outlive the designation. I am tasked with gathering testimonials from survivors and their families. This sub-committee wants to push for much stricter sentences—I'm talking about a life sentence. Would you be willing to share your story? And do you think your mom would?"

"I cannot speak for Mama, but you can count me in. And if Rebekah and I continue to correspond, maybe she'd be willing to contribute. When do you need a firm commitment?"

"If all goes according to our timetable, the board members will wrap up their homework by late February and present to the sub-committee in early spring of next year. You sure you want to do this?"

"Positive. And this will give me some time to maybe convince Mama to paint the silver lining around the clouds herself instead of waiting for the Great Paintbrush in the Sky to do it for her." Casey's smile was lopsided.

Lorelei smiled in understanding. "Meanwhile, as to what you can do now… You seem to have a good grasp of reality, on making the best life possible for yourself. That's something you can offer not only to your mom, but to the rest of the world. Just be real. Be you. Really, that's enough. What others choose to do is up to them. But I think you knew that already."

* * *

As soon as Myra sat down to complete the circle, Libby raised her hand like an eager school girl at show-and-tell time. "I just have something I want to say to the CLAMOR Girls."

Myra swept her upturned palm across her body, signaling permission.

"Last week when I left here, I was real mad and real hurt. I thought y'all were picking on me. I didn't intend to even come back tonight. But one of the things my mama taught me was to examine criticism for any germ of truth. So, every time someone from church called me to do something this past week, before I said yes or no, I stopped to ask myself why I was considering it, and whether or not I was using that as an opportunity to dodge something about myself.

"Truth is," Libby smiled generously, "y'all were right. A lot of the nice things I do for other people is so I'll feel better about myself. Not only that, I stay busy helping people so I don't have to slow down and get to know them and let them really get to know me. I know this sounds arrogant, and I don't mean it to, but I've been living on a pedestal so long, I don't know how to climb down and... I don't know how to put it...."

"Live like a mere mortal?" Celeste suggested.

"Yes," Libby agreed, smiling at Celeste, "that's it. I like to be needed and I like being looked up to, for people to think I have my act together. Isn't that sick?"

Myra responded, "I don't know that it's sick. This way of relating to others has worked for you in the past and maybe it's not working so well for you now because you're, in a sense, waking up. You're changing, growing."

"Well, anyway, I just wanted to share that with everyone, to let y'all know I'm not mad at you anymore." She smiled again, traces of sadness bordering the laugh lines already engraved around her eyes.

Myra spoke again. "Libby, it sounds as if you've already started your descent from your pedestal. I'm glad for you. It's been sort of lonely up there, hasn't it?" Libby nodded and Myra continued. "I want to remind you all that when the winds of change are blowing in your life, sometimes debris gets scattered into the lives of others— family, friends, co-workers. A good disruption in your life might be an unwelcome disruption in theirs. The best analogy I've heard describes it like this: Imagine yourself in a room full of people who are dancing, alone and in pairs."

Myra paused to allow the women to fix the scene in their minds. "You become aware that the music is no longer playing, and hasn't, in fact, been playing for some time, and yet everyone continues to dance. You stop, causing those around you to either acknowledge that the music has ended or to dance even more vigorously to 'prove' that the music still exists." She paused again. "Prepare to be misunderstood. And," she held up her instructor's finger, "be prepared to flounder occasionally as you attempt to live without the old music. Old dynamics sometimes die a painfully slow death, but we will be here for each other as you explore living with new realities."

Rebekah's eyebrows scrunched together, pondering what this might look like. Olivia interrupted her thoughts by clearing her throat, then announcing, "I left Clay this week. I guess that counts as a pretty big disruption, doesn't it?" Her smile was sad. "Actually, I asked him to leave. I'm pretty sure it's over."

All were quiet, waiting for Olivia to continue, knowing the greatest gift they could offer right then was their supporting silence. Olivia closed her eyes momentarily, searching for words, then continued in her plaintive Callahan patois, "I had already been doing a lot of thinking this past week. I realized I've been lonely my whole life. I didn't truly know that until I started coming to these meetings. This is the first place where I've known what real friendship is like. I've been practically starved for friendship, for people who really care about me. Anyway, Clay and I were arguing again. He was telling me everything that was wrong with me—again. I've heard it all before and I suggested counseling, like I always do, and he refused. He just kept telling me how fat I was and how the house is never clean. How he's tired of me bugging him about spending so much time with his buddies after work. He says that's my fault, too.

"So I asked him what he wanted, and he said he didn't know, but it wasn't this." She stopped for a moment, collecting her thoughts, then continued, "You know, I've always been the one to change my life around to adjust to him and yet, somehow, what I need and what I want always comes last with him."

Her voice cracked. "I work just as hard at my job as he does, but he thinks when he walks through the door, his work day is over. Like just because he cuts the grass and takes out the garbage, I should do the rest. I'll admit the house isn't as neat as it could be, but we have a little boy, for crying out loud." The pitch of her voice rose. "And honestly, there are days when it's all I can do to make myself get out of bed and go to work in the first place. Dealing with what my daddy did and my sister's death is like a full-time job sometimes. Clay doesn't seem to realize how that can make me feel different from everybody else, like I have emotional rabies. Anyhow, I realized how important it is for me to be around people who understand me, what I'm going through, and Clay has done so little to try to help me, to be supportive. He doesn't even *try* to understand me. All he seems to do is criticize me. I know I've put on weight. Lord, he doesn't have to keep pointing that out."

She pulled at her t-shirt so it wouldn't cling to her middle. "I think sometimes I've been trying to create a body big enough to carry around all this hurt. And when he's not criticizing me, he's telling me to get over it. Well, nobody wants that more than I do, but I either need his help or I need him to stop saying things that hurt me. So I asked him to leave. I want my son to have parents who really love each other, who listen to each other, who enjoy each other and look after each other. That should be the glue that holds us together.

"I don't want Tyler to become the kind of man who doesn't respect women, and I definitely don't want Tyler to be the kind of man who only thinks about himself all the time." Andrea, who had been jiggling her foot, nodded emphatically.

"So I told Clay that I either want my son to see his mama and daddy glad they married each other or I want him to see that sometimes it's okay to be alone. And do you know what?" Olivia cocked her head, "He didn't hardly put up a fuss. He threw some stuff in a pillow case, got in his truck, and left. I think he's been waiting for me to make the first move so I could be, excuse the pun," she smiled, "the heavy. He's been telling his buddies I kicked him out."

As if purged, Olivia stopped and hesitantly looked around the room, her eyes darting from one face to another. "Wow, that felt sorta good. Scary, but good."

Celeste's eyes danced wildly. "That was like something on the Discovery Channel, like watching a butterfly come out of the cocoon! Way to go, girl." She reached across the coffee table to give Olivia a high five.

Olivia smiled self-consciously, then her face fell. "I don't feel like I should be congratulated; I feel like a failure. But I knew I had to do something or I would lose the last shred of myself and then Tyler wouldn't have a mama at all. I know what it's like not to have a mama." Her voice trailed off.

Margot said, "I don't think you're a failure at all. I think you're very courageous. I didn't have the sense to do that when I should have..."

Myra interrupted, "Before you're too hard on yourself, Margot, try to keep in mind that there are degrees of courage in a relationship and degrees of failure." She looked around the room, unapologetically seizing upon a teachable moment. "In that none of us is 100% reliable, we will fail others. Recognizing that and what we do about it contributes to the measure of our courage. One person might be a coward for leaving, another for staying. For some, leaving is an act of mercy. Please try not to compare yourself and your situation to anyone else's. Never upbraid yourself for being optimistic; and never be afraid to be realistic, either."

Rebekah asked, "How can you know when to go and when to stay, then? I'm thinking more in terms of a job, but in any relationship?" *Did I just say that? Did I just think that? Do I really mean it?*

Myra responded, "How did you know to leave the counsel of your previous therapist?"

A look of recognition passed over Rebekah's face. "I knew we had reached a plateau and we would never be able to get beyond it."

Olivia offered, "One of the things that helped me decide about Clay is when he told me recently that he felt like he was married to his sister. That hurt." She shook her head. "I mean, it's probably true, but I don't think this is all my fault. I'm sorry I'm not exciting to him right now. I know I'm not the smartest person, but I do know that even when marriage isn't always fun and romance, it's still supposed to be—alive." Searching for an illustration, she pointed to the cover of a back issue of *Southern Living* on the coffee table, "Like the seasons."

Andrea, who had been shifting in her chair, listening in quiet agitation, spoke as if about to burst, "What is it with men anyway? God, every single one of my co-workers seems to be having problems with that *species*." She hissed the word. "As far as I'm concerned, they only complicate things. I've never met an honest one. They're all incredibly selfish, like over-grown children."

"Oh, I don't know about that. Despite everything I've been through, I still like men," said Celeste.

"What, for dessert?" Andrea shot back.

Celeste was somewhat taken aback, but amused. "I still think there's hope. In the meantime," she raised her index finger, "I enjoy the hunt." She arched her eyebrows.

"Are they really worth it? Aren't they all born brain-damaged?" Andrea responded. "If you ask me, most men ought to have their testicles ripped off and then be forced to eat them." Olivia shrunk back at Andrea's outburst. Margot looked as if she wished the sofa would consume her, help her disappear.

"I don't like where this is going at all," said Libby. *Thank you*, thought Rebekah. "I'm not a big fan of saying mean things about people, especially when they aren't here to defend themselves." Rebekah nodded. "Andrea, God created women *and* men and whatever you do to malign the other only serves to tear yourself down, too." Rebekah groaned. *Here it comes.*

"Oh, please, what is this? Touched by a Fucking Angel?" Andrea spit the words out between clenched jaws. Libby recoiled, looking to Myra imploringly. The other women, stunned at the sudden display of molten anger, looked quickly at each other, then down.

A painful silence ensued as Andrea, eyes hardened, glared at a fixed place just beyond her nose, her breathing hard. Myra smiled encouragingly at Libby, who said softly, "Andrea, why are you so angry with God?"

Andrea looked at Libby and asked, her voice dull, "What has God ever done for me? Where was he when I needed him, huh?"

"I don't know what to tell you, dear, except that you're alive, you're here. That's God."

"It's not enough," said Andrea. "It. Isn't. Enough."

Again, Libby looked at Myra with pleading eyes. "You're a minister. Help us out here."

Rebekah's head snapped up. "You're a minister?" The others watched Myra carefully, waiting for her response. Well that explains all those teachable moments—you can take the minister out of the pulpit....

Myra answered, looking at Rebekah, "I'm ordained, yes, but I don't have a congregation. Years ago I saw that there were so many hurting, lonely people sitting in the pews who needed more. They wanted to believe but they were afraid to. And they were afraid not to. I thought my gifts and my time could be better utilized working with individuals and small groups, helping people who wanted to be helped, who maybe found that faith as it had been presented to them wasn't answering their deepest needs."

"Why didn't you tell us?" asked Rebekah, her voice cracking. *I could just leave now. Cut my losses. Forget about this crap.* She listened to Myra while fingering the strap of her purse.

"I don't hide the fact. My ministerial credentials are hanging on the wall," she motioned with her head to the wall beside the credenza, "along with my diplomas. Nor do I promote myself as a pastoral counselor. Some people come to counseling only after searching for answers within a faith framework. They're disillusioned and I completely understand that. And some arrive at faith after working through some of their life struggles. I am here for anyone who wants to be well, regardless of where they are in their faith journey."

"I don't necessarily have a faith journey," said Andrea, tossing her head in Myra's direction. "No offense."

"I am not easily offended," Myra countered. "Perhaps I need to clarify what I mean by faith journey. I realize not every victim comes from a background of having been to church, but that doesn't mean at some point or another she hasn't asked the question: *Is there a God?* And if she believes that a higher power exists, the next logical question would be: *Where was that higher power when I was being abused?* For many people, that is a very pivotal question in sorting through the damage of their lives. A faith journey could lead one person toward embracing that higher power just as easily as it could lead another to conclude that God doesn't exist. Maybe a better term might be 'faith struggle.'"

"Kind of like Elie Wiesel . . .," Rebekah observed, relaxing her fingers from the purse strap.

"Precisely. The fundamental issue behind the question is who, ultimately, has power in this universe, and what kind of power is that? What did we do with our powerlessness then," she motioned back in time, "what did it teach us? What do we do with our sense of powerlessness now? And what good does it do now to sift through that wreckage?"

"Please, don't keep us in suspense," Celeste dead-panned. "Why *do* we want to do that?"

Myra offered that question to the group with a palms-up gesture. After a thoughtful pause, Margot suggested, "What if someone hit me with their pickup truck and broke my leg? I'd be pretty helpless to prevent that. But that doesn't mean it didn't happen. My leg is still broken and needs to be set—so it can heal."

"And you can bet I'll look both ways before crossing the street from now on," Rebekah added.

"Or," offered Olivia, "even if I looked and still got hit, I understand that the accident wasn't my fault."

"But not everyone who drives pickup trucks drive like a maniac or is determined to run me down," Libby suggested, glancing at Andrea.

"Good," Myra said. "So there are times when you had no real options—not about your family dynamics, the abuse itself, and not about the rip in your soul's fabric. You had no choices there," she continued, "but there's still damage. And what you cannot explain away can push you toward denial—recreating the world in your own way. Or toward numbness."

She leaned forward. "Just as your hurt and anger and longing testify to your being alive, the areas of deadness also reveal that you felt helpless. And that sets up this impossible situation of needing to be protected, isolated from danger," she wrapped her expressive hands around an invisible ball and moved it to the side, "but not left alone." She pulled the ball to herself. "So who do you trust? Who *can* you trust? How do you balance the need for protection with the need for relationship?" Her hands became the scales.

Then Myra faced Andrea and asked, "Is there something recently that triggered your attack tonight against men? Some situation where you felt helpless or unprotected?" Andrea thought for a moment, then answered reluctantly, "Yeah, there was. There's this pervert our department has been investigating for some time—we knew he's been stalking young girls, but we couldn't prove it. This past weekend, he raped an eight-year-old girl...." Her voice betrayed weariness behind the hardness. "My thing is, the chief of the department should've found some way to haul him in. He should've picked him up for jaywalking, for Christ's sake. Then that little girl wouldn't have gotten hurt. Men are either dangerous or incompetent."

"Like your brother or your father?" asked Margot.

"Yeah. Too powerful or completely ineffectual."

"And where does that leave women and girls?" asked Myra.

"At their mercy or having to do all the work."

"How might this affect someone's beliefs and feelings?" Myra probed further.

"Well, you know me. I don't trust anyone, and I get angry."

"What about the rest of you? How do you think those instances when you felt powerless affected you?"

Rebekah noticed a rage taking shape within her that hadn't been there before, at least not as the solidified mass that it now was in her gut. This wasn't mere impatience directed toward all the petty irritations that accumulate over time. And she was glad she had her father and her husband as evidence that all men weren't bad or selfish. She wasn't sure whether there was a God and if there was, how he fit into the puzzle of the universe. She was becoming convinced, however, that evil seized its power in the brew of indifference and ignorance and inaction. Having never been terribly inclined toward activism, she wondered how she might move the steel from her clenched jaw to her spine. She wondered if there was some way she could incorporate her rage into the neatly constructed world she had attempted to fashion for herself. She wondered if she really wanted that neatly constructed world after all.

The next day at work, Rebekah sat outside in a cubicle of shade provided by a fledgling oak tree. The air was tinged with the promise of fall, and leaves were just beginning to turn auburn, gold, and amber. She inhaled the smells of change as her eyes traveled from one table of corporate lunchtime escapees to another, imagining from their expressions and gestures what their conversations might be about.

She could hear the two men at the table closest to hers engaged in an animated discussion about market share losses and the need to contain those losses and reverse the trend. Smiling to herself, she momentarily fantasized interrupting their self-important talk with a little trivia of her own: *Excuse me, sirs, do you have daughters? Did you gentlemen know that by the time she is 16 years old, one out of four females will have been sexually abused, and usually by someone she knows? I know. I looked that little factoid up on the Internet. Tell me, how do you think we can contain those losses, reverse that trend?*

She abandoned the game of pretend and focused on the stationery sandwiched between her yogurt and apple. Taking a bit of apple, she wrote:

Friday, September 5, 2008

Dear Casey...

Twenty-one

MARGOT AND REBEKAH WERE THE first to arrive at Bennigan's. Myra had informed the CLAMOR Girls at the end of their last session that the following week she would be attending a week-long conference. At Celeste's suggestion, they decided to meet on Thursday night anyway. Rebekah gave the hostess her name and sat on the bench with Margot while they waited for their table for six to be set up.

Margot had traded her scrubs for a pair of jeans and an attractive sleeveless blouse, revealing arms that were well-acquainted with a free weight regimen. Rebekah remarked, "Wow, Margot, I've never seen you in civvies before; you look great. Do you work out?"

In her typical self-effacing manner, she answered, "I try to exercise almost every day. It helps keep me sane."

"Well it isn't hurting your appearance, either."

"Thanks. So, how was your day?"

"About like all the rest. The only exercise I seem to get these days is lifting the phone off the receiver. I've been thinking about walking during my lunch break, but I don't enjoy walking alone."

Margot asked, "Where do you go for lunch? Maybe I could meet you on my day off some time."

"I'd like that. Let's see, sometimes I bring my lunch to work and eat it while I work at my desk or, if the weather is nice, I'll eat outside. If I'm going to be away from the office, though, I usually try to finish up any local business I have with Regency Square Mall clients so I can take advantage of the food court."

"I'm off every other Tuesday. Why don't you call me the next time you'll be out for lunch?"

"Thank you. I will." Just as their conversation was lagging for want of more superficial topics, Andrea arrived, her usual mixture of bluster and dishevelment. Margot slid over to make more room on the bench.

"I'm beat," Andrea said, plopping down on the bench. *Well that wasn't very lady-like* Rebekah observed.

"Rough day?" asked Margot.

"No more than usual." Andrea slouched down even further on the bench, crossing her arms over her waist and extending her short, muscular legs out into the foyer. "Just the standard assault and abuse cases."

"There isn't anything standard about that—I hope," Rebekah commented, thinking *How does she do that with a skirt on?*

"No, you're right. Every case is different, but when you've been doing this as long as I have, nothing surprises you anymore. Except for the sheer volume of our caseload." She shook her head. "Jeez, you start to wonder if every family is fu…" she caught herself, "messed up."

Nice save. Too bad Libby's not here to appreciate it, Rebekah mused, then asked, "How long have you been doing this?"

Andrea looked up to the ceiling while she calculated. "Thirteen years this fall."

"Always in Jacksonville?" Margot asked.

"Yeah. The whole time in Jax. I haven't even been back to Boston since I left."

"How did you end up here?" Margot wondered. "It's a long way from Massachusetts."

"Yeah, I know. When I graduated from the academy, Duval County had a job opening in the department I wanted to work in. So I moved here and never left. Never looked back." Then, "How about you? How did you end up in Jax?" she asked Margot.

"I came here to thaw out," she smiled. "I got tired of the cold winters in Chicago. Plus, after my divorce, I needed to get away for a while. I have a cousin who invited me here to visit, and four months later I moved down here permanently."

"Don't you miss your mom?" Rebekah asked.

"I do, but she's remarried now and enjoying the Winnebago lifestyle. She and my stepfather get down here about twice a year. How about you? You're a Florida girl, aren't you?" Rebekah nodded. "Always Jacksonville?"

"Oh, no. I moved here after I graduated from college. I grew up in the Panhandle, in a little town called Founder's Creek."

"You don't talk like you're a Cracker," observed Andrea.

"Well, I lived in New York for a bit. I did an internship up there. Most of my clients are from up north, too, so between talking with them and going to college with sorority sisters from New England, I lost most of my accent." Rebekah smiled and her eyes twinkled, "But y'all should hear me when I've been home for a few days," she said, drawing out her words, exaggerating every syllable.

Andrea and Margot grinned at her self-parody. Just then, the hostess returned and indicated she was ready to show them to their table. "Oh, good," Rebekah said, "I'm starved." Like obedient ducklings behind their mother, they followed the hostess to their table. Before they had a chance to sit down, Libby and Celeste walked in together, their eyes sparkling and moist from laughing.

Celeste said, "You will never guess what Libby just told me in the parking lot. A Viagra joke!"

"I did not," Libby protested. "It's an attorney joke," she said, laughing again.

"Are you going to let us in on it?" asked Margot.

"Okay," said Libby. "Did y'all know that when a lawyer takes Viagra he gets taller?"

They laughed as they pulled their chairs out to sit. Celeste said, "I think I used to date the lawyer who was the inspiration for that joke."

The hostess suppressed a smile and said, "Your waiter, Brad, will be right with you." After they were seated, she handed out the menus and then left.

Libby said, "You know, what's really funny is my son-in-law is an attorney and he's the one who told that joke to me." As she studied her menu, Rebekah wondered what her father would have thought of the joke.

There was silence as they perused their choices. Their handsome young waiter came to take their orders. Libby looked at her watch and asked, "Has anyone heard from Olivia? Should we wait until she gets here to order?"

Brad offered to bring their drinks and come back later for their dinner orders. Rebekah looked at Celeste and asked, "Do you want us to not order anything alcoholic?"

"No, no. That's alright. I'm okay tonight. But thanks for asking." Then to Brad, "I'll have a glass of tea, unsweet," and she winked at the young man.

"Me, too," said Libby, "but make mine sweet."

"I'd like a glass of Chablis and a glass of water, please," said Margot.

"I'd like the same," Rebekah said.

"I'll take a beer, whatever's on tap," Andrea said, and then Brad left to fill their orders. They continued to study their menus intently. Without Myra's coffee table and her guidance as their buffer, they were suddenly ill at ease. As Brad was bringing his drink-laden tray to their table, Olivia arrived, looking flustered and slightly out of place. She sat down as Brad delivered the beverages.

"What can I get for you, ma'am?" he asked Olivia.

"Oh, uh, sweet tea, please," she answered, distracted.

"Everything okay?" Rebekah asked.

"Yeah," Olivia answered. "Sorry I'm late."

"Oh you're not late, Sugar," Libby replied. "We haven't been here long. As a matter of fact, Celeste and I just got here."

"Yeah," Rebekah said. "And before Celeste and Libby got here, Margot and Andrea and I were telling how we ended up in Jacksonville." She recapped their stories for the others.

Libby shared, "Well I'm a Jacksonville girl, born and bred."

"Me, too," said Olivia. "Actually, Callahan."

Rebekah turned to Celeste and asked, "So? How did you end up here?"

"Well," said Celeste, with a twinkle in her eye, "you take a sperm," she made a circle with her thumb and forefinger, "and you take an egg," she made a circle with the other thumb and forefinger and brought them together, "and voila! There's me."

After they finished laughing, Libby asked, "No, really, how did you end up in Jacksonville?"

Trying to sound nonchalant, but obviously pained by the memory, she answered, "I'm originally from California. Anaheim. After I got pregnant with Justin, I wanted to try to start over. My mom wasn't into the grandma thing and I needed a change, so I packed my car with everything I owned and got on I-10 and drove until it ended." Her smile still betrayed her hurt.

Brad arrived with Olivia's iced tea and took their dinner orders. There was a brief lull after he left. Then, changing the tone of her voice, Celeste sat up taller and cleared her throat. She assumed the role of facilitator, matching Myra's inflection and demeanor of regal serenity and wisdom. "Tonight, what I want us to think about," she said, leaning forward, placing her fingers together at their tips, "is what the best invention of all time is. We'll start with you, Rebekah."

In mock seriousness, Rebekah pondered for a moment, then answered, "Contact lenses. Definitely. The disposable kind."

"And why is that?"

"I could lie to you and tell you it's because I have better peripheral vision with them or because I can wear them to bed and actually see my way to the bathroom in the middle of the night, but in all honesty, I'd have to say it's because when I wear glasses, I look like Marian the Librarian. Besides, I've never seen really cool-looking prescription sunglasses, have you?"

"Thank you for your honesty. I can see you have been practicing our mantra that honesty is our friend..."

Rebekah interrupted, "You have to tell us what you think is the greatest invention, Oh Great and Wise One." The others agreed.

Celeste resumed her life-of-the-party identity, saying, "Let's see. It's a toss-up between Ziploc bags, Velcro, and Splenda. If I have to choose one, I'd have to say Splenda. Think of the millions of calories that have been avoided."

"Like you really need to be concerned about calories," Olivia said, tugging at her oversized shirt. "I say the best invention is air conditioning."

Celeste lifted her glass of tea and said, "Hear, hear. A toast to air conditioning," and they clinked their assorted beverage glasses in a salute to surviving brutal Southern summers.

"I think blue jeans are the best invention of all time," offered Andrea. "They're comfortable and they break down class distinctions. Everybody can wear them," she continued, awkwardly rearranging her skirt, "and it doesn't matter how you cross your legs in them. In the world of attire," she said, with mock seriousness, "they are the great equalizer."

"Well, if we're going to talk about attire, then the absolute best invention would have to be underwire," said Margot, using her hands to demonstrate its uplifting properties. "Gravity is definitely a force to be reckoned with."

"Some of us will never know," deadpanned Rebekah. She pulled her blouse out at the neckline and stared down into its roominess, then looked up, shrugging her shoulders.

"Well, I think the best invention of all time is lip spackle," Libby offered in her genteel Southern accent. Seeing the quizzical looks on her dinner mates' faces, she explained. "That's the stuff that evens out the wrinkles and creases at the lip line. Y'all are too young to appreciate it now, but just you wait and see. You won't be able to wear lipstick without it, and a girl has to have her lipstick, now doesn't she?"

"Libby, you are too much," Celeste said. "You continue to surprise me."

"And speaking of surprises," Margot said, tilting her head in Andrea's direction, "girlfriend here is wearing a touch of makeup tonight. Aren't you?"

Andrea slightly reddened and answered, "Yeah, a little. I had a court appearance today."

"Well it looks real nice, Honey," said Libby.

Soon Brad arrived with their dinners. Sensing the festive mood at the table, he served ample portions of charm along with their meals, flirting with Libby, and winking at Olivia and Rebekah. After he left, Celeste asked, looking at Libby, Olivia, and Rebekah, "Okay ladies, what's your secret? He was nice to all of us, but he was extra nice to you. What do you have that the rest of us don't?"

"Wedding rings!" Rebekah replied. "We're safe."

Olivia looked at Celeste apologetically, "I can't get mine off my finger until I lose some weight. When I do, you're welcome to it."

"Well he is absolutely jumpable, and I'm jealous," she replied.

There was an interlude of silence while they appraised the food on their plates. Then Margot raised her wine glass and proposed another toast. "To the CLAMOR Girls, and to our fearless leader, Myra." The others joined in. Then, "Andrea, can you tell us anything about the hearing today? Was it concerning an adult or a child?"

"A woman. The father of her three children beat her up in front of them. I'm pretty sure he'll be convicted, and when he gets to prison, he won't be such a tough guy. He'd better be on the constant look-out for someone lathering up a bar of Ivory."

The others flinched at Andrea's allusion. Then Margot asked, "What will happen to those children? Is someone there to help them and their mother? Does the state provide therapy for the family?"

"Depends. And sometimes, even when help is made available, some women don't take advantage of it for their children. They think if they don't have to talk about it, the children will get on with their lives quicker."

"I'm often tempted to whisper to children as I take their vitals, 'Is everything okay? *Everything?*'" she enunciated each syllable.

Rebekah looked at Olivia. "Would you have told if someone, say your favorite teacher, had asked?"

"Probably not."

"The kids I deal with usually only tell when it's their last option," Andrea said. "They want someone to know, to notice, but they don't want to have to *tell* someone. It's a pretty shitty corner to be backed into."

In silence, they munched on their dinners. *Someone please change the subject,* Rebekah thought.

After more silence and disinterested eating, Rebekah asked, "So, Olivia, how is it going without Clay?"

"Different. Tyler is handling it better than I thought he would."

"Is he with his daddy tonight?" asked Libby.

"Actually, he's with Clay's mom."

"Is that weird for you?" asked Rebekah.

"No, she admits her son can be a jerk," she smiled. "She and I were talking when I dropped him off—that's why I was late. She told me she can't believe I stayed with him this long. To tell you the truth, neither can I. I guess I was waiting for the White Picket Fence Fairy to show up and turn us into an all-American family." The others smiled, picturing which Hollywood star should play the starring role of fairy.

"And 40 years from now, you'd still be waiting," offered Andrea.

"Well, I'm glad you're still able to be close to his mother—for Tyler's sake," said Celeste, momentarily serious. "I wish Justin had grandparents."

Olivia asked, "When do you think you'll get to bring him home for good?"

Her voice was a mix of defiance and sorrow. "My caseworker, Trackman the Tyrant, is not saying for sure. He keeps saying we'll both know when I'm ready and until then, he doesn't want to ask the court's permission. I think I'm ready now, and Myra says she thinks I am, too. I don't know what Trackman is looking for. Myra says maybe he won't outline the specifics for me because he thinks then I'll, I don't know, put on a one-woman b.s. act just to get my son back. I wonder sometimes if case workers take Evasion Tactics 101 before they get their credentials." Celeste forced herself to smile, but her eyes betrayed her.

"I'm so sorry, Sugar," Libby said. "I can tell you love your little boy a lot. How does he seem when you get to have your supervised visits?"

Celeste sat up a little taller and spoke with genuine affection. "He's so good," she crooned. "He talks like he's enjoying school and making friends; and his foster parents tell me he's very cooperative. I like to think I might've done something right during that time I was using."

"I'll bet you did a lot of things right," Rebekah encouraged.

"Well, I hope so. I really do love him and I want more than anything to have him back with me. Patience has never been my strong suit."

The others regarded her statement, along with the dabs of food on their plates, which they absentmindedly pushed around with fingers and forks. Olivia looked up from her place and asked, "Can I ask y'all a question?"

"Sure," said Rebekah, looking around the table.

"Are any of y'all on drugs—for depression, I mean," she looked apologetically toward Celeste.

"Yep. Prozac. Couldn't get out of bed without it," said Celeste.

While the CLAMOR Girls discussed the merits and pitfalls of their favorite pharmaceuticals, Brad-the-waiter returned to check on his table. "My ob-gyn even says it's okay if I get pregnant while I'm on Zoloft," Rebekah said. Then, "What someone needs to do is invent the pill to make *everyone* live happily ever after. Then put it in the water supply."

"In order for that to happen," Andrea replied, "all the little pill would have to do is keep a man's brain in his northern head, keep it from migrating to his southern head." Brad smiled slightly while collecting their dinner dishes. While there, he asked them if they would be having dessert. Andrea looked at Celeste out of the corner of her eye; Celeste did not miss her cue. Quickly slipping into her entertainer persona, she touched her finger to her lip and asked seductively, "What is the most delicious thing you have to offer for dessert, Brad?"

He responded, "That depends on what you like. What are you in the mood for?"

Her expression innocent, her voice laden with coyness, Celeste answered, "I won't know until I know what my options are."

"If you like chocolate, I can bring you Death by Chocolate. It's a frozen dessert made of rocky road ice cream on top of a Kit Kat crust all wrapped in a chocolate shell. It's served with hot fudge and it's one of our most popular desserts."

"Sounds too frigid for me. What if I'm in the mood for something warm and creamy?"

Recognizing the game, he replied, enunciating the names of desserts as if from a Frederick's of Hollywood catalog, "Well, then, you might like Abbey's Apple Sizzle or Mary McClary's Very Berry Pie."

"Sizzle, huh?" Celeste traced an imaginary line down her neck and appeared to think about her choices. Then, "Why don't they call it Brad's Berry Pie?"

"Because they wouldn't be able to keep up with the demand."

"Ooooooh. So what do you suggest if someone wants something hot and wet?"

Brad arched one eyebrow and he appeared to be pensive. "Then I'd have to recommend one of our coffees like Irish Coffee or Keoki Coffee."

"Interesting concept, mixing alcohol and caffeine. Do have anything *harder* than that? You know, something *stiffer*?"

Margot leaned over and stage-whispered into Celeste's ear, "Down girl."

Fluttering her eyelashes, Celeste sighed and said, "I guess I'll pass on dessert tonight. But thank you anyway, young Brad."

"No problem." He scanned the table and asked, "Any of you other ladies want dessert tonight?"

After they all politely demurred and Brad had left the table, Rebekah remarked, "Celeste, you are merciless." Libby nodded.

Grinning, Celeste said, "I know. I can't help it. I'm an incurable flirt."

Olivia said, "I couldn't tell if you were just playing or you were trying to get his phone number."

"Oh, I didn't mean anything by it. I was just having some harmless fun. If he had acted uncomfortable about it, I would've quit. Did you notice, though? He was enjoying it as much as I was."

Olivia asked earnestly, "But what if he had taken you seriously?"

Rebekah added, "I wouldn't be able to talk like that with anyone except Cliff."

Libby confessed, "I can't even talk that way with Bud."

"You might want to read up on Song of Solomon, then," Celeste replied.

Libby's eyebrows arched.

"What?" Celeste said in mock defensiveness. "I read."

"Personally, I think that witty repartee is part self-disclosure, part foreplay," said Margot. "I wouldn't go there unless I was prepared to *go* there, if you know what I mean."

"Oh, I had no intention of going anywhere with young Brad. But if he wants to call me in a few years, I'll answer the phone. I may act outrageous, but I don't have any desire to babysit anyone but my own son."

The rest of their evening progressed with light-hearted moments mixed with self-revelations. On her drive home, Rebekah reflected on the odd fusion of isolation and kinship that being molested had created in her life. *It's like I'm one of many at a Lone Ranger impersonator convention.*

Twenty-two

THE GIANT ARMS OF OLD majestic oak trees released their hold on once-green leaves, as the hot summer had, with reluctance, finally yielded its hostage grip on north Florida. Rebekah crunched through the leaves in her front yard on the way to her car. After putting her suitcase in the open trunk, she shut it and paused to inhale the brisk air with its sweet woodsy-decay musk and to appreciate the cloudless blue sky. She marveled at the thought that even a year ago, the gathering leaves would have induced a maniacal spell of raking. Today, she chose to enjoy the fragrances of choice and change.

Cliff appeared at the front door in the outfit he favored for hunkering down to watch college football—an old pair of sweatpants, once brilliant orange but now a harmless orange-tan color, with the UF Gator logo barely visible, and the UF t-shirt he had owned since his first week as a freshman 11 years ago. "You sure you don't want me to go with you?" he asked Rebekah.

"Yes, I'm sure. I'll be fine. Besides, what would Urban Meyer do without you calling the shots from your Lazy Boy?"

He grinned the boyish, dopey grin that never ceased to melt Rebekah's heart and weaken her knees. She wrapped her arms around her husband, her hands immediately drawn to the cleft in his back above his waist. Her fingers fit perfectly into the groove created by muscle and bone. She pulled him closer to her, promising with kiss and touch a homecoming celebration to rival any halftime show.

"Mmmmm," he mumbled. "Do you have to leave for your meeting now?"

"Yes. But I'll be back tomorrow night and you can draw backfield motion patterns anywhere you like on my body and I'll show you a few strategies of my own."

"Keep talking, Coach." Then, "Bec, you okay with meeting up with Casey?"

"Yeah, I'm okay. A little nervous, but so is she. I'll be fine." Rebekah ran her hands down Cliff's arms and held his hands in hers, pulling back to look into his face. "I think this is something I need to do—now, on my own. I'll call you when I get there."

Cliff gently pulled her back for one more kiss. "I love you. You know that."

"Yes, I do know. Believe me, I do. And I love you right back."

* * *

Rebekah parked her car at the Sheraton in south Gainesville. Her business meeting had been scheduled for 2 pm. After checking into her room, she called Cliff then went to the nearly-vacant hotel restaurant. She sat in a booth and ordered a sandwich, trying to ignore the butterflies flitting over each other in her stomach. She pulled her journal out of her briefcase and began to write.

Saturday, October 4, 2008

I'm in Gainesville for a meeting and since Casey lives so close by, we're going to meet for dinner. I'm nervous about it, but excited too. It's been 20 years. So far, she has been wonderful about answering my questions and being honest about herself. I guess one of my fears is that seeing her might send me spiraling down. God knows, I've been trying to climb out of depression's dark hole for almost a year, and I have no desire to start the climb again, now that I'm beginning to see light. I have so much more to ask her, like what the past 20 years has been like for her, but I'm not sure where to begin and how to ask. And, yes, part of me hopes that we rediscover our friendship. I'd like that, I think.

Margot and I are meeting regularly to walk. I enjoy our conversations. She is insightful and also careful about sharing her insights. She isn't one who believes that others are entitled to her opinion just because she has one. I appreciate that about her. I appreciate her warmth and humor, too. Considering all she's been through, I marvel at her stability and strength. And humanity. She's just as willing to admit her vulnerability as Andrea is afraid to find hers. I believe Margot and I are becoming true friends and I feel privileged to witness her gradually-increasing forays out of her shell. I only wish we'd met under different circumstances. This is an odd sorority we're members of.

Andrea seems to be experimenting with how far she can push Libby's maternal patience. One week, she'll come in wearing a hint of makeup and be pleasant and seem at ease in her quasi-feminine attire; the next week she'll look rumpled and behave brutishly, at odds with her very skin. Those are the weeks when she seems to focus her wrath on poor Libby. I wonder sometimes if Libby reminds her of her mother. Or her need for one. I don't know how Myra does it, but she manages to referee their interchanges, allowing Andrea to vent without beating up too badly on Libby. And Libby is learning to take it more in stride. I have to hand it to Libby - she could easily assume the role of martyr, but she doesn't. Although she unwittingly seems to provoke Andrea by insisting on calling her Sugar or Honey and by making nearly everything about God, I think her patience is as genuine as her faith is, even though they both must be taking a beating from Andrea.

Olivia is struggling to lose weight and shed herself of more emotional baggage than a deluxe set of Samsonite. Somehow, the two are related.... Considering her lack of formal education, she is one of the most astute and articulate members of our group. She is wise in her simplicity. I hope one day she can go to college and realize not only her personal potential, but also her capacity to touch other people's lives. She doesn't see it, but the rest of us do; she still perceives all the ways she's deficient. She's becoming the younger sister I never had and I'm enjoying watching her bud, however reluctant she is at times to give in to it.

Celeste both amazes and infuriates me. She can be so flippant about some things but then turn right around and be completely serious. I can't tell sometimes if she's running from something or toward it. I'm not surprised if her cavalier attitude is one thing that has delayed her being able to assume full custody of her son. Her smart mouth has probably caused as many problems as her addiction has. Yet, underneath that flirtatious, wise-cracking demeanor is a woman with a heart of gold, more talented and brilliant and capable than she realizes. It's too bad she can't use some of that cocky bravado to compensate for her uncertainties over her parenting ability. She probably needs to demonstrate to her case-worker that she can be fun-loving without seeming frivolous because I'm certain that when she absolutely has to, she is able to be responsible and sensible. And sensitive. Maybe Celeste is not worried so much about her capabilities as she is her consistency. And maybe she needs encouragement from me. I've seen her talent for design and have heard her dream out loud about owning her own boutique, but I have hesitated to offer my advice or to make contacts on her behalf because she doesn't act like she takes herself seriously. But maybe she would if I did. Must think this one through....

I am finding it more and more ironic that my career is based on fashion—the attempt to present ourselves as attractively as possible. Until I started meeting with Myra and the CLAMOR Girls, I hadn't thought about how the whole idea of attractiveness can be difficult for someone who has previously been noticed for the wrong reasons. How does one find the balance between looking her best and feeling safe doing it? What kind of world do we live in where it's potentially dangerous to be feminine— female, even?

A loud whoop of collegiate loyalty from the television-engrossed staff startled Rebekah. She looked at her watch and her barely-eaten sandwich and realized she had just enough time to pay her tab and walk to her meeting. For the time being, she placed her observations about her CLAMOR friends and her anxieties about seeing Casey aside and assumed her professional persona. After the meeting, she returned to her room. As she dropped her briefcase on the spare bed, Cliff sent her a text message: *Know ur getting ready to see Casey. Am with you, Babe. Call me when you get back. Love you.* After replying to his message, Rebekah sat on the edge of the bed and knit her fingers together over one knee, leaning back on the mattress. She closed her eyes and concentrated on her breathing, trying to settle her mind and her nerves.

* * *

The Sovereign Restaurant was comfortably crowded. The two old friends easily found each other in the foyer. After embracing, they both dabbed at their eyes, then laughed. Once seated at their table, they each made a pretense of studying the menu, hiding their awkwardness behind the protective listing of entrees. The friendly waitress came to take their orders and then left with the menus, essentially removing their security blanket. Simultaneously, Rebekah and Casey looked at each other and said, "So…," then nervously laughed again.

After a brief silence, Rebekah said, "Tell me about your life as a veterinarian."

"I'm in a group practice that specializes in large animal care. It wasn't what I originally planned to do; I kind of stumbled into it when I was in vet school. One of the rotations I did was in Ocala and I did a lot of house calls to the horse farms. Barn calls, I guess you could say. I loved it. A lot reminded me of when I was younger and got to help Grandpa G in his bull stud service. Anyway, one of the doctors in that group was retiring around the time I was graduating. They asked me to consider taking his place, and made the buy-out terms extremely attractive. I didn't have to think too hard about it." Casey smiled and nodded her head. "It's hard work, but I love it. I usually spend several days a week on the horse farms, and the rest in the office. And a side benefit is that I live near my grandparents and Mama in Archer."

"How is your mom?"

"As I told you in one of my letters, I think, she's a frail woman. Old before her time. She has not had an easy life." Casey paused and collected her thoughts. "She feels very responsible for what my father did, Rebekah. Like she missed an important clue." Rebekah blanched as Casey continued, "I'm sorry. Is this too hard to talk about right now? We don't have to talk about it."

"No, no. That's okay. I *need* to talk about it. What kind of clue?"

"I've asked her that. In her defense, I'm not sure she could have known, could possibly have imagined that her husband, my father, a minister, was capable of doing something so unspeakably horrible. She had her suspicions that he had been unfaithful to her, but she never imagined his problem was so depraved, that children were involved."

"Children? Are you talking about me? Was there more than one child?"

A lifetime of sorrow showed itself in Casey's eyes, now moist again with tears. "Unfortunately, yes. Apparently he had a nasty habit of preying on teenage girls in the congregations he served prior to Founder's Creek. Most of the girls came from broken homes. They were emotionally needy and he took advantage of that." She fixed her gaze on Rebekah and spoke earnestly, "And do you know that, to my knowledge, none of them ever reported anything to an authority figure until his arrest made national news? Mama said that people at all his previous churches raved about his rapport with young people, his caring manner with parishioners of all ages. I think one reason we moved around so much was so he could outrun the consequences of his behavior. Or outrun his shadow. My poor mother had her misgivings about him occasionally, but talked herself out of them when she saw him in action at church. That's when she convinced herself she was the one with a problem," Casey rolled her eyes, "that her imagination was overactive."

Rebekah interrupted, "Casey, did your father ever do anything to you?"

"Mama and I have talked about that. I don't remember anything, but I don't discount the possibility. A part of me thinks that he didn't because he knew Mama would have killed him, even by the time she became an abbreviated version of her former self."

"What do you mean?"

"Grandma and Grandpa Greer have told me what she was like when she was a young woman. Rebekah, my mother used to be a vivacious, enthusiastic, passionate woman. I hate to say it, but I think you reminded my father of who she used to be. And what really infuriates me is that he's the one who was responsible for driving that out of her. Over the years of living with a man who eclipsed her in personality—sometimes on purpose because he liked being in the spotlight—and who never validated her intuitions, she emotionally retreated more and more. She spent her energies on being a dutiful wife and mother and on keeping the noise level of her thoughts and intuitions at a minimum. She was afraid to live any deeper; she gradually moved into survival mode and got stuck there. She's still there in many ways."

"I'm so sorry," Rebekah's voice trailed off.

The waitress arrived with their order and to refill their water glasses. They looked appreciatively at her for providing them with the brief respite they needed.

After they had each taken a few bites of food, Casey said, "You'll have to explain to me what it is you do. I don't know a thing about fashion merchandising."

"Well, let's see. My title is North Florida Marketing Representative for Petite Clothier's, Inc., a resident buying office. What that means is that I serve as the liaison between buyers—the stores—and the manufacturers. I assist in fashion direction, merchandising techniques, assortment planning, import coordination, sales promotion, and advertising. I serve as a trend tracker, too, familiarizing myself with my client stores' individual operations and needs, sort of a buying extension of the stores."

"Sounds like a glamorous profession."

"It has its moments. Typically, it used to require a lot of traveling, but now with teleconferencing and the Internet, a lot of what I do is at my desk. The rest is meeting with clients and manufacturers. It's become almost second-nature to me to discuss business and marketing and bottom lines. That takes most of the glamour out of it. About the only time it seems glitzy is when I get to actually go to shows, which is less and less often these days. And you know what, Casey, that's really okay with me. My priorities are shifting."

"Are you considering a career move?"

"No, but I would consider cutting back, or maybe job-sharing. A lot of that has to do with, oh, how do I say this?" She picked at the food with her fork, moving it around her plate, as if the words she was searching for were hidden beneath the vegetable medley. Then she took a deep breath and exhaled her thoughts, "Who I thought I was, who I thought I wanted to be, who I'm finding I really am. I mean, I realize now that part of the initial attraction of this job was that it afforded me the opportunity to be knowledgeable, to be helpful to people but without having to get involved in their lives. I can be pretty intense and that used to give me a charge, but I'm less and less satisfied with being, um, self-important. Does any of that make sense?"

"Yeah, actually, it does. I can be very driven, too. It helps block out the questions and the insecurities and the needling little voice that keeps trying to tell me that," Casey's voice assumed a cartoonish quality, "something's wrong here."

"Yes. That's it. I didn't listen to that stuff until my dad died. I just kept plugging away at the Great American Dream. Then all my defenses stopped working for me. Oh, Casey, I got so depressed, I thought I'd never be able to pull out of it, that I'd keep going down, down, down," her finger drew a spiral, "and I'd quit even trying to care."

"I've been there. Unfortunately, more than once. In high school and in college. I know how unsettling it can be to watch your hope drain away," Casey stared off into a place of the past, "to think about the rest of your life stretched out before you like one long funeral procession...." She looked at Rebekah and asked, "Is the depression better now? Despite what you're dealing with in therapy, are the dark clouds lifting?"

"Yes, I think they're definitely lifting. I'm starting to feel like a new person. I'm almost afraid to admit that, afraid that there's just been a break in the clouds and I'll be caught off guard by another storm. But I'm working with a great therapist and I'm in a support group with other women, and that is helping so much."

"I'm glad for you. I'm also seeing a counselor. I know healing can seem like full time work sometimes. I'm so glad you have a support network. Tell me, your husband—Cliff, right? Is he supportive?"

Rebekah grinned. "Yeah, he's strong in all the right places and sensitive, too. He's my greatest defender and my dearest friend. You know, if your dad wasn't already dead, Cliff would have gladly done the job."

"Oh, but there would have been other people in line ahead of him. There was a time when I would have been at the head of the line myself."

"Is that hard for you? That he died before you could kill him yourself?" Rebekah smiled again. "Or at least confront him?"

Casey returned Rebekah's smile. "It was harder years ago. Especially when I was in college. I can remember in anatomy and physiology class fantasizing about ways to harm him as much as he had hurt other people. I could never figure out a way, though, to match the humiliation he created in so many others' lives, especially those who should have been able to trust him."

"How have you managed to get on with your life, to get past what he did? Have you ever felt stigmatized?"

"Hmmm. Stigmatized? To be perfectly honest, I've always been so shy I haven't paid much attention to whether or not other people were talking about me, certainly not enough attention to know *why* they were talking about me. I guess there were people around Archer, at my grandparents' church maybe, who knew why Mama and I moved back there. But I wasn't aware of them looking at us any differently. Life there was so far removed from Founder's Creek. You know. Living in the Panhandle is like living in a different state; it's more like annexed South Georgia or Alabama than it is like the rest of Florida. Anyway, my grandparents have been very devoted to me and protective of me. But Mama—no matter how kindly other people responded to her, I guess she did feel stigmatized. Responsible. Ashamed. She seems reluctant to let go of that, though there are times when I think she has found some measure of grace to forgive herself—for what, I'm not sure. I don't think she remembers how to trust herself. And I'm sure she's forgotten how to live. She knows how to survive, but not how to live."

"There is a difference, isn't there? I thought I lost my bearings when Daddy died, but since then I've realized I've been doing more hanging in there than living for a lot longer than that. I guess when we're successful, in terms of school or career, at least, we tend to think we're on the right track." Rebekah's voice began to match the sparkle in her eyes, displaying enough passion to catch the attention of the people dining at the next table. "I'm in a place now where I'm excited about opening up my heart and discovering things about myself and about other people. But I'm also scared about opening up. If that makes sense."

Casey smiled. "You just now sounded like the Rebekah I met in third grade. The first one in line to buy a ticket for the proverbial roller coaster of life. You didn't care that you didn't have all the dips and turns figured out ahead of time, you just wanted to ride."

Rebekah reached out and placed her hand on Casey's. "Thank you. I needed to hear that. I can't honestly say that I've been enjoying life. Aspects of it, yes. Otherwise, I think I've tolerated it fairly well, but I haven't relished it. I obviously have a lot to learn from my former self, and from you, too."

There was comfort this time in the camaraderie of their silence. Their renewed admiration for each other whispered of the great affection they had known in their girlhood. Rebekah again reached out for Casey's hand and said, "Thank you for making this easier for me. For your openness."

"Thank *you*."

"For what?"

"For your courage to deal with unthinkable things. And for letting me be a part of the journey. For not shutting me out by association."

"It's the least I could do for the girl who knew what to do with my stuffed animal collection. I mean, if it hadn't been for you, I would never have known what giraffes and orcas say to one another."

"You remember that? Oh, we used to play for hours with our stuffed animals. Do you know, I still have some from when I was little? I take them with me sometimes when I'm teaching Sunday School—to help teach the lesson."

Rebekah couldn't conceal her surprise. "You go to church?" Then realizing she might have offended Casey, she continued, "I mean, I guess I assumed there might be a lot of bad associations for you."

"Oh, there have been. Sometimes still are. I don't pretend to have all the answers to faith questions; shoot, I'm still learning what the questions are. I don't understand God most of the time. Even hate him sometimes. But I still believe he exists."

"Hmm. I haven't wrestled with the faith issue much, but Myra— she's my therapist—she says that ultimately all of us will to some degree or another. I guess if I had really been raised in the church, I might've asked more of those kinds of questions by now. The whole God thing is on a back burner for me."

"Yeah, he was for me, too, until I had my college crisis. The therapist I had then helped me discover that, for me, it wasn't so much that I didn't believe in God as it was that I was angry with God. The church isn't very comfortable with that notion and I didn't know how to deal with that type of anger. Anger at my father, yeah. But how do you 'do' anger with a being you call Supreme, one you can't see, can't be sure you've heard? I was consumed by that rage and didn't have a clue what to do with it. So at first, I did the only thing I knew how to do—I shut down."

"That's how I felt after Daddy died. Like I was shutting down, swallowed up by a huge, dark pit."

"That's when you got help, right?"

"Well, not right away, but yeah, a few months after he died, when I couldn't concentrate at work and when I wanted to sleep all the time. Cliff is actually the one who encouraged me to get help. I saw this one counselor for a while, Hank," Rebekah rolled her eyes, "but that didn't work out so well. That's when I ended up with Myra, and she's great. She's a minister as well as a psychiatrist. Crazy, huh?"

"Really? How do you feel about that?"

"I was shocked at first, and I probably wouldn't have gone to see her if I'd known ahead of time, but I had already begun to admire her and trust her before I found out. She doesn't talk about faith unless the subject comes up, but there is something very serene about her. I wish you could meet her. I think you'd really like her. So tell me, where does God fit into the bigger picture for you? I mean, I guess if I knew I believed in him for sure, I'd want to know where he was when bad things were happening."

"Good question. Hard question. Legitimate one, too. My answers might make sense to one person and sound too glib for someone else. What I can tell you is that I think God is secure enough to entertain our doubts and unbelief. The gods of other cultures don't allow that. In the Bible, there are stories of people who negotiated and bargained with God, like Abraham, and people who wrestled with God, like Jacob, and people who demanded an audience with God, like Job, and people who struggled with what God was doing in their lives, not once, but over and over, like David. And all these stories, these characters, are put before us as models of faith. I look at characters like Elijah, who was strong and certain on Mt. Carmel and then seized with doubt afterwards. To imply that there was some kind of deficiency in Elijah for running scared and becoming depressed is a disservice to the whole notion of a God who invites us into relationship. That's a kind of God I can live with. That's a kind of God I can talk about. That's where God speaks to me."

"It sounds like you know him, even though you say you don't understand him. I don't think I would know if God were speaking to me."

"Well, I'm not sure I hear God speaking to me as much as I'm aware of him—when I look for him. And even that isn't always so. I do believe that there are times when God makes his presence known in obvious ways. Other times when he is more subtle. And again other times when he remains obscure. Those are the most difficult times, but I have found that I still keep the dialogue going, even when he veils himself. And I'm not so sure he doesn't purposefully cloak himself sometimes to keep us from thinking we have him completely figured out. When God becomes my talisman for good fortune, not a higher power, I find myself worshipping what I know, not who I know. So, I find God comforting some days and maddening other days...."

"I don't think I've ever heard God explained that way before. You make Him sound at least intriguing. And very real. I think I'd like to be a kid in your Sunday School class, especially on the days when you bring stuffed animals."

"The faith of children is so endearing. They help me, really; it's rarely the other way around. Life can be so hard, and choosing to live outside myself feels risky. Children do it naturally, without considering the risk."

"You almost make a believer out of me, Casey. I envy your faith. It agrees with you. You have the same poise and serenity Myra has."

Casey rolled her eyes and laughed. "Me? Poised? No. I do not think of myself that way at all. Not with people, anyway. The only time I truly feel in my element is when I'm with animals. If I come across as poised, that's evidence of the miraculous." She grinned.

"So this is hard for you—talking even with me?"

"Well, yes and no. We've talked about some very painful and personal things, but you always had a way of making me feel less awkward and timid. Special, even." Casey leaned her head toward

Rebekah and spoke conspiratorially, "I'll let you in on a little secret. I am most confident in front of other people when I pretend I am you. You had this way of riveting people's attention on you while still making them feel important. It wasn't condescension. It was a loving acceptance and a vibrancy that drew people to you without their getting lost in the process. You seemed to help people see in themselves whatever good you saw in them. That's a gift, Rebekah. A gift."

Rebekah was crying now, silent anguished tears. In a tremulous voice, she said, "It's the prospect of somehow finding *that* Rebekah again that keeps my hope alive. To be honest, sometimes I think I've lost her forever. I barely remember her at all."

"I remember her very well, and I see evidence that she's still there, patiently waiting behind the diploma and the career. And the abuse. You didn't kick her out, you just hid her away to protect her. She'll know when it's safe to return. You'll know. You'll invite her for visits enough times that she'll know when the invitation is permanent. I'm sure of it."

Rebekah smiled through her sniffling. "Do you know what a gift you are to me right now? You could not have come back into my life at a better time."

"It's the least I could do for the person who was my first surgical assistant." They both laughed, a generous release of doubts and misgivings yielded to the cords of love and friendship and divine appointment braided together.

"Casey, I want to ask you something," Rebekah hesitated, trying to phrase her question from a place in her heart she had just recently learned to read—a place that was an odd mix of regret and revelation, of something new and tender, yet eternal. "Would you say your life is full? I mean, even with your mom being the way she is and knowing what your father did, are you happy with the way your life has turned out? So far, anyway?"

Casey's eyebrows furrowed as she thought. "Hmmm. Is my life full? Yes, I'd have to say so. But full of what?" They both chuckled, then Casey continued, "I am learning that truly living means inviting the extremes to coexist, but not necessarily peacefully. When a foal is born, I feel like the buttons of my heart will pop right off. But I also know what it's like to hurt so much that my heart feels like it has blisters, like when I read in the newspaper or hear on the news about another child who has been the victim of abuse. And then there's that big open space in between, when celebrating the ordinary means the joy isn't so intense nor is the pain so pronounced. Those are the times that help me appreciate the extraordinary days more and to endure the anguishes of life better.

"I guess rather than saying my life is full, I'd have to say I am fully alive. Doesn't mean I'm not occasionally disappointed with the way my life has turned out. I didn't have the mother I needed, but I had wonderful grandparents. I learned things at an early age that no child should ever have to know, but out of that I developed great compassion. I haven't had the depth of friendship with anyone else that I had with you, but I have read some of the best literature ever written, and I have a great imagination. My father did despicable, cowardly things that hurt a lot of people, but I have learned not to let the shadow of that ghost determine who I am. So, all in all, I still don't mind getting up most mornings. I still like to discover things. And I'm easily blessed by simplicity and by acts of bravery and compassion. I am stunned into breathless excitement by those who are willing to ask, 'Is this all there is? Is it enough?' because those are the ones on the verge of really finding their way. Every day, I try to choose to live out of my heart and not my hurts, to buy a ticket for the triple loop roller coaster, even though my throat is dry and my palms are sweaty and my pulse is racing before the ride even starts."

Their conversation was interrupted by the pager on Casey's waistband. As she turned sideways in the booth to fish her cellphone out of her purse, Rebekah pushed the leftovers around on her plate, deep in thought. As Casey spoke in hushed tones on her phone, Rebekah moved two slices of yellow squash to the top of her plate, inches apart. She then sculpted the remaining mashed potatoes into a pair of lips, coloring them with some gravy left over from her roast beef. She cut the green peel off of a zucchini slice, using the pulpy middle to create a nose and the peel for eyebrows. With the remaining gravy, she painted hair around the edges of the plate. Casey finished her call and turned back toward Rebekah. A flicker of memory, a look of childlike delight, then disappointment flashed across her face. "I have an emergency. I hate this, but I'm going to have to leave. It will take me at least 30 minutes to get where I need to go."

Rebekah stood up to hug her friend. "Please let me pick up the tab. I can expense it."

"Thank you. I have enjoyed this and I have needed this more than you know."

"Me, too. We need to keep in touch." She handed Casey her business card. "I've written my personal email address and cell phone number on the back. Promise me you'll call or email."

"Promise. Be safe driving back to Jacksonville."

Their embrace was strong and tender. The reluctance to let go after rediscovering their timeless friendship was tacit, as was the regret over unasked questions and still-missing details. As Casey walked away, Rebekah noticed she was swiping at fresh tears on her cheeks. She paid for their meal and returned to her hotel room to call Cliff. After they exchanged endearments and reports on football and friends, she turned off the light and stared up at the ceiling, eager for tomorrow but reluctant to let go of today.

Twenty-three

CASEY'S EYES SPARKLED AS SHE recounted to Lorelei the details of her dinner with Rebekah. Lorelei listened, occasionally asking Casey for more details. When Casey finished, she leaned back in the chair, smiling. "That's very telling," Lorelei said, "that she gave you her work and personal contact information, don't you think? So what's your inclination about telling Rebekah that you were awake when your father molested her?"

"I still don't know. I'm torn. Will that information help or hinder her therapy? I think I'm willing to be totally honest with her, but I don't want to destroy this fresh start on our friendship, either. I guess I'll know if and when the time is right. I hope."

"I'm sure you will. Now, tell me what's next in the Casey-Rebekah Reunion Tour," Lorelei smiled warmly.

* * *

At Margot's request, she and Rebekah had forgone their usual walk in favor of shopping at Regency Square Mall. It was early November and the merchants had invested heavily in the hopes, magic, and illusions of Christmas. Sales were boosted by the last invigorating splashes of fall color and cool air before life gets buried beneath winter's shades of brown and barrenness.

"So, are you still dating the salesman—what's his name—Tim?" Rebekah asked as they absent-mindedly fondled silk scarves at a kiosk.

Margot smiled broadly, "Yeah. As a matter of fact, we're going out again Saturday."

"Oooh. Sounds serious. Where is he taking you?"

"To dinner and a concert. I'm not sure who's playing, he just told me to dress up. That's why I needed to go shopping. I haven't been to a concert in a long time and I need my fashion friend to steer me in the right direction."

As Rebekah guided her friend through several stores, they talked easily as Margot tried to find a dress that fit her budget as well as her slender frame. Rebekah had noted that, as Margot's mantle of grief had begun to slip from her shoulders, she had become more radiant and displayed greater confidence. Their conversations were sprinkled more and more with laughter and their weekly walks had become more about their friendship and less about exercise, although each made the other more enjoyable. Rebekah continued to find Margot's insight refreshing and, sometimes, disarming.

"Why do you suppose that made me so angry and sad?" Rebekah asked, relating an incident that had occurred on one of her drives back from out of town. "I wanted to slap that woman."

"Well, you said she was being verbally abusive to her child right there in McDonald's, didn't you?"

"Right. You know, when someone is so hateful to another person in public, I wonder how much worse they treat that person in private. I've witnessed parents brow-beating their children before, but I've never reacted so viscerally to a situation like I did. What was it about that day, that child?"

"Did she say or do anything in particular that, I don't know, was new on the mean mother scale?" Margot passed her hands over a selection of cocktail dresses on clearance.

"Oh, this is a nice one," Rebekah said, pulling one of the dresses off the rack. Then, "I don't think it was so different than any other time I've seen parents being cruel to their children."

"So tell me, how was the child—was it a boy or a girl?" Margot turned the dress around on the hanger to visually inspect it.

"A boy. You really should try it on."

"How was the boy reacting to his mother? Hold on. I think I will try it on; be back in a sec."

In a few minutes, Margot returned. "I like it," she said, returning the dress to the rack, "but I still want to look around. So, the boy, what was he doing while his mother was yelling at him?"

"Honestly, I usually don't pay much attention to children in those situations. I notice the parents—because they're making such spectacles of themselves—but I try to look disinterested, not get involved. This time, though, I paid attention, and the little boy looked defeated. Dazed. Confused. Oh, and get this. She told him to stop being such a sissy. He couldn't have been more than five years old." They had left Dillard's and, by some mutual homing instinct, entered Victoria's Secret.

Margot, caressing the new winter collection of lingerie, stopped and looked at Rebekah. "Great. So she emasculated him in front of the whole restaurant. And another generation of women-haters is born...."

"You're right. I wish I had stood up for him. I wanted to scoop him up and take him home with me."

"Is it any wonder there are so many mixed up, angry men in the world? We might as well wait until all male children are seven years old and then circumcise them in the mall, make it a spectator event. That couldn't mess them up any more than that lady did." Margot selected a set of lacy red thong panties with a red bustier. "Yeah. I know. I am so glad Cliff has his head screwed on straight. How did I get so lucky? Next time I talk to his mother, I'm going to thank her."

"I'll be right back. I want to try these on," Margot nodded toward the hanger.

While Margot was in the dressing room, Rebekah wandered through the store, enjoying the textures and the visual feast of colors. She sprayed a sample of Amber Romance on her wrists and was sniffing it, trying to decide if she liked it when Margot found her at the perfume display. "I'm going to buy these and then go back to Dillard's and get that dress."

While Margot paid for her new underwear, a smile spread across Rebekah's face, crinkling the edges of her eyes. As soon as they had stepped out of Victoria's Secret, Rebekah grabbed her friend by the forearm and said, "You've been holding out on me. Why didn't you tell me you were in love?"

"What makes you think I'm in love?" Margot could barely conceal her smile.

"Because you're buying underwear. And not just any underwear, but *that* underwear! Margot, why didn't you tell me?"

Losing her resolve to maintain her secret, Margot exhaled, letting her confession tumble out. "You're right. And I'm sorry I didn't tell you; I wanted to, but since I realized how I feel about Tim, I've been afraid. You know, waiting for that proverbial other shoe to drop."

"Why are you scared?"

"Because I care for Tim and it's been a long time since I felt this way. My head keeps telling my heart to be cautious but my heart keeps telling my head that he could be the one and how will I know unless I open up my heart. Sometimes I wish they'd both shut up and let me sleep."

"So you can't sleep either? You do have it bad."

Margot grinned broadly.

That Thursday evening, the air was decidedly crisp. The CLAMOR Girls crunched through a thick carpet of leaves to reach the back entrance of Myra's office, creating puffs of vapor as they chatted amiably, entering the building. They teased each other good-naturedly in the moments before their meeting officially began by Myra rolling her desk chair into their circle.

"You look like an Eskimo, Libby. If you're wearing that coat now, what do you put on in January and February, when it's colder?" asked Andrea.

"I can't help it. I've always been cold-natured."

"That's because you don't have any meat on your bones," said Olivia. "Me? I love this weather."

"I do, too," said Celeste. "It's invigorating. Only thing missing is someone to snuggle up to at night," her eyes twinkled mischievously.

"Get a puppy," Andrea deadpanned, and they all laughed.

Myra, who had been watching the exchanges from behind her desk under the pretext of finishing up some paperwork, smiled at the women as if she were the proud teacher of a brood of responsive reform school students. She rolled her chair onto the Persian rug and began the meeting. "We want to spend some time tonight addressing a question that has come up in my private session with Olivia. She has given me permission to introduce the topic because we both felt it would be beneficial to all and because I thought your insights to her question would be meaningful. Olivia?"

Olivia fidgeted with the edges of her Publix uniform top, grabbing the hem with her right index finger and thumb while running her left thumb and finger across the bottom of the garment. It was a childlike self-comforting gesture that stirred protective feelings in the others. "My question is why do I have to remember? I mean, I know what happened to me, so why do I have to go back and think about those things and look at them again? What's the point?"

Rebekah said, "I want to be sure I understand what you're asking. You're saying that you know your father raped you—repeatedly. Right?" Olivia nodded, struggling to keep eye contact with Rebekah, who continued, "so your question is, what is the benefit of remembering in detail specific times when it occurred, am I right?" Olivia nodded again.

Looking in Myra's direction, Celeste ventured, "Let me guess. This has something to do with truth being our friend and denial being our adversary, right?"

Myra smiled indulgently. "Go ahead."

There was a brief silence as they each attempted to frame Olivia's question within their own experience.

"Is it somewhat like reading a review for a movie, so you know what it's about, but you don't know what it's really like until you go see it?" Margot asked.

"What do the rest of you think?" asked Myra.

"But I *do* know what it's like. I was there," said Olivia, a tone of desperation creeping into her voice.

Rebekah offered, "I guess part of actually remembering is returning to what you were thinking and how you were feeling back then, during those episodes. Right?"

Again, Myra deferred to the group by her silence. Andrea ventured, "And that helps us think and feel in more appropriate ways now?"

"What do you mean by that?" asked Myra.

"I'm not sure, but I thought you'd like that," Andrea responded, shrugging her shoulders.

"Someone else? What is the purpose of scrutinizing the damage?"

"Well, you're always telling me to try and figure out how I came to believe certain things about myself and about the world," said Libby. "So, when we go back to those times when horrible things were being done to us and we actually relive them, we start to dig up the reasons why we think the way we think, I guess."

"How can something that hurts so much be helpful?" asked Olivia, plaintively. "If I know what happened, why do I have to hurt all over again?"

"A very good question. A very important question." Myra continued, her voice strong, yet soothing. "When you were younger, your options were seriously limited—you were children, dependent on others for your care and nurture. You had no adult perspective on your abuse. Some victims are so young, they don't even have the language to express what happened. So, when you are molested and unable to talk about it, there are few, if any, legitimate ways to silence or dull the pain searing your soul."

Myra paused for a moment and then continued, using gardening motions to reinforce her illustration, "All of that was like soil that the seeds of abuse were planted in. What grew from those seeds were the beliefs and actions that have accounted for how you've lived your life. You may have made conclusions about yourself and the world, like 'I'm too needy,' or 'I'm too weak,' or 'Trust no one,' or 'If I just try harder to be good, bad things won't happen.' That soil, the soil of helplessness, creates a predicament: 'How can I protect myself from others and yet not be alone?' Abuse survivors sometimes spend the rest of their lives trying to solve that dilemma of having her needs met without being taken advantage of. Not until you go back and stir up that soil and identify the beliefs that grew as a result of your abuse will you be able to begin laying that dilemma to rest."

She paused again to give them time to think about this latest teachable moment. "That doesn't preclude character strength also sometimes being forged right alongside maladaptive behaviors. Does that make sense to everyone?"

"So are you telling us that using the line, 'That's just the way I am' is a cop-out?" asked Celeste.

"Not necessarily. But how do you know who you really are until you go back and see who you were before the abuse and then look at the beliefs and actions you embraced as a way of dealing with the helplessness?" Myra answered. "How many of you have grown up with the sense that there was something innately wrong with you, that you were somehow deeply flawed?"

Each CLAMOR Girl ultimately raised her hand, bolstered by the honesty of each other. Myra continued, "What was that like for you, Olivia? What did you think was your defect?"

"That I was too needy."

"How about you, Andrea?"

"I shouldn't have been so stupid, so gullible."

"Yeah, me too," agreed Margot. "And the needy part, too."

"All of you probably have minor variations on those themes. Because children are just naturally the center of their own universe, that's how many of them internalize the attack on their souls—by explaining what inadequacy of theirs could account for that attack. How do you suppose that helps someone cope with helplessness?"

"I think it helps take the focus off the insanity of the abuse and onto the task of attempting to make sense out of nonsense," Rebekah offered. "It gives us something to *do* with it."

"Precisely," Myra said. "Just because it is futile to try to make, as Rebekah put it, sense out of nonsense doesn't mean we don't still try to do so anyway. We try to create order where there is chaos. That's part of our nature, how we humans are wired."

"That might explain why I'm always trying to help people with their problems, then" Libby posed. "Maybe I should open a Troubleshooters 'R Us." She smiled at her attempt at humor.

"I'd probably be your star employee," Rebekah said, ruefully.

"How does that help solve the dilemma—to be safe but not alone," asked Myra.

"For me, at least, it gives me the opportunity to be involved with people, to be valued by them, but to maintain a certain amount of distance," answered Rebekah, Libby nodding her assent.

"Hey, don't knock being in control," Andrea jested.

"Or at least the illusion of it," added Margot.

"Seriously, are you trying to tell me that everyone who enjoys helping other people is working out some kind of twisted past?" Andrea asked.

"Not at all," Myra answered. "That's why it's important to dig out the motivation, why it's important to remember. What are some other ways you all have tried to solve the helplessness dilemma?" Myra glanced at Celeste.

Like a good student, she responded, "I know, I know. By pretending I don't care. By being superficial."

"Whoops. There's that control thing again," Margot muttered.

"Explain," urged Myra.

"I control how involved I will become in someone's life and how much I allow them to penetrate my fortress. For instance, I haven't let myself become close to the other nurses at work. I was afraid that once they really got to know me, they'd be appalled."

"Does that sound familiar to anyone else?" asked Myra. Several nodded.

"If someone is naturally shy, does that mean she's being superficial?" asked Olivia, worried there was something else she hadn't known to worry about.

"By no means. The issue again becomes one of motivation. Motivation *and* willingness to overcome discomfort for a greater reward." The gentleness and assurance in Myra's voice allayed Olivia's new concern and her face brightened.

Myra continued, "Okay, now let's talk about what happens when the strategies someone adopts to deal with the uncertainty of helplessness fail to work. What then? What are we to do when what we believe and how we put those beliefs into action don't fully explain the world?"

"Is this a God question?" Andrea asked, guarded.

"It is and it isn't. Right now, I'm asking you to answer from the belief system that arose in the aftermath of abuse."

"I'm not being glib here—honestly," Celeste said, "but I can recall agreeing with that bumper sticker that says *I feel much better since I've given up hope.*"

"Fatalism?" offered Rebekah. "Instead of saying, 'This is the way I am,' I could say, 'This is the way the world is.'"

"Or maybe 'I deserve this. There's no way out,'" said Olivia.

"Is that different from cynicism?" asked Margot.

"Good question. Someone want to take that one?"

After some time, Rebekah ventured, "It seems to me that cynicism has a hardened quality to it while helplessness feels…, I don't know how to put it…"

"Actually, you're very close. Hopelessness still *feels*, but that can be so intense, it isn't infinitely tolerable. People generally want to *do* something with their despair. If the questions they ask aren't answered, or answerable, the only option that appeals to most is numbness." Myra slowed the cadence of her voice in order to underline her point. "And numbness to anger, distress, and longing brings with it mistrust of passion and of others. So the goal becomes keeping life as neat and tidy as possible with a minimum of investing one's whole self."

"That's depressing," said Celeste.

"Yes, it can be. But the reality is that uncertainty and hopelessness and numbness operate on a continuum." She stretched an imaginary string across the room. "Very few people stay in one place indefinitely; they glide in and out of them, especially as situations arise that penetrate the deadness. So let's talk, these last few minutes, about what penetrates your deadness."

Rebekah sat up straighter, a look of recognition on her face. She glanced at Margot. "Last week, when I was on my way home from a meeting out of town, I stopped at McDonald's for coffee and I saw a mother being verbally abusive to her son. That's always bothered me, but in the past I've tried to ignore the situation and get away as quickly as possible. I can't stop thinking about this incident, though. I didn't do anything, but I wanted to hurt that mom for what she was doing to her little boy. I understand murderous rage in a whole new way."

"Welcome to my world," said Andrea.

"I understand better how you get caught up in your work," Rebekah said. Andrea nodded appreciatively.

"Alright. So indignation or injustice is one thing that can get through the deadness. What else?" Myra asked.

After a brief pause, Celeste, in a rare guileless moment, said, "This may sound crazy, but when I'm shopping for material for a new design, I get a thrill out of the colors and textures. I enjoy creating something new, but when I'm walking through the fabric store, touching bolts of material and looking at all the different prints, I feel like a carefree little girl. It's an exhilaration that's pure and clean. Better than any high I ever had on drugs. Maybe even better than sex."

"That doesn't sound crazy to me," shared Rebekah. "Sometimes when I'm listening to music, I'll start to cry without knowing why."

"Ah, so beauty is another thing that breaks through the deadness. This week, as you encounter beauty and outrage and anything else that stirs you, your mission will be to notice how you deal with the stirring."

Myra's comments were met with pensive expressions. Then Libby asked, "*Do* we have options for how to handle them?"

"Yes, you do. Be aware, first of all, that something is trying to break through the barriers created by the dilemma of helplessness. Then your task becomes something as simple and as difficult as not shuttling off to the sidelines that which tugs on your heart. Not minimizing it or calling it stupid sentimentality, but to live in that moment." She stopped to take a sip of water. "That's easier to do when it's something positive, like seeing a newborn baby or smelling a rose or having a cup of coffee with a friend; it's more difficult when the thing that's trying to get through to your heart is something offensive, like witnessing an abusive parent," she smiled in Rebekah's direction, "or when someone says something at work that hurts your feelings," she smiled at the others. "These Signposts of Life are gifts, testaments to your being alive. Honor them."

Thursday, November 7, 2008

Myra introduced us to Signposts of Life tonight: pain, rage, beauty, desire. I never thought of all of them as positive intruders. I think I've tried, instead, to domesticate these wild beasts, under the pretext of being a nice girl, competent and pleasant. Now I'm aware of a solid mass of fury and grief in my belly, with tentacles that reach up to my heart and my mind.

How do I honor them, especially not let them choke out the bubble of joy that's bobbing in there, too?

I both envy and pity Olivia her task of remembering. Myra says that we must remember in direct proportion to the myths we adopted to explain what was, in reality, inexplicable. So Homework Number Whatever: as I pay attention to those Signposts, listen to the things that make me angry or sad or happy, then listen to what my head and my heart say about them; they may serve as cues to help me remember exactly what Casey's father did. I'd rather spend the rest of my life in a greenhouse or a concert hall or in bed, than where I'm headed now.

Twenty-four

DURING THE LONG THANKSGIVING WEEKEND, while Cliff trimmed hedges and performed various other lawn chores, Rebekah planted pansies in the front flower bed, reveling in their colors and cartoonish faces against the backdrop of pine straw and fading foliage. She and Cliff had celebrated the wonders of exploring the earth and each other for four luxurious, relaxed days.

The Thursday after, the moods of the CLAMOR Girls were as varied as their personalities. Libby admitted to being weary after hosting family, but of also being aware that her servitude this Thanksgiving had been borne of love instead of the need to be needed, resulting in an ease with her grown children that hadn't been present before. Rebekah glowed with fulfillment. Margot was animated, having spent Thanksgiving with her mother and stepfather and Tim and his mother. Celeste seemed distracted and distant. Andrea was agitated and thumped the foot she had propped across the opposite knee. Olivia was withdrawn and failed to make eye contact with any of the others.

Sensing the different moods, Myra commenced the meeting with, "Holidays can be very difficult, can't they?"

Andrea snorted. "Thanksgiving is misnamed. And overrated. And no," she looked directly and defiantly at Myra, "I don't want to talk about it."

Olivia spoke, dejection and desperation in her voice. "I had lost a couple of pounds before Thanksgiving, but I know I've gained it all back. All I did during my days off was eat."

Libby interrupted, "Oh, Honey, me, too. Every year I tell myself I won't do it again, but then I do."

Olivia looked imploringly at Libby. "No offense, Libby, but coming from you, that doesn't make me feel any better. You're a stick. And your husband loves you." Then, addressing the entire group, she continued, "I'm serious. I ate then slept then ate then slept. Tyler was with his daddy and grandparents, so it was just me and the TV and the refrigerator."

As if pulling herself out of a hiding place, Celeste, her voice tinged with sadness and compassion, asked, "Do you think you're making this harder on yourself than you need to—the losing weight thing? I mean, you're trying to deal with what your father did, with your sister's death, divorcing your sorry-ass husband, and you're trying to quit smoking... God knows, that's a lot at one time. Even bears and grass know sometimes the thing to do is rest."

Olivia smiled appreciatively. "It's just that I don't know why I do that to myself. I can understand pigging out on Thanksgiving Day, but even after I was stuffed and uncomfortable, why did I keep eating?" She looked between Celeste and Myra.

Myra looked at Olivia, then the others, and said, "Group?"

Rebekah smiled supportively while Libby beamed maternal acceptance. Andrea stopped thumping her foot, but kept her arms crossed. Celeste momentarily retreated back to her private thoughts and anguishes. And Margot thoughtfully asked, directing her question at Myra, "Do you think this has more to do with appetite or sabotage?"

"Ladies?"

Andrea looked at Margot and asked, "What do you mean 'sabotage?'"

Looking at Andrea and Olivia alternately, Margot answered, "It sounded to me like she, you, were punishing yourself in some way."

"Why would I do that?" Olivia asked plaintively.

"Maybe because something got close to your heart?"

Rebekah nodded. "What were you watching on television when your eating frenzy started?"

Olivia closed her eyes and leaned her head up slightly, mentally walking through the events of the past few days. "*Dances With Wolves*, with Kevin Costner. Why?"

At the mention of Kevin Costner, Celeste left her emotional retreat and rejoined the group. "Watching anything with that man in it would get close to *my* heart."

Andrea rolled her eyes, but smiled in amusement, while Libby continued to smile indulgently.

Rebekah turned to Olivia. "Sometimes everything can seem to be on an even keel until I watch something or hear a certain song. I'm consistently surprised at my reactions in those unguarded moments. I was just wondering if what you were watching uncorked your bottle, so to speak."

Myra inserted, "That might be a good thing to contemplate, Olivia. To consider what you were thinking and how you were feeling in response to the movie."

"Okay. Well, I felt like, even though the Kevin-guy was having to run for his life at the end of the movie, he was free in a way. And I thought he and his wife were beautiful together. It kind of made me sad—because Clay and I have never known each other like that. And now we're running in different directions, not together."

Several of the women nodded and smiled knowingly. "Sabotage," whispered Margot.

"Sabotage," agreed Rebekah, Celeste and Libby nodding their agreement.

"I don't understand. What do you mean?"

Margot looked at Myra, deferring to their leader to explain. "Longing," said Myra. "That movie stirred up longing in you. Or, as Rebekah put it, uncorked the bottle on your longing."

"Kevin would do that to me," offered Celeste.

"Anything with testosterone gets you going," Andrea said.

Libby intervened, "I'd like to hear what Myra is saying."

Myra continued. "All of you know what it's like when an experience that ought to be pleasurable, like sex or getting attention, is used against you as a weapon of destruction. When that happens, one often learns to equate *any* kind of pleasure with danger. We are designed for resolution; consummation, if you will. If, instead, your formative experiences with pleasure resulted in pain, confusion, betrayal, those create tremendous mixed feelings. The tendency will be to go to great effort to avoid further internal contradictions—by avoiding desire." Myra paused, looking at each of her charges for indications that she wasn't teaching too quickly. Seeing their mental wheels engaged, she continued, "If, however, you still manage to bump into longing or arousal, you might feel the need to punish yourself."

"Why?" asked Olivia.

"Would you rather experience longing and have someone take advantage of that or have no longing at all?"

"I would rather have no longing at all."

"So, what purpose does stuffing yourself with food serve?"

Olivia understood, but searched for the words. "It makes me, it helps to, oh, Lord, I don't know how to say it."

"It kills desire," said Andrea, matter-of-factly.

"Right," said Myra. Olivia nodded at Andrea's blunt assessment. "But remember, what precedes that effort to punish yourself is the humiliation and hatred that you have come to associate with longing. 'How dare I even want *whatever it is.*' That hatred is directed at both yourself and the world. The self-punishment, sabotage, is how you suppress the shame you experience for being so 'frail,'" Myra's elegant fingers made quotation marks, "as to have desires in the first place. Do you all see that?"

Celeste spoke, weariness etched into her voice. "Okay, I'm confused. Why would I punish myself for my humiliation with something that makes me ashamed of myself all over again? That doesn't make sense."

"Libby, I'm going to put you on the spot," said Myra. "You've raised children and you have grandchildren. Did you ever punish your children?"

Libby answered tentatively, "Of course I disciplined them…"

"What was your objective in doing so?" Myra pressed.

"I guess to help them make a connection between their behavior and negative consequences and to make them think about what they did."

"So…," coached Myra.

"So…. Oh, so they wouldn't do it again."

Myra waited. Her brooding group considered their lesson. In a small, girlish voice, Olivia said, "I think I get it. I'm probably trying to take my mind off of what I need. I need to be loved and I need to be appreciated. But as long as I'm mad at myself for being fat and for having no will power, I don't have to think about what I really want, what I really need. Is that right?" She looked at Myra.

Myra smiled proudly, then asked the group, "What do you all think?"

"That makes sense to me," said Rebekah, as others nodded assent, "but I wonder. Do we all take revenge on ourselves?"

"Good question. As you all think of your patterns in relationships— at home, at work, or with the world at large, and as you think of some of your more compulsive behaviors, do you detect any spark of rage beneath those behaviors? Rage directed at yourself or at others, or both? I'll give you a moment to think about this." Myra poured some water into her empty glass and took a few sips.

The usually boisterous CLAMOR Girl sequestered themselves in introspection. Some closed their eyes, visiting hidden rooms of their past, conjuring up scenes they preferred to forget. Others stared at fixed points behind the present. The room was quiet except for the sound of the clock ticking on Myra's wall. As each considered Myra's assignment, recognition registered on their faces.

"Who would like to share first? What behavior patterns do you deploy to ease the confusion brought on by longing?"

Libby volunteered, "This isn't anything y'all don't already know about me, but I guess I hadn't realized how well my constant busyness was working for me in so *many* ways. I like everything to be orderly, neat and tidy, including the lives of people I care about. Y'all know that, and how I like to be so helpful to other people."

"So, what's the payoff for you in terms of keeping internal contradictions at arm's length? How does being a busybody bring you comfort?" Myra probed.

Libby chuckled at Myra's directness. "The comfort is that I get to try to establish a little order and it gives me some sense of control."

"Okay. And how does this help you settle the score against a world that so obviously needs your help?" Myra pressed.

Libby winced. "You really do think I'm mad at the world, don't you? Okay, let's see. How am I settling the score? Well, maybe if the world weren't so harsh sometimes, people's lives wouldn't need fixing. They wouldn't need my help."

"And how are you getting back at yourself for having desires in the first place? After all, that's what landed you in the position of having those internal contradictions."

"Good grief, Myra, you don't let up, do you? Okay, um, if I'm busy fixing people all the time, I prevent others from really getting to know me better, I guess. Can I get off the hot seat now?"

Myra smiled. "Certainly. Who else wants to be subjected to this torture?"

"I'll go," Rebekah volunteered, "because I'm a perfectionist, too." She smiled at Libby. "When I am Super Woman at work, that alleviates some of the chaos that's constantly swirling around me."

"So, is that how you get revenge on your broken world?"

"I guess so."

"And how does your superior competence and business demeanor work for you in terms of easing the confusion that comes with longing? How do you try to keep longing from even knocking at your door?"

The smile on Rebekah's face faded. Myra's words had stung. After some thought, she answered, "If I am so thoroughly capable at work that nobody ever sees my frail, human side, then I have set myself apart from them. They think that they have nothing to offer me, that I don't need them."

Myra smiled warm encouragement. "And how does this help you get even with yourself?"

The exercise was stirring the hard knot of grief inside her. Rebekah cringed, but continued, slowly gaining the awareness Myra was probing for. "If I am unapproachable, then that also means I don't have the closeness with others I really want." A light came into her eyes. "Oh. So if they don't know that what I really want is not their professional admiration, but their friendship, then at least I won't get hurt. But I've also 'proven' to myself that I am not capable or worthy of their friendship. Or they of mine." She smiled bitterly. "Who knew desire could be so dangerous?"

Friday, Dec. 5

Didn't sleep very well last night. Sort of a refreshing change after trying to sleep-walk my way through the last year. Tossed and turned so much I finally got out of bed to let Cliff sleep and to attempt to put into words what was keeping me awake.

I thought I had turned the corner in this depression/abuse thing. Until the group session last night. Now I'm more aware of where I'm not, who I'm not, what I'm not. I had no idea I was so afraid of passion. In some respects, I envy Celeste in that department. She's not afraid of her passion, she just doesn't know how to draw boundaries around it. Olivia kills hers with food, Libby funnels hers into doing nice, safe things for people so her passion won't gallop all over her, but underneath she is seething with rage. Sometimes I'm not sure who she's trying to convince when she mentions Jesus and God—herself or us. I guess Andrea has made her passion her work. Other than that, she doesn't impress me as being a very vibrant person. Margot seems to be comfortable letting her slumbering dragon of desire wake up. I thought I was comfortable with that, too, but I realized last night that I'm afraid—afraid that if I sparkle with life, someone will try to steal that life away from me. The dilemma is this: how can one be inconspicuous but have her needs met legitimately at the same time? Problem is, I've lived meticulously for so long, I'm not sure I'd know how to live larger than life. Casey said she still saw that in me. Don't know....

Celeste seemed to zone in and out of what we were doing. I could tell something was bothering her and she finally told the group what her caseworker had told her yesterday. He told her he thought she was unstable. He told her she needed to stop being a dreamer, stop spending so much time designing clothes and concentrate her energies on bettering herself. So she asked the group if we thought she was crazy to want to have a career at something she had never actually gone to school for. She asked us if we thought she was just plain crazy. She was actually beginning to believe him. We spent a good deal of time trying to encourage her; I even told her I'd look at her sketches and see what I could do for her. That seemed to lift her spirits.

We were all feeling a little better until Myra asked the group, "What gets your passion?" Is it protecting myself? If so, that's just sad. Is it about keeping things in my world well-defined? What am I missing by doing that? She really put the screws to us when we were confessing the ways that we try to avoid passion and what we do when we can't avoid it. I simply had no idea I was so afraid of it, and I wasn't the only one squirming. I think we all were. Then Myra asked, "How beautiful do you feel when you are all alone?" I'm not sure we were ready to think about that one. How can she expect us to think about our thwarted desires and our unrecognized rage and our beauty all in one session? Entirely too unsettling.... Thing is, I know too much to continue living the way I've been living and not enough to know what to do about it. And I can't sleep this one off. Damn.

Twenty-five

THE CITY WAS SHROUDED IN hues of cold and gray and trees stretched their bony, bare arms in supplication to the sky. The Christmassy glitter and lights almost seemed mocking by contrast. Head down and muttering to herself, Rebekah shuffled and kicked her way through the leaves that lay between her car and the office building. When the receptionist called her back to Myra's office, without sitting down, she angrily tossed an email print-out on Myra's desk, eyes flashing and nostrils flared. Myra looked up, calm and questioning.

"Read it. Just read it," Rebekah clenched her teeth. "I don't know what the hell she expects me to do."

Myra read:

9 Dec. 2008

Dear Rebekah,

I hope this email finds you happy and well. I'm guessing this Christmas, like last year, will be bittersweet for you as you remember your father and miss him.

As usual, I will spend Christmas day with my grandparents and Mama. I am on call for the office Christmas Eve. That's what I get for being the newest kid. I would ask Mama to go to the Christmas Eve service with me, but if I'm called out on an emergency, she'd feel awkward sitting through the rest of the service without me. Even if I weren't on call, though, she probably wouldn't go, even with Grandma and Grandpa Greer. There's something about the Word arriving wrapped in a defenseless baby that haunts her, I think.

Will you spend part of Christmas with your mother and brother? Where do Cliff's parents fit into the celebration? It must be strange, but kind of nice, to marry and begin traditions of your own. I remember the first few Christmases after my father died. It was therapeutic in a way to create new routines for the holidays. But I'm rambling.

Rebekah, there's no easy way for me to ask you this. I had hoped to tell you about it the evening we met for dinner. (Damn that pager!) My counselor, Lorelei, has been asked to gather testimony from abuse victims so a legislative sub-committee can draft stricter penalties for abusers. The current sentencing guidelines are so loose that if a man rapes a little girl, he could be eligible for parole before she's old enough to vote. That means, if my father were still alive, he could have conceivably been out of prison by now. This sub-committee wants compelling enough testimony to convince the legislature to change the law so that someone convicted of being a sexual predator is automatically imprisoned for life.

So, the question I have for you is this—will you consider coming to Tallahassee with me and letting Lorelei's committee interview you? They've already begun collecting testimony from child psychology experts, but they need to hear from people who have actually been victims. They need to hear that the damage stays with people long after the actual events. I sense that you have become an intensely private person, but my hope is that you would find it easier to reclaim the joyful, open girl you once were if you share your story with people who care. Please think about it. I know you could make a difference.

If this is asking too much, though, I understand. I look forward to hearing from you after you've had time to think it over. I treasure you, as much now as then.

Love,
Casey

Myra set the pages down and searched Rebekah's face. While Myra read, Rebekah had remained standing, arms crossed over her chest, tapping her left foot. "Well?"

"Rebekah, while I understand your alarm, I want to say how marvelous it is to see that sparkle in your eyes. You look so alive right now."

"Alive? Shit. I want to know how Casey could ask me to do such a thing! Why did I give her my email address? And my phone number, too? Oh, crap."

Myra continued to smile at Rebekah. "Sit down, Rebekah, and tell me what it is about Casey's email that makes you uncomfortable."

Rebekah sat obediently and immediately tears began to form small puddles at the edges of her eyes. Fighting to control her voice, she started, "For one thing, it's an invasion of my privacy…"

"Which she acknowledged," Myra pointed out.

"How much has she told her therapist about me, I wonder. She had no right."

"She didn't indicate they had discussed you. If she mentioned you, I'm guessing she didn't divulge your identity."

"I'm scared," Rebekah squeaked, her voice suddenly small. "I don't even want to talk about my abuse with you or Cliff or my mom or the CLAMOR Girls; I want it to go away. I'm coming in here every week, hoping I'll turn the corner and see the proverbial light and I can get on with my life. I sure don't want to talk about it in front of a group of strangers. How could she even think of asking me?"

"Rebekah, you *are* getting on with your life and somewhere deep inside you know that. You'll miss the best parts of today if you think life starts 'when,' because life is going on all around you. It just stinks sometimes." Rebekah smiled through the film of tears. "And as for turning the corner, you also probably know by now that you will turn many corners and there will be a light on in a window around each one. And you will follow that light to the next corner."

As Myra, with cadenced voice and calm inflection, imparted the truth her client needed to hear, Rebekah's breathing returned to normal. Still, she protested, "But if I tell those people what happened to me, that means it's all real."

"Ahhh. The search for denial has become harder than the search for truth. Progress."

* * *

The following Thursday, Myra presided over the group much as a Mother Superior over her classroom of eager, talkative novitiates. The light-hearted conversation was infused with a depth and warmth that belied the separate aches in each of their lives.

"I've got to tell you all, I should be awarded the C3BW Award," said Celeste.

"What's that, Sugar?" asked Libby.

"The Could've Been a Bitch But Wasn't Award." Andrea's eyebrows cocked. Celeste continued, "I met my caseworker, Mr. Trackman, today and he pissed me off so badly I wanted to scratch his beady little eyes out. Remember that time a few weeks ago when he told me I was unstable? Usually when he criticizes me, I argue with him. Okay, I yell at him." She smiled at her confession. "Today when he started to criticize the way I dress and tried to tell me that proved I was an unfit mother, instead of yelling at him, I just smiled real nicely and looked at him like this," at which Celeste modeled sweet innocence, "and asked him how I should dress. I mean, I've done everything he has asked me to do to prove that I'm ready to have Justin back full time, unsupervised. And every time, he adds another condition. I suddenly realized today, he's the one with the problem. Probably not getting any at home, not that I blame the missus. So he's making my life more difficult 'cause his is so freakin' pathetic. It's a power trip. He can't stand it that I'm doing so well, so he wants to make me miserable—as miserable as he is. But I decided I wasn't going to give him the pleasure of making me upset, that I'd be so nice it'd make him die of sugar shock."

"Well, how did he respond?" asked Margot.

"Yeah, what did he do?" asked Rebekah.

"He nearly had a stroke, he wanted so badly for me to argue with him. And no matter how hateful he was to me, I was sticky sweet to him."

"So you made him squirm. Good for you," said Rebekah. "I wish I'd been a fly on the wall."

Olivia winced, maternal pain in the creases of her eyes. She said, "It doesn't seem fair for him to be changing the rules on you all the time. Seems like there's something you ought to be able to do about that."

"Really," agreed Andrea. "Doesn't he have a supervisor? And isn't your input supposed to factor into his decision?" she asked, looking accusingly at Myra.

Myra held Andrea's gaze, smiling sympathetically. Celeste interrupted, "Oh, Myra and I talk about this all the time. She's been trying to help me see that it isn't worth it for me to play his little game. But I like to have the last word. Damn, I like to have the last word. Today," she raised her index finger to emphasize, "I had the last look." She batted the lashes of her large innocent-looking brown eyes.

"That's your answer to this man's power trip? To act all innocent and demure? Jesus, that makes me ill," said Andrea. "What are you going to do about getting your son back? What are you going to do about him moving the damned dangling carrot?"

Libby flinched, but involuntarily sighed with relief, grateful for once that someone else was the object of Andrea's scorn.

Myra spoke. "What are you reacting to, Andrea?"

"Oh, crap, here we go again. What is Andrea's problem? Am I the only one here who's pissed that this guy is misusing his authority? My God, if I did that in my job, I'd get fired in a New York minute. He can't keep changing the standards. He can't keep setting you up like that. He knows how important Justin is to you and he's taking advantage of your soft spot."

"You're right. Of course, you're right." Celeste was sincere. "And I'm right, and Myra's right. I haven't been handling this the appropriate way, though—until today." Celeste stopped smiling and looked directly at Andrea. "And Justin is my child, not my soft spot. You don't have a child, so how would you know the fear of never being able to take care of him again? I know that little pecker-head of a man has been using my fear to manipulate me. I know that. But you have to understand that I have to at least act like I'm playing by his rules. My son is at stake. That turd already thinks I have an attitude. And I know he's been waiting to see if I'll crack under pressure and either start using again or offer him a blow job. Nothing would make him happier than to write on my paperwork *custody denied*," she wrote in imaginary ink on her palm. "I simply decided to start acting like he thinks I'm supposed to act so he can't delay the process any longer. No more attitude from me, no more lip, no more short 'floozy' dresses—on appointment days, anyway. He'll crack before I do. Guaranteed."

"You go, girl," said Margot. The others nodded agreement while Andrea continued to fume.

Myra offered, "So, Andrea, what is annoying you about this?"

Andrea shrugged her shoulders.

Myra continued, addressing all of them, "Mr. Trackman's behavior may seem like deliberate deceit. Acts of betrayal will strike a nerve with all of you, reminding you of a time when an offer of help or hope or intimacy was the very same act that, instead of touching your soul, destroyed part of it. How can anyone help but feel defrauded in these instances? To feel set up?"

The room was quiet as they all remembered instances when this was true. Rebekah sat up straight, recognition dawning in her expression. "My God, Myra, that's why I was so upset with Casey's letter. It felt like a set-up, a betrayal. And I ended up angry at myself for believing that we could be friends the way we used to."

Myra nodded at Rebekah. "Would you like to share this with the group?"

Rebekah related the story of Casey's email and her request. "I think you should consider going," said Margot.

Rebekah, jerking her head around as if she'd been slapped, asked, "Why? Why should I talk about this with people I don't even know?"

"You didn't know us before you started coming here. None of us knew each other," Celeste reminded her.

"I thought y'all would understand," Rebekah's voice trailed off.

"I couldn't do it," said Olivia, nodding toward Rebekah.

"I'm not saying I think I could do it," said Margot, "I'm just saying you should consider it. If it might get the law changed...."

"It might not be so bad," Libby offered. "I'll ride over with you if you want me to."

"There you go, trying to fix everything," said Andrea. Then she looked at Rebekah, "Don't do it if you don't want to."

An edge of strength and sureness in her voice, Libby countered, "Who said anything about *wanting* to do it? Maybe she should do it because it's the right thing to do." Margot nodded in agreement. Olivia looked frightened just by the idea. Rebekah suddenly longed for a soul-deadening nap. Andrea scoffed, while Libby continued, "I would think that you, of all people, would want Rebekah to testify. Couldn't that potentially make your job easier?"

"Have you ever been deposed, lady? Do you have any idea what that's like?" Andrea shot back.

Libby persisted, "What's the worst thing that could happen? You could open your mouth to speak and no words would come out, or you could start crying. But, like Margot said, if it gets the law changed, wouldn't it be worth it?"

"I feel like she's asking me to stand naked in front of a bunch of people—people I don't know. How do I know I'll never run into them again? How do I know they won't tell other people?" Panic had returned to Rebekah's voice.

"Maybe if you prepare a speech—like reading them a story... And make sure they know ahead of time your conditions for agreeing to talk to them," Libby offered. "I know God will help you."

Andrea looked at Libby. "I've got it," she said derisively, "why don't you go instead of Rebekah?"

"All I was saying," Libby responded evenly, "is that if she prepares for it, it might not be so bad."

"And what I'm saying is you might not know what the fuck you're talking about," Andrea shot back, mocking Libby's refined Southern pronunciation of *might*.

With determined politeness, Libby turned and faced Andrea squarely. "You've been picking at me for weeks and weeks, Andrea. If you have something to say to me, why don't you say it now? Let's just get it out in the open so we can stop taking up these other ladies' time."

Andrea was slightly shocked by Libby's directness. She looked to Myra to intervene. Myra played the role of wise judge, allowing two arguing attorneys to make their points. She widened her eyes at Andrea, encouraging her to answer Libby's accusation. The others collectively held their breath.

"Fine. I'll tell you. For one thing, I'm sick of you always trying to stick God in everything. That's bullshit. And you act like you've had such a hard life. What do you know about being raped over and over, anyway? I mean, for Christ's sake, an uncle felt you up one time. Get over it!" Stricken, tears welled up in Libby's eyes, but she held Andrea's glaring gaze. Andrea continued in her rapid-fire volley of Bostonese, "And I'm tired of you acting like fucking Dear Abby, with an answer for everything. I don't need another mother, okay? So just back off."

Libby wept silently, too stunned to respond. Myra started to speak and was interrupted by Olivia's small, plaintive voice. "I think that's just what you do need. A mother, I mean. I know a day doesn't go by that I don't miss my mama." She looked at Myra, "You've told me we're never too old to need our mom."

Myra smiled warmly at Olivia. The others applauded her bravery with their approving smiles. Despite Andrea's desperation to use her icy floe of rage to keep her pain dammed up, she shuddered involuntarily as it shifted, thawed somewhat by Olivia's childlike perceptiveness. She swiped angrily at gathering tears.

After a brief silence, Myra spoke. "That was painful for all of us, I think." She paused, then, facing Libby, continued, "Out of fairness to you, I'd like to offer you an opportunity to respond to Andrea."

"That's okay." Libby reached for a Kleenex.

"In that case, I'm going to use this as one of those teachable moments. We were discussing Rebekah's feelings of betrayal by her friend, Casey. Once one has been betrayed by someone she should have been able to trust, whether that occurred once," she nodded in Libby's direction, "or multiple times," she nodded in Andrea's direction, "the dynamics have begun that, over the course of time, result in a host of trust issues. Your radar will work overtime in assessing every situation for dependability. Along with that, you might develop a fear of intimacy or tenderness; your reluctance will speak louder at times than your need for closeness. A persistent voice will tell you that, eventually, everyone important in your life will choose to leave you in some way. It will tell you how foolish you are for having needs or for trusting someone in the first place. If you continue to listen to that voice, you will have difficulty asking for help. You will carry around with you a general sense of unfairness about the world, all the while questioning your value as a person, as a woman. And, again, how this plays itself out is as individual and unique as each of you is. Is any of this sounding familiar?" Myra looked around the circle. Some readily accepted what she said while other struggled against it. None spoke.

Myra continued, "And I want to caution you against comparing your history of abuse with that of another. Your journey is just that—yours. No one else's." Again, no one spoke. After a brief pause, Myra looked at Rebekah and said, "You do not need to make a decision right now about helping Casey out with your testimony. It's okay right now to feel at odds about it and not know what you will decide. But it would be helpful for you at this time to determine whether or not she has actually betrayed you. Has she?"

Rebekah placed her fingertips across the bridge of her nose. *It would be easier to stay angry at Casey if I thought she had*, she thought. Rebekah searched her mind for answers. After a moment, she looked up at Myra and answered, "No. She just scared me."

"How?"

"By suggesting I talk about what her father did to me, with people I don't know. By making me think about it more than I already care to. By making it more real, whatever 'it' is."

"You mentioned her asking you to stand naked in front of a crowd. What is that about?" Myra probed.

Rebekah shifted uncomfortably in her chair. She looked down at the floor, hoping it would either swallow her up or reveal great truths. Finally, she looked up at Myra and responded, "The idea of talking to this panel of experts makes me feel naked. Makes me feel, um...."

"Vulnerable?" Margot guessed.

"Exposed," suggested Celeste.

"Yeah," Rebekah agreed. "Both."

"So your radar was on high alert," offered Myra.

"Yeah, it was. Is."

Myra turned to the rest and asked, "Can you see how a request for your involvement, even if it doesn't seem outwardly harmful, can suggest to that little voice of alarm inside your head the idea of being taken advantage of?"

Her charges nodded obediently. They were well-acquainted with the voice.

Olivia spoke next, unsure at first of how to phrase her question. "When I... Does the... How..." She paused for a moment, then tried again. "How do you know when to listen to that little voice and when to tell it to shut up?"

"Good question. Do you have a specific instance in mind?"

"Well, last week when I stopped by Clay's to pick up Tyler, Clay was in the back of the house and Ty was in the living room, watching TV. I noticed two *Playboy* magazines on the coffee table, right there where Tyler could see them. It made me sick on my stomach, like I used to feel after my daddy did things to me."

Margot stiffened in her chair. Libby shook her head sorrowfully.

"That's wrong. Leaving those out where your son can see them," Margot said. Her voice almost growled with fury. "When I was a little girl, that apartment superintendent used to let the boys in the complex come to his apartment and look at all the dirty magazines he left lying around. They bragged about it, too, how Mr. Jackson let them hang out with him, smoke cigarettes, look at magazines. My ex-husband was into that stuff, too. When we were making love I always felt like I was competing with those air-brushed images." Margot looked directly at Olivia. Her voice had an earnest fierceness in it. "You've got to put a stop to that right away. Unless you want your son growing up to look at women as objects and not people."

Almost relieved, Olivia nodded. "Something felt wrong about that, but I just couldn't put my finger on it. And I know what you mean about competing with those pictures. Clay was forever looking at those magazines. He thought he was careful about hiding it, but I caught him a couple of times. That was my fault, too," she said, halfway smiling, "that he was looking at them."

Andrea leaned toward the edge of her seat and added, "Many of the perverts we arrest got their start looking at that trash. It's like a gateway drug or something. You keep that stuff away from your son." Again, Olivia nodded, grateful to have her intuition validated.

Celeste asked, "I'm just playing devil's advocate here, but if men are visually stimulated, and those women agreed to pose, what is wrong with them looking?"

Myra swept the air in front of her, offering the question to the CLAMOR Girls.

Libby shifted in her chair. Olivia looked between Margot and Celeste, willing Margot to speak. Rebekah rested her chin in the cradle of her palm, unable to conjure an opinion or answer.

Andrea and Margot spoke at the same time, "Because...." Andrea yielded the floor to Margot, who continued, forcefully, "because it's not real, that's why. They don't look for merely aesthetic reasons. They look because it makes them feel more masculine, more virile. They look because they're curious and they want to explore without getting their hearts involved. They look because it's easier to live in a fantasy world than in the real world. Pornography is cheap, imitation intimacy." She rested back in her chair, breathing hard.

Andrea looked at Margot to see if she was finished, then said, "And because one look becomes two. Then something goes wrong in their lives, and they spend an evening, alone, looking, cruising the Internet. Then they have trouble relating to women because they have this image of the perfect woman sex kitten in their small brains, which have long since migrated to their peckers. So they become more obsessed, some of them to the point that the only female they feel comfortable with is someone they can control. God, they're so pathetic. I've met men who even became obsessed with getting into the tightest space possible." Libby flinched and Olivia winced. Rebekah squeezed her eyes shut against the idea. "Yeah," Andrea continued, "you wouldn't believe some of the things I've seen. Little girls ripped and bruised, kids with gonorrhea."

Libby interrupted with a whisper, "Please stop."

Myra looked at Andrea. "Unfortunately, we get the picture." Then to Celeste, "Of course, not all men who look at pornography reach such a low point," then to the entire group, "but when you consider that over $1 billion is spent on pornography every year in this country alone, we have to acknowledge an industry that leaves many victims in its wake. Victims of betrayal to the very essence of femininity and beauty."

12/11/08

Hard to believe a little over a year has passed since Daddy died. And yet a whole lifetime seems to have passed before my eyes, some shadowed, some Technicolor, some good, some bad, some sweet, some difficult.

Sent an email to Casey tonight and told her I just couldn't go with her to meet the committee, but to please keep me informed. Not sure why I said that.

Mom seems to be adjusting to the empty nest. Says she's staying busy. She hinted the other night that she wished she had grandchildren to shop for at Christmas. It's too early to know for sure, but she just may have her wish by next Christmas. At least I hope so!

The group session tonight was interesting and intense. Everyone's nerves were raw, if not before the session started, then definitely afterwards. Seems like some weeks instead of resolving things, we end up excavating more junk. Makes me wonder sometimes if there's anything inherently beautiful left in this world or if everything is tainted. Myra says all women, all females, are inherently beautiful. Is that something that's dormant in someone who's been traumatized or does that have to be recreated? And she also says embracing one's beauty, feeling safe with it, and being able to trust are all tied together. Then she left that for us to figure out while we break for the holidays. She tried to pull the past few weeks together for us—her Christmas gift to us, she said. I should've taken notes. What I can remember her saying is something about how things appear and how things really are not always being the same—like in winter, when things look dead on the outside, but new life is lying underground, germinating. There's cause for hope!

I have mixed feelings about not meeting with the CLAMOR Girls until January. I'm looking forward to taking a break from so much thinking and wrestling. Question is, will it take a rest from me? I feel like I'm on a tightrope between an old way of life that no longer satisfies me and a new way of living life that both frightens and lures me—inching, creeping—forward. So, my gift to myself this Christmas is to just try to enjoy my family for the holidays and stay, as Myra encourages, in the moment.

Rebekah spoke the words, "in the moment," aloud, imitating the cadence in Myra's voice, musing that Celeste would be proud.

Whatever the hell that means.

Twenty-six

THE NEW YEAR BEGAN WITH optimism and resolutions marking time with unease as winter unfolded in fits and starts. Days of warm, radiant sunshine were interspersed with spells of crispness and cleanness interrupted by intervals of drab, bone-penetrating wet and cold. Coats left idle over the backs of chairs were ushered back into short-term duty, then replaced by sweaters, then both layered on together again. It was a typical Jacksonville winter.

Myra had given the CLAMOR Girls an assignment—to describe how they interacted with the people they encountered on a regular basis, focusing their observations on their own personal actions and responses. They were to share their revelations during their first February meeting. The women arrived with their journals and a sense of expectation and dread. They knew that whatever mirror they, as members of a group, would be reluctant to hold up to each other, Myra would gently, firmly suspend before them.

As the session began, Myra listened as the women talked to each other about the previous week. The conversation easily flowed from Olivia's meeting with her divorce attorney to Andrea's plan to attend a local celebration to watch one of the children she had worked closely with march in a parade. Libby talked about her daughter's relapse and how that had affected her granddaughter, then Celeste shared that she had been assigned a new caseworker due to allegations of Mr. Trackman's inappropriate behavior with another client.

Margot glowed when she spoke of Tim and of taking a class at the University of North Florida in preparation for her studies as a Nurse Practitioner. And Rebekah revealed that she and Casey had remained in contact about the upcoming closed hearings before a select committee of the state legislature. She shared this information non-committally while patting her slightly thickening midriff and joking about the Butterball seeds she must have swallowed during Thanksgiving.

Myra, in her melodic, rich voice, said affectionately, proudly, "Good! I'm glad none of you has avoided the assignment. You should have lots of observations written down in your journals." A collective moan went out from the group as they anticipated the scrutiny that was to come. "I'd like for each of you to share some of the things you learned about yourself. Remember, I want you to describe your own behavior in your personal transactions over the past few weeks. We'll give everyone a turn in the hot seat," she said, smiling. They groaned again, good-naturedly, realizing they were captive to Myra's caring and persistence. "And in order to take some of the pressure off of you, I'm going to describe three kinds of animals and I want you to be thinking about which one best describes you in most of your interactions. Okay?"

The CLAMOR Girls shared a sigh of relief, thankful that Myra would initiate and guide the discussion. *We're all a bunch of chickens, that's the kind of animal we are,* Rebekah thought, smiling.

"The first kind of animal is a new puppy. She's so glad to be rescued from the pound, she pees all over herself trying to please everyone." Rebekah stole a glance at Libby, who sat smiling benignly through Myra's description. "She comes when called and cowers when scolded. The second kind of animal is a porcupine, who bristles when someone gets too close." Several women peeked at Andrea, who was stoically listening, unreadable. "She's a solitary animal, proficient in her self-protection. And the third kind of animal is the cartoon hyena. She's the life of the party. Hilarious." With that, a smile broadened on Celeste's face, aware that others were looking at her. "And sometimes sneering beneath the laughter and jokes." The corners of Celeste's mouth turned down slightly. "Now, we all know we aren't always the same way with all people, but think about which animal you most often resemble. Then let's talk about the nuances of your style of relating."

The room was quiet for a moment, several of them thumbing distractedly through their journals, looking purposefully absorbed so as not to make eye contact with Myra. Then Libby spoke. "I bet y'all didn't think I saw you looking at me when Myra was describing the puppy, huh? Well, I know that describes me. The people-pleaser. What else is there to know?"

Myra answered, "Why don't you tell us about a recent interaction, one where you were the puppy, and tell us about what you offered of yourself in that interchange and, just as importantly, what part of yourself you kept tucked away."

A shadow fell across Libby's face. She closed her eyes, struggling to find an example other than the one that occurred to her first, one that was more innocuous. She couldn't find a suitable alternative. Sighing in resignation, she opened her eyes and said, "Bud. He was angry with me for 'interfering' with Rachel and her husband when Rachel told me she was maybe going to have to go back to the hospital. I was trying to be helpful, so I told her I'd watch Courtney for her if she had to go. Bud got mad and said I was making it easier for Rachel to not eat. That I should stay out of it." Fresh tears of motherly anguish spilled down her cheeks. "But she's my daughter. How can I not help her?"

"How did you handle Bud's anger, Libby?" Myra wanted to know.

Reaching for a Kleenex, she answered, dabbing at her eyes, "Well, I tried not to let it get to me. He doesn't get mad with me very often. He could tell I was upset, so I told him we would cross that bridge if we came to it. I mean, it may not come to that—you know, Rachel having to go back into the hospital."

"So, you were pleasant?"

"Yes, I guess you could say so. At least, I hope I was."

"So that's what you offered him. Your pleasantness."

Libby, guarded, answered, "Yes," but her voice said *So?*

"Did you keep anything from him that he might have needed?" Myra asked, her voice calm, gentle. Libby looked puzzled. She shrugged her shoulders, almost reluctant to ask herself.

After a brief pause, Margot hesitantly said to Libby, "Maybe what Bud needed was for you not to keep the peace at all costs, but to resolve the issue then and there. Or at least discuss it, regardless of whether or not he was angry and you were hurt...." She and Libby looked at Myra at the same time.

Myra smiled deeply, nodding, "Your passion. Maybe he needed your passion, Libby?" Libby flinched at the word. Myra continued, "You obviously feel very strongly about helping Rachel and Courtney. Your husband needs to be the recipient of some of that passion, that fire. If you think you're right about Rachel, tell him. Tell him why. Don't shrink from his anger for fear that...." She made a move like handing an empty vessel to Libby, willing her to fill it with the truth.

Libby looked pained, but she accepted Myra's challenge. She squinted as if peering into a shuttered room in her mind for the answer. "For fear that, for fear that..." she coaxed herself. Her eyes opened widely. "I'm afraid that this husband of mine, that I've lived with and loved for all these years, won't like me anymore. That he'll leave."

"Why would he do that?" Myra asked.

"Because I disagreed with him."

"So, you think his anger will go away if you simply choose not to acknowledge it, right?"

"I don't know. I guess so. I hope so."

"Well, it might go away, but it might not. I can assure you that there's a greater chance that *he* will go away if you don't talk to him and really share yourself with him. I don't mean he might actually leave, but he may give you less of himself if he thinks you don't respect him enough and trust him enough to let him see what, who, you are behind all that pleasantness. Besides, you are depriving both of you the privilege and fun of making up," Myra winked, causing some of the others to smile.

After a brief pause, Margot spoke. "I'm sitting here trying to decide which animal most fits me. I feel like I'm in a period of transition where none of them really describes me adequately."

"Well, that could be a good thing. Tell us about one of your recent interactions with someone."

"Okay." She turned to a page in her journal, smiled, and then said, "Tim was over for dinner one night last week. I was finishing up in the kitchen and he was relaxing in the living room. He saw the print he'd given me for Christmas still propped up against the wall. I just haven't taken the time to hang it up yet, and he offered to hang it for me, and I said no, it wasn't necessary."

Celeste interjected, "What's up with that? A man offered to help you and you turned him down?"

"I guess you could see it that way, but I've hung every other picture in that place without any help. Besides, we were getting ready to eat."

"Let's give it the test, then," Myra said. "What were you offering him, in response to *his* offer?"

"The opportunity to continue relaxing."

"But he offered his help," said Celeste. "He was willing to do that for you. What'd he say when you told him 'no thanks'?"

"Hmm. He was pretty quiet. He fiddled with the knobs on the stereo instead, like he was doing something important there."

"So," Myra asked, "was there anything you withheld from him that he might have needed?"

"I guess the opportunity to help me, to feel useful," Margot said, disappointment in her voice. "I've gotten so used to doing everything for myself, I hate to be a bother."

"A new puppy," said Myra. At Margot's quizzical look, she continued. "A new puppy wants to please, doesn't want to inconvenience the people who were gracious enough to invite her to come live with them. The thing is, Margot, in any relationship, there are times when what you need or what you want *are* going to be inconvenient. And so that has to be balanced against what the other person needs right then. In this particular case, as Celeste pointed out, Tim offered his assistance."

"Oh, ouch," said Margot. "No wonder he was so quiet during dinner."

"There is nothing wrong with letting someone feel necessary. Sometimes letting them do something for *us* is a gift to *them*. Letting others be kind to us may also be good practice asking for help, for when we really do need it."

"So, I'm a new puppy, too," Margot said, smiling at Libby. "I'm hearing Barbra Streisand singing People Who Need People...."

"Are there any other new puppies in our midst?" asked Myra, her smile encouraging.

Rebekah and Olivia looked at each other, polite and smiling. Rebekah broke the stalemate by offering, "I'm definitely not the hyena," she said, glancing at Celeste, who nodded, "and I don't think I'm the porcupine. But I'm not sure I'm the new puppy, either."

"Why don't you share one of the interactions you wrote about and see if that helps," Myra gestured, palm up.

Rebekah flipped through several pages of her journal, then stopped. "Okay, here's one," she said, pointing to a page from her private world. "I went into Ross's office—he's my boss—to tell him I'm pregnant, so we can start to strategize my maternity leave. I guess I expected him to be happy for me. I at least expected him to be accepting. He acted so indifferent, like I told him I had a hangnail. That hurt."

"What did you do about that?" prodded Myra.

Rebekah scanned her notes briefly, then responded, "I assured him that the pregnancy wouldn't interfere with my work, in case he was concerned about that."

"A puppy," said Celeste.

"A puppy," agreed Andrea. "And your boss is a bastard."

"How so?" asked Myra. "What about Rebekah's response tells you she's a puppy?" She looked between Celeste and Andrea.

"I have this wonderful news," Celeste said, playing docent of Rebekah's mind, her voice whispery and enthusiastic, her face animated, "at least, to me it's wonderful. It might change things around here, but I promise you it won't inconvenience you. I'll try to make sure your life can continue without interruption."

"Bastard," Andrea muttered. "God forbid he might have to make some adjustments."

"Okay, so I was a puppy. Was there some other way I could have handled that?"

"Without being a porcupine, a hyena, or a puppy, you mean?" asked Myra. Rebekah nodded and Myra continued, "Rebekah, there is nothing wrong with being polite—especially to your boss," she smiled. "Please don't get me wrong, ladies. I'm not suggesting any of you be anyone but yourselves. What I'm attempting to help us see is the internal motivations behind the way we relate to others. As far as this episode with your boss is concerned," she faced Rebekah, "perhaps his insensitivity just didn't warrant a response at all. Perhaps if you had ignored his lack of enthusiasm, his self-centeredness would have echoed in that office. And even if he couldn't hear how ridiculous he sounded, at least you didn't make his 'problem' your problem. Because it isn't."

Some of the others were nodding. Rebekah said, smiling, "Okay. I see. I 'deprived' him of the opportunity to see what an ass-wipe he was being."

"Possibly," said Myra. "And, again, even if he didn't pick up on that, his selfishness is *his* problem, not yours."

Olivia fidgeted with the edges of her sweater, preparing to be the object of scrutiny. She looked down at her hands first, then at Myra. "This just happened today, so I haven't written anything down in my journal. Okay, so there's this woman at work, Maelene." In her girlish drawl, she said the name as if it were a question, not a fact. "She's been at Publix since before I started working there. She's kind of like everybody's mom there," Olivia smiled quickly in Libby's direction. "Anyway, she's been after me for a long time to go to church with her. She says it's important for Tyler to be in church at his age. I know my Mama would want that. So, anyhow, today Maelene was already on her lunch break when I went into the break room for mine. She asked me to sit with her, so I did. She invited me to her church again, saying, 'I know you'd just love it if you came, and there's lots of little kids Tyler's age.' So I told her I might come. Then she started telling me what the preacher talked about yesterday—the be-at something," she looked between Libby and Myra for help.

"Beatitudes?" offered Libby.

"Yeah, that's it. So, she was telling me the preacher talked on the be-at-i-tudes," she pronounced the word slowly, carefully. "I told her I didn't know what that was, so she was trying to explain it to me. All those 'blessed are's.' And then Vienna, one of the cashiers, came in for her break. She really can't stand Maelene, makes fun of her all the time behind her back, and so she was standing there in the doorway, behind Maelene, where she couldn't see Vienna making fun of the way Maelene was talking and moving her hands. Even making fun of Maelene's hairdo—Maelene has some big hair," she said, smiling at Celeste. "You'd have a field day with her, Celeste. Anyway, I don't think Maelene even knew Vienna was back there. I was having a hard time paying attention to what Maelene was saying. But I remember one of the things she said was, 'blessed are those who hunger and thirst for righteousness.' I was pretty interested in that."

"And why was that?" Myra interrupted.

"The part about being hungry—for righteousness. I just never thought about being hungry for anything except food. But then Maelene had to go back to work and Vienna came and sat down with me. The first thing she said was, 'I wish she'd lay off that religion crap. How can you stand it?'" Olivia paused, glancing at Andrea to gauge her reaction. Andrea showed no evidence of irritation, so Olivia continued. "The thing is, I like Maelene. She's been like a second mom to me, and I know she really cares. But I like Vienna, too. We're about the same age. She doesn't have any children, but she makes me laugh. She's always cutting up. Anyhow, I didn't know what to say. I didn't want to agree with her, but I didn't want to disagree with her, either."

"So what did you do?" asked Margot.

"I just said, 'Oh, she's not so bad.' Then a new guy came in to get something out of the snack machine. While he had his back turned to us, Vienna was admiring his butt, making all these faces, making me laugh."

"My kind of girl," said Celeste.

There was a brief pause, then Olivia asked, "But what should I do? I mean, if it happens again. I don't want to hurt Vienna's feelings but I don't want to hurt Maelene, either."

"The issue here isn't so much what you should do—there may not be a right or wrong thing to do. The issue is more *why* you don't want to hurt either of your co-workers' feelings." Myra spoke gently. "Is it to keep the peace? Or is it because you want them both to like you? Or is it because you care about both of them? Or is it a mixture of all those? While you think about that, if you're okay with it, I'd like to hear from our other two members. Then, I promise, I'll try to wrap this up for all of you." Her smile was broad, reassuring.

"Sure."

"Let's hear from Andrea and Celeste." Myra looked to one, then the other.

"Oh, hell, I'll go," said Celeste. "Everyone already knows I'm the hyena and Andrea is the porcupine," she tilted her head in Andrea's direction. "Actually, when you mentioned Maelene's big hair," she nodded in Olivia's direction, "it reminded me of something that happened a while ago, but I never wrote it down." She turned and faced the entire group. "You all know how I like to flirt. Well, this really cute guy came into the salon for a haircut one day. I'd never seen him before, so I assumed he was a first time customer. That was the day after I had told myself I would be on my best behavior so that Trackman couldn't say I wasn't professional and serious about my conduct. I was getting sort of paranoid that he was sending snitches in to spy on me. So, I was being real business-like with this customer, but I was dying to find out if he was married, attached, whatever." Andrea rolled her eyes. Celeste, noticing, smiled, saying, "Well, I'm not dead yet." Then, "So, anyway, I was cutting his hair, making polite conversation, really watching myself around him, when *he* started to flirt with *me*! Asking me questions about where I like to go, what I like to do for fun, raising his eyebrows at me, winking."

"And what did you do then?" asked Myra.

"Oh, God. I didn't know whether to give him the full Celeste charm treatment or to keep playing it cool. I mean, if he was sent in there to set me up, I didn't want to take any chances. I really wanted to play along, but before I had to even decide, he looked over at the door when he heard someone come in and started acting all stiff and formal. After I finished cutting his hair, he whispered, 'I want to apologize for my behavior earlier.' Said he'd had a fight with this girlfriend right before the appointment and when he'd seen her looking through the window, he wanted to make her jealous. When she came in the shop, he could tell she had been crying and he felt bad. They walked out arm in arm, all lovey dovey."

"Jerk," said Andrea.

"A victim of reverse flirting," Rebekah observed.

"I guess. I should've given him my phone number. In case he wasn't able to patch things up with his girlfriend. He was gorgeous."

"Have there been other instances of flirting since then, or have you been cured?" Margot asked, smiling.

"Oh, don't you know I'm making up for all those wasted opportunities, now that Trackman is off my case."

"So, when you're flirting, what are you offering of yourself?" asked Myra.

"A little appetizer," quipped Celeste. Rebekah and Olivia stifled a laugh.

"And in flirting, is there anything that you withhold?"

Turning serious for a moment, Celeste thought, then said, "Yeah, the real me. The part of me that doesn't want to get hurt."

"So you do see that you might be keeping a sort of depth and honesty from infiltrating your cocoon of superficiality..."

"Yeah, I know," Celeste said, her eyes clear and sad. "I know." Her momentary vulnerability touched the others and they were quiet in their compassion.

Myra spoke. "Andrea? Would you care to share something with us?"

"If we already know I'm a porcupine, what's there to share?"

"Do you see yourself as the porcupine?"

"Geez, I don't know. I'm sure not the puppy, and I'm definitely no hyena. Does that automatically make me a porcupine?"

"Not necessarily. These are general styles of relating that result from some sort of emotional damage. Tell us about a recent interaction, why don't you?"

Andrea rolled her eyes again and sighed, cornered. "Okay. There's this girl on the volleyball league who keeps asking me to do things with her—like go to a movie or meet her for dinner; that sort of thing. Now, I don't mind going with the whole gang for a beer after the game, but I'm not real interested in being best buddies with any of them. Anyhow, the last time she asked me if I wanted to do something over the weekend, instead of telling her I was busy, like I usually do, I told her no. I could tell she was hurt, even though she took it pretty well. I guess some people can't take a hint; you've got to be direct with them."

"Can I ask you something?" Olivia asked.

"Sure."

"Why don't you want to be friends with her?"

"I'm just not into the being friends and baring your soul to someone else. I like to keep things…" she searched for the word.

"Safe?" asked Margot.

"At arm's length," stated Celeste at the same time.

"Casual," said Andrea, defensively. "I'm just not the palsy walsy type. I go to work, I do my thing there. I'm good at it. I play ball, I do my thing there. I'm good at that. Then I go home. I really don't need to be with other people."

"And that is legitimate," said Myra.

"But?" Andrea responded, hearing the pause in Myra's voice.

"To the extent that you don't need other people, but not because you don't *want* to need other people. It all has to do, again, with how you handle both offering and protecting yourself." Myra turned to the entire group. "Some questions to ask yourself are: am I pleasant, but not passionate?" She nodded in Libby's direction, the dulcet tones of her voice soothing in her frankness. Then she continued, "Why am I reluctant to ask for help?" She smiled at Margot. "Am I so nice that I enable people to avoid the truth about themselves?" She looked at Rebekah, then turned to Olivia, "Why am I acting as a peace-maker in this situation?" Then facing Celeste, "Do I use my sexuality as bait or ammunition, or am I expressing my femininity?" Then to Andrea, "Why do I prefer for others to enjoy me for my abilities and not for myself?"

She paused and let her words penetrate, then continued, her voice warm and rich, "In the very act of protecting yourself, you are avoiding pain. But when your motive is solely to avoid pain, you are also lying to yourself, telling yourself that *pain* is the worst thing in the world. I'm not advocating that you don't guard yourself in situations that call for it, but in your everyday dealings with acquaintances, co-workers, loved ones, self-preservation can deprive you of a depth and quality of life that we're all meant to enjoy. And *that* is the worst thing in the world to do to yourself. When the cost of opening yourself up is not calculated ahead of time, when you can include others in the bigger picture of your life, you are not only free to love, but free to *be* loved. And, after all, isn't that the very cry of our hearts?"

Myra's loving gaze and the invitation in her sparkling eyes to find the truth in her words was met with tear-glistened eyes. "I know it's a scary proposition to fully give of yourself after having been betrayed. I *know* that. Just as I know that giving of yourself is not a problem-free, pain-free proposition, especially if you've been in the business of protecting yourself for a long time. But I promise you that if you will ask yourself—why do I offer myself? why do I not? where and how do I protect myself?—an ever-so-subtle shift will begin to occur and you will find yourself, rather than being on the periphery of your own life," with her index finger, she traced a circle around the upturned palm of her other hand, "being right in the middle of it." She poked her palm with the finger and then finished with a confident stage whisper. "And that's a really grand place to be."

Rebekah slept fitfully at first. Myra's exhortation turned over in her mind, thumping and thudding like sneakers tumbling in the clothes dryer. She absent-mindedly reached over to Cliff's side of the bed and, feeling the cold spot, remembered he wasn't due back from his business trip until the next afternoon. In her subconscious fog, she took his pillow to her and inhaled, comforted by the familiar smells of his cologne and pheromones. Hugging the pillow to herself, she turned on her side and gave herself over to sleep and to pleasant dreams. In the morning, in the unguarded moments between deep sleep and alarm-clock reality, as one dream sequence segued into another, a sylph-like harbinger flirted with her consciousness, slipping behind her dream screen, drawing a scene more harrowing than she had ever imagined.

Twenty-seven

REBEKAH SAT IN MYRA'S OFFICE, staring vacantly. She impassively held her purse on her lap while Myra read her most recent journal entry.

Friday, Feb. 6, 2009

I remember. Oh, God, I remember. I spent the night at Casey's house and Pastor Wes kept winking at me during dinner, kept trying to make conversation with me. Casey had a puzzled look on her face. Why didn't her own father ask about her day? She was unusually quiet, like she was listening more to something inside her mind than to the dinner conversation, and she had a scowl on her face. He kept asking me questions about how I felt about becoming a big sister. After dinner, he left to go to his office at the church. As he left, he promised Casey he would look in on her when he got home—something about an angel watching over her. Miss Annette flinched. I remember that clearly. Just as I remember being relieved when he left.

Casey and I took a bubble bath after we helped Miss Annette clean up the kitchen. Then we got into our pajamas and played in Casey's bedroom until it was bedtime. Miss Annette came in and said prayers with us, sitting on the twin bed I was in, and I remember her stroking the back of my hair. She'd never done that before. Casey looked at her mom like she was sad and hungry.

Casey and I whispered and giggled for a little while, until the pauses between our words became longer than our sentences. She fell asleep first. I was holding her stuffed tiger and she had a unicorn. I rolled over on my side, with my back to Casey, and held the tiger while I sucked my thumb. The only time I sucked my thumb was when I had trouble falling asleep—a leftover habit from being a colicky infant, maybe.

The next thing I was aware of was a quick sucking in of air and a gasp. Then my face wet. I opened my eyes and Pastor Wes was standing beside the bed, wiping at the puddle beside my cheek with the sheet. His pants were unzipped and his penis was dangling in front of my face. He quickly pulled his shirt over it and then he patted my head and smiled at me, whispering, "Shhh, it's just a dream; go back to sleep." I was groggy, so I rolled over and went back to sleep. I don't remember the next day— waking up, what Casey and I played. I just remember this sense that there was something I was supposed to say or ask or do, like when you walk into a room, but forget what you went there for.

So, now I know. That Casey's father, my pastor, my parents' pastor, my best friend's father, pulled my thumb out of my mouth while I was sleeping and stuck his dick in. And he did the same thing the night Robert was born, I'm sure of it. I don't know how many times he previously violated me, how many times he stole my innocence then tried to make me think he was comforting me from a bad dream. And if Miss Annette hadn't walked in on him the night Robert was born, how many more times would he have gotten away with it, how far would he have taken it? The night Robert was born, I remember Miss Annette, turning on the lights, shrieking, "Get away from her!" I thought I had done something wrong. And Casey was sitting up in her bed, looking bewildered.

I am sick. I am sad. I am angry and scared. I want revenge. I want Casey's father to be alive so I can kill him. I want my mom and my daddy, and I need Cliff to hold me.

Myra looked up at Rebekah, tears moistening the edges of her eyes, and in a gentle voice said, "I am sorry. I am so, so sorry."

Rebekah nodded and said, quietly, "I called my mom yesterday and told her everything. She cried. I cried. She's coming to see me."

"What did Cliff say?"

"He was mad. And he was sweet, too. He offered to call you for me Friday night, and to stay home from work for a few days if I needed him. I told him I'd call when I leave here and let him know. He says that what Casey's father did to me, he also did to *us*. My husband is a good man," Rebekah smiled weakly.

"Yes, he is. I have met spouses who wanted the victimized spouse to just get over it, like getting over a headache." Then, pointing to the open journal, "Can we talk about this some more? You okay to do that?"

"Yeah, okay. I guess."

"As you were writing this, what were you thinking, how were you feeling?"

"Nauseated. Sad. Angry. Dazed. Hurt." Rebekah paused. "Before I had this memory, I think I used to be sad for *that little girl*, but," her voice squeaked with the tightening of her throat, "that little girl was me. Me. That," she pointed at her journal again, "didn't happen to her, it happened to me." She touched her finger to her heart.

"Yes, it did. Yes. It did."

"And part of me wants to die right now so I never have to hurt like this or think about it again." With her fingertips, Rebekah wiped at the tears collecting beneath her eyes. "But an even bigger part of me wants to get through this and emerge on the other side stronger and better. So he can't have won—not in the long-run, anyway."

* * *

The CLAMOR Girls gathered for their usual Thursday night group. Rebekah and Myra had spent an extended session talking about Rebekah's memory of being violated. Rebekah acknowledged the hard knot of anger and grief that had pushed itself out of exile and into a place of prominence in the fabric of her daily routine. With Myra's assurance that the anger and grief would, in time, fade into the background, Rebekah vowed to embrace their presence until they had been allowed to speak themselves into exhaustion.

The group was listening to Rebekah's retelling of her flashback, horrified at her ordeal. They were supportive in their silence and in their questions. "And so," Rebekah concluded, "I have decided to meet Casey in Tallahassee in March and testify before her committee."

Libby smiled broadly, reaching over to squeeze Rebekah's hand. "Good for you, Sugar."

"I've been to this kind of thing before. I could go with you, if you'd like," Andrea volunteered.

"No, that's o… Okay, thank you. I'd like that." Myra smiled broadly at her brood, pleased they were looking out for one another.

Tentatively, Olivia offered, "I have some vacation time coming up. I could go, too."

Celeste enthusiastically suggested, "Why don't we all go? We wouldn't all have to testify, but we could go to support Rebekah—and the cause." She looked at Rebekah, then Myra, who looked at Rebekah and raised her eyebrows—*well?*

"That's okay with me. Let me talk to Casey and see what she says."

Andrea, Libby, Celeste, and Olivia nodded their agreement, excitement sparkling in their eyes. Celeste turned to Myra, asking, "You're coming, too, aren't you?"

"No, my dear. I will leave this to you all and eagerly await your report when you return."

They were momentarily disappointed, until they heard Rebekah speaking to Margot, who had been sitting solemnly, her head slightly bowed. "Margot, are you okay? You aren't sick, are you?"

Margot looked up. Exhaustion and pain were written into her smooth mocha features. In a voice devoid of animation, she answered simply, "No."

"What's wrong?" Rebekah asked.

Tears began to slip down her cheeks. She croaked, "It's Tim."

"Did something happen?" asked Rebekah.

"No. Well, sort of." Margot stopped. Reaching for a Kleenex, she continued, "I don't know how to explain this." She stopped again, faltering, then continued, "Tim has to be out of town for Valentine's Day this Saturday, so he wanted to celebrate with me last Saturday. He picked me up for dinner and took me to Juliette's."

"Ooooh," said some of the others.

"Nice," said Celeste.

"Yeah. You'd think I'd be the happiest woman in the world. I mean, he treats me so well—almost too well."

"Meaning . . .," said Celeste.

"He says he loves me, but it's almost as if there are strings attached. I can't quite put my finger on it, though. It's not that he's pressuring me. I have this sense that he wants something from me that even he's not aware of." Margot paused. "It's difficult to describe. It's just that lately, after we've spent time together, I'm almost relieved when he leaves to go home or he takes me home. I feel so drained. And I made the mistake of trying to talk to him about it when we went back to his apartment after dinner. He got his feelings hurt and kept saying, 'I don't know what you're talking about. All I know is I love you.' And it's true. I know he loves me. And I love him, but I told him I needed some time apart. I'm so confused."

The others waited in silence. Margot added, "You'd think, wouldn't you, that after what I went through with my ex-husband, I'd latch onto the first man who treats me so well, who's so decent and thoughtful." She looked at Myra and gave a half-hearted smile.

Celeste, sensitivity and confusion in her voice, said, "I'm not sure I understand what you mean by feeling drained. Usually, if I've been with someone I care about, I feel almost euphoric. How is he draining?" She smiled apologetically, "Is it the sex?" Libby gasped and Olivia's face colored red.

"No," Margot responded matter-of-factly, "it isn't the sex. Tim is very attentive. Again, almost too attentive."

Celeste's brow furrowed. "Too attentive? How can… What does… I sure wish I knew what you were talking about."

Myra asked, "Without invading your privacy, can you give us an example?"

Margot closed her eyes for a moment and inhaled sharply, selecting a scene from her recent date. "Okay, for instance, after he kisses me, instead of quietly talking or, you know, basking in the afterglow, I feel like a piece of him gets up and walks across the room to observe us. Does that sound crazy?"

"So you feel like he's not fully there?" asked Myra.

"No, it's not that. It's like he's waiting for something more, no matter how perfect the moment seems. Like there's a comma there instead of a period."

"And what do you think might be after the comma?" Myra pressed.

"I'm not sure. That's what got me confused. It doesn't feel like he necessarily wants more than that perfect moment. It's more like he wants…" she searched, "like he wants to know something. I guess after the comma, there's a 'well?'"

"'Well' what?" coached Myra.

"I think, 'well, how am I doing?'"

"A report card?" asked Myra.

"Yeah, a report card. And God knows, I'm the first person to understand insecurity, but how many report cards does someone need in order to believe he's really okay? Every time we kiss? Every time we make love? Every time we talk? Sometimes I feel like I'm drowning in a sea of his self-doubt. And I keep waiting for the day when I disappoint him and he decides it isn't worth it. Maybe I'm just too idealistic. Maybe relationships are just this way.…"

"Oh, I don't think so," countered Rebekah, looking intently at her friend. "First of all, if you sense that something isn't quite right, don't disregard it. Haven't we all done enough of that?" she scanned the room. "—not listening to that place inside of us that says, 'something's wrong here.' And, no, not all relationships have to be that way. I'm so lucky to have Cliff in my life. When we're together, he loves me well, he loves me all the right ways, but I also know when we're apart, even though he still loves me, he continues to know who he is as a person and a man. He doesn't live in a state of suspended animation. And that takes a lot of pressure off me—not being his entire world. Does that make sense?" she asked, looking between Myra and Margot.

"Honey, you aren't lucky, you're blessed," said Libby.

"Yeah, I guess I am. I know that he is strong and masculine and gentle, with me or without me. And *he* knows it, too."

"That's it," Margot said. "I think Tim wants to draw life from me, but what kind of friend, what kind of woman, would I be if I let him believe that I was the source of his life, his masculinity? Why can't I be *a* source of peace and happiness and joy? Why can't he know who he is even without me?"

"Very astute observations," Myra crooned. "All of you are familiar with how it feels to be used. In a healthy relationship, there's give and take. In the very act of sexual intimacy, for instance, you are inviting another to partake of you; you are giving a part of your soul away. Only when the other person is able to offer you the same level of involvement will you be able to stay 'full,' to avoid being used or being used up." She paused, panning the room, then continued, "As much as each of you has to offer other people, the reality is, as Margot said, you *will* disappoint people, significant people in your life. If they have made you the center of their universe, there will be hell to pay when the disappointment occurs."

"What do you recommend I do about Tim? I really care about him. I want to be a part of his life."

"Send him to Myra. She'll fix him," offered Celeste.

Myra smiled appreciatively, then faced Margot. "Only you can decide what to do about having him in your life and at what level. In the meantime, ask him to talk about his relationships with the important men in his life—his father, grandfathers, uncles, brothers, Scout masters, teachers, coaches. Who were his mentors? What have they taught him to believe about himself? Were any of them distant or disapproving? That type of information serves as clues to how he defines manhood; and what he didn't learn from them, he might turn to peers and to women, to prove things to himself he's not certain of."

Margot nodded. "That makes sense."

Olivia, who had been quietly, intently listening, remarked, "That helps explain a lot about my daddy. And about Clay. I really need to make sure Tyler meets other men who know how to be good husbands and daddies. Where else will he learn it?"

"Exactly," said Myra. "And they're out there, aren't they, Rebekah?"

"Yep. They sure are."

Olivia said, "If Margot is finished, I'd like to share something with the group." Margot nodded at Olivia, then slouched back into her chair, spent. Hesitantly, Olivia unfolded a single piece of notebook paper. "Do y'all remember I told you about how Maelene at work was telling me about the be-a-ti-tudes and about how I was interested in the one that said, 'blessed are those who hunger and thirst for righteousness'? Well, that got me thinking about being hungry; I had never thought about all the ways I could be hungry. The other night, after Tyler was in bed, I went to the refrigerator about 30 times, like there was something in there I hadn't seen five minutes before." The other women smiled, recognizing themselves. "So, I stopped to ask myself what I was hungry for. And I ended up writing this little poem." Self-consciously, she began to read:

> *I heard hunger call my name.*
> *I think it wants to play a game.*
> *What am I really hungry for—*
> *A hamburger? Or something more?*
> *These are things that I want now:*
> *A cigarette, not meat from a cow;*
> *A walk in the woods; a gentle touch—*
> *Is that asking way too much?*
> *A conversation with a friend;*
> *A little garden I can tend.*
> *There is so much I'm hungry for*
> *That I can't buy at the grocery store.*
> *'Cause if I could, and it's no joke,*
> *I would soon be very broke.*

Olivia looked up at the others, who were smiling supportively. A few dabbed at the corners of their eyes. "Olivia, that's great," said Rebekah.

"Yeah, Honey, that's real good," agreed Libby.

"How did you feel after you wrote the poem, Olivia?" Myra asked.

"A little sad. Sad and lonely. And a little smarter."

"What did you do with the sad and lonely?"

"Nothing, really. Well, I mean I stopped going to the refrigerator every five minutes."

"You could have called one of us," offered Rebekah.

"I know that in my head, but I hate to be a bother," Olivia said to Rebekah, then to Myra, "but, no, nothing else changed."

"Oh, I think a lot changed," said Myra. "You listened to yourself. And you allowed those feelings to be recognized and to exist without trying to numb them. And you lived to tell about it. Rebekah's right, Olivia. You are allowed to 'bother' anyone in this room."

"So it's okay to have all that want in my life?"

"It's not only okay, it's acceptable, it's normal, it's human. It's life," Myra breathed the words like an incantation. "You are waking up,

Sleeping Beauty. And that is a good thing. Not always an entirely pleasant thing, but a good thing."

"Well I guess I'm waking up, too, then," said Andrea, hesitantly.

"How so?"

"Remember that parade I told you I was going to?" The other CLAMOR Girls nodded. "I went to it. It was a little community thing about an hour away. I had told the little girl, Beth, that I would come watch her twirl her baton. Honestly, it's a wonder the child can walk after what her father did to her." The others flinched. Andrea continued, "Anyway, I thought I'd stay long enough for her to see me waving to her from the crowd, then I'd leave, but I ended up staying for the whole parade." Andrea's face softened. "Before I even saw Beth, when the first band marched by, playing *Stars and Stripes Forever*, I started crying. Not misting up. Full-blown bawling. God, I was so embarrassed."

"Why is that?" asked Rebekah.

"What kind of crying was it?" prompted Myra, "happy crying or sad crying?"

"I'm not sure. I'm not particularly patriotic. I was glad to be there; that much I know. Glad I could be there for Beth, but also glad, I think, just to be out on a pretty day, away from the burdens of my job. And glad that Beth is well enough to march with her baton troupe. Beth's mother has done a remarkable job of helping her. But why would that make me cry?"

"Because, Sugar," said Libby, "we all need to feel like a part of something bigger than ourselves. That's one reason Bud and I go to some of the Jaguar home games instead of watching them on TV. It's much better being there in person, part of the crowd, making fools out of ourselves with the other fans. And," she added, "it's one reason we go to church."

While Andrea was acknowledging Libby's remark with a nod, Margot asked, "Do you think you might have also been a little sad about missing out on all those kinds of activities when you were her age?"

"Yeah, that's possible. I sure wish I had waited until I got home to cry, though," she smiled wistfully.

"Actually," said Myra, "that was a very good thing. By the time you'd gotten home, you might have found a way to avoid having that good cry." Andrea shrugged her shoulders. "Tenderness can feel like a trap, a snare. Remember, we are wired to enjoy and to be enjoyed. If that desire has been taken advantage of, we may learn to mistrust our softness, leading us to experience tenderness as dangerous at the same time it's inviting."

"What do we do when those feelings march all over us?" asked Olivia. "I mean, sometimes I don't even know what I'm feeling. I just know that it hurts and it's scary and it won't go away."

Rebekah and Margot nodded emphatically. Celeste added, "Or when I know what I'm feeling, but there are so many of them at once, I don't know what to do with them."

"Ellis Island," said Myra.

"Huh?" asked Olivia.

"At the turn of the century, most immigrants who were coming into this country had to stop at Ellis Island to be processed first. They had to say who they were and where they were from. Sometimes they were given Americanized names. The point is, one by one, they were acknowledged, they spoke, their names were recorded, and most of them were allowed to enter the country. You have your own Ellis Island of emotions; they've been there, sometimes for years, waiting for you to open your little ledger book and hear them speak their names. So you listen to them, one by one, making note of them. Then you will tell them where to go."

Myra turned to the entire group, "What I'm getting at is this—in the midst of the noise those emotions are making, intruding into your life, demanding your attention, you have the choice of ignoring them, killing their voices, as it were. You can smother your longings under a mountain of television or food or booze, you can refuse to care about other people, you can offer others your mind but not your heart or soul, you can refuse to want or need anything or anyone. Or, you can go watch a little girl march in a parade," she smiled in Andrea's direction, "or have a heart-to-heart conversation with someone you care about," she said, nodding toward Margot, "or write a poem," she looked at Olivia. "Or you can go talk about your story in front of a group of strangers, hoping that some change for the better might come as a result," she said, nodding at Rebekah.

As the CLAMOR Girls were leaving the meeting, inspired to open their Ellis Island ledgers, Andrea walked up beside Libby, tentatively placing her arm around Libby's shoulders. In a low voice, she said, "You're okay, Libby. You're okay."

Twenty-eight

THE PLEASANT WEATHER HAD COAXED azaleas and daffodils into a resurrection of their previous season's glories. March hadn't come roaring in but, rather, floated in gently on balmy ocean breezes. The CLAMOR Girls' post-Ides road trip to Tallahassee began on a Monday evening after all had gotten off work. The legislative sub-committee was scheduled to convene the next morning.

The support group members checked into two adjoining rooms in their hotel and immediately divested themselves of the bondage of pantyhose, high heels, and bras, changing into a vast array of nighttime wear, from old t-shirts and athletic shorts to spaghetti-strapped nightgowns, cut low to reveal impressive cleavages. While Olivia was washing her face in the bathroom and Rebekah was hanging up her dress, Libby brought a Ziploc bag of homemade chocolate chips cookies into the room being shared by Andrea, Celeste, and Margot, offering them around. "I like the way you think," said Celeste, as she pulled a large bag of M&M's out of her overnight bag, throwing them on top of her bed. Their squeals of laughter brought Olivia and Rebekah into the room.

"Oh, Lord," said Olivia, smiling, "what are y'all trying to do to me?"

With that, Margot lifted a bag of baby carrots out of an insulated lunchbox and handed it to Olivia.

"Spoilsport," teased Rebekah. "Chocolate is medicinal, or didn't you know?"

"Somehow I know that no matter how many of these I eat," Olivia lamented, taking a bite of carrot, "they won't taste like chocolate."

In short order, they had all situated themselves around the room, settling into chairs and on the two double beds.

Taking another bite of carrot, Olivia asked Rebekah, "Are you nervous about tomorrow?"

Swallowing a bite of cookie, she answered, "Uh huh. But I'm glad you all are here with me."

"I'm glad we're here, too," said Libby, smiling affectionately at the younger women.

"Do y'all think you'll say anything?" Olivia asked, addressing the others.

Libby answered, "I thought I might. It depends."

Margot shrugged her shoulders. Andrea made a non-committal gesture. Celeste said, "I'm not sure. You?"

"Not me!" said Olivia, shuddering.

Celeste jumped off the bed and went to her cosmetics bag. "One thing's for sure, we're going to look good tomorrow. I'll do everyone's hair and makeup—if you want me to."

Eyes widening, Andrea said, "That won't be necessary. But thanks."

"Oh, come on. I won't make you look like a hooker or anything," Celeste winked, holding her hairbrush in the hand she had on her hip. "C'mon. I'll show you."

Delighted with the idea, Libby said, "Ohhh. Please, Andrea. If you don't like it, you can comb it out and wash it off." Andrea was holding up both her hands in an attempt to stave off Celeste and Libby's intentions.

"Actually, I'd like to see you all dolled up myself," said Margot. Rebekah and Olivia nodded agreement.

Groaning, Andrea relented, saying, "Where is Myra when I need her?"

"Oh, goody," exclaimed Celeste as she fished her curling iron out of her bag and plugged it in.

"What all do you have in there?" asked Olivia, amazed at the bounty of beauty supplies.

"Look for yourself. Use whatever you want." Celeste was giddy with the prospect of transforming Andrea. "Sit here," she commanded, pointing at a spot in front of the bureau mirror.

Mutely, Andrea complied while Olivia and Rebekah explored the contents of Celeste's makeup bag. With deft, sure movements, Celeste brushed and curled Andrea's hair, all while engaging in conversation with the women in the room.

"What's this for?" asked Olivia, holding up a comb with assorted-sized teeth.

"That's supposed to give your hair more body. You lift from underneath. Try it." While the others munched and chatted and primped, Celeste continued to work confidently with her reluctant charge.

"Do you believe every woman is beautiful, like Myra does?" Olivia asked Celeste, biting into another carrot. "I mean, you must have seen some really beautiful women in your business—at the hairdresser's, I mean." Olivia blushed. "And you must have seen some who aren't pretty at all."

Celeste laughed good-naturedly. Margot interrupted, "Myra believes all girls are born beautiful, but the way Myra defines beauty has nothing to do with being pretty."

Olivia's brow furrowed. "What do you mean? I thought Myra was trying to get us all to believe in ourselves, to give us some self-esteem. You know, how a mama tells her little girl she's beautiful—'cause she's her mom."

Andrea snorted, "Some mothers."

Rebekah spoke. "I think Margot's right. Myra wouldn't necessarily associate what we call pretty with being beautiful. Like being beautiful is who you are and being pretty is how you appear."

"Oh. Well, do y'all believe every woman is beautiful?"

"Sugar, every girl starts out that way," Libby interjected. "I think that's what Myra wants us to realize. But sometimes, along the way, we stop believing it. We either don't hear it enough or we learn to equate being beautiful—being female—with danger. Wouldn't y'all agree?"

"Well I don't think I'm very pretty at all," said Olivia, matter-of-factly. "So, if being beautiful is who I *am*, how do I *do* that? How do I know I'm beautiful?"

Rebekah, once again touched by Olivia's simple, yet astute, observations, responded, "Good question. How *do* we know we're beautiful?"

"Tenderness," Margot responded. "For one."

Andrea squirmed in her chair. Celeste, who was trying to apply eye shadow to her eyelids, said, "Hold still." Then, "But can't men be tender, too?"

"Being receptive. That's part of it, too, don't you think?" offered Libby. "After all," she blushed, "look at the way we're designed—physically, I mean."

"Ahhh," said Margot, "that's where the danger lies." Some concurred by the nodding of their heads.

"Where does our strength, as women, lie, do you think?" asked Libby.

"Hmm," said Rebekah. "Another good question. Ladies?" She performed a perfect imitation of Myra's broad, sweeping gesture.

"Well, first of all, look at all of us," said Celeste. "We've all survived some really bad things. And here we are, alive to tell about it. So maybe, part of our strength is in the sheer will to survive."

"Tenacity," offered Andrea, wincing with Celeste's application of eyeliner.

"Yeah, but without losing our sensitivity," said Rebekah. "And without telling the whole world to go screw itself."

"Just parts of the world," quipped Andrea.

"Yeah, different parts on different days," said Margot.

"Maybe part of our strength is being able to still see the good things in the middle of bad things," Olivia thought out loud.

"And staying intact in the midst of insanity," Rebekah added. "Still smiling at the bank teller or the dry cleaner when really you're crying on the inside."

"Or still appreciating a gorgeous sunset, even though nights are the most difficult and lonely time of day," offered Margot.

"Yeah," Celeste agreed.

"Yeah," Olivia chimed in. Then, "So we're beautiful because we're alive, right? Not because we're particularly attractive."

"I think so, Honey," said Libby. "At least, that's probably what Myra would say."

"I think Myra would also remind us," said Margot, "that being alive is a choice. The kind of alive that is evidenced by a generosity of heart and spirit, not just by breathing. That's willing to take a chance on people."

"Insanely involved," Celeste said, putting the finishing touches on Andrea's mascara, "even though so many things have told us to drop out of life, to give up on people, including ourselves. To keep working at our lives without our hearts sealed off."

"Which means we can grow," said Libby, who then gasped in wonder as Celeste stepped away from Andrea. "My Lord, child, you are a sight to behold!" Libby clasped her hands together like an excited child on Christmas morning.

Celeste smiled appreciatively as the rest of the group expressed their amazement. "See, I didn't use much make-up at all. I just tried to accentuate her natural features. And, Andrea," she added, "you have great hair."

Andrea smiled self-consciously, looking between Celeste and the others at the mirror, trying to reconcile the image staring back at her with the one she had seen for so many years in her mirror at home.

"Well? What do you think?" asked Rebekah.

"This would take some getting used to," said Andrea. Then, to Celeste, "What I mean is, I like it. I think. But I don't see myself this way. You're really good. A magician."

Celeste smiled. "Thanks. But I'll tell you what I tell my customers. I'm not a miracle worker; it all depends on what you have to work with. In your case, you have good hair, good skin, and pretty features. They just need a little attention. And don't we all… ?"

Twenty-nine

THE NEXT MORNING, AFTER A quick continental breakfast at the hotel, the CLAMOR Girls met Casey and Lorelei outside a meeting room in the Senate office building. The session was to be presided over by Senator Harvey Burkhalter, chair of the Senate Crime Prevention, Corrections, and Safety Committee. Lorelei introduced the women to the senator while Casey clasped Rebekah's hand between her two, occasionally giving it an affectionate squeeze.

Lorelei turned to the women and assured them, "This will be real informal. You'll come to the seat where the microphone is because the proceedings are being tape-recorded, but there won't be any video recording." Her voice reminded Rebekah of Libby's—deeply Southern and cultured and caring. "At any time during our time together, if you want to say something for the record, just slip out of your seat and come to the front. Our transcriptionist will record your name, but identities will be kept strictly confidential. She already knows Casey and Rebekah intend to speak. Anyone have any questions?" Upon getting a mute response, Lorelei said, "Good. We'll get started in a few minutes. You're telling a story that badly needs telling, so thank you. Thank you for your great courage and willingness." She smiled at the CLAMOR Girls. Despite the gravity of the occasion, her warmth helped set the women more at ease. *Now I know why Casey is so fond of her*, Rebekah thought.

The meeting chamber was set up with two long tables, end to end, at the head of the room. At the table sat Senator Burkhalter, two other

Senate subcommittee members, Senators Hall and Paris, Lorelei, and Dr. Elaine Warren, a Licensed Marriage and Family Therapist with a Ph.D. and ten years of experience in counseling victims of sexual abuse. The transcriptionist's desk was to the right of the long tables. A chair and a single, smaller table with a microphone were positioned directly across from the long tables. Two rows of chairs had been set up for those testifying or observing. Each table had been set with a water pitcher and glasses. Another table with coffee and water was set up at the back of the room, near the door. Boxes of Kleenex had been strategically placed at every table and at both ends of each row of chairs. The CLAMOR Girls, by some tacit prearrangement, homed in on the second row of chairs, while guests from counseling and law enforcement sat in the front row. Despite the pleasant temperature outdoors, the room was chilly. Margot leaned over to Rebekah and whispered, "I think our legislature is doing experiments in cryogenics."

Rebekah responded, "That might explain why we can't get rid of some of them."

As the proceedings commenced, the mood in the room was somber and anxious. With her left thumb, Rebekah nervously twisted her wedding band around and around her ring finger. Her heart pounded wildly inside her chest and her bagel threatened to reintroduce itself.

Before Senator Burkhalter could make his preliminary remarks, the transcriptionist indicated there was a problem with some of her equipment. The Senator called for a brief break while a member of the Information Technology team brought in replacement equipment. Rebekah slipped out of her seat and across Casey's lap and went to the restroom, followed by her Thursday night cohort. "You okay?" Margot asked, as Rebekah exited a stall.

"I guess. As okay as I can be under the circumstances. I'd almost rather be getting a root canal, though." Her smile didn't convince anyone.

As Rebekah went to the sink to wash her hands and splash some water on her face, Margot asked, "How come you didn't want your mom to come today?"

"I thought I'd be able to speak more freely if I wasn't worried about her feeling incriminated somehow. As much as I'd like her here with me, I just don't think she's ready to be immersed in this."

Libby sidled up next to her and whispered, "You'll do just fine. I'm praying for you."

"Thanks. I'm sure I need it."

Andrea, who had opted for Celeste's hair-taming and a light application of lipstick, but not, as she put it, "the full froufrou," was the first to leave the restroom. With her hand on the door, she turned around and said to the others, "All you have to do is tell it like it is. That's usually what I tell the kids who have to testify against a perp. Let's go get 'em." With a pilot's thumbs up, she left the restroom.

"Yeah, let's go get 'em," said Celeste.

Once the women returned to their seats, Burkhalter was ready to resume. In his booming, central Florida, gentleman-farmer voice, giving each syllable its own due, he called, "Dr. Greer, please step forward." Rebekah turned to Casey and smiled as Casey stood up. Rebekah grabbed her friend's hand and squeezed encouragement.

Casey stepped up to the single table and adjusted her seat so that her arms folded comfortably on top of the table. She pulled the microphone close to her mouth. Senator Burkhalter cleared his throat, then spoke. "Please state your name clearly for the record."

"Casey Greer."

The senator turned to his peers at the table and said, "I had the privilege of eating dinner last evening with Dr. Greer and Dr. Mackenzie—Lorelei. I've known Lorelei for years. She's from my district and worked on my campaign for re-election. She has more energy in her pinky finger than I have in my entire body." Rebekah couldn't help comparing his considerable girth and double chin with Lorelei's trim body: *Go figure.* "Her tireless efforts have made these proceedings today possible. Dr. Greer has also shown a tremendous amount of courage, not only in rising above her circumstances, but also in helping make today possible. I thank you both for taking time out of your busy schedules to come, to help us address the need for a change in sentencing guidelines."

Casey smiled. "Thank *you*, Senator Burkhalter. And please, call me Casey."

"Okay. Casey it is. Dr., uh, Casey, please tell us how you became involved in these proceedings."

"I'm a client of Lorelei's. Twenty-odd years ago, my father abused a childhood friend of mine. He was arrested and he hanged himself in prison before his case ever went to trial. As I grew into adulthood, I became interested in how crimes of this nature are prosecuted. Lorelei asked me to speak."

"Now, for the record, Casey," intoned Senator Burkhalter, "what do you mean when you say your father abused a friend? For the record."

Rebekah shifted uncomfortably in her chair as Casey answered, "He sexually molested my friend."

"So we are talking about capital sexual battery on a minor," he said, reminding the panel seated at the head table, who all nodded their understanding. "Please tell us, Casey, did your father ever do something similar to you?"

"No, sir, not to my knowledge."

"Then, may I ask, what is your personal stake in this?"

Casey looked surprised, unsure of whether or not to be shocked or defensive. She looked up at the members of the panel, her eyes passing between Lorelei and Senator Burkhalter. The two other senators attended to the note pads in front of them. Dr. Warren, neatly manicured and highlighted, dressed in a stylish lightweight winter wool suit, was the picture of professional composure, as if years of hearing similar stories had permanently prevented her from becoming ruffled. Lorelei smiled quizzically, but encouragingly. Finally, Senator Burkhalter broke the silence, "Tell this panel what you told me at dinner last night."

Casey expelled the doubt from her lungs in one long sigh, and then said, "My personal stake in this is that, even though I was not sexually molested by my father, my family was still a victim. What I mean by that is his actions affected every aspect of my family life. Not only did his actions cause tremendous embarrassment to my mother, they resulted in him losing his job, our only source of income. We had to move to central Florida, in with my mother's parents, Grandma and Grandpa Greer. I was not allowed to contact my best friend. My mother had a nervous breakdown and spent months in a hospital. And I struggled for years trying to find a place to put all my questions and reservations. After all, if a little girl cannot trust her father, cannot trust her pastor, where can she go with that? What change machine can I put those coins in and get something back that fits the slots?"

"Excuse me," interrupted Senator Paris. She was a short, overweight, friendly-looking woman with more-salt-than-pepper hair. Her glasses, with a silver-colored chain wrapped around the back of her neck, were anchored by some mysterious force to the very tip of her nose. "You lost me. You father. He was a pastor?"

"Yes, ma'am. He was a pastor."

Senator Paris scowled. A brief flicker of disgust crossed Dr. Warren's face. Senator Hall scribbled on his note pad. Senator Paris asked, "If I may ask, what have you found to be the, uh, peculiar implications of that?"

Casey nodded in understanding. "As a child, growing up in church, I was taught that Jesus loves the little children." She smiled and continued, her voice gentle and sure. "Church is viewed, wrongly or rightly, as a place that offers refuge from the insanity of what's going on in the world," she pointed at the window—*out there.* "If nothing else in life makes sense, children are taught that God knows, God cares, God numbers the hairs on their sweet little heads. And whatever sense you can't make of the insanity going on in the world, there's amazing grace to undergird you. But, you see, if that insanity has infiltrated the minister's home, where can his family or a member of his congregation turn to? Where, now, is their refuge?"

Aware that she was failing in her explanation, Casey paused, pouring herself a glass of water. She took a few sips, then continued, leaning farther in toward the microphone. "In some ways, being a preacher's child or a preacher's spouse isn't easy. You invite a lot of scrutiny into your life. People watch what you do, how you act, what you say, even what you wear. There are worse things in life, granted, and one of the ways you turn the fishbowl into a positive experience is to make yourself articulate why you do the things that you do. If it's because you're being watched, and you'd choose another way if you weren't always being observed and evaluated, you have an opportunity to know yourself better. And to know what your faith is really about. If, on the other hand, you do what you do because it grows out of what you believe, then you sacrifice some of your privacy for a higher cause. You're generally okay with the scrutiny.

"My father, though, refused to scrutinize his own heart but he let Mama and me believe that it was important that we continue to represent him and his profession respectfully. So when he was arrested after molesting my friend, everything we thought we had stood for as a family marched off to jail with him. It all felt like a lie. If amazing grace wasn't enough for him, what did that mean for us? I have spent the last 20 years of my life and will probably spend the rest of my life trying to answer that question."

Senator Paris smiled warmly at Casey. "Thank you for being so honest. I know it has nothing to do with this hearing, but I'd sure love to know if you attend church or if you quit going."

"I didn't for a long time. But I'm learning to separate out what is human and what is divine, or at least ought to be. It has been a long, excruciating journey, I'll tell you that. And it still is, at times."

"I must say, I admire you."

"Thank you. I don't think I've done anything particularly admirable. My friends," Casey turned around and smiled at Rebekah and the others, "the ones who have been molested. They're the real heroes in this room."

Rebekah stiffened in her chair. Clutching her purse to her chest, she stood and quickly moved to the door and exited. Her friends looked at each other with concern. By invisible poll, Margot was selected to follow her.

Senator Burkhalter cleared his throat, drawing attention back to the front of the room. "Dr. Greer, uh, Casey, is there anything else you'd like to say to this panel?"

"I don't think so, sir. Just thank you for the opportunity to talk about a subject many people hope will go away if they ignore it."

"Then we'll hear from the next person." As Casey pushed back her chair, the senator looked at the transcriptionist and asked, "Who's next on the list?"

"Rebekah Wilkins-Standifer."

"Rebekah Wilkins-Standifer, please step forward."

Casey turned around in the aisle and faced the long table. "I believe she's stepped out, sir."

Casey looked at the other CLAMOR Girls questioningly. They apologetically hunched their shoulders, just as puzzled and concerned as Casey. Senator Burkhalter spoke again. "These are not formal hearings, so if anyone else would like to speak, may I ask that you come up to the center table now?"

They looked among each other. Lorelei tried not to show her disappointment at the prospect of having only one person's testimony. She crossed her fingers underneath the tablecloth skirt. Presently, Libby stood up and moved out into the aisle. She stood at the small table in front of the panel. Lorelei exhaled relief.

Senator Burkhalter asked, "What is your name, please?"

She nervously replied, "Libby Hopkins, your honor, um, sir."

He looked at the transcriptionist, who nodded her head. "Please have a seat, Ms. Hopkins," he said, indicating with his hand the chair at the table. Libby pulled the seat up to the table and folded her hands uncertainly in her lap.

"Now, Ms. Hopkins, would you please tell this panel what your personal interest is in this issue?"

"Um, okay. And it's Mrs. Hopkins, or Libby." Lorelei smiled reassuringly at her. "My personal interest in this issue goes back lots of years, to when I was a little girl, about five years old. I was molested by my mother's uncle. It happened once, and I didn't tell anyone about it until I started seeing a therapist about a year ago. And, honestly, I forgot about it until then. At least, I thought I had forgotten about it. But in the last year I've come to realize that, while part of your mind forgets or tries to forget about something like that, the rest of you remembers."

"Would you elaborate on that for us, please?" the senator asked.

For comfort, Libby rubbed her forefingers and thumbs together in a circular motion in her lap. "Well, I learned not to trust my body. I mean, I didn't listen to it. I felt at odds with my body; ashamed of it, really. Looking back, I realize that ever since I was five, my body has been trying to tell a story, trying to get me, someone, anyone, to recognize that something bad happened." She paused, attempting to still her quivering chin, then continued, "It's really stunning when you think about it, how one event can shape the rest of your life, even when you've tried to push that event into a foot locker in your mind. It's still in there, tapping, knocking, demanding to be heard. And I'm sorry to say, my daughter became an unwitting victim. All my misgivings about my body, I passed on to her. To the point where she was hospitalized for an eating disorder."

Libby swallowed hard, blinking back tears, and forced herself to continue. "Even my husband has been a loser in this. In all the years we've been married, I can't say that I've really enjoyed sex." She tried to clear the knot in her throat, then staring at a spot above the heads of the panel members, explained, "Oh, I've never refused him. Sexually. I have been a dutiful lover. But I've never initiated sex with him, and I've never really let myself go with him, either. Frankly, I usually count the dots on the ceiling tiles or make my grocery list," she admitted. "I endure sex."

Dr. Warren smiled knowingly—a story she had heard repeatedly. Senator Burkhalter, uncomfortable with such a forthright confession, cleared his throat. Lorelei kept her steady gaze on Libby, willing her strength. Senators Paris and Hall continued their note-taking. At that moment, Margot and Rebekah re-entered the room, Rebekah ashen. As they returned to their seats, Casey, Olivia, and Celeste leaned over to whisper their concern.

Senator Burkhalter cleared his throat again. "Ms., ur, Mrs. Hopkins, thank you for your honesty. Is there anything else you'd like to say to this panel?"

"Yes, sir, there is. What I need for y'all to know is that the toll from sexual abuse cannot possibly be calculated at first. No insurance adjustor in the world could assess the damage. It reveals itself over time, even in the best of family situations. And since sex offenders are one of the most difficult prison populations to rehabilitate, they need to remain incarcerated to allow their victims to get a handle on life. I cannot imagine what it would be like trying to deal with something like this knowing that the person who molested me was out, free to do it again, to me or to anyone else. They don't belong out here," she motioned around the room, "with the rest of us. They just don't."

"Thank you, Mrs. Hopkins."

As Libby was returning to her seat, Senator Burkhalter asked, "Would Ms.," he leaned over to look at the transcriptionist's list, "Ms. Wilkins-Standifer like to testify now?"

Margot stood up and spoke. "Rebekah, Ms. Standifer, is not feeling well. She asks to be excused from speaking, sir." Margot sat as Libby returned to her seat. The others patted her on her shoulders.

Disappointment flooded Lorelei's face. Burkhalter spoke again, "As I stated earlier, these are not formal hearings. This is more like a fact-finding mission. No one is under any obligation to speak, but if anyone else from your group would like to speak, please step forward now."

They looked among each other. Casey placed an arm around Rebekah's shoulders as Libby whispered, "What happened? Are you okay?"

Rebekah, deflated, whispered back, "I just can't do it. I thought I could, but I can't." Libby patted her arm, smiling weakly.

Margot, gulping in a lungful of air, stood up again and made her way to the center table. She sat in the chair and placed her trembling hands in her lap.

Senator Burkhalter's voice boomed, "Name, please?"

"My name is Margot Jeter."

The transcriptionist looked toward the senator, who asked, "How do you spell that, please? For our records."

"M-A-R-G-O-T," she paused, "J-E-T-E-R."

"Thank you, Ms. Jeter. Now then, please tell this panel what your personal interest is in these proceedings."

Margot looked down at the table, bracing her hands against her knees. She closed her eyes then, after exhaling slowly, looked up, directly at Senator Burkhalter. She then scanned the panel, stopping at each face to make eye contact. Lorelei smiled warmly at her. The others tried to maintain their professional composure. Then Margot spoke, "For several years, when I was a young girl, the superintendent of the apartment building where my mother and I lived molested me. He used the threat of eviction to insure my silence. That abuse continued into my early adolescent years, until he, Mr. Jackson, the superintendent, was fired. I suffered his abuses in silence to protect my mother and myself, but the cost to me was greater than I could have realized at the time. I could not have imagined, at eight, nine, ten, eleven years old, how great my shame would be."

Margot's voice, gathering strength and assurance, continued, "Unless you have experienced this particular form of degradation, you cannot imagine how the base behavior of a one-man demolition crew can affect almost every aspect of your life. It still amazes and infuriates me that someone can take advantage of a child, in such a deeply personal and private way and, yet, it is the child who is left feeling foolish, afraid, and deeply ashamed. It really is as if *they* do the crime, but *we* do the time. I have, in many ways, been imprisoned by my fears and humiliation. I don't trust easily. I am not just cautious, I am wary. For me to allow someone to get close to me, I have to override an automatic response to keep everyone at arm's length. And that has, at times, made me a very lonely person."

Margot paused, inhaled and exhaled deeply. "So, when someone robs you of your sexuality when you are too young to make that choice for yourself, within the confines of a loving relationship, that person is also robbing you of your future, your peace of mind, your sense of well-being." Margot sat back.

Senator Paris leaned forward. "I know this is a deeply personal question," she said, peering over the edges of her glasses, "and by asking this, I'm confessing my ignorance, but what do you mean when you say you were molested?"

"For me," Margot replied, leaning again toward the microphone, "it meant I was fondled and sodomized repeatedly. To this day, I still have difficulty even going to the dentist."

Dr. Warren and Lorelei nodded, unsurprised. "Thank you," Senator Paris croaked. "I appreciate your candor." Senators Burkhalter and Hall squirmed in their chairs.

Senator Burkhalter then asked, "Is there anything else you would like to say to this panel, Ms. Jeter?"

"Yes, sir. I would just like to add to something my friend, Libby, said a moment ago. She mentioned that, statistically, sexual predators are a difficult population to rehabilitate. I believe we," she looked back at the other women in the room, "would all say that these people—molesters, abusers, pedophiles—are good at what they do. By that, I mean they are good at lying, good at manipulating, good at pretending, good at intimidating their victims. While they are in prison, they are in a very controlled environment. They are not faced with choices about whether or not to act on their impulses. Where there are no children, there are not choices. I firmly believe that they have used up their opportunities to exercise choice and I don't think they should have that chance again."

"Thank you. Thank you, Ms. Jeter." Margot nodded and stood up. As she returned to her seat, Senator Burkhalter asked, "Is there someone else who would like to speak?"

There was a stirring in the row of seats occupied by the CLAMOR Girls as Olivia stood up. She tugged nervously at her sweater, wrapping it around her as if a hard wind had just blown into the room. When she reached the center table, she stood by the chair hesitantly, unsure of what to do next. She looked behind her, almost as if looking for the unseen force that had propelled her there.

"Name, please?"

In a voice that was reedy with panic, she said, "Olivia Franklin."

With a quick glance at the transcriptionist, he boomed, "Have a seat, please."

Olivia started. Then, placing her hands on the table, she lowered herself into the chair, not trusting her wobbly knees to support the effort. Senator Burkhalter waited for her to get settled then, in a more restrained voice, continued. "Now, tell us, young lady, what is your personal interest in this subject?"

"Um," she squeaked, "after my mama died, my daddy, he, um," she coughed to clear her throat, "he started coming in my room at night to, um, have sex with me."

The members of the panel waited for her to continue. After an uncomfortable silence, with the two male senators shifting in their chairs, Lorelei spoke gently. "Harvey, Senator Burkhalter, would you mind?" she gestured with her head toward Olivia.

"By all means. Go right ahead."

"Olivia. It is Olivia, right?" Olivia nodded and Lorelei continued. "Olivia, how old were you when this started?"

"Twelve."

"And how long did this continue?" Lorelei's voice was soothing, calm.

Olivia stopped to count years in her head. "About six years."

Senator Paris sat up straight. "Six years?! My God, however did you endure it?"

Olivia, childlike, answered, "At first, I didn't have a choice. But when I thought about telling him no, I was afraid he'd go after my baby sister." She paused. "I bet you people are wondering why we," she motioned with her head toward her friends seated behind her, "why we didn't tell somebody. You've got to realize that they have their way of keeping you from telling. They tell you lies—sometimes lies you want to hear, sometimes threats. You're more afraid to tell than not to."

"Is your father still living?" asked Senator Burkhalter.

"As far as I know. I figure he'll work at the paper mill until his retirement kicks in. After my sister died, I quit having anything to do with him."

"Would you ever consider a lawsuit against him?" Senator Paris asked.

"I never even thought about it until a couple of months ago. I don't think I'm ready to do that right now, but I still might some day. If I knew that *he* knew he was the cause of my sister killing herself, if I knew that would haunt him 'til his dying day, I'd say that was punishment enough. But who knows? Maybe I will."

"Can you help us understand—I assume your father told you he loved you. How did he excuse his behavior?" Senator Paris asked.

"Well, for one, I don't remember him telling me he loved me. Maybe he did, but I kind of think maybe he didn't—doesn't—even love himself. He probably thought he loved me. *I* probably thought he did. But one of the things I tell my son—he's eight—is that some monsters smile at you. Not all monsters have scary faces. If it feels bad, if it feels wrong, I tell Tyler, 'you tell somebody,'" she said firmly. "I wish somebody would've told me that."

"That's very good advice," Lorelei said, smiling. "Very good advice."

"Well, if I can keep my son from going through what I've gone through…. I never want him to feel as lonely and as different as I have. That's the crazy thing. Someone does something bad to you, and you're the one who ends up thinking there's something wrong with you."

There was another silence. In a voice tinged with paternal compassion, Senator Burkhalter asked, "Miss Olivia, is there anything else you'd like to tell this panel?"

"No, sir, I don't think so."

"Thank you for talking with us today. You may return to your seat."

Lorelei caught Olivia's eye as she rose, thanking her with her warm gaze. As Olivia walked back to her seat, Senator Burkhalter asked, "Is there anyone else who would like to address this panel? Please step forward."

Celeste stood up quickly. She strode to the front with a false bravado that fooled several panel members, but none of her friends. They saw the vulnerability masquerading behind her poise.

"Your name, please."

"Celeste O'Farrell, O apostrophe F-A-R-R-E-L-L," she responded, then sat, positioning herself close to the microphone.

"Now, Ms. O'Farrell,"

"Celeste," she interrupted.

"Celeste, please tell this panel what your personal interest is in this subject."

"I'm one of those people that therapists say doesn't have complete resident memory of her abuse. My memories return in bits and pieces. But like my friend, Libby, mentioned, a person's body remembers. Somewhere deep down, I've known for years that something was wrong. And for years I assumed what was wrong was the environment my mother was bringing me up in—alcohol, multiple boyfriends, no ambition in life except to figure out who was going to provide her with the next bottle of booze. So I thought that as soon as I could get out of there, my life would turn around."

She paused for effect. "And it did. For a while. But I ended up with a son born out of wedlock and a drug habit. I knew I wanted a better life for my son, but it wasn't until he was put into foster care and I was admitted into a drug treatment program that I began listening to what all the years of hurt and neglect and abuse were trying to tell me."

Celeste reached for a Kleenex and dabbed at her nose and eyes. "And what they were trying to tell me was, 'Pay attention. We have a story to tell.'" She blew her nose. "But who wants to listen to that kind of story? Who wants to get bummed out and hurt all over again? But my therapist convinced me, over the course of many, many months," she smiled, remembering Myra's patience and persistence, "that if I didn't let that pain tell its story, then I'd spend the rest of my life on the run. So," she added, "I could hurt like hell right now, while I deal with the past, or I could have a low grade hurt forever and keep looking for ways to shut it up."

Senator Paris and Dr. Warren smiled at Celeste's frankness. Lorelei continued to smile supportively. The men on the panel fidgeted.

Senator Hall leaned forward. "Are you telling us," he asked, a hint of skepticism in his voice, "that there is a direct correlation between your drug habit and being, um, molested?" He rocked back in his comfortable desk chair, elbows on the armrests, and parked the fingertips of his slender, short body on his slight paunch.

"Yes, sir, I am. I am telling you that after burying the memories of my mother's boyfriends doing unspeakable things to me, I was attempting to keep those memories anesthetized. Really, if it weren't for my son, I'd probably still be selling my body for my next hit," she responded, her voice cutting. "That's what I'm telling you."

Dr. Warren nodded slightly. Lorelei reached for a Kleenex.

"And I'm telling you that, even with motivation, like trying to regain custody of my son, it isn't easy. I know I put on this show of self-confidence—almost like 'to hell with 'em'—but the truth is, that old adage of three steps forward, two steps back is true. I'm scared every day of my life. Scared of messing up, scared of hurting, scared to get out of bed but even more scared not to. Scared to try; scared not to. And the truth is, I do mess up."

Celeste stopped to settle an internal debate. "As badly as I want my son back, it wasn't enough a few months ago to keep me from relapsing." She heard a few gasps from the CLAMOR Girls seated behind her. "It's true. The only people who knew that up until now were my case worker and my therapist. Just as you die little by little inside when you are molested, you learn how to get your life back in little slices. Little slices with big gaps in between. God, how I hate those gaps."

Senator Burkhalter glanced at his watch and broke the ensuing silence by saying, "Well, Ms. O'Fa . . ., Celeste, you have certainly engaged us with your honesty. If you have nothing else to share, I suggest we take a brief break." Celeste shook her head. Relief in his voice, the senator continued, "In that case, let's take a 15-minute break. We may have some wrap-up questions," he said, looking down the row of panelists.

Several members of the panel compared notes while Casey and the CLAMOR Girls convened in the hallway outside the conference room.

Rebekah apologized to her friends. "I just can't do it. I'm so sorry I dragged you all here to support me and then I chickened out."

"Honey, you didn't drag us here," said Libby, while the others nodded. "We offered to come."

With assurances from everyone that they understood, Rebekah added, "I just knew that I would throw up if I had to talk to them." She turned to Casey and said, "Lorelei is great. She smiles and listens; she seems to really get it."

Celeste said, "That Dr. Warren has heard it all before, did you notice? Why is she here, you think?"

Casey spoke. "Lorelei told me the senators on the subcommittee asked for a local therapist to be on their committee so she can offer her professional expertise on the validity of our testimony and assist them in crafting their legislation. They hope to make the cross-over deadline by the fall term. And you're right. So far, I don't think she's heard anything here today that she hasn't heard in her practice. They're probably picking her brain right now."

Margot spoke next, "Okay, I like that Senator Paris, but what is going on with those other two?"

"They're men," said Andrea, by way of explanation. "I've seen it before. When testimony involves what men, grown men, have done to children, every man in the courtroom squirms."

"I find Senator Burkhalter almost patronizing, though," said Margot. "Almost too eager to prove that he's sympathetic. Do you think he's uncomfortable with the subject of their 'fact-finding mission'?"

Casey answered, "He is. He's trying to act professional, but the fact is he has a young granddaughter he adores, and he knows the statistics. It's difficult for him to separate the grandfather out from the legislator. He's really a marshmallow inside."

"What's the deal with Senator Hall?" asked Rebekah, looking sympathetically at Celeste. Then, "I think you sort of threw him for a loop, Celeste."

Andrea's usual caustic tone about men was replaced with generous insight. She said, "Oh, him. He just doesn't get it. He grew up in the school of 'so something bad happened; get over it.' None of what we've been telling him today squares with that. He's lost, really, but I think he's fairly harmless."

The proceedings resumed and Senator Burkhalter reminded the women that anyone who wished to speak was allowed to, including anyone who had thought of something else she wanted to say. There was a brief lull. The women sat quietly, turning thoughts over in their minds. Hesitantly, Andrea stood up. She pulled at the edges of her sleeves while making her way to the small table. After she sat down and pulled the microphone closer, Senator Burkhalter asked, "What is your name, please?"

"Andrea Robinson," she answered in her typical clipped Boston accent.

"What would you like to tell this panel about your experience with the subject?"

"The subject of sexual predators? And how so many of them get off with light sentences? That subject?" Andrea questioned.

Senator Burkhalter's eyes widened and he involuntarily moved his head back. "Uh, yes, ma'am. That's what I'm talking about."

"What I can tell this panel," Andrea began, matter-of-factly, "is that as both a survivor of sexual abuse by my older brother and his friends and as a professional law enforcement officer in the Duval County Sex Crimes Unit, I see effects of sexual abuse every day." Senator Paris sat forward. Andrea continued, "The toll sexual abuse takes on victims and their families is too broad, too wide, too deep to comprehend unless you are walking in their shoes. And I will tell you, as a professional, one of the concerns of young victims who have had to testify against their abusers is when those perpetrators will get out of prison. You can see the parents calculate in their heads how old their son or daughter will be when the abuser gets out. As far as I'm concerned, these children shouldn't be asking *when* their abusers will get out; the question they should be asking is *why* their abusers will get out."

"May I ask," Senator Hall cut in, "is your professional opinion somehow clouded by the fact that you are also a, as you put it, survivor?"

Dr. Warren, visibly angry, made a move toward her microphone. Then Andrea answered brusquely, "Yes, sir, you may ask that. And, no sir, it does not cloud my judgment. That is an issue I settled within myself a long time ago. If anything, it makes me better at my job. I know what questions to ask kids to set them at ease; I know what signs to look for in families where abuse is occurring with a parent's blind consent."

"I'm sorry," Lorelei interrupted. "Could you clarify what you mean by blind consent?"

"That's a phrase I use to describe some families where there are signs the child is being abused, but certain family members choose to ignore those signs. Sometimes it's a father who is the abuser, and the mother, fearing for her own security, overlooks the signals the child may be using to cry out for help. Sometimes," her voice suddenly cracked, "an older brother is the abuser and neither parent will take note of the ways the child is trying to indicate something is wrong."

Another hard block of grief, for years kept in check by stoicism and anger, shattered, releasing hot tears down Andrea's made-up cheeks. The room was quiet except for the sound of her sobs, along with the shared sniffling of her friends. Her voice husky with emotion, Andrea leaned toward the microphone and said, "I'm sorry. I don't usually do this," and a fresh wave of emotion rocked her body. Libby made her way up to the table. She leaned down and put her arms around Andrea's shoulders.

At that moment, the door at the back of the room clicked open and a small, round face, wrinkled with age, creased with years of hard work and compassion, peered in. The women seated together looked back. Casey stood up, "Grandma!"

Grandma Greer smiled broadly, opening the door wider. With her was a tall, elegantly weathered gentleman and a diminutive woman, scarecrow thin, years of sorrow etched into the crepe paper wrinkles around her eyes. "Grandpa! Mama!" said Casey, making her way to the back of the room. "What are y'all doing here?" she asked, hugging each of them tightly.

Senator Burkhalter spoke. "It appears that this would be a good time to take another brief break. Ten minutes?" The other panelists nodded in agreement.

After the break, the panel reconvened to find Annette Greer, Casey's mother, seated at the small table. Casey was seated in a chair she had removed from the row of chairs and placed beside her mother. She leaned over, holding the frail woman's hand.

"What is your name, please?" asked Senator Burkhalter. "Annette Greer."

"And are you Dr. Greer's, Casey's, mother?"

"Yes, sir," her voice was as tiny as her frame. She squeezed Casey's hand.

Senator Burkhalter glanced between Annette Greer and the transcriptionist, who nodded to indicate she had recorded the name. He then continued, "Please tell us, Ms. Greer, what your interest is in the panel's attempts to explore the possibility, the merits, of changing the sentencing guidelines for sex offenders."

Annette Greer nodded in small, jerky movements. Everything about her existence seemed spare—her wrists and ankles and neck, noticeably birdlike, even clothed in garments seemingly too bulky for her frail form to support; her mannerisms; her facial expressions; her timid, tremulous voice; her emotional demeanor. All were indicators of a shell of a woman, a person reduced to the frame of her existence. The room was quiet as Annette withdrew her hand from Casey's and placed both on the table in front of her, every knuckle and vein and tendon accentuated by premature aging and frailty.

She clasped her hands together and leaned forward. "I was married to a man who was a sex offender," she stated. "Casey's father," she inclined her head slightly in Casey's direction. "If he had not killed himself in jail… If he had stood trial and been sent to prison, he would probably either already be out or at least eligible for parole while the little girl he molested in our home is, as a woman, still coming to terms with what he did to her." She rotated in her chair stiffly and looked over her shoulder at Rebekah, smiling sadly, almost apologetically at her. Tears trickled down Rebekah's cheeks.

Because Casey had talked openly with Lorelei about her childhood with her father, and because she had shared a meal with Senator Burkhalter the previous evening, they had already made the connection that the other panel members were just beginning to make between Casey and Annette and Rebekah, the woman who had abruptly left the room earlier—the very woman who had, since, declined to speak. Lorelei smiled warmly at Annette then Casey then Rebekah. Senator Paris sat at full attention. Dr. Warren, intrigued, picked up her pen and note pad. Senator Hall, who had been leaning back in his chair, polishing his glasses lenses with a handkerchief, stopped mid-smudge and placed his glasses back on his face, sitting up straighter.

"Now, Ms. Greer, I'm just playing devil's advocate here, so please bear with me." Senator Burkhalter spoke, using a softer voice than usual. "How can you be sure of the truth of your statement—that she's still coming to terms with what your husband did to her?" His fear of upsetting this delicate woman was nearly palpable, as if one wrong word from him would cause her to snap like a brittle twig. "It has been about 20 years, hasn't it?"

Pulling her small frame up to its full height, Annette spoke in quiet, distinct, sure tones. "Yes, it has been 20 years. And I am still haunted by what he did to her. And if I am haunted, then there is a strong likelihood that she is, too. I don't know how much you know about the after-effects of sexual abuse, but the victim's recognition of damage and the healing from that tends to come in waves. When a man molests a little girl, he is not only molesting her as a child, but he is also marking her adolescence, her child-bearing years, and other times of transition in her life."

Dr. Warren was nodding in agreement, sure that this Annette Greer had done her homework, had thoroughly researched 'the subject.' "He is handing her a life sentence of self-esteem and trust issues." As an afterthought, almost to herself, she added, "When a man rapes his daughter's best friend, he is also raping his own family."

"Excuse me?" said Senator Burkhalter. "I'm not sure I heard you. Would you mind repeating what you just said?"

Annette paused and tried to remember what she had last said, tried to determine if she had uttered her last thought or had just thought it. Tentatively, she replied, "I think I said that when a man rapes his daughter's friend he is also raping his own family."

There was a brief pause, then Dr. Warren leaned forward and, with a soothing, gentle voice, asked, "Would you mind elaborating on that for us?"

Annette took a deep breath, held it, bit her lower lip, and let the air out of her lungs, deflating her personal reservations. "When I caught my husband, Wes Bourkline, molesting Casey's friend while both girls were sleeping in our home, I had to make an instant decision. Call the police, regardless of what that might mean for our family, or try to protect my family and our future. I knew what the right thing was to do. I turned him in. At that time, I could not know that I would wind up in a hospital due to a complete mental breakdown, or that Casey and I would need to move in with my parents and be dependent on them."

In the back of the room, Mr. and Mrs. Greer nodded. "My daughter was forced to learn about things when she was a little girl that most adults don't even want to know about—rape, nervous breakdowns, suicide. I never imagined that Wes would kill himself; just like I never imagined that he was a monster, a sexual predator. Inappropriate, maybe, but a pedophile?"

By now, a surge of dammed-up words and worries, of guilt and grief, competed for first-place utterance out of her small mouth. They tumbled out in a torrent of agony and urgency. "When he died, part of me died, too. Who I thought I was, what I had staked my life on. My desire to serve right alongside him. There was no opportunity for resolution, or even confrontation. There was just death. There was no clarification of my role in the good things he had done in his years in the ministry. And about his dirty secret, I never got to ask, 'why?' or 'how many?' or 'how long?' There was no explanation of my part in his misdeeds. No chance to ask if I, by ignoring years of vague suspicions or believing his contrite apologies for flirting with young girls, had become a co-conspirator."

Pain and regret colored her voice. "I never got the chance to make any kind of sense of it. None. It's like the train running from "I do' to "happily ever after' ran out of track somewhere in the middle. My daughter lost her father *and* her mother—in increments. I wavered for years between the world I had invested myself in and the world that I ended up with—where my husband let me believe his flirtations were really harmless, although he always said he was sorry if I had been hurt by them; where he let me believe my intuitions were flawed, my suspicions unfounded. I gradually retreated into my self-doubt. At least that was a place I was sure of," she said ruefully.

"I had thought I had known my husband, had known his heart and everything he was about. I met this man who was raised in an orphanage and said he wanted to take the message of the gospel to hurting people everywhere and I wanted to be a part of that. I wanted to give him the home he'd never known. I wanted to share a lifetime with him. I thought I had it in me to be a good wife and a good mother. But that slowly got stripped away. My retreat was as much about saving my daughter as it was about my confusion. And now, 20 years later, I still can't seem to find my way." Audible sniffles and soft sobs could be heard behind Casey and Annette. Casey reached over to take her mother's hand.

Dr. Warren smiled warmly. "Thank you. Thank you, Ms. Greer."

Senator Hall leaned forward and asked, "Is it possible that your husband was a victim himself, at an earlier age?"

"I suppose it's possible," Annette answered. "But that does not excuse what he did. He had the opportunity to get help. And he didn't. I don't know what makes a grown-up look at a child and think sexually about that child, but people who do so know it's wrong. Why else would they shroud it with such secrecy? All the more reason to talk about it. If he was a victim himself, he should've sought help before his impulses became actions. Deep down, he knew what he was doing was wrong and he chose to try to get away with it rather than try to get help. I firmly believe he reached the point where his greatest agony was not over what he was doing to another human being but over being found out. And a victim's agony is that they *won't* be found out."

"So you are saying that even if your husband couldn't help being, um, attracted to children, he should have known he needed help?" Senator Hall asked.

"Yes, sir, I am."

"Thank you very much for coming here today, Ms. Greer," said Senator Burkhalter. "I'm sure I speak for this entire panel when I say we admire you for your courage."

Before she could respond, before she could say to the panel she did not think of herself as courageous at all, rather thought herself a parasite, a drain to her parents' retirement account, to the state's disability funds, to her daughter's infinite patience and understanding, Rebekah came up behind Annette and Casey.

Startled by her sudden presence, Annette turned around to face Rebekah. Rebekah reached out to touch Annette Greer's shoulder, an uncertain gesture at first, but when she felt the woman's bony arm, felt her tremulous grasp on life, Rebekah leaned down and hugged the frail woman.

She spoke softly into Annette's ear, "Thank you. Thank you for catching him. Thank you for screaming at him to get away from me. Thank you for calling the police. Thank you for giving life to my dear friend, your daughter." Tears dangled from Rebekah's lashes. Casey pushed her chair back and helped her mother stand, and the three women stood together, lost in the timelessness of defining moments, the flood of relief and pardon and grace, the washing away of years of uncertainty and waiting.

Rebekah whispered something into Casey's ear and Casey nodded. Casey helped Annette to a chair beside her parents and then returned to the table in the center of the room where Rebekah stood, waiting. Rebekah turned to face the long table and the five people seated there. She sat in the chair, pulled it close to the table, and spoke clearly into the microphone. "My name is Rebekah Wilkins-Standifer, and I would like to tell you my story."

Senator Burkhalter smiled kindly. "Alright, Ms. Wil…, Ms. Stan…"

"Rebekah. Please call me Rebekah."

"Okay, Rebekah. We're listening." The panel members all smiled indulgently.

Rebekah took a deep breath. Casey placed her hand on Rebekah's forearm, as much to steady her own nerves as to provide support for her friend.

Rebekah began, "As you already know, Casey's father molested me in their home. I was eight, nine years old. Casey was a frequent spend-the-night guest in my home and I was just as often a guest in her home. One night, while I was sleeping in the twin bed next to Casey's, I woke up when he, her father, ejaculated on my face."

Senator Paris gasped; Dr. Warren and Lorelei kept their steady gaze on Rebekah. The two male senators shifted in their chairs. "I was an occasional thumb-sucker and he, when he tiptoed into the room late at night to look in on Casey, would slip my thumb out of my mouth and put his penis in instead." Rebekah paused to take another deep breath. Annette Greer and her mother sobbed silently, as did Libby and Margot and Olivia. Celeste drew her knees up into the chair and wrapped her arms around herself, rocking rhythmically. Andrea, spent from crying earlier, listened in silent anguish, unused to the new tenderness within. Mr. Greer sat grimly, numb with rage and a father's protective desire to participate in vigilante justice. Fresh tears splashed on Casey's lap.

Rebekah continued, "There was no place in my upbringing, no place in my little girl world, to put this. I didn't know that men would do these things to little girls. I barely had knowledge of what two consenting adults might do. My innocence was ripped away and he bought my silence by making me believe it was all just a bad dream...."

The ensuing silence hung like a pall over the room. Rebekah stared straight ahead, again twisting her wedding ring around her finger—in part, self-comforting gesture, in part to focus her nervous energy on one small project. Senator Hall broke the silence. "I hope you won't take this the wrong way. Please be patient with my ignorance but, if you were sleeping when all this happened, what is the serious harm? I'm not condoning what he did, mind you. I'm just wondering why it was so traumatic. Please help me understand."

Libby stood up quickly and leveled her gaze at Senator Hall. Her voice exploded with anger, filling the room. "I'll tell you what the serious harm is, Mister Hall," she emphasized the Mister like an epithet. "The serious harm is that regardless of whether or not you're awake when someone molests you, your body, your mind, your very soul knows an indignity has occurred. And you still bear the marks of that indignity." She gathered control of her voice and continued, her eyes still flashing, "If someone sneaks in your room and cuts your hair while you're sleeping, your hair has still been cut." Andrea reached for Libby's hand and gently pulled her back down to sit.

Dr. Warren's eyes danced with approval as Senator Hall spoke feebly. "I apologize, Ms. Rebekah. And to all of you ladies. I'm just an old guy who obviously needs an education in these, uh, matters. To be honest, I never thought about all the ways my grandchildren can be harmed. Suddenly, today, I am very afraid for them. I feel like calling my family and telling them to stay inside with the doors locked. I do apologize."

Rebekah smiled graciously. "*My* education about abuse issues has been a long process. For 20 years, I kept what happened at Casey's house locked up inside me. Disconnected from the rest of my life. What I did not know, though, until very recently, is that, in the process of tearing my innocence from me, Reverend Bourkline tore with it a part of my soul. That rip has stayed there for 20 years, slowly, slowly bleeding out. Up until recently, I had blanked that segment of my childhood out of my mind, but the wounds were still there, oozing. I just didn't know where the hurt, the lack of trust, the confusion, the depression, the need for control and certainty came from."

Rebekah paused, then spoke again. "And it will take time to heal." She patted her belly. "And with each little healing comes another set of questions, another set of issues. Like this baby—who will I trust to hold her? How can I protect her, and allow others to delight in her at the same time? How can I gradually let her go if I don't know *whom* to let her go to? There will probably be a lifetime of questions."

She paused again, then took Casey's hand in hers and squeezed. "He sacrificed me on the altar of his tainted, sinister desires. He took what wasn't his to take, and he left, in its place, this almost-person who has spent the past 20 years afraid to let go and live, barely scratching the surface of life. I have a lot of catching up to do." Rebekah sat back in her chair.

After watching the two friends hug, Senator Burkhalter, exhausted, said, "If nobody has anything else to ask or to say, these proceedings are concluded. I want to thank you ladies again for taking the time out of your schedules to come speak to us today. I applaud you all for your courage, your strength. And I assure you, your testimonies have lent credence to our case. We will work tirelessly to get stricter sentences enacted."

He waited for any last moment discussion and when there was none, said, "Thank you again for coming. Be careful on your drive back home. I wish you all the best."

While the panel members and the CLAMOR Girls were mingling in the meeting room, Casey walked with her grandparents and mother to their car. Dr. Warren, upon overhearing Andrea confess her embarrassment to the group at "breaking down" in public, said to her, "Your tears, believe it or not, said as much as your words did."

Before the CLAMOR Girls left the building to carpool back to Jacksonville, they stopped in the restroom. From her stall, Rebekah phoned her mother. "It's over, Mom. I did it," she said, whispering her excitement. "And guess what? Miss Annette came. I'll call you when I get home and tell you all about it." Then, "I love you, too, Mom. Bye."

Thirty

THE EXPLOSION OF SPRING TO summer colors reached a
dizzying pitch as April ended. Azaleas and dogwoods conspired to
take the city's breath away. With spring-fevered excitement, citizens
of Jacksonville nurtured their new geraniums in pots by the front
door and watered new plugs of Bahia and St. Augustine grass.
And lovebugs made their semiannual appearance, sensing nature's
permission for their return.

Myra had asked the CLAMOR Girls to prepare for their final group
meeting by reflecting on what the Wizard of Oz did for Dorothy and
her traveling companions—bequeathing to them symbolic tokens
of gifts that already resided within them. So the women arrived
at their April 30 meeting, each carrying the gifts they would give
to each other. "Tonight, we will celebrate each other," Myra said,
beginning the meeting. "And I'm going to invoke my leader privilege
and designate that we will go in alphabetical order. When it's your
turn to play Wizard, you may bestow in whatever order you choose.
And," she added, "I know you all are going to want to get up and
hug each person after each presentation, but let's wait until the end,
shall we?" Then, "Andrea, you first. What have you brought for your
group mates?"

Andrea reached down to the floor beside her chair and brought up
a large manila envelope. She opened it and slid out several pieces of
paper with pictures clipped from magazines glued to them. "I, um,
'borrowed' some women's magazines from the break room at work,"

she said, smiling. "Now I know," she invoked a beauty consultant's sincerity, "what color eye shadow goes best with my skin tone." She winked at Celeste, picked up the page at the top of the stack, and then turned to face Margot. "Margot, I want you to have this," and she handed Margot a sheet of plain white paper with a picture of a pair of milk-chocolate brown hands glued to the middle of the page. "This represents one of a physician's most valuable tools—her hands. I know you will continue to touch, literally and figuratively, many lives when you are treating your patients."

Margot accepted the gift and said, "Thank you," as Andrea looked down at the next name on her pile of papers.

"Olivia," she said, handing Olivia a picture of an airline ticket, "this is your ticket to be whatever you want to be. I know you can do it."

"Thank you," Olivia responded. She ran her fingers through her newly-styled hair, foregoing her old habit of yanking at her clothes.

"Rebekah, these eyes, ears, and heart represent what kind of mother you will be. You will see everything your daughter needs you to see, and hear everything she needs you to hear, and you will love her the way she needs you to love her." She handed the paper to Rebekah, who acknowledged the gift with tear-moistened eyes and a grateful smile.

"Celeste, this woman looking into a mirror represents me, because I'm spending more time than I used to in front of a mirror." The others laughed softly, appreciative. Although Andrea's choice was minimal makeup, versus the glamour girl look Celeste had given her in the hotel room, it was clear she was no longer comfortable with her previously disheveled appearance. "And I wouldn't be doing that if it weren't for you, you know, helping me like what I see." She handed the paper to Celeste.

"Good Lord, have you gotten a manicure?" Celeste asked.

Andrea blushed. "Yeah, It's no big deal. One of my co-worker's mother-in-law just started selling Mary Kay. She came to work today to do demonstrations during lunch."

Then she picked up the last sheet of paper and handed it to Libby. It contained a picture of a blow dryer. "Thanks for helping to melt my heart. Mom," she added.

Libby let out a little cry of astonishment, smiling at Andrea through her tears.

Celeste pulled a sandwich-sized Ziploc bag out of her voluminous purse. "I guess I'm next." The baggie contained single letters of the alphabet, cut out with the aid of a stencil. On each letter, one word was printed on the front and the intended recipient's name was printed on the back. Separating the letters with her fingers, she selected one and drew it out of the bag. "C," she said, "for Courage." She handed the letter to Olivia. "I look at you—a mom, like me—and all you have been through, and I'm amazed at your courage. And I've got to tell you, girl, nobody was more surprised than me when you sat in front of those people in Tallahassee and told them your story." Olivia smiled gratefully.

Celeste picked another letter out of the baggie. "D, for Dance," she said, handing the letter to Margot. "I never met anyone before who so badly wants to let go and dance. Throw her head back and boogie. So I am giving you permission to do that. If it's with Tim, great. But if things don't work out between you two, stand in the middle of your living room with the music pumped up and dance anyway, okay?" Margot laughed, relishing Celeste's enthusiasm and at the image of herself given over to that long-dormant girlish desire to abandon herself to joy.

The next letter was a B. "B is for Belief." She handed the letter to Rebekah. "Rebekah believes in people. Even, sometimes, when they don't believe in themselves." She smiled warmly at Rebekah. "Or when they might, but they're afraid to do something about it. She looked at my sketches of the clothes I've designed and she had helped me make my dreams come true."

Rebekah took the letter from Celeste and said, "What was it you said about having the right material to work with?" Celeste puckered her lips and kissed the air between them.

She pulled an O out of the baggie and handed it to Libby. "This O is for Orgasm," she said, continuing to talk through the ripple of laughter in the room, "'cause one day soon, you're going to have the Big O. I only wish I could be there the morning after to see the look on your face. And Bud's." She picked up an imaginary phone with her hand, spoke breathlessly, "Yes, pastor, this is Libby. I won't be at the meeting this morning. Something's c-come up." She hung up her phone and winked at Libby. Libby blushed deep red, both at Celeste's offering and at the fluttering in her heart, the tingling warmth between her legs.

"This S," Celeste continued, pulling the last letter up, handing it to Andrea, "is for Soft. For all your bluster, you are really soft on the inside. And I feel privileged to have witnessed that softness push itself to the surface."

Andrea mouthed the words, "Thank you."

Libby, still clutching the O to her breast, looked startled when Myra called her name. "You're next, Libby." She was obviously enjoying the interplay of the women, who were vainly trying to conceal their amusement at Libby's stargazed expression.

Flustered, Libby put the letter down on her lap and picked up a stack of index cards she had placed next to her in the chair. Blinking away her reverie, she took the first card off the stack. "I did sort of the same thing as Celeste," she drawled. "I wrote one word down on each of these cards." She held up the first card. It said *Class*. "This is for you, Celeste," she said, handing her the card. "I know you've probably thought of yourself as 'The Tart with a Heart,' but I know, we all know," she said, nodding around the room, "that you are a class act. You just never had the chance to perform on the right stage. Now you do." It was Celeste's turn to be embarrassed. Her cheeks colored red.

She held up the next card—*Faith*. "As much as we've butt heads," she said, handing the card to Andrea, "I just know you'll find your way. And He'll wait for you while you do." Andrea graciously accepted the card.

"Let's see. What's next?" Libby lifted up the card that said *Mom*. "Y'all know I don't think there's any higher calling in life than being a mother. And I'm honored to be the oldest gal in this group. If y'all want to think of me as a sister, that's okay, but I know sometimes who you need is your mom." She handed the card to Olivia. "And I'll be your mom any time you need me." A soft cry escaped from Olivia as she nodded her thanks to Libby.

Knowledge, the next card read. Libby held it up then said, "You have a lot of knowledge, Margot. About medicine and about people.

About yourself. And deep down, you know you are worth knowing. You have so much to offer. Share yourself and what you know with the world. It'll be a better place if you do." She handed the card to Margot, who smiled gratefully.

"The last card I have says *Compassion*." She turned and faced Rebekah. "I know you wonder if you will be a good mother to your baby. Every mother wonders that." Olivia and Celeste nodded agreement. "You'll be fine," she continued, "because you are gentle and nurturing. And because you are compassionate. You will be sensitive to what your daughter needs from you." She handed Rebekah the card, then added, "And you will know when to hold her and when to let her go. You will." Libby smiled. "Oh, and remember I'm available to babysit!"

"You're in line after me," chirped Celeste.

"And me," Margot and Olivia said simultaneously.

"You'll all get to take turns," said Rebekah. "I better tell Cliff to start planning one night out a week."

Margot lifted a plastic Allegra bag from the floor onto her lap. "I raided the supply closet at work." She reached into the bag and withdrew a sticker with a butterfly on it and handed it to Rebekah. "It has been amazing watching you find your wings. You thought you were getting along just fine before, crawling around like a caterpillar, eating leaves. Now you're able to fly. And I'm enjoying watching you." Rebekah smiled through her tears, mouthing, "Thank you." Margot replied, "Thank *you* for showing me it's okay to leave the cocoon, even if it's scary."

Next, Margot pulled out two magnets. Both bore the inscription of a popular children's allergy medication. She held them up and said, "Andrea, you have resisted people getting close to you," and she demonstrated by trying to hold the positive ends of both magnets together. "And now you are experiencing the magic of letting people get close," she demonstrated with the magnets. "And you are learning," she said as she handed the magnets to Andrea, "that people are 'attracted' to you just because of who you are." Margot cupped one of her hands underneath Andrea's and dropped the magnets in with the other, closing her fingers around Andrea's hand. Andrea swallowed hard and smiled at Margot.

"This is for Olivia," Margot said next, taking a piece of paper out of a bag. It resembled a page from a prescription pad. It read, "Rx: Friendship" and it was signed, "Love, Margot." "I know you have been lonely for a very long time. Believe me, I do know. And it has touched my heart seeing you come in here week after week, smiling at us, sharing tears with us, letting us see into your heart, being our friend when you could have been bitter at the world. And I hope you know now that you have five new best friends." She offered the paper to Olivia, who, half stood to accept it, pulling a Kleenex out of the box on her way back to being seated.

Margot fished around in the bag and next pulled out a toy watch. "This is from the little treasure chest of toys we have on hand to give our patients," she said, handing it to Celeste. "I know you love your son very much and have worked really hard to prove that to him. You both have a lot of lost time to make up for. Make every minute count." Celeste thanked Margot, who added, "Personally, I think he's very fortunate to have a mom who has such a terrific sense of humor."

"And last, but certainly not least," she said as she pulled a paper measuring tape out of the bag, "I want you to have this, Libby. You have measured your worth by what you were able to do for others, and now it's time for you to measure your worth just by who you are, which is a wonderful, warm, caring person in her own right. And since my mom lives in a different state, I'll take you up on your offer to be my other mother." She handed the measuring tape to Libby.

"Just wait 'til Bud hears we now have five more daughters," said Libby, her eyes twinkling.

Olivia picked the brown paper Publix grocery sack up off the floor next to her chair and parked it ceremoniously in her lap. "Well, as y'all know, I work at Publix. Sometimes I think it's my home away from home. So, anyway, I went shopping for y'all." She leaned the bag toward her face and peered inside, taking out a baby bib. She held it up then passed it to Rebekah. "I just know you're going to be a good mama. I think your baby is real lucky to have you as her mama."

"Thank you, Olivia," said Rebekah. "Wow, my very first baby gift!"

Olivia rummaged through the bag again and took out a box of Kleenex. "I want Andrea to have this 'cause I think you're going to need more of these." She winked at Andrea. "I know sometimes you think that isn't such a good thing, but I sort of think all those tears wash out some of the hurt. So it's a good thing." She gave the box to Andrea.

"Next thing I know," Andrea joked, "you'll be buying a bib for *me* because I'm such a crybaby."

Olivia returned to her bag, removing a box of Lucky Charms. "Celeste, this is for you, 'cause I think you're charming and because I'm lucky to know you." Celeste received the gift with quiet gratitude, uncharacteristically speechless.

Next, Olivia pulled a bottle of store brand lotion out of the bag. She handed it to Libby, saying, "Lotion is supposed to make you soft. I think you're just about one of the softest ladies I know. Soft-hearted, I mean. I want to be like you when I'm your age." She added, "Mom."

Libby, eyes gleaming, accepted the gift. "That's one of the nicest compliments I have ever received. Thank you, Dear."

"You're welcome." Olivia responded. Reaching into the bag, she took out a bag of balloons and gave it to Margot. "Margot, I admire you. You had dreams of what you wanted to be and you're making them come true. I know you're gonna soar above all the bad things that have happened."

Margot wiped away a tear and whispered, "Thank you," smiling tenderly at this seemingly simple woman's profound observations about the members of the group. "There's enough balloons in here for both of us, girlfriend."

Next, Rebekah opened her purse and withdrew five hand-written cards. "I couldn't decide what to give each of you," she scanned the room, "so I wrote thank you notes. Each of you has become very dear, very special to me. Each of you has given something valuable to me. So I want to recognize that tonight." She took the first card, opened it and read out loud, "Dear Andrea, Knowing what I now know about all the dangers lurking for children and knowing that I am bringing a child into that world, it gives me great comfort that there are good people like you doing everything they can to make this world safer for children. Thank you for using your indignation to protect them," she read, unconsciously patting her stomach. "Love, Rebekah. P.S. Will you move next door to me?" They all laughed and Rebekah handed the card to Andrea.

Rebekah opened the next note and said, "This one's for Margot." She began reading, "Dear Margot, It has been a long time since someone has given me the precious gift of genuine friendship. While I have many fair-weather friends, I have few who would be at ease going with me through difficult times. These past months have been difficult, haven't they? You not only offer me your understanding, you also offer me your presence and your patience. You're not afraid to make me think and you're not afraid to let me feel. That is a gift. Thank you, my dear friend. Love, Rebekah. P.S. After the baby is born, you've got to help me get back in shape." Rebekah gave the note to Margot, who smiled warmly while flicking a tear off her cheek.

"Okay, this one's for Libby," said Rebekah, picking the next card up off the stack. "Dear Libby, You have shown me, all of us, how it is to be both tough and tender. I will never forget you standing up and shouting at that 'Mister' Hall on my behalf. My hero! You are our own steel magnolia and I love you. Rebekah. P.S. I love your accent. When I am around you, I almost pick up my Panhandle patois again. And that's a good thing, Sugah."

Libby laughed out loud, delighted. "I'll be happy to give you lessons—so you can learn to talk right again," she said, winking, as Rebekah handed her the card.

"And I might take you up on it, my deah."

Rebekah opened the next card and turned to face Celeste. "Dear Celeste, Remember when you asked if we thought you were crazy? Especially to hope that you might be able to do something with your childhood fantasy of designing your own clothes? When I offered to look at your sketches and give you my professional opinion, I thought I was doing you a favor. Little did I realize that you were doing *me* a favor. Thanks to you, we both have a career change coming in our lives. And what timing, too! I can't wait until our boutique opens and your designs start decorating women in town. Celeste, you aren't crazy. Just as our label says, you are Insanely Beautiful. Love, Rebekah. P.S. Have any maternity sketches?"

"As a matter of fact, I do," said Celeste, taking the card from Rebekah. "You see, I have this gorgeous redhead for inspiration...."

"Okay, I guess that means this note is for Olivia," Rebekah said, opening the last card. "Dear Olivia, I think of you as the younger sister I never had. Big sisters are supposed to share their wisdom with their younger sisters, but I have learned more from you than I could ever possibly have taught you. You deride yourself too often for being 'undereducated,' but I think you are one of the sharpest, most observant, most insightful women I have ever been privileged to meet. I will depend on you often for childrearing advice, as well as wanting to know your thoughts about all sorts of things. Love, Big Sis, Rebekah. P.S. Have you ever considered a career in early childhood education? I want my daughter to have you for her teacher."

Olivia let out a little squeal of surprise. "You aren't going to believe this, but I was talking to a counselor just the other day about getting my GED. I want to go to college. I was just too afraid to tell anyone. Oh, Lordy, it's been my dream since I was a little girl to teach Kindergarten." She took the note from Rebekah's extended hand and hugged it to herself.

Rebekah reached under her chair and brought out a wrapped garment box. "Now we have something for you, Myra."

Genuinely surprised, Myra accepted the box, looking at each woman seated in her office. "Thank you. Thank you all."

"Open it!" said Celeste.

"Yeah," said Olivia, "you've got to open it."

Myra turned the package over and carefully peeled the wrapping paper away from the box. Then turning it back over, she lifted off the lid. Inside, lying on top of a tissue-wrapped garment was a DVD containing rare footage of jazz performers at the New Orleans Jazz Festivals. "Oh," she exclaimed, "this is just too much. How did you know I've been wanting this?"

"Your receptionist was bribed with chocolate," Celeste stated in mock confession. "Now you know she can be bought. No secret is safe around Ghirardelli's."

"Well thank you all," Myra said as she unwrapped the tissue around the garment. She took out a handsomely designed dress, rich with earth tones to accentuate the richness of Myra's ebony complexion. The label inside the dress read *Insanely Beautiful*.

"You are our very first fashion model, Myra," said Rebekah.

Moved to tears, Myra held the dress up and admired it. "I love it. I absolutely love it. I can't wait to wear it. Thank you."

"Actually, thank *you*," said Celeste. "We could use all the free advertising we can get."

"And thank you, too, for all those teachable moments, Myra," said Rebekah, smiling impishly. "All of them."

Myra smiled in return. "I am deeply touched. And I have enjoyed sitting back tonight, watching you all care for each other. I am so very proud of each of you." She took a folder from the glass-topped coffee table and opened it. "And now I have something for you, as part of our final ceremony." She handed out certificates printed on parchment paper stock. All that was printed on the certificates was one word, in large, bold script: *Permission*. "As you all know by now, wellness is on a continuum. And the path to wellness is not a quick trip, it is a journey. A lifetime journey that is not at all linear."

She traced an imaginary line across the room with her finger. "Instead, it resembles the course of a roller coaster ride, scary and exhilarating." She made waves with her hand. "It is work. Sometimes painful. Sometimes crushingly lonely. This certificate is your permission. Permission to hate the journey sometimes. Permission to fail, to fall down. You have earned the permission to reinvent yourselves as often as necessary. You have permission to remain in or re-enter counseling whenever you want, for as long as you want, as often as you want. This certificate entitles you to have needs and wants; and to cave in to insecurity once in awhile. This certificate gives you permission to climb out of whatever hole you stumble into and rediscover life, in all of its madness and intrigue. This certificate allows you to be imperfect and passionate people. And that is not my gift to you. That is your gift to yourselves. You have earned it."

Myra's words rolled over in their minds, gentle and soothing in their honesty and exhortation. Myra let her words to them take root as they thought over them. After a comfortable silence, she spoke again. "And now it is my turn to play Wizard. Rather than attempting to wrap up what we know from our last nine-plus months together— that would imply some kind of finality to your growth as people, as women—my parting comments to you as the leader of this group will be in the form of questions. Questions to ask yourself when you reach a bend in the road. Questions to ask yourself each time you bump into another piece of damage that was done. And here they are."

She held up a fist. "First," she unfurled the forefinger, "what will I do with what has been done to me?" She paused for effect. "Second," she raised her middle finger to accompany the first, "what will you do with your beauty?" Again, she paused. "Next," she raised another finger, "where will you focus your wrath?" Then, "And finally," she held up all four fingers, "how will you practice forgiveness in your life—of yourself and others?"

While they were still quietly storing Myra's words away, like squirrels gathering acorns in fall, she continued, "We all realize now that sorrow and pain are inevitable. It's what you do with them that counts. Sorrow can be the pathway to living tenderly, or it can be the gateway to living a self-protected life. Surviving. Existing. If you will remember, when you encounter rage or pain or desire, they, in and of themselves, are not your enemies but, rather, opportunities. You choose how to appropriate them into your lives."

She waited again for them to mull over what she had said, then asked, "Questions? Comments?"

Andrea spoke. "Yeah, I have a question. You said something about forgiveness. I have a real problem with that. Why should I forgive my family for what they did to me? Why should I forgive my parents for having their heads up their asses?" she glanced at Libby, who was trying to conceal a frown. "I'm sorry. I mean, for neglecting me."

"Good question. The answer, I believe, depends on how you define forgiveness. I prefer to think of forgiveness as 'letting go of getting even.' It's not permission to harm you again nor necessarily an invitation to relationship. It also doesn't mean you don't want justice served. It means you refuse to let revenge consume you. If you use that as your operating definition of forgiveness, does that help answer your question?"

"Yeah. I can live with that. Thanks."

"I have a question. Or more like a comment. I don't know. Anyway," Olivia said, running her fingers through her hair, "I went to Maelene's church a few times. I liked it okay. I think Tyler enjoyed it. He says he did. So, my question is for you, Myra. Or you, Libby. I think I'd like to believe in God. I might already. I don't really know. How do I know? If he exists, where do I find him?"

With a tilt of her head, Libby yielded the answer to Myra. Myra sighed. "We will never, I believe, know all there is to know about God. But as to where to begin looking…. One of my disenchantments with many churches in general is their emphasis on getting things 'right.' Like doing things right is an end in and of itself. Some churches are often more interested in making God look good, but I firmly believe God honors the search. They leave out all the good parts about exploring what is in your heart, even mixing things up a little to get to the places in our souls that are parched." She paused, collecting her thoughts. "I believe that God honors passion over precision. God is okay with us goofing up as long as we are involved in an honest, authentic pursuit of meaning and purpose. Does any of that make sense?"

"Yeah, I think so. Just do it. Get out there and stumble around, but get out there, right?"

Relieved, Myra said, "Good. Yes." Then, "Remember, passion is a good thing, and if you will resist the urge to mistrust or hate passion because of what happened to you, your search will be exciting, revealing. And so, my final word to you all is this: I endow you with the right to live passionately without the fear of being abandoned."

Amidst the many hugs and affectionate pats and the plans for Rebekah's baby shower, the realization that their Thursday nights would seem empty for a time hadn't yet dawned on the CLAMOR Girls. They all left Myra's office that night laden with the gifts of love and friendship and hope.

Thirty-one

MARGOT, LIBBY, OLIVIA, AND ANDREA all converged on Rebekah in *Insanely Beautiful*, the tiny boutique located in a wharf refurbished to house unique shops and restaurants along the St. John's River. They had all agreed ahead of time to meet together as a group periodically. It was almost closing time and the friends snooped around the little shop, oohing and aahing appropriately over the items for sale. "Where's Celeste?" asked Olivia.

"She's running Tyler to soccer practice," Rebekah answered.

"How are things going for them?" asked Libby.

"Great. They're getting adjusted to being a family again. She really is a good mother."

"Speaking of mother, when are you going to have that baby?" Andrea asked.

"My due date is August 20th, less than two weeks away. Do you all want to see the nursery we have set up in the back?"

While Rebekah was showing them the room in the back that doubled as office and nursery, Celeste returned. When Rebekah heard the bell on the door jangle, she called out, "We're back here. Looking at the nursery."

"Well hurry up," teased Celeste, "it's closing time and I'm hungry."

***

Casey's cell phone rang in her modest two-bedroom home at 6:30 a.m. on Monday, August 17. Weary from being on call the night before, she answered groggily without looking at the display, "Hello."

"Casey?" She heard. "It's Rebekah."

Casey sat up. "Hey. What are you doing up at this hour?"

"I'm sorry to call so early, but I wanted you to know that Cliff and I had a baby girl at 4:30 this morning."

"That's wonderful! Tell me, how is she? How are you?"

"We're all doing great. Casey?"

"Yeah?"

"Her name is Casey. Casey Theodora Standifer."

A Note From The Author

SOME OF YOU MAY QUESTION my decision not to capitalize he, his, and him when referencing God. First of all, original Hebrew and Greek scriptural texts do not do so; that grammatical affectation came along much later. More importantly, though, as it relates to the story, many abuse victims already struggle with God questions. I felt it imperative to be sensitive to abuse victims, many of whom naturally tend to conflate abusive authority figures with God, making it doubly difficult to tweeze out truth when one is simultaneously trying to get past specific gender references. You may have noticed that Myra is able to talk about God without making gender references and without sounding stilted. Myra does this because she's been trained to do so, and she is aware of survivors' additional struggle to sort through their beliefs when God is presented as having gender.

Best,

Dede

Meet the CLAMOR Girls— snapshots of the main characters in *Reawakening Rebekah: The Gift of the CLAMOR Girls*

- Celeste: Brassy, creative hair stylist by day; single mother; recovering addict
- Libby: Grandmotherly and genteel; self-appointed mother-figure
- Andrea: Hard-nosed, athletic, loner law enforcement officer
- Margot: Smart, subdued pediatric nurse; divorced
- Olivia: Young, timid, guilt-ridden grocery store assistant manager; married; mother
- Rebekah: Young, intense fashion merchandiser; married to Cliff Standifer; best friends with Casey in third grade
- Myra: The CLAMOR Girls' tireless leader; psychiatrist; jazz- and travel-aficionado
- Casey: Best friends with Rebekah in third grade; large animal veterinarian; single; honorary CLAMOR Girl

Readers' Guide for *Reawakening Rebekah: The Gift of the CLAMOR Girls*

1. When a phone call or an email will suffice, what are the merits of a hand-written letter? What about Casey's unique character would lead her to write her sentiments in a letter rather than call, text, or email?

2. Have you ever been in a situation where someone thinks they know more about you than you do about yourself? What was that like? How

might Hank's demeanor with Rebekah make working through her issues easier? Harder?

3. Do you have any childhood memories of worship services or of religion in general? How might Casey's observations about her parents' interactions at home compared to their interactions while on the road contribute to her sense of family, faith, and of self?

4. One of Myra's first assignments for Rebekah is to look at photos of herself from childhood to present and record her impressions. What are some adjectives you would use to describe yourself as a young child? What are some adjectives you would use to describe your childhood? What were Myra's reasons for this particular first assignment, given Rebekah's stated reason for seeking Myra's help (depression over her father's death)?

5. Even before her father's death, Rebekah has lived more increasingly in her head. Why do you think she wasn't aware of this shift – from the joyful, exuberant, tender-hearted child to the calculating and precise adult?

6. Why do you think Faye Wilkins, Rebekah's mother, isn't more forthcoming about the events surrounding Casey's father and the family's sudden departure from Founder's Creek?

7. Rebekah states to Myra that she feels like a stranger to herself. Have you ever felt like a stranger to yourself? When? What was that like? How did you work through that experience/time?

8. What are the merits, you think, of "talk therapy"? What about in a group setting? Why might that be a good idea? Could it also be a bad idea?

9. What types of situations cause in you the oppositional "do something; don't move" response? What do you think of the adult Casey fretting over her childhood inaction twenty years after the event of her father molesting Rebekah?

10. What smells do you associate with parts of your childhood? Are there any odors that have a negative association for you? Why do you think Rebekah's subconscious responds more strongly to smell than to Myra's assertion that there's more to Rebekah's depression than meets the eye?

11. Rebekah is new to the world of journaling, and feels some trepidation about doing so. Do you journal or write or otherwise engage in any sort of creative process that helps you make sense of your life? What are the merits of doing so? Are there any inherent risks?

12. Given an outsider's view of Rebekah's seemingly perfect life and that some might be measuring their lives against hers, why would Rebekah be concerned with whether or not she is normal? Have you ever struggled with what is "normal" and what isn't? How do you determine what is normal?

13. Did anyone encourage your childhood dreams? Were there adults in your childhood who served as a second set of parents or of encouragement and nurturing? How did the influence of Casey's grandparents help mitigate the damage done by her self-absorbed, dishonest father and her frail, distant mother?

14. What do you think of Casey's mother, Annette Bourkline/Greer, as a woman, a mother, a daughter?

15. Are there any members of the CLAMOR Girls you are drawn to or put off by more than the others? Why? What connection do you make between their stories of abuse and their current lives? What do you think of the labels "victim," "survivor," and "thriver"?

16. Why is Rebekah initially so ambivalent about remembering the details of her abuse? Are there parts of your life where ambivalence affects your decisions?

17. Why do you think some people are more willing to seek help and others are so reluctant? What role does Cleopatra Syndrome (denial)

play in that decision? Does a pronounced self-awareness like that which Casey possesses play a role as well? What do you think of Myra's exhortation to fear denial more than reliving the abuse?

18. What has been your experience with shame? Is there a difference between guilt and shame and, if so, what? Why do you think innocent victims of sexual abuse struggle so much with shame?

19. How are beauty, femininity, human longing, and danger linked? How can we encourage young girls to embrace their inherent beauty and femininity while also keeping them safe from being taken advantage of?

20. What connection do you see between the secret, shameful events of Rebekah's abuse and her adult perfectionism?

21. Rebekah struggles with being vulnerable to emotion. What is the connection between being vulnerable and living a "three-dimensional" life? Can one avoid vulnerability and still live a life of breadth and depth?

About the Author

While *Reawakening Rebekah: The Gift of the CLAMOR Girls* is my first novel, it is not my first literary effort. I have written a short children's story (unpublished) as well as several articles for our local college newspaper—under the pen name Madonna Nachomama. I have contributed to textbooks on student success as well.

I live in Athens, Georgia and, by day, I am the Director of Learning Support for University of North Georgia and by night I am an adjunct professor of UNG's student success course. When I am not directing or teaching, I enjoy listening to an eclectic mix of music and radio programs, doing word puzzles, reading, taking long, soul-cleansing power walks, and doing Pilates. And writing. I cannot not write; it's the way I try to make sense of the world and determine what I think and know and believe. I have three accomplished, brave, and beautiful grown daughters, one cat, one grand-cat, and four grand-dogs.

CPSIA information can be obtained at www.ICGtesting.com
Printed in the USA
LVOW12s0920211113

362235LV00004B/9/P